THE DRAGON PIT

By
Gerhard Plenert

Outer Banks Publishing Group
Raleigh/Outer Banks

FIRST EDITION – August 2024

Library of Congress Control Number: 2024940659

ISBN 13 - 979-8-9907093-2-4
eISBN – 979-8-9907093-3-1

Dedication

This Book is dedicated to Renee
And the 8 Kids and the Yet to be Numbered Grandkids
Who Work Hard to Make Life Our Own Personal Dragon Pit

Acknowledgements

This book has been many years in the making and there are numerous individuals that need to be recognized. The first being my conscience who validated the flow and identified any holes in the plot, Renee Plenert.

The names of individuals in this book are fictional and have nothing to do with individuals that I have known in the past. I used names that are common and familiar with no intended parallels.

Also by the author

Dawn of the New Templars

Dawn of The New Templars is a mystery novel, where a terrorist group engages mercenaries to assist them in world domination. Unfortunately, their efforts are hampered by religious radicals and international executioners. Which of these groups would you think is the CIA?"

The XLs

A patient with a brain tumor is operated on and the surgery results in the unexpected result where the patient ends up with super mental powers, including the ability to communicate telepathically, retain information with a photographic memory. Even worse, the patient becomes the target of computer industry moguls who see him as a threat because these new super mental powers may eliminate the need for computers and cell phones.

Both books are available on Amazon and fine bookstores everywhere.

Table of Names / Key Actors

The Dragon Pit
A sub-group of academics at the Colorado Engineering School

- Gene Wiseman – Pit leader
- Gage Davis – Navy Seal, part of Seal Team Six, body builder, 5'11", single & hot
- Carlos Santiago – Puerto Rican, Ricki Martin look-a-like, Boeing / Lockheed Martin employee, developed AMG-114 Hellfire helicopter
- Livy Cobar – FBI agent, radical, cute 5'6" bombshell, long hair, not married, living in her one bedroom apartment
- Lincoln Travinski – Army Ranger, Special Forces, rugged looking, scars, scary, conservative
- Brian Pearson – wife and 2 kids (7 and 4), 6'4", Air Force Captain, flies stealth planes
- Gerd Plet – Brian's new identity
- Jenny Plet – Brian's wife's new identity
- Brian Colter – Brian's fake Provo, Utah identity
- Glenn Pierre – Marine, Pentagon connections, wife and 2 kids
- Cynthia Pierre – wife of Glenn
- Boston George – techie genius, poor writing skills, exceptional computer and math skills – wife and 2 kids

FBI team members

- Alvin Foller – Livy's boss, 50's, 5'5", graying beard and mustache, bald
- Jonathan Lusere – Livy's boyfriend, 5'10" with black, slightly balding hair. His features & skin color had a hint of Indian
- Edward Colton – sneaky, mousey, 5'5"
- Gerick Johannes – agent in charge of the Denver office

Other players

* Jimmy - Orlando
* Judy – North Dakota
* Muneersha Shammari – in Medina

Muslim Brotherhood and Their Connections

* Imam Sami Abdulaziz
* Mohammed Abdul Kalam – suicide bomber – Orlando
* Nayef Dehar – suicide bomber – North Dakota
* Niran – Muslim informant in Golden
* Nadia – Muslim roommate to Niran
* Shihab – Sami's brother
* Akil – Cathedral attacker / suicide bomber
* Abdullah – Muslim warrior deserter
* Kadeem – Muslim warrior deserter
* Uday – Muslim Brotherhood member resident in LA

Muslim Kidnapping team

* Abdul-Wadud – killed in the crash
* Yusuf – injured and later shot
* Fatih – messenger who picked up Muslim Brotherhood
* Husam – kidnapper and pervert
* Nawwaf – Muslim Brotherhood who take over kidnapping
* Rasil – Muslim Brotherhood who take over kidnapping

Three Muslim Ann Arbor warriors that go to LA

* Najid - plane
* Taqiy - train
* Uthal - car

Two additional Muslim Brotherhood that join in for LA

* Qasim
* Kahil

Chapter One

Nukes
April, 2017, Thursday, Ann Arbor, Michigan

"I need the bombs," insisted Imam Sami, the Imam for one of the many mosques in Ann Arbor, Michigan close to the State University of Michigan. Sami was tall for a Saudi, nearing six feet. He had attained his U.S. citizenship. He was overweight like most Americans, a little on the chubby side. Nevertheless, his Muslim and Arab roots came through in his facial features and his personality. "I have been requesting your support for years." He was pleading with the Egyptian Branch of the Muslim Brotherhood. The phone conversation was on a secure, encrypted line, which was routed through Europe thereby avoiding suspicion.

"Why should we support you?" replied the caller on the Egyptian side of the conversation. "What have you accomplished that is worthy of us giving you some of our most critical weapons? For all we know when we send them to you, you will just sit on them. It will be a complete waste of opportunity and resources."

"What you don't understand," explained Sami, "is that it is exactly the fact that we haven't drawn attention to ourselves that makes us dangerous. The FBI, CIA, and NSA do not have a spotlight on us. We are obscure and unknown. We can pull something like this off and they will not think to look our way until it is too late. We're exactly the secret weapon that can be successful at an operation of this type." Even with the secure phone line, the callers knew better than to get too specific about any planned missions.

The Egyptian sounded skeptical and condescending, but that is the way he always sounded. "I would like to believe you, but you have to realize that giving high priority weapons of this nature to someone who is unproven is extremely risky. I will send you two small low-yield nuclear bombs, not the twelve dirty bombs you requested. I will send them with a representative who will get me the details of what you are doing. If anything sounds suspicious, we will not deliver the weapons to you. Is that understood?"

"Understood," agreed Sami who was excited at the prospect that he may finally get the nuclear weapons that he so badly wanted. He understood that these would be very limited use weapons with a small range, but they would be powerful enough to have an impact and to send a message. The infidels had to be stopped. Their corruption was devastating to the high standards of his ideal Muslim culture.

Originally Sami wanted access to a dozen dirty bombs. He stressed that he could have a large impact on American soil if he could just get the bombs. But the Muslim Brotherhood headquartered in Cairo worked at a snail's pace and it frustrated him. First they criticized him for wanting something as weak as a dirty bomb. They told him that he should have a better understanding of what he was requesting. Dirty bombs wouldn't have a very big effect. They generally don't kill anyone except the person standing right next to the bomb. They tended to be more of a scare tool than lethal. The Brotherhood insisted that Sami needed to get something that would have a larger impact.

"So you're going to send me two of the small nukes that we discussed with an impact radius of about ten miles?" Sami asked. Sami had agreed with the Brotherhood's recommendation on the bombs. "You told me this was something we could fit into a roller suitcase so it would be easy to transport and relatively unnoticeable because it is so common. Is that what you're sending me?"

The Muslim Brotherhood had acquired some nuclear material from old Cold War bombs that were positioned in the Ukraine. In the Ukraine they had been disassembling nuclear missiles and occasionally some of the nuclear material would disappear. This material was broken down and repackaged into smaller nuclear devices of the type that the Brotherhood was suggesting for Sami.

There was a long pause on the phone and then unexpectedly the phone call dropped off. Sami waited for the Brotherhood to call him back. That was the protocol. If the call dropped off it was assumed to be because they had to get some additional information and they would be calling back. At long last Sami received a generic text message on his phone, which read, "Your request has been approved for two units of the items requested. The materials are currently in Canada and will be carried across the border to you within the next few days. Further similar orders will be processed based on current performance."

Sami knew what the message meant. He had to prove himself. He had to have as large an impact as possible and he had to receive extensive international press recognition for his cause. He had to make Allah proud.

As the day dragged on, Sami became more and more excited. He hoped the bombs would arrive that day, but he wasn't sure. As usual, he went to the mosque for daily prayers. But he couldn't get his mind off of the bombs. He was concerned they wouldn't get across the border safely. He was afraid someone would recognize the bombs and divert them. He was afraid the car would get into an accident and not be able to deliver the weapons. There were so many variables to worry about that Sami was starting to get anxiety chest pains. In the end, the self-inflicted stress was unnecessary and unfounded. The bombs arrived as promised in two roller bag suitcases that were thrown in the back of a car. They arrived late in the night, but that didn't matter because Sami was having trouble sleeping anyway. The excitement was keeping him awake.

The bombs were successfully driven across the border by a western looking couple carrying United States passports. They looked like tourists and they claimed they were on a honeymoon. The border agent didn't get suspicious.

When the transporters arrived with the bombs it was about four in the morning. Sami came rushing to the door and invited the driver in. "I am delighted that you made it," he exclaimed.

"The trip went smoothly," explained the male driver of the vehicle. The woman who was his wife stayed in the car. She had no business being part of this conversation. This was "men's" business. "Explain to me how you're going to use these devices," challenged the driver.

"We have two very prominent targets in mind, and I have several individuals who can act as my delivery system," explained Sami. Then he went on to explain the potential targets and how the bombs would be delivered.

"When do you plan to execute?" asked the driver.

"As soon as possible," explained Sami. "I want to hit the first target in the next few days and the second target in a month or so. These infidels are so gullible they would have forgotten about the first hit in that amount of time. The second hit will be a reminder to them that we are here for the long haul, not just for a quick hit and run. And they will go crazy wondering where the third target will be one month later."

"I like it," explained the driver. "The bombs are yours."

They two said their customary farewells and the driver departed.

The bombs were low yield nuclear explosives with a destruction radius of only a few miles. They were Unranium-235 based and had an equivalent blast of about one ton of TNT. It wasn't much, but it was enough to do the job that Sami had planned. He wanted public recognition more than he wanted deaths and he wanted to get as much of it as possible. He wanted to make Allah proud.

Tomorrow was Friday, a holy day of worship. Tomorrow he would find out how many warriors he had that he could trust. It would be an exciting day. A day he would never forget.

Chapter Two

The Imam
April, 2017, Friday, Ann Arbor, Michigan

"The Koran is explicit. It is the word of Allah and there can be no confusion. Infidels are corrupting our wives and children. They are degrading our world. The Koran explicitly states that we must act. We must take revenge on the infidels. They must be wiped out in order for us to retain our purity. Our youth are losing the faith. And it is because of the pornographic visuals that are on television, in movies, on billboards, and in magazines. What westerners call science is a complete distortion of the truths that can only be found in the Book. It cannot be avoided. It is in our faces. And the more our children see of this degradation, the more they hear about it in the schools, the more they will become numb to the danger of the lies. The more acceptable it becomes. The more they will think it is a reasonable element of any society. It cannot go on. It must be eliminated. Allah will curse anyone who does not take revenge against the infidels. It is stated clearly in the Koran and there can be no doubt about its meaning. We must act or we will be cursed along with the infidels. And I don't want to be numbered with the infidels. Do you?" The Imam was on a rant. He knew he had the attention of his audience and he was not about to let up, not until everyone was nodding their heads in agreement.

The audience was primarily made up of young men in their late teens and early twenties. They were adaptable and moldable. They believed the Imam. They thought of him as the authority on the Koran and on the will of Allah. They knew he spoke the word of Allah. What he said was truth and no one wanted to fail in a call from Allah. They wanted the promises of heaven and not the condemnation of hell.

This life was temporary. It was meaningless unless it was devoted to the service of Allah. The Imam successfully had the heads of each of these sixteen young men nodding in agreement. The Imam was on top of his game today. He knew he could get these boys to do anything he wanted. He wanted action. He wanted revenge. He took it as his personal mission in life to get as many of these youth fired up as possible. He wanted them to be his own personal army. He wanted them to execute suicide attacks for him on the infidels of America. He could see that he was getting a positive response.

The Imam Sami Abdulaziz and his congregation were primarily from Saudi Arabia. He had lived in Saudi as a child until his parents migrated to Michigan, where he received the remainder of his education and where he had lived ever since. He had lighter skin than the rest of his congregation. He was somewhat overweight and loved to eat, especially the delicacies of the fatherland.

Sami had a stare that demanded direct attention to every word he was saying. These youth were young and moldable. The boys were trying to find some important meaning to their life; some direction where they could have a significant impact. The Imam had identified two of the sixteen individuals that he thought were ready for action. He directed his sermons toward these two. Once these two were off on their assignments he would work on the rest of the group. But for now, he needed and targeted just them.

***

Nayef Dehar was from Dammam, Saudi Arabia where his father was a high-ranking Vice President at Aramco, the world's largest company by revenue. Aramco was the company that ran the country. It was a strange reversal of roles, but it worked for them because the Chairman of the Board at Aramco was the King of Saudi Arabia.

Nayef's father would have had mixed feelings if he knew what Nayef had gotten himself into. He would be proud that his son was dedicated to Allah. But he would be afraid of losing his son in a suicide attack. He didn't believe that the way to repress Western influence was by killing people. Rather, he believed that the true believers of Allah should avoid Western influences by isolating themselves from infidel environments. That's why the Kingdom of Saudi Arabia (KSA) didn't allow visitor's visas. They only wanted believers in their country. Unfortunately they were forced to bring in temporary workers. Work visas were allowed for the infidel workers, but no visitors. Western visitors would just be an unnecessarily bad influence, like what occurred during the first Gulf War when the negative influence of the United States military swept into their country. Females dressing like males and acting like males, making eye contact, not subordinating themselves properly, and dressing inappropriately. That wasn't going to be allowed to happen again. KSA had to be isolated from the corrupt infidel influence.

His father had sent Nayef to the United States to study in the best universities with the hope that he would come back some day and be a leader in his own country, possibly even following in the footsteps of his father. But a suicide attack was not what his father had in mind for his son. He would have preferred Nayef to be a good missionary. He would have preferred Nayef to bring the infidels to the truth and have them share in the glory of Allah. In his opinion, killing them off was too easy. He didn't consider himself a pacifist, but he believed, as did many Muslims, that violence only bred more violence. He believed everyone should have a chance to learn the truths found in the Koran and that required missionary work, not suicide bombers. However, there was one exception to this pacifistic philosophy, and that was Israel. In the case of Israel, anything was fair game.

Nayef had been introduced to Sami when he attended the local mosque close to the university and he had learned to trust in his teachings. Nayef believed every word that came out of Sami's mouth. After all, Sami knew the Koran better than anyone Nayef had ever met and he was convinced that Sami spoke for Allah.

***

The second youth that Sami was targeting was Mohammed Abdul Kalam. Mohammed was from Riyadh, Saudi Arabia, which was the most conservative city in a country that was already extremely conservative. His father was a Saudi "Prince" which afforded him high status and a unique set of privileges, which included unlimited funds. But according to Sami, all that money meant nothing if Mohammed's life was not dedicated in service for Allah. Mohammed had to be willing to sacrifice everything, which included money or even his own life in a mission to revenge the degradation of Allah and Mohammed was more than willing to do that.

Mohammed had a jealous streak. He wanted to be greater than his father. He wanted to make his mark. He didn't want to just inherit his father's riches and live off what his father had. He knew that if he carried out an attack against the infidels, his family would be both disappointed and at the same time proud. But he knew he had to do this thing that Sami wanted, whatever it was and however hard it might be. Mohammed was ready and willing to sacrifice everything.

***

Sami could see that Mohammed was eating up every word of the sermon. He was ready to go. Sami wanted to act while Mohammed was hot. He didn't want to wait too long for fear that Mohammed might cool off. He had to put something together with him and he had to do it now.

Sami had revenge in mind. He wanted to send a message to the infidels that the Muslim world was tired of its influence. The hit on the twin towers on September 11 was a great example, but this time he wanted to hit them where it hurt even more. He wanted to hit their entertainment centers. He thought of Hollywood, but that was a spread out mess and it would be hard to really hit at the core of that industry with a low yield bomb. He thought of Las Vegas, but resisted a hit on that location because he enjoyed his personal visits to that sin capital. He knew it was sinful to go there, but he felt justified in a little decadence and he knew Allah would forgive a little sin when considering the big hit he was going to make on the infidels. Plus he was planning another vacation trip back to Vegas in a couple months so he didn't want to ruin his outing. Next he thought of the world's favorite theme park in the Anaheim area. This was a center of Western decadence because it was strictly focused on pleasure. He finally decided he would target a different theme park in Orlando. That would be his first target.

As Sami's lecture drew to a close he suggested, "I need two of you to come help me in my chambers." Then, before anyone could volunteer he said, "Nayef and Mohammed, would you join me?" He specifically wanted to talk with just the two of them.

Once the three of them were in his private office, Sami sat behind his desk and he looked directly at Mohammed. "Are you ready to make a difference?" he asked.

"Guide me," replied Mohammed. "Show me the way."

"We need to attack Western decadence. What if we make our first attack on one of the biggest entertainment centers in the world?" Sami suggested and then paused to see Mohammed's reaction.

But Nayef spoke up first, "I'll do it!"

Then Mohammed spoke up, "Of course I'll do it. What location are you thinking about?"

Sami turned to Nayef and said, "First I want to establish Mohammed's mission. Then we will talk about a different mission for you." Then, turning back to Mohammed he said, "You know what theme park I'm talking about. Do you think that will make a noise heard around the world, maybe even bigger than the successful collapse of the twin towers?"

"Yes," replied Mohammed. "Theme parks are a place where Westerners from all over the world congregate in order to be entertained. I love it. What do you think we should do there?"

Sami continued, "I think we should explode a nuclear bomb right in the middle of the whole mess. We'll wipe out the park and leave it unusable for years into the future."

"Are you thinking suicide bomb?" asked Mohammed.

"Of course. Wouldn't you want to take advantage of the chance to die a hero?"

"Yes indeed. I love the idea. What do I need to do to get ready?"

"Do you have a vehicle that you could use to drive to Florida?"

"Yes," replied Mohammed, thinking about the Lexus he had received as a present from his father when he came to study at the university in Michigan. "Will I be taking the bomb with me?"

"Yes," replied Sami. "It's the size of a carry-on roller bag like what you would take on an airplane. You would never need to open the bag. You would take it into the theme park, head for somewhere in the middle of the park, and set off the bomb. We detonate it by making a phone call, which will activate the bomb. It's all packaged up and ready for you to go. So when would you be ready to leave?"

"I can leave right now," replied Mohammed. That was the answer Sami was hoping for. Any delays and he may get cold feet. But if he took off immediately there was a much better chance for success.

Sami looked back at Nayef and said, "Can you wait a few minutes? I want to get Mohammed on the road and then we can talk a little more."

"Of course," replied Nayef. "I'll be right here waiting."

Sami and Mohammed stood up. Sami walked over to a coat closet, opened the door, and rolled out a roller bag. He handed the handle of the bag over to Mohammed. Then he wrote down a phone number on a small piece of paper and gave it to Mohammed as well. He explained, "If you dial this phone number it will detonate the bomb. That's all there is to it. But you need to stay with the bomb at all times so that some over-anxious security guard doesn't walk off with it." Sami wanted to make sure Mohammed would give his life with the bomb thereby eliminating any chance of him getting picked up and confessing. Sami didn't want to be exposed.

"Understood," said Mohammed. He grabbed the handle of the roller bag and headed for the door. He knew what he had to do and he was excited to get started.

After Mohammed had left and closed the door behind him Sami sat down again and returned his attention to Nayef.

"Do you have a mission for me?" asked Nayef.

"Not yet," replied Sami. "We need to space out our missions so that we maximize the effect. We want to show these decadent infidels that they can't let their guard down. We want to remind them on a regular basis that Allah is in control and that his will is the only thing that matters. We need to have a strike every few months. That's about how long it takes for these whores of the West to get complacent. When they start to get comfortable, we strike again. We remind them that we are still around. What I want to do is to work with you on a second target that we can hit in about three months."

"If Mohammed is hitting The Orlando theme park, I could hit a Los Angeles theme park."

"No. The theme park is a hit on their fantasy life of pleasure. I think we should hit them where it hurts even more. I think we should hit their pocket books."

"How do we do that?" asked Nayef.

"Oil," replied Sami. "They are sucking our home country dry and then when they have all the Saudi Arabia oil sucked out, they want to come up with their own cheap oil. I think we should hit their oil industry. That affects everything. That affects their plastics industry, their cars, their airplanes, and on and on. But not in a way that would hurt Saudi Arabia. What we want to do is make them even more dependent on us. We can control them if they become more dependent on our oil. Then we can set whatever price we want."

"Cool! How are we going to do that?"

"The Americans have two major sources of home grown oil. One is in Alaska, and the second is in North Dakota. The other splattering of oil that exists in the U.S. is in places like Texas or Montana, which are not as significant. That oil is hard to get at. We need to hit one of these two big locations. What I want you to do is research where in the U.S. they have the most concentrated oil source. We want to put as much of their oil production out of commission as possible and we want to do it with one strike. We want to hit them fast and hard and we want the hit to be overwhelming to the economy. We want to hurt the money."

"I love it," replied Nayef. "I'll get right to work on finding the best location."

"No rush," responded Sami. "We're not going to hit the site for a few months. So there's no big rush. Be careful and be discrete. Let me know what you learn."

"Will do. I'm excited to work out my target so I'll let you know what I learn as soon as I learn it." Nayef jumped out of his seat, stood up, and headed for the door.

Chapter Three

The Orlando Theme Park
May, 2017, Wednesday, Orlando, Florida

At long last Jimmy, his father, mother, and sister walked through the gate. Jimmy was hyped. He had been to the Orlando theme park once in the past. That was many years ago when he was a little kid. But this time would be the first time he would be tall enough to go on the "big boy" rides. He was stoked. He wanted to do them all: the Scary House, the Water Log Ride, the Storm Railroad Ride, and lots more. He wasn't going to miss any of them. He was here with his little sister who wouldn't be able to go on those rides. She was just too small. It made Jimmy feel good to be able to do things that she couldn't do. She wouldn't be able to follow along behind him the way she always did at home. He wouldn't have to babysit her this time. It made him feel more grown up. He would have his dad all to himself on these rides, which made it even more exciting. His mom had stressed that she didn't like the scary rides and his dad would have to go with him. Jimmy liked the idea. He liked leaving the women behind and doing the manly things with his dad.

The line was long. It would be about a sixty-minute wait to get on the ride. Jimmy looked down at his new sneakers, which his parents had purchased for this trip. They were bright green and really "cool." They were just an added bonus. But he noticed some dirt along the side of his left sneaker. That was not acceptable. He bent down and brushed off the dirt. Using a little spit on his finger he was able to clean it off. The line dragged on. But the excitement of going on the ride with his dad made it all worthwhile. After fifty-five minutes of winding back and forth on the trail to the logs, Jimmy and his dad finally arrived for their turn. They quickly jumped on the log ride, and it wasn't long before they were off, being pulled up high and then when they arrived at the top they were released for a short ride. Then they were again pulled upward and wound their way through the inside of the mountain, working higher and higher each time. Eventually they arrived at the high point of the ride. They were out in the open, no longer in a cave inside the mountain. They were able to look out over some of the scenery and activity that was going on around them in the amusement park. They were about to take the final big drop when, off in the distance they could see a large puff of smoke followed by a loud bang. It was so loud that it made the log they were riding on shake badly. It scared Jimmy. When he looked at his dad he could see that his father was also scared. "What was that?" asked Jimmy, but the noise was too loud for his father to hear the question.

As their log started to drop off for the "big splash" a wave of strong hot wind struck Jimmy. It felt like the blast of a really strong burst of air. But it was hot; really, really hot. He looked at the source of the blast, which was slowly forming into a mushroom cloud. But the heat was too much. Jimmy blacked out. He never knew that the log hadn't arrived at the bottom of the drop-off. The heat was so intense the log melted right around Jimmy and his dad. The hot wind burnt Jimmy and his father. They were both gone before they ever realized what happened. Fortunately, it all happened so fast that they never felt any pain.

At the bottom of the drop, next to a wire fence, stood Jimmy's mom and sister. His mom looked up, initially in excitement but then in horror as she saw her husband and son hit by what looked like an enormous flame. Her horror was short lived. A fraction of a second later she was also hit by that same big wave of heat and both her and her daughter were incinerated before they were able to mentally process what was happening. It was over before they knew it. It was over in an instant.

* * *

The explosion was centered in the middle of the theme park. It was a small nuclear explosion often referred to as an A-bomb, which incinerated everything within a three-mile radius. But the fallout from the radiation would affect a ten-mile radius. Orlando and the surrounding areas would need to be evacuated. The inhabitants would need to be tested for radiation poisoning. Areas around the theme park would become a radiation wasteland for decades. The death toll was in the thousands and the damage in the billions of dollars.

It took two months for the investigators, cloaked in their radiation suits, to work their way through the destruction. But the damage was so complete that there was very little they could learn. Fortunately, the theme park had an underground world, which was their activity hub. The heat and radiation had been strong enough to cause severe damage even in the underground bunker, but fortunately the critical area known as the security room survived. It was here where the theme park's thousands of cameras stored their recordings and for this investigation, these recordings would prove to be instrumental tools in tracking down the events leading up to the explosion.

The lead FBI investigator on the scene in the security room was Livy Cobar. She was a cute little five-foot six bombshell that triggered more than one male to take a second look. She had long hair, but it was usually up in a bun to keep it out of her way when she worked. Today she was decked out in her unattractive yellow radiation suit. She sat in what was left of the security room, trying to work her way through the damaged remains of the equipment. She would take one CD at a time and test it on her computer to see if it was readable and if it contained anything that might be useful in the investigation. She was specifically interested in the recordings within the park on the day of the explosion. She would test out each CD, putting aside ones that were not readable or damaged, and labeling and saving any that were readable into her briefcase. As she was rummaging through the CDs, the one she was currently testing started to display the area of the explosion and she yelled out, "I think I found it!" In her excitement she forgot that she was in her protective gear and that everyone communicated through a microphone and earpiece. So, when she yelled out, she blasted a few eardrums and was answered back by a barrage of cusswords.

"What was that good for?" reprimanded Alvin Foller. "We all have ear pieces on and you just blew out half our eardrums." Alvin was in his fifties and a short five foot five inches with a graying beard and mustache, but his head was bald. He was the fire that kept his small group of twenty FBI investigators at the top of their game. Livy was a key player on his team.

"Sorry," she responded. "I was a little excited. I think I found the recording that's pointed directly at the area of the explosion." Livy was slightly taller than Alvin. She was in her forties and loved her job as an investigator. She made it her obsession to never leave a stone unturned. She was relentless in her pursuit of answers.

In her mind she knew without a doubt that the Muslim Brotherhood was behind this attack in the Orlando theme park. She was convinced this was an act of terrorism and she wasn't the only one who felt that way. She had made it her mission to find the evidence that would prove it.

"Super," replied Alvin. "Let me know if you see anything specific. Then we'll send it to the lab and see what they can learn." The lab had the equipment that could zoom in and pull-out details even when the recording wasn't the best. They were the hi-tech gurus behind the FBI's crime team.

Livy was fast-forwarding through the video. It wasn't a continuous play. It had recorded at four shots per second so the movement was a little choppy, but good enough to see all the activity that went on during the day. She saw everything right up to the time of the explosion. Unfortunately, the area around the explosion was crowded and it would require detailed analysis to see if the bomber could be spotted and hopefully identified.

"I see the explosion, but the area is too crowded for me to zoom in on the bomber," explained Livy.

"Have one of our runners take the disk over to the lab as quickly as possible," instructed Alvin. "You keep looking to see if there are any other recordings from a different angle."

"Will do," replied Livy, but she was already on her way finding a runner who could take off with the disk. Having sent the disk on its way, Livy returned back to the security room to continue her search.

The FBI team was a collection of specialists. Some of them were experts in bombs, others were experts in the effect of heat on buildings and people, and so on. Each agent investigated their piece of the puzzle looking for clues. They wanted to know what the bomb was made of, what the detonator was, was the bomb remote detonated or a suicide bomber, and so on. After each specialist completed their investigation they would generate a report on their findings. Then, all the specialist reports would get pulled together to see if there was a consensus on what happened. Often these consensus meetings would become heated debates and the members would argue about conflicting evidence.

Livy's personal specialty was in video and audio recordings. She loved working in this area because her evidence would often trump the other sources of evidence. If she could come up with a video recording of someone planting the bomb, then any question of whether it was anything but a terrorist attack would be eliminated. A recording would put them on the trail of an individual or possibly a cell they could now chase. That's what had happened in Boston at the marathon bombing a couple years earlier. The video evidence had trumped all the other sources of evidence in identifying and finding the bombers. However, Livy also realized that all the other evidences were also critical and it all became crucial when it came time for getting the necessary convictions.

Livy continued her search for videos of the area and came up with a couple more that were usable. She sent these off to the lab as well. She considered the lab workers as her very own miracle workers. They were able to take a recording, which seemed like garbage and build incredible pictures of the event. That happened again this time. It took a couple of days, but eventually the lab was able to take the three recordings and identify an individual with an overstuffed roller bag who seemed nervous and confused. This individual ended up in the middle of the blast zone and everyone was quickly convinced he was the source of the explosion. They saw him place the bag in a central location and then he made a phone call. The call must have been what triggered the explosion because just as he pushed what must have been the send button, the bomb went off.

A good picture of the terrorist's face led to his identification using passport files. This in turn led to the identification of his friends and associates back at home, which led to the identification of the mosque he attended. This evidence led the FBI to the Muslim Imam who was in charge. As the spiritual leader of his community, the Imam immediately came under suspicion. The Imam was already believed to be a member of the Muslim Brotherhood and the connection had been made. As far as she was concerned, they should "nuke the mosque." But who was the "they" that should do this deed?

Chapter Four

A Second Bombing
July, 2017, two months later, Minot, North Dakota

Judy loved J Cents. It was a store that always had lots of variety and reasonable prices. It was not like the overpriced clothing she found in the more expensive stores. She was in her forties and J Cents seemed to feature the styles she liked. She was always able to find something there that she just couldn't live without. She had already picked out six items she wanted to try on, four shirts and two pairs of shorts. But she wasn't finished looking.

Judy worked as a secretary for one of the oil companies and her husband worked out in the fields. It was a good life. The money was good, but the winters were killers. You just had to make the best of it indoors during seven to eight months of the year. The two of them looked forward to retirement in Arizona or New Mexico where the weather was a little more to their liking.

She headed over to the dresses and on the way saw her neighbor. Normally the two didn't talk much, but this time they both felt chatty. Their conversation lasted a good fifteen minutes. They talked about the weather and, of course, the oil production. There was little else to talk about in Minot. Running out of things to say, Judy continued over to the dress section. She started browsing through the dresses. She had come to the store because she needed a new dress for the wedding next weekend but she had become distracted by all the other clothes she felt more comfortable wearing. She hadn't yet picked out a dress to try on for the wedding and she didn't want to go back into the dressing room twice. She would need to find a couple options. A full-length green dress with an open back caught her eye and she started to check to see if they had her size. Just then she heard a loud crackling sound followed by rumbling. She looked up and started to look around. She noticed everyone else was looking around as well. Then the entire building started to creak and shift. This left her confused. What would do this to a building? Just as she turned her head upward she noticed the ceiling burst into flames. That was followed by an enormous surge of heat, which crashed down. All the clothes around her burst into flames, and her last thought was, I just found the perfect dress and now it's going to be ruined. But that was all she thought. She didn't even have time to scream. It all happened too fast.

***

Across town at the golf course Judy's husband was just wrapping up the eighth hole. It was a beautiful day for Minot. There weren't a lot of perfect days here, and you had to enjoy every one of them. It was usually snowy or at least freezing cold most of the year, and when it wasn't cold, it was windy. But today was neither. It was beautiful, sunny, and calm. It was the type of day he expected every day to be after he retired and moved to Arizona or New Mexico. Then he could play golf every day all day long.

But here in Minot, when you had a nice day like today, the golf course was always crowded. It seemed like everyone within 100 miles wanted to go golfing when there was a good day. The course was packed. This meant everyone was on a timing schedule. You had to keep moving or you would hold up the entire rhythm and flow of the course. In his mind it turned golfing into something similar to a production line. Everything had to flow smoothly.

As he picked up his ball and started heading to the ninth hole, he heard an unusual sound, one he had never heard before. It came from the southwest. Looking in that direction, he saw what looked like a dust cloud starting to form from the ground upward. It started to form into a mushroom. At first he didn't register what it could possibly be. There were no manufacturing facilities down in that direction. There was nothing there that would explode. The idea of a terrorist attack never entered his mind. A terrorist explosion in North Dakota was out of the question. It seemed ridiculous. There's nothing worth destroying. But the cloud was undeniable. There it was forming in the distance.

As soon as he realized that the explosion was real, his mind flashed to thoughts of what to do next. But it was already too late. The searing heat came at him like an ocean wave. It was visible. He could see it coming. The wave scorched the green grass, setting it on fire. Then it blasted him as well. It was unforgiving, leaving nothing but a pile of ashes behind.

Chapter Five

The Dragon Pit
July, 2017, Golden, Colorado

It was the first time in months that the Dragon Pit team of students was together again in full force. Each pit member had been off in different directions. A couple had taken summer courses, others had returned to their regular roles in the military or in their professional life, and a couple of the pit members had taken a hiking vacation along the Pacific Crest trail in Northern California near Mount Lassen. The impromptu reunion wasn't something that was planned. The members trickled in as they came back from their respective activities. But the reunion was just as warm as if it had been centered on a major celebration.

Gene, their faculty mentor, entered the room in the late morning, which was normal for him, and unceremoniously went directly to his desk without saying a word. He justified his silence by saying he didn't want to disrupt the work that the team was doing. He checked some messages and then, looking up from his desk, which was his signal that he wanted everyone's attention, he asked the question, "What are we going to do this school year which will make a difference?" He scanned the room. Everyone was looking in his direction, but no one was willing to offer an answer. They all knew what he meant. Gene was after some significant team based improvement project which would affect as much of the world as possible. He was looking for something innovative. He wanted "out of the box" thinking. Gene wasn't necessarily expecting an answer at this time. He just wanted to start everyone thinking.

"I know that in economics everything is fair game, but how about we try to narrow down the scope a little bit," suggested Gage, looking at Gene. "Are we talking financial, political, social, or operational?" Then he looked at the larger group and asked, "Let's hear some suggestions about an area of focus and then it will be easier to identify our goal." Gage saw himself as Gene's right-hand-man and was trying to help Gene get some answers to his question. Gage was a body builder, about five feet eleven, but strong as an ox and even Brian, the Air Force Captain, at well over six feet had no interest in challenging him. Gage was single and was considered "hot" by the girls that looked him over.

After a few minutes of waiting some suggestions started flying out from the various team members. One suggested they fix a failing automotive company, like one of the big three American automotive manufacturers and bring it back to financial success. Another team member suggested they work on modeling a complex international supply chain for some hi-tech company and identify its key shortcomings. Then they could share their findings with all supply chain organizations in an attempt to help them try to optimize their processes.

The debate went on for another fifteen minutes without Gene saying a word. That was the way he worked. He would start the discussion, and then he would break a fast exit. He didn't care about the debate circle. He didn't want to be drawn into the discussion. He just wanted to hear the conclusions of the team. Then, in the end, he would get them to do whatever he wanted anyway. That was the way he liked it. He wanted the team to think. But he reserved the power and right to change any of their suggestions and do what he felt was best.

The PhD program at the Colorado Engineering School (CES) Department of Economics was conducted differently than any other PhD program. It was a team of up to ten students and they were all physically located in one large room sitting together at individual desks with the chairman of the program sitting at his own desk in the same room. Their desks circled the wall with a large conference table in the middle. It was somewhat informal and often you would find various team members getting into discussions which sometimes turned into heated debates. They were a team. They learned as a team, attended classes as a team, and worked their way toward their degree as a team.

The PhD program focused on interaction and not individual study. They took individual tests, but the learning process was team based.

The chairman of this unusual PhD program was Gene Wiseman and he was always heavily engaged in the creativity that occurred. Currently the team had seven students which included Brian Pearson, an Air Force Captain, Livy Cobar, the FBI agent who had been temporarily called in to help with the Orlando theme park and later the North Dakota bombings, Gage Davis, a Navy Seal who had been part of the Seal Team Six that had found and eliminated Osama Bin Laden in Pakistan, Lincoln Travinski, an Army Ranger with special forces training, Glenn Pierre, a Marine who had served in the Pentagon for five years of his career and who still had exceptional contacts with the top brass, Carlos Santiago, an employee of the Boeing / Lockheed Martin complex which developed AGM-114 Hellfire helicopter mounted missile, and Boston George, the techie genius who had trouble writing a coherent sentence, but whose exceptional computer and math skills continually amazed everyone.

This team of students, along with their leader, was located in their one-room conference bunker which was incorporated as part of the Economics Department in the center of the Colorado Engineering School campus. This team had affectionately come to be known as the "Dragon Pit."

As usual, Gene's departure from the room didn't end the debate. With Gene gone the conversation took a sharp detour. Carlos went over to the door of the pit room and closed it, which was a strange and unexpected move. The door was rarely closed, but Carlos had something he wanted to share privately. Carlos was from Puerto Rico. He was a single Latino "stud" that was the spitting image of the singer Ricki Martin. When he and Gage went out shopping for girls, they would usually get into heated competition. They always seemed to like the same girls, or maybe they just liked to compete with each other. Sometimes it was hard to tell which was more fun.

Carlos walked back to the center of the room with a suggestion, "The world is going to pot and we're sitting here debating the wonders of corporate America. What we need to do is to have an impact. We need to make a difference."

"What are you suggesting?" asked Gage.

Carlos continued, "I look around this room and I see a group of the brightest America has to offer. And we're spinning our wheels on mathematical models. I'll tell you what really upsets me."

"What's that?" This time it was Livy that stepped into the conversation.

"Just last week we said 'they' should do something about the terrorists that hit the Orlando theme park. Well, I keep looking around and I can't figure out who 'they' are."

"Spit it out, Carlos," suggested Gage. "What do you think we should be doing?"

Carlos slapped his hand on the center conference room table in order to put emphasis behind what he was going to say next. He wanted to make sure he had everyone's attention. Slowly looking at the eyes of each of his team members, he said, "We should be the 'they.' Orlando was bombed months ago, and our politicians are still running around debating who did it." Looking at Livy he asked, "We know who did it, don't we?"

Livy, who everyone knew was part of the FBI investigation team, was caught off guard. She knew that some of the investigative information was secret and she could be accused of treason if she revealed it. After a long pause she decided to break with protocol and nodded her head yes. Then she decided this group of friends deserved to know the truth so she verbalized it and said, "Yes, we know. And I don't think it's a big secret. History keeps repeating itself. We helped Egypt get free elections. As a thank you they voted in the Muslim Brotherhood who swore their hatred for America. We helped install a government that in the end hates us. Then two years later a military coup kicked them out and executed most of them. Then a very similar thing occurred in Syria. History keeps repeating itself. This Muslim Brotherhood or ISIS or the Islamic State or whatever they call themselves keeps rearing its ugly head when we least expect it. They use a radicalized Koran to justify their actions. They focus on a Koran, which stresses revenge rather than love. In fact the word 'love' does not even appear in the Koran. It's all about revenge. And many Islamic Imam's focus on the revenge aspect of the Koran so much so that they can get people to die for their religion by doing things like suicide bombings in the name of Allah. They believe that executing revenge is the way to get to paradise in the next life."

"Are you saying the Muslim Brotherhood is responsible for the Orlando theme park bombing?" asked Gage.

"That's strictly confidential information that I'm not allowed to share. I didn't say anything like that," responded a politically correct Livy but everyone knew how to interpret her smile. "You know I can't talk about an active investigation." Again she shared her smile.

Lincoln, who was holding back until now, jumped in, "What can we do? We're just a bunch of PhD students with no political clout. And worse yet, no money." Lincoln was rugged looking. He had the appearance of someone who came from the back streets of some tough inner-city neighborhood. He had a scar across the left cheek and another above his right eye, both of which occurred during a badly planned military training exercise. But they made him look like he had been in more than one knife fight. In his heart he was a pussycat. But his outside appearance was scary and caused most people to avoid him.

"Our obscurity is our advantage," responded a supportive Brian. "We are in a position where we could get away with things that our obsessive bureaucracy in Washington and our hamstrung military can't get close to."

"Wait. What are we really talking about here? Are we talking about analysis, or are we talking about some kind of hit squad. I'm thinking you guys are talking about something that borders on insanity. Are you guys talking about taking on the Muslim Brotherhood all on your own? This is crazy talk."

Livy, who was starting to get both excited and scared about where this conversation was going, came back with a suggestion. "We don't need to take on the Muslim Brotherhood. We just need to send a message. These Muslim radicals don't take us seriously. You have the radicals attacking us, like 9-11 or like the recent attack on the theme park, and what do we do? We go into weeks and months of debates, which often lead nowhere. And then the non-radicalized Muslim community talks us into backing off and doing nothing. We become afraid of appearing to be religiously racist. Sure, we went into Afghanistan and Iraq, and we occupied the countries forever, but did we squash Al-Qaida or ISIS? No! They just moved somewhere else and continued planning their attacks. We had Bin Laden sitting in Pakistan right next to us and we didn't even know it. He was practically our neighbor and we didn't know it. We're doing this all wrong. The radicals aren't selectively targeting us. They're randomly hitting 'symbols of Western decadence.' The only way we're going to get them to stop is if we do the same to them. If we retaliate by also hitting targets that are the symbols of the Muslim Brotherhood, we'll hopefully find that the Muslim community will take it upon themselves to suppress the radicals. That's the bottom line. Every time a Westerner strikes a blow against a Muslim radical, the radical becomes a hero and a martyr. But if we can mobilize the Muslim community to clean their own house, then we will have a chance at winning this war on terror. We won't have to chase the Bin Ladens all over the globe. That's a waste of time. We need the Muslim community to chase and eliminate the Bin Ladens instead of hiding them and protecting them."

Lincoln was more conservative. "This is crazy talk. Are you seriously talking about us starting our own little vigilante organization against the Muslim Brotherhood? We'll probably end up doing more damage than good. We'll just create more Muslim radicals who are out looking for revenge against the Western infidels. According to the statistics, only about five to ten percent of the Muslim community is radicalized. How can we attack the entire Muslim world because of a few crazies?"

Livy wasn't giving up. "True. But we also need to remember that at Hitler's peak only seven percent of the German population was Nazi, and we see how well that worked out. In the end a lot more than just Germany suffered. We need to ask ourselves if anything we are doing now is working. We live in fear in our own country. Twenty years ago we laughed at the countries that had armed guards in their airports. We thought of them as underdeveloped and uncivilized. Now we're the country with the armed guards at the airports. We're losing the battle against terrorism. We've allowed terrorism to change our world. It needs to stop and I say we need to fight fire with fire. Most other religious communities police themselves. For example, the Roman Catholic Church, the largest church in the world, when it was accused of child molestation, went to work identifying and eliminating it. But the Muslim community, the second largest religious group in the world, expects the Westerners to clean up the Muslim radicals. It will never work that way. It will just drag this war on terror on forever and ever. I'm glad Carlos opened this door and started this conversation. I may be crazy, but I think Carlos has an idea here that could work."

Brian, playing the neutral role between Lincoln and Livy, jumped in, "How are we going to make a difference? We don't have the money, the tools, or the technology to do anything. We can't even get into most of these countries without an extensive visa process. We're talking nonsense here."

Livy turned and was staring directly up into Brian's eyes. Leading the thought process she said, "Tell me, Brian, how do we get into a country without them knowing about it? Do we need to be physically there? We don't need to be suicide bombers. We just need bombs." Everyone knew what she was referring to. They knew Brian flew remote aircraft for the Air Force and that they could sneak into any country below their radar system.

"How in the world do you expect me to get approval for something like that?" Brian asked.

"Who's talking about getting approvals?" responded Livy.

Brian and Lincoln were both taken back. They were surprised by Livy's aggressive approach. She had taken Carlos's suggestions to the next level. She was not just talking about retaliation, now she was talking about stealing military equipment. The entire room went silent as they processed what Livy had just said. Livy was advocating an all-out frontal terrorist attack of her own. She was pushing for an-eye-for-an-eye type hit against not just the Muslim Brotherhood, but against the Muslim community. She was suggesting that the Muslim community needed to clean their own house and the only way to get their attention was to hurt them the way they were hurting the United States.

"We are talking crazy nonsense here," blurted Lincoln.

"Are we?" asked Gage, who was starting to see Livy's logic.

"Absolutely. You don't fix stupid by being stupid. They attacked us, which was wrong. And if we attack them, that's also wrong. There is no logic in the world that would say that two wrongs make a right. What you're proposing would just make us terrorists too, just like the Muslim Brotherhood."

"But that's just the point. What we're doing now, which is using Western morality to fight Muslim terrorists, is not working. Maybe our Western morality needs to shift. Maybe we need to think like the terrorists do. Maybe we need to focus on revenge like they do. Maybe then we'll get their attention."

Lincoln just shook his head in pretended disgust. Then Brian jumped in. "Where do we get the equipment and money to do anything like this? The stealth planes that I fly don't grow on trees. They are tightly controlled and monitored. And the weapon systems are even tougher to get."

"But they do crash, don't they?" suggested Carlos, who was loving all the turns this conversation had taken. He was hinting that maybe a pretended crash would be the way to acquire a plane. "And they do fly below radar so even we wouldn't be able to follow them. We need to be a little creative and I'll bet we can come up with something."

At this point Gene walked back in the room. Unknown to the rest of the team he had been standing outside listening to the conversation and he liked where it was going. But the conversation seemed to be stalling out and he thought it was a good time to let everyone call it a day and think. He knew this subject wasn't dead, but he also knew they would stop the conversation as soon as he returned to his desk. True to expectations, everyone stopped talking and returned to their respective desks pretending to get back to work. But their minds were still processing the conversation that had just occurred. They would keep processing it for days to come.

Chapter Six

The Dragon Pit Accelerates
July, 2017, Golden, Colorado

Boston was raised in Sacramento, California and lived there all the way through his college years where he attended the California State University, Sacramento. After college he moved and worked in the Silicon Valley for a hi-tech company where he met his wife and married. He was then hired by another hi-tech company and moved to Seattle. He was a techie genius but he wanted more. He had met Gene Wiseman at a conference and was completely enamored by the program he described at the Colorado Engineering School. Additionally, his wife developed bronchitis in the damp cold of Seattle, so he decided to return to school and get his PhD. In the end, Boston left his position in the Pacific Northwest and moved his family to Colorado to join the Dragon Pit.

Boston was at home in the evening, having returned to his small apartment where he lived with his wife and two children while he worked on his PhD. He was following his normal end-of-day ritual. He was standing in the kitchen, leaning against the counter, and watching his wife make dinner. He started a conversation with her by saying, "The world is going to pot. We were having a conversation in the Pit today and we basically came to that conclusion."

"So what's new about that?" questioned his wife.

"Not much, I guess. It's just that we were saying that there are a lot of things out there that need to be done, and there's no one to do them. We keep saying 'they should do this' or 'they should do that' but who is 'they'?"

"Maybe it's you." His wife was not willing to let him off the hook.

"You sound like the guys in the Pit. What can I do?"

"You have a group of buddies in the Pit. You guys are supposed to be the best and the brightest. Why don't you put your heads to it and come up with something?"

That comment left Boston speechless. It set his mind reeling. He wasn't sure how to react to that comment. What was it that he could do? What was it that the pit could do? They were just a few individuals in this big bad world. If the big boy politicians couldn't fix the problems, what could this little group of academics accomplish?

The children were watching TV in the living room and their show, "The Kids Club House", was interrupted by a special news broadcast. Of course the children let out a cry of complaint. They yelled for their dad, "Our show is messed up. Can you come fix it?"

Boston went into the living room to see what they were complaining about. Regular programming had been interrupted by a special news broadcast about another bombing. Boston shushed his children, sat down on the couch, and listened intently. Then out loud he said to no one in particular, "Minot, North Dakota? Who would want to bomb Minot, North Dakota?"

The noise brought his wife into the room as well. As she was drying her hands off with a kitchen towel she asked, "What's going on?"

"They bombed Minot, North Dakota. Can you believe that? Minot, North Dakota. How does that make any sense?" Boston asked.

"Tell me one more time where it was," requested his wife sarcastically.

Boston looked at his wife and could see the smirk on her face telling him that she was being sarcastic. "What the heck was worth bombing there?" This time he avoided mentioning the name of the city. He didn't need any more sarcasm.

"That's terrible," she responded. "The only thing that's out there is those enormous oil fields that they've been working recently."

"We want to see Club House," whined the children.

Without responding to the children, Boston looked at his wife with a flash of insight. "You're right. It's the oil fields. They are trying to disrupt our oil supply so that we remain dependent on OPEC oil. That has to be what it is."

"So back to our conversation in the kitchen," his wife added. "What are you people in the Dragon Pit going to do about it?"

"What can we do?" questioned Boston. But his mind was already on a roll trying to formulate a solution. Then he punched in a text message and sent it out to his entire Dragon Pit group. It said, "Can we be the 'them' that needs to do something? Let's meet at my house at eight p.m. to brainstorm, after the kids are in bed."

***

Livy was out shopping in downtown Denver with her live-in boyfriend Jonathan when she received the text from Boston. She didn't like shopping; that wasn't why she went to the mall. She would go out to walk and browse in order to take a break from her studies. It gave her headspace. Often she would walk into stores and scan them front to back looking for nothing at all. She would walk around for a while, and then leave again.

The two of them didn't talk a lot. Jonathan was used to this routine. When Livy was focused on something, it was better to leave her in her little world thinking through what she needed to think through. If he interrupted her he would often get blasted by some rude remark. So he just walked with her and looked.

Normally Livy would be absorbed in thought with no particular subject in mind. But today there was a subject that bothered her a lot. There was another bombing. It was getting to be a monthly occurrence. Every month somewhere in the world a major bombing occurred. More often than not it would be Muslim radical inspired. Often it would be in countries where you would expect attacks. But when the attacks were in Western countries like Europe or the United States it was especially bothersome. Not because these countries were somehow better than anyone else, but because they were a little stupid. The Westerners thought differently than these radicals. The Westerners actually thought that if they treated these radicals with respect that they would receive the same kind of respect in return. That was way off. To these radicals, infidels were infidels no matter how nice and respectful they behaved. According to their radical interpretation of the Koran, it was appropriate to take revenge on these infidels who were trying to corrupt their religion, their standards, their wives, and their children with satanic Western ideas. Women's rights and the education of women were considered anti-Allah behavior. Western television and movies were insulting, immodest, and had to be suppressed. Retaliating against these corrupt Western infidels was not just a good thing, in their view it was required by the Koran.

Livy was especially troubled now that there had been two major hits in the United States within three months' time. This was unacceptable. The president wanted to sweet-talk the radicals. Couldn't he see that they would love nothing more than to blow him up; that the individual who suicide bombed the U.S. president would be the ultimate all-time hero?

Livy knew she would be called on any minute to go to North Dakota to help in the investigation of the bombing there. But this time there would not be an underground bunker filled with recording tapes like in Orlando. This time it would be a matter of stumbling around in the debris in radiation suits hoping to find a miracle.

Jonathan was also in the FBI. He was in a different division and was stationed in the Denver area. He was part of the local Denver force. He wasn't exceptional in any way; just a plain ordinary looking five-foot ten male with black, slightly balding hair. His features and skin color had a hint of Indian. But Livy saw him as someone who was stable and always on track. She envisioned him as Mister Reliable, and she felt that was what she needed in her life to keep her grounded.

Livy outranked Jonathan and her DC area position gave her a lot of prestige. She would fly off to use her investigative techniques in all corners of the United States as required. Jonathan envied her traveling because he rarely traveled outside of the Denver, Colorado area.

The text from Boston came just as Livy was at her peak of irritation. Thinking about the bombings had her blood boiling with frustration. She was ready to do something. But she didn't know what. She wanted to talk about it. She was a good forty-five minute drive away from Boston's house, but she was going to be there at eight no matter what. She had something to say, and she wanted to be heard.

"What was that?" asked Jonathan.

"Boston wants to get together," responded Livy. Jonathan was used to her receiving calls from the Dragon Pit members. The program was very team oriented, and they were always ready to help each other out. But this wasn't something Jonathan enjoyed. He had been to some of these Dragon Pit meetings in the past and had found them extremely boring. He preferred to watch the Broncos on TV.

"Drop me off at home on the way," Jonathan suggested. He was sure this was going to be another one of those boring economics discussions, and he hated them, mostly because he had no idea what they were talking about.

"Sure," Livy responded. She wasn't sure where the conversation at Boston's place would go, so she didn't want Jonathan coming with her and spending his whole time waiting to leave. It was better to drop him off.

Sometimes Livy wondered why they were together. Jonathan was more of a jock, and she enjoyed the intellectual challenge of the PhD program. She would be reading when he watched his ball games or when he was out playing basketball for long hours at a time with his friends. What she liked about him was that he left her alone. She could space out when she felt like thinking, and he had learned to leave her in her thoughts. But other than occasionally being a social companion, she didn't feel strongly connected. He was more like a neighbor or a friend, which was also important. But their connection was extremely weak. She didn't feel the passion for him that she felt was a requirement if they were going to get married, which she assumed was the ultimate goal in their relationship.

Jonathan had asked her about marriage in the past. It wasn't in the form of a proposal. It was more like an informal conversation. He would ask questions like, "Do you think we should get married at some point?"

or "Are your parents bugging you about getting married?" She was glad that he didn't formally propose, because she wasn't sure what she would say. She really didn't feel like "yes" was the right answer.

They started their long walk to the opposite end of the mall where her car was located. Her thoughts had shifted. Now she was working out what she planned to say when she met with the Dragon Pit team.

Chapter Seven

The Dragon Pit Organizes
July, 2017, Golden, Colorado

The evening set in and eight rolled around quickly. Everyone who was coming to Boston's house had mentally formulated their perspective on what had happened with the bombings. Each felt they knew what needed to be done about it. But each had a completely different solution.

The first to arrive was Gage, followed closely by Livy and Brian. Boston invited them into his small apartment, and they all found a place to sit. The living room only had a two-person couch and a recliner, but that didn't bother anyone. They were used to living on student budgets. A couple of them unceremoniously grabbed chairs from the kitchen table and seated themselves around the small coffee table in the center of the room.

"So what's up?" started Gage, kicking off the conversation.

"I'm really irritated by the bombings and my wife keeps telling me that we should quit talking and start doing something about it," responded Boston. "I don't have a magic answer. I just thought we'd kick it around a little away from school. Maybe there's nothing we can do. But then again, maybe there is. I just felt like bouncing ideas around."

"I think there are too many people already feeling like they can't do anything," jumped in Livy. "Our government is spinning their wheels trying to be politically correct and not offend anyone. They just want to make sure our Middle East oil supply doesn't get disrupted. In the meantime our own oil supplies here at home are being destroyed so we're even more dependent on the Middle East. I only see this going from bad to worse for us if we don't do something soon. By the time our government figures out what's going on it will be too late."

"So what are we going to do about it?" inserted Brian. "We're just a bunch of nerds. What power or influence do we have?"

"We're a lot more than just academic nerds," replied Boston. "When you look at the Dragon Pit team we have someone from each branch of the military, and someone from the FBI. And we have someone who has walked the halls of the Pentagon. We probably have a better group of heads here than our own government. And we don't have to kiss up to the bureaucrats."

"Okay but so what? What are WE going to do?" challenged Brian.

"Hit them back," Livy responded.

Everyone paused for a moment letting her comment sink in. "What does that mean?" asked Brian.

"They hit us and we hit them back," replied Livy. "The Muslim radicals are a culture focused on the importance of revenge; an eye for an eye and a tooth for a tooth. We need to show them that we can execute a little revenge of our own."

"And how do you propose we do that?" Brian wasn't sure he liked where this conversation was going. It was starting to sound a little crazy. But he wasn't the only one who was nervous. Boston and Gage were starting to see through the rhetoric. They were starting to see what Livy was hinting at.

"Hold it," Gage started. "We heavily criticize the radical Muslim Imams that are responsible for radicalizing the youth and getting them to perform acts like suicide bombings. We blame them for undue influence on their members. I'm starting to feel a little like I'm being radicalized," he said with a smile.

"You're not exactly what I would call radical-izable youth," replied Livy. "But you are correct in assuming that I am suggesting a radical solution. I think it's time to think like the radicals. I think an eye for an eye is appropriate. I think that if they're going to hit us where it hurts, which is the Orlando theme park and our oil resources, then we should hit them in the same places. Let's hit them where it hurts them the most. Let's hit their theme park, which is Mecca, and let's hit their oil resources. And in the future every time they hit us, we immediately strike back in kind. That's the way to end this terrorism nonsense. Politicians have not been able to do it with their big talk. The United Nations and the Federal Government haven't accomplished anything. I'll bet we can accomplish more than the both of them put together."

Just then the doorbell rang and Boston opened the door to Lincoln and Carlos. "Sorry we're late," said Lincoln.

"It's okay," Boston replied. "You arrived at the right time. Livy was just suggesting that the Dragon Pit get organized into our own little terrorist cell and that we bomb Mecca and the Arab oil fields."

Lincoln looked over at Livy and exclaimed, "Have you lost your mind? How on earth do you think we could accomplish that? And don't you think it would just make things worse?"

But Livy suddenly had defenders when Carlos jumped in. "It's not so crazy. No one else has been effective against the radicals. And we would just be reversing their eye for an eye philosophy against them. It's a language they would understand. It might be the only language they understand." Then turning to Livy he asked, "But how in the world would our little group be able to accomplish something so crazy?"

Livy picked up the conversation. "Actually, I was thinking we have all the pieces in place right here in this room. We start with Brian somehow ditching one of the remote controlled unmanned aircraft that he flies and then we use that aircraft to fly in under the radar and hit the locations we're talking about. I think that's the easy part. The hard part is deciding which locations to hit."

Everyone looked toward Brian to see his reaction. His past negativity made it seem questionable that they would have his support. But he surprised everyone, "I like it. Let's do it. I've always thought that it would be amazingly easy to steal one of these drone aircraft. I think I've been radicalized. I'm convinced that we may actually be speaking their language if we do something like this. I'm willing to risk my career to save thousands of lives, like the lives that were lost in Orlando or North Dakota. That's what I signed up with the military to do: save American lives. And this may just be the best way to accomplish that goal, better than what I'm currently doing by flying surveillance planes over Afghanistan and Iraq." Looking around the room he said, "I'm going to need some help in accomplishing it. We need to steal not just the aircraft but also the control computers with their software and of course the weapons systems. And we'll need a place to land the plane that no one will find suspicious."

"Okay," said Carlos. "Let's talk this through one step at a time to see if it's feasible. Let's get all our heads together to see if we're totally crazy or if we can formulate a plan."

Again to everyone's surprise Lincoln also jumped in. "I have the landing site covered. My family has a 5,000-acre tract of flat land in Texas and I'm sure we can find a spot that's remote where no one will see us land or take off. In fact, I can think of the perfect place, complete with a small cabin, which we can clean up and make workable. I'll take care of that piece of the puzzle."

Brian jumped back in, "Getting the aircraft is fairly simple. All we need to do is disable the GPS tracking devices. If we do that, it will seem like the plane crashed or was hit. No one will go searching for it if we lose it in enemy territory. We need to find an aircraft that is on a mission in Afghanistan or Iraq and which is fully loaded with weapons systems. Then, while en route we disable the GPS, and then fly it on to our target, whatever that is, do our mission, and then fly the thing back to our base in Texas. We may have a fuel problem, depending on where the plane took off from, but even if we drop it into the ocean after our mission, we'll have accomplished what we set out to do, which is send the radicals a message."

"That's a better plan then flying it back into the United States. If we just drop it into the ocean after it accomplishes its mission no one will be able to track us. But how do we disable the GPS?" asked Livy.

Now it was Boston's turn. "I can build a mechanism that will disconnect the GPS whenever we decide. We send a signal to the plane and GPS drops off the radar. That's my baby. Then we can switch control over to our own computer. But someone will need to install it into the plane after I build it. And we don't want to put it into the wrong plane because we don't want anyone to find it afterward. Maybe I can build a self-destruct feature into it that gets activated after the GPS has been eliminated and our mission has been successfully completed."

"I knew a techie would come in handy," replied Livy.

"What about weapons systems?" asked Carlos. "We'll have the weapons for the first strike. But what about future strikes. We'll have the plane but we won't have the weapons."

"We may be better off just ditching the aircraft in the ocean," suggested Gage. "I like that idea. That also solves the weapons systems problem for repeat missions. We'll have to find a drone already equipped. Ditching offers less chance of anyone finding us in Texas with the aircraft. I vote we do the hit, ditch the plane, and live to fight another day. We'll just have to single use the aircraft and if we need a second mission we'll have to steal a second one. I think we'll be putting these planes to better use than how they're being used now."

"That probably makes the most sense," responded Brian. "Now for the next big issue. How do we get a control computer?"

"Any suggestions?" asked Carlos, looking directly at Brian.

"I can probably figure out a way to get access to the software. But we also need a computer with the correct configuration. Since we'll have eliminated the GPS we're going to have to do all the guidance ourselves. This is going to be harder than it originally seemed. We need to think through how we're going to control and fly this thing after we disconnect it from the base."

Boston jumped in again, "I can help with the computer and making the software work. But we are going to be flying blind. That's going to be tricky."

Livy and Carlos had become really excited. This was no longer a wild dream. These guys were actually trying to figure out how to make this work. They were past the point of resistance and were now focused on the success of the effort. This team was actually going to "make a difference." It wasn't some "they" that was going to do this. The Dragon Pit team was the "they"!

Gage jumped in, "What if we left the GPS alone, but rather cut the communications cord and reconnected it with our communications connection? How would that work?"

"Doable but riskier," responded Boston. "There is a tracking signal that will allow satellites to track the bird using GPS. It would be better to eliminate it. Probably the easiest thing to do is for you to get your hands on one of their current communications boxes and I'll modify it to accomplish what we're talking about. Then we just need to swap it out sometime. I'll fix it to look like the original box so it won't be suspicious."

Brian continued, "I'll have to figure out how to get my hands on it. The boxes are not tracked so it should be easy. And I assume you'll get the flight control computer to sync with the modified equipment as well."

"You bet," replied Boston.

The room went silent for a few minutes while the team thought through other possible glitches to the plan. It seemed as though the plan was doable.

"Looks like we have an executable plan," suggested Carlos. "Now what are we going to hit? What's our target going to be?"

"Mecca," blurted out Livy. "Why not hit them where it hurts?"

"You realize that it's the most tightly controlled site in the world," responded Lincoln. "I'm more for giving them a warning shot across the bow. Then, if they don't take the hint we may have to get more drastic like Mecca."

Carlos jumped in, "What site can we hit that will hurt the radicals the most? We want them to get the message."

"That's the problem," responded Livy. "There is not one site that will effect the radicals and not also sting the rest of the Muslim population. But that's the same with the sites they have been hitting in the US. They haven't targeted military sites. They're hitting sites like the Orlando theme park in order to maximize the civilian casualties. They're trying to hurt us as much as possible. I still say we hit the big one. We shouldn't avoid offending the larger Muslim community. In fact we want to get them excited and involved. We want them to feel the pain that we're feeling. That will get them to react. That's what will get them moving. I say we hit Mecca. That's their Orlando theme park."

"How about Medina?" suggested Lincoln, still trying to get the conversation off of the Muslim world's holiest site. "Or how about the Dome of the Rock in Jerusalem?"

"We can't hit a site in Jerusalem without getting Israel on our tails," responded Brian. "That doesn't work. We don't want to get into a conflict with them. And besides, they'll probably track us even better than the Saudi's who are protecting Mecca."

"Okay," responded Lincoln. "Let's stay away from Mecca and from the Dome of the Rock. But Medina is still in play and what other site choices do we have?"

"What about hitting them in their pocket books?" asked Boston. "What about a hit on their oil industry?"

"The problem with that is we would hurt a country, and not the radicals at large," replied Livy. "A hit on their religion would hit everyone. It's the kind of hit that will make one part of the Muslim world blame another part of the Muslim world. And that's what we want to accomplish."

"Well then, Medina it is," replied Lincoln. "I guess we have our target. The second most holy site in Islam. What are we going to hit them with?"

"Whatever our captured plane is carrying," replied Brian. "We'll have to make do with what we have on board."

"True," replied Livy. "So let's pick a plane with a good payload."

"Let's avoid nukes," suggested Lincoln. "That's too drastic. We just want to give them a warning shot."

"We haven't used the unmanned planes for nukes so I doubt that will even be an option anyway," responded Brian.

"I'm concerned about the timing," Lincoln continued, his hesitation showing through. "Should we wait until there is another attack? We want to make sure they tie our response to their attack so there's no question about what happened."

"Are you kidding?" Livy jumped in all excited. "Are you telling me that 3,000 deaths in Orlando and another 2,000 in North Dakota aren't enough motivation for us to move forward? Are you telling me we need another few thousand deaths before we respond? We can't wait any longer. We've already waited too long. We need a response and we need it now." The rest of the team members were nodding their heads in agreement with Livy's statement.

"I guess I've been outvoted," replied Lincoln. "Actually I agree, but I just thought I'd explore the question to see what the rest of you thought."

The team proceeded to draw out a plan of attack which included acquiring a spare communications control module, modifying it so that it could be switched to communicating with the team, getting it inserted into an aircraft that was expected to go on a mission in the near future, acquiring a computer which could be used for loading the control software, copying the software and loading it on to the computer, and waiting for the ideal opportunity for the team to take over control of the aircraft. The target had been selected. The plan had been made. Now it was time for execution.

As they were nearing the end of their planning Livy's phone started ringing with her Jason Mraz ring tone, which told her it was a call from the "boss". "Here we go," she said to no one in particular as she pushed the "Talk" button. "Hello!"

She listened intently and then said, "On my way." Then she turned to the rest of the team and said, "I'm off to North Dakota to see the mess there. I'll keep you posted on what I learn. In the meantime, let's execute on our plan as quickly as possible. I know that what I will be seeing up north will be enormously irritating.

"But we need to be smart about this. We're stepping into a clandestine world that requires extreme secrecy. We can't be blundering around like idiots that are eager to get caught."

"What are you suggesting?" asked Boston.

"First, we each need to get a second secure phone. We each go to Superstore Mart and purchase one of those throwaway phones and we purchase it with cash. Then we sync up all our phones so that we have each other's phone number in that phone. We use these phones only for communicating with each other and never call anyone or anything else on them. If anyone's phone is compromised in any way, for example a call comes in or goes out that was not one of the team members, we all throw our phones away and replace them immediately. We still use our regular phones to talk to each other about schoolwork. We use the throwaways for conversations about our clandestine activities."

"Understood," replied Carlos. "I can see we are getting ourselves into a world that requires extreme secrecy."

Livy continued, "It goes without saying that we talk to no one, and I mean no one else about what we're doing here. Everyone suddenly becomes suspect."

"Agreed," answered Brian.

"Another precaution we need is to have a code system. What I mean by that is that each one of us has to pick a favorite book. Then, if we need to send a coded message for any reason, like if a phone has been compromised, we use that book to send out a message. We always refer to the book of the message sender. Here is how it works. If I need the letter 'a' I say something like 37c. What that means is that on page 37, the first letter of the first word on line 'c', which is the third line, is the letter that we're looking for. So we can send an entire message and anyone listening in won't be able to interpret the message without knowing what book we're using. As a precaution, we never write down the names of the books we're using. We need to memorize each of our books. Make them easy books to access so we don't have to search the world for the book. And don't be too generic. For example, there are hundreds of versions of the Bible, so don't use that. One more precaution: we should use this system as infrequently as possible because the use of it could also raise suspicion."

"I understand the importance of secrecy," replied Brian. "We're endangering not just ourselves, but our entire families. This is going to be risky. I think we should each make sure we're committed to this cause before we go any further. Can I get confirmation from each of you?"

He went around the room looking for each person to say they agreed. Everyone said the customary, "I'm in," some more enthusiastically than others.

"I have to go," said Livy. "But let's get the phones and the books figured out as soon as possible. My book will be 'The Goal' by Eli Goldratt, which all you operations gurus know about and have a copy of. And let's work with Brian to develop the details of his plan."

"We'll keep you posted," replied Carlos. "I'm wondering if our communications should be masked by creating a name for our team that won't be too revealing. Do we need a name for our mission?"

"I have an idea," suggested Gage. "How about we call ourselves the Nerds?"

"Yes," interjected Boston. He took it as a joke and threw in some sarcasm, "and then we could use code words like having Grandma picking up the kids at the babysitter means we have acquired control of the aircraft. And Grandma has delivered the kids to school is the successful dropping of the bombs."

"Sure," came back Gage playing with the humor, "and Grandma has returned home is when we dropped the plane into the ocean. And Grandma is ready to get the kids is when everything is in place with the computer operationally and the aircraft control box has been replaced."

"I like the Grandma thing," commented Carlos. "But I'm not sure I like the Nerds label for the team."

Gage continued, "I was thinking that NERDS could be the initials standing for Necessary Evil Retaliation Delivery System."

Brian jumped in, "Oh my gosh, that's a stretch to force fit an acronym. We are definitely nerdy if we're resorting to these types of word games."

Livy responded, "I love it! But I think it's dorky. We are a group of nerds called the NERDS and we are getting Grandma ready to deliver the kids. We're getting a little carried away." With that she bid her goodbyes and headed for the door. She would drive directly to the Denver airport. En route Livy received a text, which informed her about her flight reservations. She was off to see what was left of Minot, North Dakota.

Chapter Eight

The Devastation
July, 2017, Minot, North Dakota

The Minot airport was shut down so air travel required Livy to go to Bismarck and then take a two-hour drive north. The FBI team convened at the local Holiday Inn where they were outfitted with the necessary protection gear. Then, when they were about two-thirds of the way to Minot they put on their gear, switched vehicles getting into one, which was labeled "contaminated", and finished the drive. Riding in any vehicle with full radiation gear including oxygen tanks was extremely uncomfortable. But no one was going to complain. The alternative of not wearing the suits was out of the question.

As they approached the point of impact near the mall, the team was awestruck by the devastation. "Looks like Orlando all over again," said Livy into her microphone which was used for communication between team members. No one responded.

When the FBI team arrived at ground zero of the explosion they identified a large crater and noticed about one third of the shopping mall missing. Livy went to work immediately searching for a control room in hopes that something survived. A floor map of the mall that she had pulled off the internet helped her in her search but she was disappointed to learn that the control room had been destroyed during the blast.

Other team members searched out their own aspects of the blast and each came away equally disappointed. About the only thing they could conclude was that it was a nuclear blast, which originated in the shopping mall, and based on measuring out the location of ground zero it occurred inside of an empty store that was being remodeled. Further investigation would reveal that the store was rented out by an unknown entity a couple months earlier and the FBI team concluded that this explosion was in the planning cycle for at least that long. It left them not knowing if this had been a suicide bombing, if the bomb was set with a timer, or if it was remotely detonated.

The next phase of the investigation would follow the only available lead, which was to try to identify the tenants of the rented store. This would lead to a nonexistent organization that had dummy bank accounts with only enough money in them to cover the rent until the time of the explosion.

At the end of their day on-site, the FBI team returned to Bismarck silent and frustrated. Each was in their own thoughts and each was disappointed that they hadn't found anything significant. At the two-thirds point a changeover station had been set up. The team climbed out of their protective suits and took showers. Then they went through a decontamination chamber after which they were allowed to get redressed. It was a lengthy but necessary process. After that they were allowed to return to their hotel.

Livy had done what she could, which turned out to be very little. In the evening she documented what she learned and sent the file over to her superior Alvin. This would become part of the larger report on the investigation. But because there were no surveillance recordings she was no longer needed on site. She planned to return to Colorado the next day.

Chapter Nine

North Dakota
July, 2017, Minot, North Dakota

Alvin Foller, the FBI lead investigator in Orlando, was also the lead in Minot. He ended his investigative day by rounding his team together in Bismarck for a strategy session. They all knew the routine and came to the conference room for a debriefing shortly after they arrived back at the hotel. Once they were all together Alvin started the discussion by saying, "What have we learned today?" Each of the team members knew that they would have to report their activities for the day, especially if they had something valuable to share with the team.

The first agent started up, "It seems pretty obvious that this attack was triggered by a device that was identical to the one used in the Orlando theme park. The signature of the bomb is identical. The blast is the same and the radiation tests that we've taken at the two sites match exactly. It seems we may have a serial suicide bomber cell in play. What we learned from our investigation of the earlier site has suddenly become extremely relevant here at this site. So I'm going to share some of your previous findings because they may help here as well. What we learned in Orlando was that the bomb that was used was made from materials extracted in the Ukraine and sold by the former Soviet territory now known as the North Caucasus. They in turn had stolen the bomb triggering mechanisms from the Chechen republic. The bombs and triggers were transported to Vladivostok on the East coast of Russia and shipped to Vancouver, British Colombia, Canada. The bombs were smuggled into Canada using a sealed cargo container, which was shielded in lead thereby making the radiation undetectable. The bomb was mixed in with a shipment of coffee products, which suppresses any smells that the dogs might pick up. The bombs were assembled in Canada and driven across the border into the United States in cars using roller bag suitcases. Once the bombs were in the United States, they were delivered directly to Detroit. Whether the bombs ever made it all the way to Detroit or not, we don't really know. The next thing we know is that a suicide bomber has the bomb in a roller bag, the type that passengers use for air travel. Now it appears that there were at least two bombs and possibly more that we don't know about."

A second agent spoke up, "Then we need to focus on finding the bombs, not on studying the destruction."

Alvin stepped in, "We need to do both. Our Crime Scene Investigator team needs to see if there is anything else that can be learned at the bombsite, and the rest of our agents need to put all their efforts into retracing the path of this bomb. Let's start by seeing what we can learn from any surveillance equipment that may have been posted along the Vancouver BC to Detroit route. Let's see if there are any gaps in the travel time. Then we'll know where to drill deeper, looking for a point where the bombs may have been off-loaded."

Livy spoke up, "Can't we use what we already know about the Orlando bomber to help us in our investigation here?"

Alvin continued, "Actually, we do have a separate team working on the assumption that the Ann Arbor mosque which was the source of the Orlando bomber may be the base of operation for a terrorist cell. If we can connect the North Dakota bomber to the same mosque then we can zero in on their activities. But I don't want the North Dakota team to start with that assumption. If it is the same mosque, then I want this team to independently come to the same conclusion."

"We should at least check airports, trains, car rentals, roadway video recordings, or anything else we can come up with between here and Detroit, just in case," Livy suggested. "For example, if we see a car with Michigan plates driving from the eastern border of North Dakota we should take a closer look at its registration."

"Excellent suggestion," responded Alvin. "I'll put someone on that as well. And I'll have them send any recordings to you so you can go through them."

"I'd love to take a look at anything suspicious. We shouldn't assume that all the bombs were off-loaded in the same place, which isn't necessarily a good assumption."

"Good point. I like your suggestions. We shouldn't just follow the path of the nukes. We should investigate all options. But that includes our looking for gaps in time during the transfer of the bombs. We can't quit looking after we've found the first one." Alvin went to the white board and listed out the tasks and activities that would need to be accomplished. Once the list was complete he started to put names next to each of the tasks. Knowing their assignments the agents disbursed and went to work.

Livy's assignment was to review and analyze the videos that were found. She liked this assignment because it meant that she could return to Golden and her degree program wouldn't be disrupted. She could easily work the video analysis between her coursework as long as she was in the Denver area. The video tapes would be transmitted to her digitally via a secure drop box. Then she could go to work looking for clues around any trucking activities.

Livy checked for flights home but there was nothing so late in the day. She would have to wait till the next day before she could return to Colorado.

Early the next morning, she packed up her materials and headed for the airport. She was anxious to learn what the NERDS had put together.

Chapter Ten

The Dragon Pit Plans
July, 2017, Golden, Colorado

During her flight, Livy had sent out a text to the pit members inviting them to her apartment the morning after she returned. She wanted to share what she had learned and find out if the NERD team had made any progress. Her apartment was small, even smaller than Boston's because it was just for her. It was on the third floor of her apartment building. It had a living room / dining room combination, a small kitchenette, a bathroom, and a bedroom. The laundry was centrally located in the apartment complex and had coin operated machines. It wasn't much but for now it was home.

Jonathan wouldn't be there. He had his own place and he only called her apartment "home" when she was around. Livy didn't want to tell him that she was around until after her meeting with the team. She would let him know later, after her meeting with the Dragon Pit team. Then he could come over and hang out with her.

She had set the meeting time for ten in the morning, knowing that it was during a break time where there would be no requirement for them to be present on campus. She didn't feel it appropriate that the conversations they were having should be held on campus and so she volunteered her apartment, at least for this meeting. Maybe in the future someone else who had a larger living room would volunteer.

Almost as if on cue, the team members started showing up shortly before ten. Gage, the Navy Seal, was the first at the door followed by Lincoln, the Army Ranger, and Brian, the Air Force pilot. In Livy's mind she thought, *The military guys are always first in line. That's cool.*

A few minutes later the rest showed up including Glenn the Marine, Carlos from Boeing, and Boston the techie. Livy started the conversation by saying, "Wow. I'm impressed. The entire team is here. No one is backing out of our crazy idea."

Brian, who was often the spokesman for the group, spoke up with, "What's crazy is that it's taking a group of geeky college kids to do what our government is too bureaucratic to accomplish. What we're doing isn't so much crazy as it is critical. I've been losing sleep over this crazy idea that we've come up with and I have a plan for how we can execute."

It was Carlos who spoke next, "Before we go into plans, let's hear what the FBI learned in North Dakota." He was suggesting that Livy give an update to the team, and she was more than willing to do so. She felt this Dragon Pit team was made up of trusted companions. This group's activities had become a higher commitment for her then the FBI. She wanted the Dragon Pit team to have all the information possible so they could be as successful as possible.

Livy started by summarizing the FBI findings, "Looks like we have a serial suicide bombing cell. It looks like this cell acquired their explosives in the Ukraine and the Chechen republic and that they're nuclear. We have no idea how many of these bombs are out there but we do know how they moved them into the country and how they arrived at the sight of the explosions. What the FBI is working on right now is to trace the movement of the explosives through Canada and on into the Detroit area. And we're looking for spots when the bombs may have been off-loaded. We're expecting to find out that all the explosives were delivered to a cell in the Detroit / Ann Arbor area and that these explosives are now in the hands of a cell in that location."

"Why Detroit?" questioned Lincoln.

"Our suicide bombers seem to have originated in the Ann Arbor area. We have the most information about the Orlando bombing and we know that the bomber came from Michigan. He left his car in the parking lot at the theme park and it was easy to make the connection."

"Then wouldn't we be the most help if we found this cell," questioned Lincoln, "rather than talking about becoming international vigilantes?"

Brian responded to the questions, "Actually, the FBI has much better resources to accomplish that then we do. What's missing is that once they know about the cell, the Muslim Brotherhood will shut it down and create another cell in another location. But our bureaucracy never goes the next step, which is to keep another cell from springing up. They never take that step, which would keep these terrorists from creating another cell. Shutting down the cell in Ann Arbor is a small patch on a very large problem."

"And what is that problem?" questioned Lincoln, looking straight at Brian.

"The problem is that there is no deterrent." This time Gage jumped in. "The desire for revenge, even if it seems ridiculous and unfounded to us, is very real in the radical and extremist Muslim culture. That desire will continue to be there even though we shut down one or two terrorist cells. We need a deterrent. Currently the balance of power is with them and unless they feel the pain of a deterrent, they will continue targeting us in their need for revenge."

"So basically you're comparing this to the Cold War era where the U.S. and the Soviet Union counterbalanced each other with a nuclear deterrent and both sides hesitated to strike because they knew what the retaliation would look like," continued Lincoln.

"Exactly," continued Brian. "And our play has to move into the area where our government will never move. We need to focus on the deterrent. We need to figure out what the trigger point is that will keep the radical Muslim community from striking out at us. We need to figure out how to get the larger Muslim community to stop the radicals within their faith." After a pause he continued, "The common thread in all of this is the religion. I don't want to sound like a religious bigot, but it seems to me that the deterrent has to be a religious deterrent."

Livy was tuned into this conversation. The Dragon Pit members were expressing something she had felt for a long time. It simply was not right that the extremist Muslim community like the Muslim Brotherhood was able to promote terrorism from half way around the world and then have any American retaliation be centered strictly on the fools who were willing to die for the cause. The leaders never seemed to volunteer their own bodies to the cause. They just sat in their remote locations cheering when the twin towers fell. But the fools on the ground died. To her it just did not seem right, and she always felt that some retaliation was needed that struck the leaders where it hurt. They needed to feel the pain in their own homes, not in Ann Arbor, or even in Afghanistan. They had to be touched personally. So she was excited to see what the team had been scheming, "So what's the plan? What have you guys come up with while I was vacationing in beautiful radioactive North Dakota?"

Brian, since he was the Air Force pilot, took the floor and started the explanation, "What we have in mind is to deliver a little pain. They hit us economically in North Dakota, and they hit our entertainment industry in Orlando. We need to hit them back in their centers of importance. Economically that would be the oil industry, and entertainment would be their religious sites."

"Hitting their oil industry would hurt us more than them, wouldn't it?" questioned Lincoln.

Brian continued, "That's what we were thinking too. Besides, we may not need to hit more than one site in order to generate the deterrent that we're after."

Livy suggested, "Then, like I suggested the last time we were together, let's hit the holiest site of all. Let's hit Mecca."

Brian, being more logical than emotional, responded, "That would dilute our deterrent. We want them to be afraid that we may hit Mecca next. That would be a deterrent. We want to hit their second or third most holy site. But since the third site is the Dome of the Rock in Jerusalem, I think we need to stick with what we said before. I think we're stuck with the second most holy site, which is Medina. That would hit the entire Muslim community and maybe the Muslim's themselves will try to solve the problem of their radicals."

"Understood," returned Livy. "Medina hits at the radicals and it establishes a deterrent. Then Medina it is. Now, have you done any more in figuring out how we're going to hit them?"

Brian responded, "Actually we're well on our way detailing out our plan of attack. We acquired a spare communications control module and Boston is modifying it so that it can be switched to communicating with our team. We've identified a window of opportunity during a building maintenance cycle when no one will be in the hangers. We'll use that opportunity to get the module inserted into an aircraft that is expected to go on a mission in the near future. Then we wait. Our only glitch is that the facility is monitored by cameras. We have to make it look like we're maintenance workers doing normal maintenance on the plane, so we'll need to go in dressed in overalls and we'll need to prevent the cameras from seeing us directly. But I think it's doable."

"You've forgotten a key piece," jumped in Boston. "We also acquired a computer which we are going to use as a controller. We've loaded the control software on to the computer and we tested it out to make sure it communicated with our new controller. As soon as we get the control module inserted we will be ready to go. We'll just be waiting for the ideal opportunity for the team to take over control of the aircraft."

Livy jumped in, "With that planning in place, what have we done about security?"

Carlos handed Livy a burner phone and said, "We have the burner phones the way you suggested and here's yours. All were purchased with cash from various store locations. I already programmed in all the phone numbers for the entire team into your phone. We're ready to go." Next they went around the room and identified their favorite book, which would be used for future encoded messages. The NERD network was established and was now operational.

*****

Later that evening Livy met up with Jonathan and they did dinner and a movie. She didn't mention her earlier meeting with the Dragon Pit team because it would make Jonathan jealous. He would want to know why she didn't call him first, and she was nervous about how he would react to the radical approach the team was taking. Sometimes it was smarter to keep work, whether its school work or FBI work, and pleasure separate.

Chapter Eleven

The Dragon Pit Executes

November 2017, two months after the Minot bombing, Golden, Colorado

It was several months before the big day finally arrived. Brian was off duty and at the gym when the remote plane with the modified control box took off on a mission to Afghanistan. Boston had rigged a messaging system to the airplane's control unit, which sent a message to Brian's phone to notify him upon take-off. Brian had placed the mission in the back of his mind because of the long delay. But Brian was ready. He quickly jumped into his car and drove to his apartment. He knew he had about an hour before he would need to take control of the plane but he wanted to be ready. He didn't want to miss this opportunity.

The computer system that would take control of the airplane was set up in Brian's one-car garage. Once he arrived he quickly jumped into action. He started monitoring the plane's activity until it was deep into the Afghanistan countryside. He wanted the take-over to look like an accident so he had to wait until the plane was deep enough into enemy territory to make its disappearance look like an enemy strike. Since he did not know the plane's target he also couldn't wait too long. If the plane released its missiles then Brian would have nothing to shoot at Medina. So the timing had to be perfect.

Brian was taking over operations of a plane known as a UAV (Unmanned Aerial Vehicle) or Drone for short. It was remotely controlled by a pilot somewhere on the ground. This particular plane was known as the Reaper Drone and when Brian was flying it he would normally be based at Creech Air Force Base near Las Vegas, Nevada at the Ground Control Station (GCS). The Drone contained both a weapons system for recognizance and a high-powered camera for surveillance. At an altitude of 20,000 feet it had the capability of reading the license plate of a car driving on the ground.

The General Atomics MQ-9 Reaper, also known as the Predator B, had the ability to fly 1,800 kilometers (over 1,100 miles). The Reaper used a 950-shaft-hoursepower (712 KW) turboprop engine. It could hunt for targets and observe terrain using a number of sensors, including a thermal camera. An operator's command took 1.2 seconds to reach the drone via a series of satellite links. The MQ-9 was fitted with six stores pylons. The inner stores pylons carried a maximum of 1,500 pounds (680 kilograms) each and allowed carriage of external fuel tanks. The mid-wing stores pylons could carry a maximum of 600 pounds (270 kilograms) each, while the outer stores pylons could carry a maximum of 200 pounds (90 kilograms) each. An MQ-9 with two 1,000-pound (450 kilogram) external fuel tanks and a thousand pounds of munitions had an endurance of 42 hours. The Reaper had an endurance of fourteen hours when fully loaded with munitions. The MQ-9 carried a variety of weapons including the GBU-12 Paveway II laser-guided bomb, the AMG-114 Hellfire II air-to-ground missiles, the AIM-9 Sidewinder, the GBU-38 JDAM (Joint Direct Attack Munition), and the AIM-92 Stinger air-to-air missile.

One of the main features of the RPV was that it could fly over a combat area night and day waiting for a target to present itself. In this role an armed RPV complements the piloted strike aircraft. A piloted strike aircraft can be used to drop larger quantities of ordnance on a target while a cheaper RPV can be kept in operation almost continuously, with ground controllers working in shifts, carrying a lighter ordnance load to destroy specific targets.

When Brian took control of his selected RPV the Air Force had over 400 in use allowing Brian to assure himself that they wouldn't miss this one. Beyond Iraq and Afghanistan the RPV was being used all over the world for everything from humanitarian search and rescue missions to anti-piracy patrols off the shores of Somalia. They were also deployed in Benghazi, Libya after the attack that killed the U.S. Ambassador in that city. Brian had been involved in many of these missions. Close to fifty of these Reapers had been lost in combat operations or during training operations. For example, one was accidently shot down over Israeli air space October 6, 2012, and Brian knew that he had to stay as far away from Israel as possible.

Brian was involved in one of the RPV losses on December 13, 2011 when an Air Force MQ-9 Reaper crashed at the Seychelles International Airport in Mahe, located in the Indian Ocean, 1,500 miles east of mainland Africa. The MQ-9 was not armed and no injuries were reported. The cause of the incident was listed as unknown. This experience gave Brian the confidence to know that the Air Force would also write off the loss of his hijacked drone as an MIA.

The RPV aircraft that Brian was after had been flown from Creech Air Force Base in the United States to an Aircraft Carrier in the Gulf of Oman where it was refueled and where it was weaponized. From there it headed straight north over Pakistan and on into the southern end of Afghanistan. Brian was confident that the target would be somewhere in Northern Afghanistan since that was where the most recent hits occurred. Brian waited until the plane was about one-third of the way into the country and traveling over an area that was known for its rebel activities.

When the time was right, without a word, Brian switched control of the plane to his computer. He knew the previous pilot who had control of the plane up to this point would assume the plane had been hit and was now destroyed. That was the standard explanation for a loss of communication over enemy territory. Mission command would simply fire up another remote aircraft and send it out on the same mission without giving the missing plane a second thought.

Once Brian had control of the plane in Afghanistan he quickly turned the plane to the south going back over Pakistan and back out into the Gulf of Oman. He needed to avoid Iranian air space. He also needed to avoid being spotted by the American carrier, which had launched the plane. Once in the Gulf he headed west toward the Strait of Hormuz, took the plane around the horn, and headed into the Persian Gulf, also called the Arab Sea depending on whether you were looking at the water from the southern or Arab side, or from the northern or Persian side.

He continued west toward Kuwait and as he approached Kuwait he turned north traveling over the thin strip of Iraqi land between Kuwait and Iran. He was now in Basrah, Iraq. He knew the Americans would not take notice of his aircraft because of its American markings. After all, it was an American military drone that he was flying.

Brian traveled along the western border of Iraq into an area that was completely deserted on both the Iraqi and the Saudi sides, and then crossed the border into Saudi Arabia. His plan was to sneak into Saudi from the top by going back northwest through Iraq, then turning south into Saudi from the north. This was a desolate part of Saudi and was the weakest point in the Saudi national defenses. The Saudis' would not expect an attack from United States dominated Iraq.

Brian dropped the plane low below the capabilities of Saudi radar. Unfortunately taking it low risked the possibility of someone on the ground taking notice of the flight. So he kept the plane away from any populated areas. He checked the weapons load. There were four missiles on board. That was enough weaponry to send the message he wanted to send. He didn't want to create a lot of casualties. He was focused on creating a deterrent that would discourage future attacks on United States targets. He wanted the Muslim world to realize that they were also vulnerable and that they had something to lose if these terrorist attacks continued.

Once inside Saudi the plane traveled straight down the middle of Saudi Arabia through the area known as the Empty Quarter. This was a desolate area with nothing to offer. Brian often wondered why it was called a Quarter when in reality ninety percent of this land was empty nothingness. It should be called the empty ninety percent. He continued flying through this region until he was horizontally opposite to where Medina was located. Then he turned west, straight toward Medina.

Medina was located along the eastern side of a mountain range that traveled along the western coast of Saudi Arabia. Traveling along the edge of this mountain range was an ancient trading route known as the Frankincense Trail. This was the trading route used by Frankincense merchants bringing their precious material from the southern coast of the Arabian Peninsula to the eastern shores of the Mediterranean. From there the incense was shipped to the Pagan temples in Italy and Greece. The Frankincense Trail was composed of a series of way stations or watering holes called wadis where water and some small agriculture were available. Medina was one of these wadis. But what made Medina special was that it was the birthplace of Mohammad. Because of that special distinction, Medina was built around an enormous complex which contained Mohammad's Mosque and numerous other structures that had special significance to the Muslim community. It was this central complex that Brian would be targeting.

As Brian's plane approached Medina he could see the two traffic circles that were distinctive in the city. There was an outer traffic ring and an inner traffic ring. The inner ring tightly circled the sacred and holy sites of Al Madinah and Al Masjid al Nabawi. This was where the Prophet's Mosque Al Haram was located. Brian headed straight for these most revered sites.

As he saw the city off in the distance he wondered once again how two extremely ritualistic religions, who worshiped the same God, even though they called him by different names, could hate each other so much. How could the Jews and the Arabs have such strong death wishes toward each other? But that would have to be a question for a different day.

As Brian's plane approached Medina he took it to a higher altitude. At this point it didn't matter if he was detected by radar. By the time the Saudi's detected him and reacted to his intrusion it would be too late. He just wanted to quickly drop his missiles and urgently fly out over the Red Sea and into the Mediterranean where he would ditch the plane. He was now close enough so that he could clearly see his target off in the distance.

Chapter Twelve

The Deterrent
November, 2017, Medina, Saudi Arabia

Muneersha Shammari lived in Medina, Saudi Arabia, officially known as al-Madīnah al-Munawwarah, transliterated as Madinah, which was the second holiest city in the Islamic world after Mecca. The city was named by the prophet Muhammad and was known as the city of the prophet, or the radiant city. It was the Prophet's final religious base and was also his burial place under the Green Dome. It was the initial power base of Islam

Medina was home to the three oldest mosques in Islam, namely Al-Masjid an-Nabawi (The Prophet's Mosque), Quba Mosque (the first mosque in Islam's history), and Masjid al-Qiblatain (The Mosque of the Two Qiblahs). Just like in Mecca, entrance to the sacred core of Medina where the Mosques are located was restricted to Muslims.

Medina was 210 miles (340 km) north of Mecca and about 120 miles (190 km) from the Red Sea. It was situated in the most fertile part of all the Hejaz territory. The streams of the vicinity tended to converge in this locality. An immense plain extends to the south and in every direction the city was surrounded by hills and mountains.

Medina was a historic city formed in an oval and surrounded by a strong wall dating from the 12th century CE. It was a castle flanked with towers. Beyond the walls of the city, west and south were suburbs consisting of low houses, yards, gardens, and plantations. These suburbs also had walls and gates. Sadly, almost the entire historic city had been demolished during the Saudi era. This was because of the Saudi government's religious policy and its concern that historic sites could become the focus for idolatry. This caused much of Medina's

Islamic physical heritage to be destroyed since the beginning of Saudi rule.

Saudi Wahhabism was the Saudi policy that was hostile to any reverence given to historical or religious places of significance for fear that it may give rise to shirk (idolatry). As a consequence, under Saudi rule, Medina suffered from the loss of many buildings that were over a thousand years old. Critics described this as "Saudi vandalism" and claimed that in Medina and Mecca over 300 historic sites linked to Muhammad, his family or his companions had been lost.

The rebuilt city of Medina was centered on the vastly expanded mosque of the Prophet. It also contained the tombs of Fatimah (Muhammad's daughter) and Hasan (Muhammad's grandson) across from the mosque at Jannat al-Baqi. This mosque dated back to the time of Muhammad, but had been twice burned and reconstructed.

Medina, in addition to being the second most important Islamic pilgrimage destination after Mecca, was an important regional capital of the western Saudi Arabian province of Al Madinah. In addition to the sacred core of the old city, Medina was a modern, multi-ethnic city inhabited by Saudi Arabs and an increasing number of Muslim and non-Muslim expatriate workers.

For twelve-year-old Muneersha Shammari, Medina was home. He lived with his mother in one of the Hotels in Badaah which was in the inner circle. The two of them lived there together and his mother worked in the laundry department of the hotel. It was an extremely exclusive hotel, but Muneersha knew that with the Saudis you had a lot of money only if you were in the right tribe. But if you weren't in one of the ruling, oil rich tribes, then you were dirt and that's where Muneersha and his mother were classified. They were outsider Arabs.

The inner circle was an exclusive area filled with resorts and hotels and every building had a heliport on the roof. After school, and before his mother came home from work, Muneersha loved playing on the roof. On the occasion when a helicopter would arrive at the hotel, usually transferring some rich guy who didn't like taxis from the airport, he would stay out of the way and hide behind one of the roof air conditioning units.

Today was one of those days. His playmate who usually joined him on the roof was sick and couldn't come out so today Muneersha was on his own. But he didn't mind. It allowed him to create his own daydreams of someday being a hero to his family. Family pride was everything and he didn't just want to be a member of the family, he wanted to stand out; he wanted to make a mark. This was an unusual attitude in a society where the pride of the family and its status were more important than the wants and desires of the individual.

It was quiet on the roof, if you ignore the steady howling of the wind. But Muneersha didn't even notice the wind. He was so used to it that it had become part of the quiet. In fact, the hum of the wind tended to calm him.

Suddenly the rooftop quietness was disrupted by a loud bang, followed immediately by three more bangs. Looking south in the direction of the noise, toward the central square where the Prophet's mosque was located, Muneersha could see a growing puff of dust engulfed by flames. His mouth dropped open in horror. What had happened? Has something happened to the Prophet's mosque? Fear engulfed him. This wasn't possible. A chill ran down his spine causing him to openly shiver in spite of the 100 plus degree weather. Who would dare to attack such a sacred and holy place? Allah would surely retaliate. Allah was great and powerful and whoever did this would pay. "I would hate to be that person," Muneersha said out loud, knowing no one would hear him.

He wanted to run downstairs and out into the street. He wanted to somehow protect the holy shrine. He didn't care about his own safety. He just didn't want this most sacred of all shrines to be damaged. He was proud of the shrine and an attack against it was personal. He hoped someday he would be privileged to be the individual who killed the infidel that brought this destruction down on Islam. How could something so horrible have happened?

Chapter Thirteen

The Celebration
November, 2017, Golden, Colorado

Brian had dropped the payload and had scored a direct hit on the Prophet's mosque in the center of Medina. It could not have been more perfect. Now he had to get out of there and make his way to the Red Sea as quickly as possible. But he could see that this wasn't going to be easy. He was barely out of the Medina area when radar indicated several planes scrambling at the local airport. He knew these had to be fighters because commercial aircraft would not take off so close together. He knew his RPV was in trouble. Unfortunately if they captured the plane it would mean the United States would be blamed for the attacks, since the plane would have U.S. markings. But Brian wondered if this might not be a good thing. *If the United States was blamed, it would make us seem as though we weren't going to put up with any more of these terrorist attacks.* So, according to Brian's thinking, at this point it didn't matter if his RPV was shot down and if the U.S. was blamed. The mission had been a success. Let the Saudi fighters come. It would be too little too late.

Brian was able to fly the RPV about halfway to the Red Sea when it was hit, not once but several times. It was literally blown out of the sky. Brian knew his efforts were over when he lost signal from the RPV. He shut down the computer and went into the house to listen to the news.

The news spread fast. The tragedy of it all was played repeatedly over the liberal channels. Reporters kept saying, "How could such a cultural tragedy occur? Who would destroy such a sacred and revered site?"

"What about the Orlando theme park? What about North Dakota? What about the twin towers in New York? What about the Boston

Marathon?" asked Brian of no one in particular. But the public media had not yet made the connection between the hit on Medina and the destruction of these other locations. They tended to be a little slow in making these types of connections. Eventually they would figure it out.

Brian was proud of his success, not that he had killed innocent victims, but that he had given the Islamic community a taste of revenge on their own turf. The mission had been a military one with non-military casualties. That part of it was sad. But sadly this conflict could no longer be evaluated using Western morality. If they were going to put a stop to this terrorist behavior, then they would have to look at the morality, or rather the lack of morality, of the extremists. These individuals had no problem with collateral casualties, in fact they celebrated them, and so that same level of morality had to become part of the Western mindset if they were going to successfully win this war on terror.

The outcry of the Muslim community was horrendous. The airplane parts of the RPV were quickly identified and the plane was tied back to the United States. They were even able to find identifying markings on the wreckage to determine which RPV had been involved in the attack. It was quickly traced to the RPV that had disappeared in Afghanistan just a few hours earlier. The Air Force was doing a song and dance around how one of their RPVs could not possibly have been involved in this attack on Medina. But the evidence of the plane was undeniable.

The Arab world was in an uproar. Their precious Temple of the Prophet had been destroyed and they were already blaming, cursing, and threatening retaliation against the United States. The Muslim Brotherhood made several broadcasts declaring they would retaliate and get revenge.

"Then so will we," said Brian out loud to himself.

"We will what?" asked Brian's wife who was a short way away in the kitchen.

"If they take revenge on us we'll have to take revenge again back on them," replied Brian.

"Well, I am proud of you. I'm glad you didn't let these attacks on United States soil go unpunished. I'm glad someone is trying to solve this terrorist issue. And I'm proud that my husband is a part of the solution." Brian had reservations about including his wife in knowing about his activities. But it was hard to hide the computer in the garage. In the end he had decided to bring her in but stressed that secrecy was critical or it would put the entire family in extreme danger.

"We'll have to see what kind of a solution it really is. Time will have to tell on this one."

There was a knock on the door. The entire Dragon Pit arrived unannounced and started to convene at Brian's home. They had heard the news and they wanted to hear Brian's take on the operation. They wanted to offer him their congratulations. This would be a great day in the fight for freedom. The radical Islamists would always remember this day.

Lincoln was the first through the door and he high-fived Brian, and then gave him a hug. "I can't believe our plan actually worked," he said to Brian.

"Of course it worked," replied Brian. "We know what we're doing."

Boston entered next and after expressing his congratulations he said, "Did you see the issue of Scientific American about the RPV? It's in the November 2013 edition. It specifically talks about how easy it is to steal an RPV and turn it into a weapon of terrorism." Lincoln and Brian shook their heads no. "I guess our little adventure just added credibility to that article."

"That's no surprise," commented Brian. "I always felt the RPVs weren't controlled very tightly. But we'll be seeing changes to that in the near future. The fall-out from what we've done is going to make it a lot harder to intercept RPVs in the future. If nothing else, we at least increased awareness of that security problem. "

Next to enter were Livy, Gage, Carlos, and Glenn. Everyone wanted to know the details of the mission and Brian was thrilled to oblige them. He told the Dragon Pit the story of the capture of the plane and the attack on Medina in agonizing detail. The Pit was thrilled to learn the details. They all wished they could have had a more active role in the entire operation.

As they were finishing their discussion about the attack on Medina, Livy received a text from her boss Alvin. The text read, "You're operational. Make contact immediately and plan to come in."

Chapter Fourteen

The Deterrent Aftermath
August, 2017, Washington DC, USA

For Livy the message to "come in" meant she would have to travel to FBI headquarters in the DC area. Fortunately, Denver was a United Airlines hub and she would be able to get a direct flight to Dulles. This message from her boss meant several days of long meetings discussing what had happened and what they should do next. But that was her job and she knew she would not be able to find anyone that could do it for her. Besides, she loved her work. She loved digging into the cases. She loved searching out new ways to look at an old problem. She loved the feeling of solving a problem. She was addicted to success.

Before leaving she spent a couple hours with Jonathan. Since they were both in the FBI she felt comfortable sharing her experiences in Orlando and in North Dakota. She told about some of her findings and about the connection to a mosque in Ann Arbor. Jonathan also shared his work in Denver. It wasn't as big or as dramatic as hers, and wasn't as critical to national security, but it was his job. It was what he did, and Livy tried her best to act interested.

In an attempt to keep Jonathan in her life, Livy gave a token invitation for him to attend the next Dragon Pit meeting with her. Maybe he could be helpful and involved. But she was still concerned that he wasn't ready to share in the Dragon Pit's efforts to counterbalance terrorism. She wasn't sure how he would react. She feared he would react negatively. But she felt obligated to invite him anyway. She would have to see how his involvement played out. Maybe he would become a valuable participant. But she was also relieved when he refused by saying, "Maybe some other time."

The overnight plane trip was always draining, but it had to be. There was no other way to give Jonathan the attention he deserved, and still meet her obligations to her boss at the FBI. She arrived at Dulles airport and took a taxi directly to the headquarters office.

She normally looked forward to a lengthy, analytical day. But today would be different. As Livy, Alvin, and the rest of the team settled into their chairs in the conference room, there was an eerie silence in the group. Alvin started the conversation. "This is going to be challenging. We have no data and will not be allowed to go into Saudi Arabia to see the crash site. The FBI and CIA always had trouble getting into Arab countries in the past, but after this incident it's going to be impossible."

Edward Colton, one of the agents who always reacted negatively, spoke up, "Why are we even involved? This should be a military inquiry. And they should be supported by the CIA which does the international investigations, not the FBI which focuses primarily on the domestic issues." He was the pessimist of the group, and he looked the role. He was five foot five with squinty eyes and a sneaky, mousey look about him. People meeting him always suspected his intentions because he could never find the positive in any situation. He spent his life squirming around issues trying to find a way for someone else to do the work.

"Our boss, the director of the DOD, has made a special request that we have our own independent investigation," replied Alvin. "He wants more eyes on this because of the enormous international impact this may have on our relationship with the Arab world."

"What resources are we going to have to work with?" questioned Edward. "The CIA isn't going to share anything with us. You know they don't like working with the FBI. They consider us their underlings. I can't see anything good coming out of our working this case."

Alvin explained, "The DOD has already stressed that the Secret Service be the repository of all information and that they make sure all data is distributed amongst all the players in this investigation, which includes the Air Force, the CIA, the FBI, and of course the Secret Service."

"That sounds like a bureaucratic nightmare," burst in Livy. "Nothing good will come out of this mess." Secretly Livy was glad to hear the news. This meant that she would have inside information on how the investigation was going. She would be able to monitor everyone's activity and stay on top of any problems that might affect the Dragon Pit team members.

Alvin suggested, "This comment is not to leave this room but the thing that bothers me is, why we are investigating this at all? This was obviously a retaliatory attack done by someone who is frustrated with the lack of results of our war on terror. And this approach of using 'revenge' to fight fire with fire is the only approach which may actually get us some results. The war on terror can't be won as long as we're fighting an enemy that has a completely different set of morals than we do. They have no problem asking women and children to blow themselves up when these same Imams are too cowardly to strap the same bomb onto themselves. We really shouldn't even bother with this. We should congratulate whoever did this, not hunt for them."

Livy's mind was racing. Alvin would be an incredible ally to have on their side. She knew she would have to pull him aside at some point and tell him about the Dragon Pit. But she was torn. *Would the rest of the Dragon Pit members be offended if an outsider was involved?*

Several of the agents nodded in agreement with Alvin. "But," Alvin continued, "we have to do our job and sometimes we don't like it. Sometimes I think what we're doing is more for show than anything else, and that's how I feel about this assignment. Regardless, we have been given a mission, so let's figure out a plan of attack."

The rest of that day, and the next day, were spent going through what little information they had about the attack. This included satellite surveillance videos and the news media videos which were made available through public sources.

The team received regular updates from the Secret Service which Livy studied carefully. She wanted to stay on top of anything which might affect the safety of the Dragon Pit members. It was on the third day of the team's working together when Livy saw a report that was extremely disturbing. The military had traced the attacking RPV back to its base location. They had surveillance cameras in the RPV's hanger and they were going through those videos to see if there was any point where the plane had been tampered with. Livy knew there was a distinct possibility that they would see Brian tampering with the unit. They would see him swapping out the control units and they would be connecting this activity with the Medina attack. Livy knew she needed to act quickly, but what should she do? She left the conference room where the team was working and went outside to an atrium area where she knew she could have a private conversation. Then she placed a call to the Dragon Pit conference room at the Colorado Engineering School. She knew she would be able to get a hold of someone there.

Gage answered the phone with the usual greeting, "Dragon Pit."

"Is that you, Gage?" asked Livy, thinking she recognized the voice.

"You bet," he replied. "What's up?"

"We have a big problem," Livy replied. "Can we get everyone together and have a quick conference call?"

"When?" asked Gage.

"The sooner the better. Right now would be best."

"I'll get right on it. We'll give you a call as soon as I have the majority of the team in place. I'll try to conference call in anyone that's not here."

"Perfect," replied Livy as she hung up the phone. She went back to the conference room which had become the war room for their combined efforts. She pretended to participate but her mind was focused with concern about Brian's safety.

About twenty minutes later Livy's second phone rang and she stepped out of the conference room and walked out to an atrium area where she was confident there was no monitoring. The conference rooms all had cameras and private conversations were always held in the atrium. She closed the outside door, and answered the phone with, "Is everyone there?"

"Yes," replied Gage.

"Including Brian?" asked Livy.

"I'm on the call," responded Brian.

"Here's the problem," started Livy. "Brian, you are in danger. The Air Force is going through a video of the hanger where the RPV was stored. They're looking to see if anyone tampered with the unit. I know it was several months between the time you changed the control box and the time the plane took off, but eventually they are going to get to where you made the switch. I know you tried to disguise yourself by dressing as a maintenance worker, but you know that there's an excellent chance they're going to pay you a visit. Since this investigation falls under the Patriot act, there won't be a formal arrest. It will be a military arrest and a military tribunal and you may be tied up for a long period of time, and possibly even convicted. Worst case they may call it treason, but I would hope not. Anyway, Brian, you need to go to Canada ASAP. Pack up your family and move, and move quickly. The rest of you in the Dragon Pit will need to help him out by giving him the vehicle he needs for his escape, and by helping him move his house to wherever he decides to move. Brian, I know this is a shock, but you don't want to get caught. Grab your family and run. And after you're in Canada, don't tell anyone where you're located. We can communicate through the internet using our code system, but never reveal your location to anyone. Don't even use this burner phone anymore. For your safety you should assume it has been contaminated. Get rid of all your phones, credit cards, anything that might be traceable. Then, if nothing comes of it, if they don't connect you with the attack, you can always return. But for now, the safe and smart thing to do is to flee."

"Great," replied Brian. "I was afraid this might happen. I'm not sorry for what I did. But I was hoping we wouldn't have to go through this hassle. But, like I said, I'm not surprised. How do I get into Canada without my passport being flagged? And do I really want anyone to know that I went to Canada?"

Livy paused for a moment and then suggested, "I'm positive my boss here in the FBI is in agreement with what we've done. He doesn't know it was us doing it, but he agrees it needed doing. I'm going to have a conversation with him about getting you and your family a different identity. He may even have some suggestions about where you should go in order to avoid detection. I know we didn't want to bring anyone else into our little circle of trust, but I'm afraid we probably don't have a choice at this point."

"Agreed," replied Brian. "I'm going to need some serious help to get out of this mess."

Chapter Fifteen

The Imam Strikes Back
November, 2017, Ann Arbor, Michigan

The Imam Sami Abdulaziz was once again on a rant. His young Saudi congregation inhaled every word. These were youth who were trying to find meaning to their life. Their martyred friends had destroyed the Orlando theme park and the oil fields of North Dakota and were heroes. But there were still fourteen more followers that the Imam had available to him. These individuals claimed they were willing and ready to make the ultimate sacrifice for Allah. They wanted to be heroes too. But the Imam wasn't so sure they were ready.

The Imam screamed at the boys who sat around him on the floor, "Do you realize the sacrilege that has been committed by the destruction of Medina? Do you realize how insulting this event is to Allah? This is not an attack on the Muslim people; this is a direct attack on Allah. It cannot be tolerated. Who amongst you is strong enough and brave enough to defend Allah with action and not just with words?" Sami paused to see the response, which was overwhelmingly positive. "Are you ready to defend Allah? If you are, stand up and follow me. I have a mission for you."

The Imam stood up and started walking to his chambers in the back. He realized the act of standing up and following him would be similar to making a commitment. He knew this act was more than just a stage show. He was forcing the followers to take the first step to being fully radicalized.

Once in the chambers the Imam waited to see if the boys would all follow him. Every one of the fourteen ended up in the chambers with him. It was a tight squeeze. It was not as roomy as the mosque. But no one seemed concerned about being pressed closely to each other. They all sat on the floor anxiously waiting to hear what the Imam had to say. Each individual wanted to know how they could become Allah's hero. Each wanted to take revenge for the destruction of their holy site in Medina. Each had a special hatred for the infidel who would do something so horrible, so devastating.

The Imam started, "Yesterday a friend and hero of Allah who has a high ranking position within the FBI contacted me and warned me about two things. He informed me that the FBI had placed listening devices throughout our sacred mosque, in this very building. He informed me how I could get access to a tool that would identify the locations of these devices. I quickly identified, removed, and disconnected those devices. I find it extremely offensive that the FBI would stoop so low as to plant listening devices in our sacred mosque.

"The second thing I learned was that the Air Force has identified the individual who flew the plane into Saudi Arabia and dropped the bombs on our sacred shrine. The Air Force has found video tapes that show this individual swapping out a control unit in the airplane that executed this disaster. Apparently, he tried to shield himself from the cameras, but through a reflection on a stainless-steel plating that was on the plane they were able to get a clear picture of his face. He is a pilot of these types of planes. The Air Force believes this monster took control of the aircraft and deliberately flew it under the radar and attacked us. And I do feel as though it was a personal attack on each of us. I'm sure every Muslim in the world feels that way."

"I was able to get this information in secret using Muslim Brotherhood contacts that are in both the Air Force and in the FBI. The Air Force will probably arrest this blatant attacker. But I feel we should hit him where it hurts. I feel we should attack his family. If we make them pay, we make him pay."

"What can we do to help?" asked one of the young boys.

"You can find the family of this infidel," replied the Imam, "and you can make him suffer just the way we are suffering. Hit him where it hurts. Hit his family. Can you all go and attack his family?"

"Can we rape his wife?" asked the youth.

"Do whatever you want," responded the Imam. "She's just a woman. I personally would find an infidel woman repugnant, but do whatever you want. When you get done with her, make sure she watches her children die and then kill her too."

"Should we all go together?" asked another youth.

"I don't think that's necessary," suggested the Imam. "Select three or four of you and the rest can stay in communication and help out with the directions, etc."

"I'll go," yelled out the first youth, followed by six others who quickly volunteered. The Imam selected four of them, gave them the information about Brian, and sent them on their way to Denver to take revenge.

The four were given a rental car that the Imam had rented using a false name in anticipation that he would find sufficient volunteers to go on this mission. He also supplied them with pistols, an automatic rifle, and four grenades. "This should help you accomplish your mission," commented the Imam.

"What exactly do we do?" questioned one of the believers.

"Eliminate the family of the infidel! I don't care how," responded the Imam. "I have some prison insiders which will be able to take care of the infidel. But we will do this after the family is gone. We want to maximize his pain. So your mission is to go to Golden, Colorado, kill the family, and then return as soon as possible. I will know when the mission is completed because I'll hear it in the news. Then I will dispatch our prison believers to eliminate the terrorist who destroyed Medina."

"Understood," replied a different one of the four youths. After that the four left the mosque, climbed into the vehicle Sami had acquired, and immediately left Ann Arbor, using Interstate 94 heading west. They traveled through Indiana and on into Illinois. In the Chicago area they encountered the anticipated congestion which cost them a couple additional hours of travel time. Then they switched to Interstate 80 which crossed Illinois and Iowa. From there they traveled into Nebraska switching freeways to Interstate 76 which led southwest directly into the Denver area. Golden, Colorado was west of Denver so they traveled through the congestion of Denver on to Arvada, a town known for a mass murder occurring at a movie theatre. Here they switched to state highway 58 and passed through the foothills to find the small and hidden community of Golden, Colorado.

Golden was hidden enough to give the impression of a small mountain community, but still offered the easy accessibility to the large metropolis conveniences of Denver. Golden had two recognizable landmarks, which have become the reason for the entire town. The first landmark was the Carters Brewery, which the Islamists passed as they traveled into Golden. The second was the Colorado Engineering School (CES), an internationally recognized university with a specialization in resource engineering and economics. They specialized in mining and oil extraction. CES graduates were in demand by companies and countries all over the world because of its reputation for high quality graduates.

The total travel time was over twenty hours. The foursome didn't want to stop except for the occasional bathroom and food break. They were obsessed with the completion of their mission. They picked up the occasional Subway sandwich and ate while they traveled. Bathroom breaks and driver changes occurred at the rest areas along the freeway. They alternated their sleeping times so the drive would not be interrupted. They were on a mission and their mission was for Allah. Their mission had to succeed.

During the drive the remaining two volunteers who were not driving to Denver were given the mission of tracking the travelers and helping them in any way possible. This included mapping directions and searching out Brian and his family's location.

***

During this time the Imam also had a mission of his own. He was going to find a Muslim brother who had connections with the federal prisons in the Denver area. He wasn't sure which prison Brian was heading toward but he wanted to be ready. He was confident he would be able to find a Muslim brother who could help. He wanted someone to punish

Brian, but not until Brian had learned about the torture and death of his family. The Imam wanted Brian to feel that pain. Then the infidel must die.

Chapter Sixteen

Arresting Brian
November, 2017, Golden, CO

Brian had a lot of regrets. But the regrets weren't because of the mission of attacking the Mosque of the Prophet in Medina. His regrets were centered on him not getting rid of the physical evidence associated with the attack. He should have immediately eliminated the computer equipment in the garage. He should have gotten rid of the search engine records on his personal computer which tracked the location of Medina and the surrounding Saudi Arabian terrain. These items would prove to be extremely damaging if he went to trial. He should have been more careful. He tried to hide his identity by avoiding the cameras in the hanger, but apparently he had missed something. Somehow Livy was sure the Air Force would be able to identify him in spite of his efforts. It was better to be safe than sorry. He needed to take his family and run. If at some future point Livy sends him the message that all was clear, he may still be able to return to Golden and rejoin the Dragon Pit.

It was the day of his son's birthday when Brian arrived home and his small apartment was filled with half a dozen screaming boys all having fun playing video games on the Wii. The knock on the door was loud and abrupt, giving the message that someone serious was knocking. Brian's wife answered the door and saw four Air Force police standing there fully vested out with bulletproof vests, riot helmets, and rifles at ready but pointed down.

"Is Brian Pearson home?" asked the officer, standing near the front of the group who was obviously in charge.

"Yes," responded his wife. "What do you want with him?"

"Please step aside," replied the Security Forces officer, which was the name given to Air Force military police, as he forcefully pushed his way into the apartment followed by the other three members of his team.

Brian was now sitting on the floor with the boys, sharing in their fun. He didn't expect the Security Forces to be this quick. He mistakenly assumed he would have a little time before they found him on the video. So he stupidly decided to not interrupt his son's birthday party.

Brian and the boys were all taking turns bowling on the Wii. The boys would get serious, stand up, and pretend they were rolling bowling balls down an alley. Brian, when it was his turn, would sit and flick his wrist in a specific way, and get strikes almost every time.

The Security Forces stomped into the room. Upon spotting Brian, the Security Forces officer went directly up to him and said "Brian Pearson, you are under arrest for terrorist activities under the Patriot Act. Please stand up and come with us."

Brian knew it didn't make any sense to resist. He stood up and joined the arresting officer. He was quickly handcuffed and escorted out of his home and to the back seat of the Security Forces vehicle. His wife and sons were in a panic asking a barrage of questions like, "Where are you taking him? What are you going to do with him? Why is he being arrested?"

The arresting officer did not respond to any of the questions. Instead he ordered the other three officers to search the apartment for evidence. It wasn't long before they reappeared with the computer equipment from the garage and also with the personal computer Brian had set up at a desk in the living room. It was upon seeing them haul the equipment out of the apartment that Brian regretted not having cleared and disposed of it sooner.

With the search complete and Brian tucked away in the back of the vehicle the arresting officer turned to Brian's wife and said, "He is being taken to a detention center in Denver. We cannot tell you anything about what he is being charged with. You'll hear from us within twenty-four hours and we will update you on his status." With that he took her phone number and the Security Forces team unceremoniously jumped into their military police vehicles and drove off.

Brian's wife was left in shock. His wife knew why he was arrested. It had to be related to the attack on Medina. But she was surprised they had discovered who had executed the attack so quickly, and she had no idea what this meant. Would she ever see Brian again outside of a prison? What if they sent him to Guantanamo Bay which was where they held terrorists? Would she even be able to visit him at all? What was she going to do in her life? Would his pay be taken away, which would leave her without any source of income? How would they survive?

Her son was also in shock. He kept asking his mom the same kinds of questions for which she had no answers. He asked, "Where are they taking Daddy? Why are they taking Daddy away? What's going to happen to him? Why are the police mad at Daddy? Will Daddy be home for dinner?"

The birthday party was over. The children, who all lived close by within the same apartment complex, were sent home. It wasn't long before the phone calls started followed by visits from her neighbors. They drilled Brian's wife with questions like, "What's going on? Why have they taken Brian away? What are the charges against him? What did he do?"

She stayed evasive saying she didn't know what the charges were or why he was arrested. She kept saying that it was all a big mistake. She dreaded the questions because she either did not know the answer or didn't want anyone else to know what Brian had done. They would find out soon enough anyway. The news media would be broadcasting their accusations soon and his picture would be plastered all over the television.

As she closed the door to her most recent neighborhood visitor and gossip queen she could see a car off in the distance with Michigan license plates pulling into the apartment parking lot. She didn't attach any significance to the four individuals that were in the car.

Chapter Seventeen

Helping Brian
November, 2017, Washington, DC

Livy approached Alvin in his office. She asked if he had a few minutes for a private conversation and he invited her in. She shut the door behind her giving Alvin the message that this was going to be a serious conversation.

Alvin had always felt a spark for Livy but he kept the spark under control because he knew she had a relationship with Jonathan. Additionally, boss-employee relationships were frowned upon in any workplace, and he really wasn't sure how she felt about him. But when she wanted this private time with Alvin, he was thrilled to oblige.

"What's up?" asked Alvin.

"We need an 'off the record' conversation," replied Livy, more as a request and a question than a statement. "Can we do that?"

"Of course," replied Alvin. "What have you been up to that we need to be 'off the record'?"

"Do we need to go somewhere else? Are we being recorded here?"

"We are secure here. Besides, just to make sure, I'll turn on my signal scrambler so that any listening devices will be disrupted." He turned on the device at the side of his desk. "Now we're safer in here than anywhere else around here. Tell me what this is all about. You've piqued my curiosity."

Livy continued, "You know the bombing in Medina? I know who did it."

"I had a feeling you knew more than you were willing to share. You had a suspicious and resistive look about you, like you weren't fully engaged. It was as if you really didn't want this investigation to go forward."

"Correct on all counts."

"Tell me why you would keep something so critical a secret," urged Alvin.

"Okay but we've agreed to stay off the record and completely confidential," Livy reminded him as she paused to see his nod of agreement. She knew she had to have this conversation, but she feared that it might not go as hoped. "There's a small group of us students at the Colorado Engineering School known as the Dragon Pit and we are all very frustrated about the lack of understanding and the lack of response associated with the bombings in Orlando and North Dakota. We were voicing our opinions to each other and came to the conclusion that no one is going to do anything meaningful. So we decided to take matters into our own hands. Within our group we have an Air Force Pilot, a Marine, a Navy Seal, and an Army Ranger. We also have a tech guru and a few other highly trained individuals."

"Like you," interrupted Alvin.

"I'm afraid you're right. I'm part of the problem. I am also an important resource behind this mess."

"So why are you telling me all this? Why disclose this now?"

"Because I need your help. This all stems from our belief that the only language that the Muslim radicals will understand is an-eye-for-an-eye and so we planned to give them some of their own revenge focused medicine."

"First off," commented Alvin, leaning forward on his desk and acting as if he was extremely interested and fully engaged, "I want to congratulate you guys on your initiative. I don't necessarily approve of vigilantism, which is what this amounts to, but I also agree that if you didn't do this then no one would be doing anything. I know how frustrating it is to see the liberals whine about the deaths on American soil and at the same time talk about tolerance for the individuals who are behind these tragedies. I actually am excited and willing to join you and be a part of the solution. I'm glad you're bringing me in. Maybe there is some way I can help out. I'm tired of being part of the bureaucratic problem. I'm tired of doing all these investigations and in the end nothing changes and we sit around waiting until the next time we get attacked. There has to be some action taken. So, I agree with and support what you are trying to accomplish. Why did you come to me at this time? What do you need?"

"The Air Force pilot who commandeered the drone in Afghanistan and flew it into Saudi Arabia is in trouble," Livy explained. "We tried to be careful by disguising him but apparently there was a video taping of the hanger where the drone was stored and they caught him swapping out the modified flight control box. There were several months between the time he did the swap-out and the actual flight, so they will be going through a lot of video to find him, but unfortunately it looks like eventually they are going to find him and he is in serious trouble."

"What do you want me to do?" asked Alvin, already having a good idea of the help Brian was going to require.

"Passports and fake IDs that will get him and his family into Canada. And of course money. I know you have a slush fund somewhere for emergencies. Then from Canada they can travel to anywhere in the world and find a safe haven. Maybe you even have some suggestions of where they should go to avoid detection."

"Absolutely. Not a problem. There are some great places in Costa Rica where they can hide out. But the less we know about where they go the better."

Livy left the meeting feeling good about the support that Alvin was offering. She walked out into the hallway only to get discouraged by the text message she received from the Dragon Pit on her burner phone informing her that Brian had been arrested. She spun around and went right back into Alvin's office and closed the door behind her.

"That was quick. What's up?" asked Alvin, seeing the stress on her face.

"Brian's been arrested," she replied. "Air Force Security Forces have picked him up and they are holding him somewhere in Denver."

"I understand. I'll find out where they have him and see if I can take him under the care and comfort of the FBI." Alvin immediately picked up the phone and placed a call to the Denver FBI offices. Livy, now feeling even more stressed, sat down on a chair waiting to see how this would proceed. She was also interested in knowing if there was anything she could do to help.

Livy could only hear one side of the conversation, but that was enough. There was an answer at the other end of the line and Alvin introduced himself. "Hello, this is Alvin Foller at Washington, DC FBI headquarters. I would like to talk to the agent in charge of the Denver office." Then after a short pause he continued the call. "Yes, this is Alvin Foller. Am I talking to the agent in charge?" After another short pause he continued. "I need your help with something extremely sensitive and urgent. We have a contact and informant that has been picked up by the U.S. Air Force Security Forces in Denver and we are responsible for his safety." Alvin was concocting a story that would sound convincing. "He is one of our informants and we need to protect him. The Air Force will not be treating him gently if we leave him in their care. I need you to get your hands on him and get him to a safe house in the Denver area as soon as possible. Let me know the minute you have him. This is a matter of national security. So make it a top priority item." Another pause and then, "His name is Brian," and looking at Livy he hesitated waiting for her to fill in the last name.

"Pearson," said Livy.

"Brian Pearson. Thank you for jumping right on this and again let me know as soon as he is safe." Alvin hung up the phone and looked at Livy. "Now we wait to see what they come up with.

"Thanks," Livy responded as she stood up and started for the door. "Let me know as soon as you know something. Let me know how I can help."

"No problem," replied Alvin. Then he went on to explain, "We need to do something different here. Your Dragon Pit team is a group of highly trained military individuals, and I don't want to discredit their abilities, but they're not trained in clandestine operations. You need someone running this effort who knows how to manage operations of this type which amounts to a spy operation. I don't want you guys blundering into any more mistakes like this last one. What your team did was heroic, but next time let's try to not end up in trouble."

"What are you suggesting?" asked Livy.

"I'm suggesting that the Dragon Pit has just become a secret black operations reconnaissance branch of the FBI. I'm suggesting that I am now the team leader and we're going to make this an overwhelming success."

"I'm concerned about bringing in any more people."

"I'll run this show, and you'll be my right hand man, but no one else needs to be brought in at this time," suggested Alvin. "It will be our secret. But I want you discuss any further operational activities with me before you proceed in order to avoid mistakes."

"Thanks," responded Livy. "I am excited to have you involved. I don't want to see anyone else get arrested."

Livy left the office and headed back to her own office hoping they would be able to find Brian quickly and get him away from the Security Forces. She knew that the longer he stayed with them, the rougher it would get. They would try to force additional information out of him. They would be looking for some major international plot, and there really wasn't any type of plot involved. It was simply the retaliatory activities of the Dragon Pit.

Chapter Eighteen

Disaster

November, 2017, Golden, Colorado

Brian's wife was in a panic. She didn't know how to interpret Brian's arrest. What was going to happen to him? Will they consider him a terrorist? She regretted having encouraged him to take action against the Muslim Brotherhood. Were they too large a force to deal with? Or was the Air Force just being stupid, not realizing that Brian was taking action that Washington, DC wasn't strong enough to take.

She could also see the terror in her boys' eyes. The arrest of their father had left them crying. They were filled with questions and their mom couldn't answer any of them. She did her best to comfort the boys but it was difficult when she also felt in turmoil, and she knew they sensed her stress level was at a maximum.

Brian's wife placed a few calls to friends in the Air Force Security Forces they knew from their home base in Nevada hoping they might be able to provide some information. They didn't know anything. They comforted her by telling her they would try to find out what had happened, but they let her know that information would be very restricted and hard to get at.

She learned where the Air Force Security Forces detention center was in the Denver area. Feeling desperate and not knowing what else to do, she decided to go there and try to find someone that could help her. She grabbed her two sons and went in the garage to strap them into the car seats. She had just gotten them into their seats and was climbing into the driver's seat when an enormous explosion rocked the apartment. The door and most of the wall between the apartment and the garage was blown into the garage and debris battered the side of the car. The front passenger window of the car was immediately smashed in but fortunately the window next to each of the boys remained intact. Glass was thrown across the front seat of the car hitting her. Luckily there were no serious injuries to anyone in the car.

Her mind reeled. What was that? Was the explosion caused by a gas leak inside the house? Then she realized that this guess didn't make any sense. The apartment was completely electric. There was nothing else in the apartment that should explode. She continued to analyze the situation at high speed. Within seconds she came to the conclusion that the explosion had to be the result of an attack. Someone was after Brian and possibly his family too, in revenge for the attack on Medina.

In shock and desperation, and not knowing what to do next, she pushed the garage door button and the door started to slide upward. But it didn't open all the way. It only opened about two-thirds of the way and then jammed because of damage to the garage door tracking mechanism. Fortunately she was smart enough to realize that she couldn't hang around. This explosion had to be the result of an attack. Whoever had attacked may still be out there. She gunned the car in reverse, tearing out the bottom panel of the partially opened garage door. She knew there was damage to the side of the car from the explosion. Now the back of the car was also damaged from hitting the garage door. But she also knew she had to make a run for it.

A quick glance at what was left of her apartment as she pulled out made her realize that this was no accident. The apartment was completely destroyed and was now on fire. She could never return to this location again. Even the relative safety of her home had now been eliminated. There would be no returning and even if she could return, there would be nothing to salvage. She said a short thank-you prayer when she realized how fortunate she was to have been in the garage at the time. Otherwise her entire family would have been wiped out.

Once out of the garage she put the car into drive and spun the tires heading for the parking lot exit. On the road she gunned it and headed toward downtown Denver, not really knowing what else to do or where to go. To her dismay she noticed a car following her and trying to catch up with her. She knew this could not be good so she accelerated, soon passing the 100 MPH mark. The pursuit car continued to follow her, matching her speed as she flew down the freeway heading for downtown.

Mentally she was programmed to visit the Air Force detention center, assuming that was where Brian was being held. Now that she was being chased, she decided the best thing for her to do was to stay on the freeway rather than pull into the downtown area where she would need to slow down and stop. She hoped a highway patrol officer would see her situation and come to her rescue.

It wasn't long before she achieved her wish. By this time she was close to 120 MPH and a stream of four Highway Patrol cruisers was chasing the two cars. The second car didn't seem to care. They had no interest in slowing down and losing her. Instead the passengers in the pursuit vehicle pulled out weapons and started shooting in her direction.

She was a mom and no one, not even the Air Force or Islamic terrorists were going to be able to hurt one of her kids. She started swerving back and forth across the freeway but soon realized that maneuvering in this manner wasn't very smart because she could easily lose control of the car and end up in a crash. After a little thought she came up with the idea that rather than run away from these guys, she was going to take them out. She allowed them to catch up with her and when they were only a couple car lengths back she smashed on her car brakes. The result was what she hoped for. The second car didn't anticipate this move and suddenly and abruptly crashed hard into the back of her car. Then she accelerated once again trying to get away. Her pursuer's vehicle was out of commission. Their radiator had been jammed back into the engine. The pursuit car was quickly surrounded by two police cruisers while the other two police cruisers continued to follow her.

Seeing that she was no longer at risk, she pulled over and stopped her car. The police quickly blocked the front and back of her car. Using their speaker system they yelled, "Get out of the vehicle and lay down on the ground!"

By now there were a dozen more police officers at the scene. The freeway had been blocked off in both directions because of the shooting. But only two of the officers had followed Brian's wife since she hadn't been doing any of the shooting.

She eagerly complied and the police were next to her within seconds. They asked her to explain why she was being chased.

"Can I check on my kids first?" she asked.

The Highway Patrol officers, not realizing there were children in the car, but also not willing to have her find a hidden weapon in the car suggested, "We will check your children for you. For now you will have to stay away from the vehicle."

One of the officers went to the vehicle while the other remained with Brian's wife. He yelled back, "The children seem to be fine but they look like they've been crying." He opened the car door and spoke with each of them asking them if everything was okay.

Happily the boys weren't hit by any of the random shots of the pursuers. They were shaken up and scared, but no physical damage. The only thing the officer could get the crying boys to say was, "I want my mommy."

He checked the car for weapons and, turning to the other officer said, "Let her come over to comfort the kids." She didn't even wait for approval from the second officer. That was her cue and she was off to the car in a flash, hugging and holding the two boys.

After a couple minutes one of the officers said, "Ma'am, we need your driver's license and car registration and we need you to explain to us what's going on here."

She eagerly complied, giving up her license and registration, and then said, "I have no idea who those guys are. I was putting the kids in the car when all of a sudden my apartment exploded. I drove off in fear for our lives and we were pursued by that other car. I don't know what they want, but I drove really fast hoping you might spot me, which you did, and here we are. That's all I know which isn't very much."

The officers checked her license and registration and found everything in order. She didn't even have a traffic ticket to her name. There was no reason to mistrust her now. They continued to stay with her waiting to hear from the other officers.

The officers asked to send someone to Brian's home to investigate what had happened there. They learned that the fire department and sheriff's office was already on the scene. They confirmed what she was saying. The home had been destroyed.

The officers questioned her about her safety. She obviously couldn't return home. Where could she go? What would she do? Assuming that the threat on her family's life would be ongoing, what were her options?

She informed them she needed to get to the Air Force detention center so she could learn more about her husband's situation, and they promised her they would stay with her until they knew she was safe. There may be others waiting to attack.

Her car was badly damaged. The police weren't going to allow her to drive her car away. They offered to take her to the detention center and have her car towed. She was distraught but appreciated the help.

Chapter Nineteen

The Chase Disaster
November, 2017, Denver, Colorado

At the other end of the chase, two patrol cars had parked at each end of the stranded pursuit vehicle blocking it in. They could see that the vehicle was disabled, but just in case, they made sure to block the vehicle at both ends. With weapons drawn they blasted a command over the loudspeaker, "Come out of the vehicle with your hands in the air."

Nothing happened. It seemed as though the driver and passengers in the pursuit vehicle didn't care. The police could see movement in the vehicle and they knew the vehicle contained weapons so they had to remain cautious.

The police officers stayed behind the protection of their vehicles and broadcast another message, this time a little more assertive, "Throw out your weapons, put your hands out the windows, open the car doors, and come out of the car."

Nothing happened. Another ten minutes went by with the same message being repeated every half minute. By now the local Denver SWAT team had arrived.

Freeway traffic had become a nightmare. No one was allowed to travel through the area in either direction and the freeway had become a four-mile long parking lot in both directions. It was a nightmare and looked like it would become even worse.

Suddenly two of the passengers in the vehicle opened their doors and stood up out of the car with their hands raised. "Where are your weapons?" asked one of the officers. The passengers pretended they did not understand the request. "Walk over here and keep your hands raised," commanded the officer.

Slowly the two individuals walked toward the police car, acting as if they were complying with the request. However, just as they passed the front of one of the patrol cars, the other two members of the foursome opened fire at the police. The police quickly retreated back behind their vehicles and started returning fire. The two remaining attackers, who were pretending to surrender, jumped into action. Picking the police cruiser that was closest to them, they quickly jumped in before anyone could react, started the car which was easy because the keys had been left in the ignition, and accelerated down the freeway.

The SWAT unit opened fire on both the stranded vehicle and the hijacked patrol vehicle. Shooting from the stranded vehicle had stopped, but the patrol car had escaped. The SWAT members quickly picked a couple of the other patrol cars and sped off after the stolen vehicle.

The diversion had worked. The two escaped assailants had hidden their pistols in the back of their pants and they were now armed and dangerous. As the stolen vehicle flew past the location of Brian's wife and her vehicle they swerved over close to the vehicle and before the officers realized what was happening, the attackers let off a volley of bullets, killing one of the officers and seriously wounding the other. Luckily, Brian's wife and the boys were tucked down into the back seat of their vehicle. They weren't visible and none of the bullets struck them.

The remaining SWAT team members snuck up to the stranded car, which was now badly shot up. Peeking into the vehicle they saw the two youths who had created the diversion were now both dead, obviously the victims of the volley of SWAT bullets. The SWAT team proceeded to pull the boys out of the car and laid them out on the ground. They needed to confirm their deaths. There would be no additional threat from either of them.

Some of the police who had previously been watching the pursuit vehicle drove over to Brian's wife's vehicle to see if there was anything they could do to help their fellow officers. They called for an ambulance, which was already on its way, and quickly helped the injured officer as best they could. Then they took statements from Brian's wife about what happened. But she was not much help because she didn't know who the attackers were or why this attack happened.

***

Back at the apartment, the fire department and police swooped in on the site of the explosion and fire. The fire was devastating. It not only destroyed Brian's home, but also four homes surrounding their home. Sadly one of the homes had children asleep and two of the children were killed by the fire. A quick examination of the area looked like someone had planted a high explosive in the center of the living room. The police interviewed the neighbors who informed them that they had seen someone jumping out of a car that contained four youths. That individual ran up to Pearson home and had thrown something which looked like a large rock through the front window. This was followed immediately by an explosion. The police recognized that it was probably a grenade.

The police also learned that this same vehicle with the four boys was seen leaving the apartment parking lot in pursuit of Brian's wife who, in a surprise move, had crashed out of her garage and had sped away. The four boys seemed intent on catching her because they immediately took off after her.

The Pearson residence was completely destroyed. There was nothing left to salvage. There would be no reason for Brian's family to ever return.

***

Back on the freeway, the car chase after the stolen police cruiser by the two SWAT cruisers was on. The freeway was empty in the eastward direction because it had all been blocked off and clogged a little west of the shooting. The freeway was shut down. Across to the other side of the freeway, the lengthy highway parking lot continued for miles and miles. One of the youths laughed out loud saying, "Look at all those infidels. They are like ants on parade. How I would love to squash them right in their tracks."

But the other boy was more practical and complained, "Don't worry about them. Worry about us. What are we going to do? We can't stay on this freeway forever. Eventually we are going to have to do something that will help us escape."

Slowly traffic on their side of the freeway started to pick up. As they drove further along the freeway they passed on-ramps which had remained open because they were past the original danger zone. The freeway was no longer free of traffic.

The SWAT teams were following close behind with lights flashing and sirens blaring. The boys realized it would be difficult to shake them by jumping off the freeway.

The driver of the stolen police cruiser also switched on the police sirens and lights, hoping this would cause the cars to pull over to the side and give them a free run of the road. They continued to streak forward at full speed.

Eventually they encountered the inevitable; a roadblock. Two police cruisers were parked sideways across the freeway. How would they deal with this new problem? They decided to crash right through it at the junction of two of the vehicles. Unfortunately when they crashed through they heard a noise which sounded like ripping and tearing. At the same time they felt a jerk, like something had suddenly grabbed the vehicle. In spite of the driver's attempt to accelerate the car it slowed down and they could feel that they were no longer driving on tires. They were now driving on the rims. They had run over a tack strip that had been laid across the freeway and their tires were in shreds. Without good tires the car would no longer drive as fast as it had in the past.

The stolen police cruiser decelerated quickly and the SWAT team members were able to catch up with it. Now the assailants realized they had cops in front of them and behind them and they had a vehicle which was no longer operational. They struggled to decide what to do next.

One of the youths, in frustration, yelled out, "Death to the infidels. Death to those who would disgrace Allah." Then he started wildly and randomly shooting at the police cars. The police were hesitant to fire back because they were on both sides of the vehicle and there was the risk of missing their target and hitting a fellow officer on the other side. So they resisted taking random shots. But two marksmen from the SWAT team snuck over to the side of the road in such a way as to avoid having fellow officers in their line of fire. They took up prone shooting positions and took aim. They counted off, "three, two, one, fire," and in an instant the battle was over. Both shots rang true and the two remaining youths in the stolen patrol car slumped down with bullets in their heads.

***

The news media had a hay-day. They were full of stories and they all had their own explanations with plenty of opinions and theories. As always, they completely messed up the facts and twisted them to add as much drama as possible. The media described it as, "The destroyer of Medina had been captured and arrested after a long and drawn out battle with police who were aided by Muslim youths who were just trying to help. The US military has the attacker captive and they are going to take him to Guantanamo for further questioning. The gun battle on the freeway was between the police and the radicals that attacked Medina. The home of the radical had been destroyed during a confrontation between Muslim youths who were defending their homeland and the attacker of Medina."

Everyone who knew Brian Pearson and his family had trouble believing anything that was reported by the news. Unfortunately, there were plenty of people who didn't know the Pearsons and did believe the news media version, especially in the Muslim community. The Pearsons would no longer be safe in the United States.

Chapter Twenty

Reaction
November, 2017, Washington, DC

As soon as Livy heard the news about the attack in Golden, Colorado, and a fire that had destroyed several homes, she ran to Alvin to update him. Alvin was in a meeting with two other individuals who were investigating the Medina bombing. Alvin had to continue business as usual. He couldn't let on that he knew all about the attack and who was behind it. He had to allow his staff to continue searching or they would all become suspicious. But when he saw Livy come to his door he could tell that she was excited and anxious. He asked the other two individuals in his office to step out for a moment. Then he beckoned Livy in, turned on the signal disrupter, and asked, "What's new?"

Livy explained, "It looks like Brian's home was attacked and destroyed. Looking at the news footage, the destruction looks like a war zone, which suggests maybe it was a grenade that was thrown through the front window. Luckily the family wasn't in the house at the time but there were some neighbors who were killed by the resulting fire. It's a tragedy. But the question that's bothering me is who would do something like this? Surely not the Air Force. This hints of a leak in the Air Force that somehow made it to the Muslim Brotherhood who then went on to initiate a full-fledged retaliatory attack."

Alvin switched his computer to the Denver local news and he and Livy started watching the latest updates. The reporter described the attack at the Pearson home and then went on to describe a freeway chase that resulted in five dead including a highway patrolman. Four of the dead were described as Arab youth.

Livy and Alvin looked at each other in understanding. But the question remained and was immediately voiced by Alvin, "Two questions. First and most important is, what happened to the Pearson family? And the second question is, were those four youths from the same mosque as the bombers in Orlando and North Dakota?"

Alvin picked up the phone and placed another call to the Denver office of the FBI. There was an answer at the other end of the line and Alvin introduced himself. "Hello, this is Alvin Foller at Washington, DC FBI headquarters. I would like to talk to Gerick, the agent in charge of the Denver office." Livy was listening and only heard Alvin's side of the conversation. After a short pause he continued, "Yes, this is Alvin Foller. Am I talking to Gerick, the agent in charge?" After another short pause he continued. "Yes, we spoke briefly earlier today and I understand that you haven't had enough time to take care of that issue yet, but I have another problem I need your help with, and it's related to what we discussed earlier. You had an incident today on your freeway where some individuals were chasing another car and there were several shootings involved. I need several questions answered. First off, who was doing the chasing and the shooting? What do we know about them? Can you send me their identifications? And second, and more importantly, who were they chasing? And what is the status of the people who were being chased? We think they were the family of Brian Pearson, the guy we want you to get away from the Air Force. We think today's attack was retaliatory so we need to know the who, what, and why. And we don't want the news media version. So get in there with the police and let me know what's going on ASAP. I need this entire family, which includes Brian, his wife, and two kids tucked away in a safe house by the end of the day." Apparently there was confirmation on the other end of the line because Alvin responded with, "Thanks. I look forward to hearing from you."

Alvin looked up at Livy and said, "I'll let you know when I learn anything. Maybe there is something we can do to help this situation."

"Thanks," Livy responded as she stood up. Leaving the office she stressed, "I'm really worried about them. They're close friends and I don't want to see any of them get hurt.

***

About two hours later Livy received a call from Alvin beckoning her to his office. She dropped everything and went. She entered the office and stood directly in front of his desk. She was so anxious to learn about any news that she didn't take time to sit down.

Alvin explained, "Brian's family is all right. They were being chased and were shot at. They're traumatized but physically not hurt. The Denver team has taken them to a safe house in the Denver area. The FBI team on the ground is in communication with local law enforcement. Apparently, the attackers were a group of four Saudi nationals attending the State University of Michigan which we believe were radicalized by their local Imam, which we think is the same Imam that was connected with the two previous bombings. All four of them were killed in the firefight with the local police. So, for now, Brian's family is safe. But they'll never be able to return home or return to a normal life in the Denver area. We're still working on getting our hands on Brian and we're going to get him to the same safe house with the rest of his family as soon as possible. Then we'll get the entire family out of the United States and up to Canada. I have people working on the new identity papers and that should be completed in the next day."

"Incredible," replied Livy. "Thanks so much for the help."

"Obviously you should now know that I am in support of you guys, but you need to be a little more careful. We don't want another incident like this Brian affair."

"Agreed. Do we have any idea about the leak?"

"You mean how the Muslim Brotherhood found out about Brian?" asked Alvin. "That's been on the top of my mind as well. However, I'm hesitant to dive into that until Brian is safe. If we show our interest in him it may draw attention to us and our efforts, and we really do not want that at this time. There is a time and a place for that investigation, but it's not now. Let's get his family somewhere safe and then we'll jump into a mole hunt with both feet."

"Makes sense," responded Livy. "Thanks for the help and let me know when Brian is safe."

"Will do," answered Alvin and Livy turned and left the room.

Chapter Twenty-One

A Completely Different Reaction
November, 2017, Ann Arbor, Michigan

Imam Sami Abdulaziz was outraged as he watched the news report. The reporter said, "There was an attack in Golden, Colorado which left several people dead, shut down the freeway system for hours, and burned down most of an apartment building. From what news we have gathered from neighbors and witnesses, a man was arrested and pulled out of his home by Air Force Security Forces. Within minutes of the arrest, the home was destroyed by an enormous explosion, followed by a fire which destroyed the larger part of the apartment complex killing three individuals who were caught in the blaze." The newsreel displayed a picture of the apartment where Brian had lived.

The reporter continued, "Immediately following the explosion, the wife and two children of the man arrested were seen driving away from the apartment complex pursued by a second vehicle with Michigan license plates. The second vehicle contained four Saudi nationals who were attending the State University of Michigan. This pursuit ended up in a chase and a gun battle on the Denver freeway system resulting in the deaths of the four students and one police officer. The mother and children are fine but I'm sure they are heavily traumatized by the entire affair. We have attempted to contact them for questioning but were unable to learn of their whereabouts. Police indicate that they are in hiding because of the possibility of future attacks. No reason was given for the attacks.

"The entire freeway system was closed for hours and is still reduced to one lane causing miles of backed up traffic. Speculation has been raised that this was an attack in retaliation for the attack on Medina, but at this point these are all speculations and nothing has been confirmed. Our understanding is that the FBI has taken over the case and will continue pursuing the investigation. They claim that they received word that the Muslim Brotherhood has taken credit for the bombings." With that the reporter went on to discuss the local Ann Arbor weather.

Sami was livid. How could these idiots he had sent to do a simple task have messed up something so easy and made such a big disaster out of it. They didn't even get their target. The family of the terrorist who attacked Median was still alive, and so was the terrorist. They had accomplished nothing. The only thing they did was to get themselves killed. What a waste.

The Imam was now late for prayers. He left his office inside the mosque and hurried off to lead the prayers. He arrived and led those in attendance through their ritual of standing, kneeling, bowing to the ground, and expressing their oblations to Allah. It was the same ritual that had been done for nearly 1,400 years by Muslims all over the world. There was no deviation in the ritual or the words that were said.

Once finished, the Imam went over to the microphone and started his sermon. He had two sermons. The one he shared with the larger group, and the one he shared with his select group. He went through his first sermon, teaching from the Koran. Then he waited till the larger portion of the congregation had departed. Next he summoned the remaining, focused group back into his chambers so they could have a more detailed discussion.

His focus group was down to eight people. Four had been killed and two had disappeared. "What happened to Abdullah and Kadeem?" he asked his small congregation.

"They heard about the trouble in Colorado and they were scared off," replied one of the eight.

"I don't want them as part of our group if they're not committed. But I also don't want them running around with the risk that they could expose our plans. Do you think they would reveal what we are doing?" Heads started nodding but to his dismay they didn't all nod in the same direction. Some were positive and some were negative. He continued, "It looks like we have disagreement as to the danger our two missing revolutionaries may present. I think the best thing for us to do is to eliminate the potential risk. I think we need to eliminate these two before they expose our efforts to appease Allah." Again the Imam waited to see their reaction and to get their confirmation and agreement. "In the name of Allah, who can help me solve this problem?" There was hesitation by the group. Sami was asking them to kill a couple of their friends. But eventually intimidation won out and two individuals raised their hands. Then the Imam, speaking directly to the two volunteers said, "You know what is needed. Leave now and do your duty and report back to me when the task is completed. Now go." With the wave of the Imam's hand the two stood up and headed for the exit.

Next the Imam turned his attention back to the remaining six team members. "I need four of you to go and complete the task that your companions failed to complete. The remaining two should stay behind and act as a support team helping with mapping or any other problems that may come up." Four volunteers were quickly selected and were once again given weapons and a vehicle and sent on their way retracing the previous team's travels for the long drive to Golden, Colorado.

The Imam was upset with the failures of his team. He wanted to manage these bombings by himself. He wanted to prove to the Muslim Brotherhood that he was a great Islamic leader. Now he regretted not bringing the Brotherhood in to help out. He looked like a fool. But he wasn't done. He was going to give this new effort one more try before he asked for help.

Chapter Twenty-Two

Plotting another Attack
November, 2017, Golden, Colorado

Livy set up a conference call with the rest of the Dragon Pit members using the burner phones. She had promised to keep them updated and she wanted to see what they learned as well. Once everyone had dialed into the call, she started the conversation, "I can see which phone numbers are on the call and I want to confirm who is listening in so I'm going to do a roll call and tie each of you to the specific phone number I have listed here. In the future we need to be more careful, especially in light of what has happened to Brian and his family." Livy proceeded with the roll call and had every phone number accounted for on her register.

Livy started the update with, "What's happened to Brian is tragic. Somehow there must be a leak in the Air Force or the FBI or both because his family was apparently attacked by Muslim Brotherhood supporters and they knew about it well in advance of when the Air Force picked up Brian. There is a significant amount of travel time between Michigan and Golden. We believe it's the same cell that executed the attacks in North Dakota and Florida. We can't allow this to happen again."

Lincoln jumped in, "What happened to Brian and his family? Do you have any updates? We really don't know much except what we hear on the news and they spend five percent of their time on the facts and ninety-five percent of their time giving their twisted interpretations. The news media is pretty much worthless if you're trying to get news facts."

"Brian is being held by the Air Force Security Forces under the Patriot Act. He is being treated as a terrorist, even though the attack wasn't against Americans or on American soil. But since Saudi Arabia is a partner with the United States, he will be treated as an American terrorist. It's too bad that money and oil blinds the politicians to the reality of the situation. Anyway we in the FBI are trying to get him away from the Air Force. His family has already been moved to an FBI safe house and they will stay there until Brian can join them. Then they will be given new identities and moved to safe locations outside of the United States where they can't be found. Sadly he and his family will need to spend the next few years in hiding until all this blows over. And we have no idea how long that will take. He will no longer be able to be a part of our team.

"On the more positive side, we have a new team member. Alvin, my boss here at the FBI has joined our cause."

"Why did you bring in someone new without discussing it with us first?" questioned an obviously distraught Gage.

"Sorry but I had to act quickly," replied Livy. "I mentioned it to all of you earlier, and because of Brian's situation I had to act. I needed Alvin because he can authorize the use of the safe house and he had access to the resources that could create valid new identities for Brian's family. I really didn't have a choice if I was going to get Brian's family to safety. Besides, you'll find him a strong supporter."

Lincoln jumped in again, "The deed sounds like it's done and we're going to learn to live with it. What scares me is that one minute you're saying the FBI has a mole and the next minute you say Brian is being taken care of by the FBI. That doesn't seem consistent. I hope you really do get Brian and his family to safety. His entire life has been destroyed by this. I feel sad for him but at this point there really isn't anything else we can do. It's best to get them out of here because you can be sure the Muslim Brotherhood will be back. They're not going to give up that easily. And next time they may be successful in killing Brian and his family."

It was Glenn's turn to speak up, "It's a shame that we can't even say goodbye to them. I understand why we can't but it's just too bad."

Gage chimed in, "Assuming that Brian is taken care of as best as possible, we now need to ask ourselves how we respond to this attack. Our original hard talk stressed that if they came back with an attack then we would retaliate. We didn't expect that attack to be against one of our team members. But nevertheless, we need to respond. And what will our response be? What do we do to retaliate for this attack on Brian's family? We obviously can't attack Mecca without an aircraft. And we lost our pilot. So how are we going to respond?"

Glenn responded, "That's a hard question to answer isn't it. What should we do? What options do we have?"

Livy jumped in, "It looks like the cell that's causing all the trouble is in Ann Arbor, Michigan. There's some Imam up there that sent the four guys after Brian's family. We're only guessing at this point but we're pretty confident in our guess, that this same Imam is the source of the other two attacks as well."

Gage jumped in, "Well that answers it, doesn't it? Our retaliation has to be against the mosques in Ann Arbor."

"But would it be fair to attack mosques that had nothing to do with the attack on Brian's family?" challenged Lincoln.

"Fairness fell out of the equation a long time ago," responded Livy. "There was nothing fair about the attacks on Orlando or North Dakota. You're taking us back to what started all this in the first place. They only understand revenge, not fairness. And we're only going to get their attention if we focus on revenge too."

It was Carlos's turn to speak up, "I'm with Gage and Livy. We need to react and we need to react quickly so they know there was a connection with what happened here in Denver."

"But we need to plan this a lot more carefully than we planned our last expedition," chimed Livy. "We don't want anyone else to end up the way Brian's family ended up. Let's start with the target. Are we in agreement on the target?"

"The mosques in Ann Arbor," suggested Gage emphatically.

"Any disagreements?" questioned Livy.

"How about just hitting a few, rather than all?" asked Lincoln.

"If we're going to hit the mosques of Ann Arbor, then we have to make sure we hit the mosque of the guy causing all the trouble," replied Livy. "But, as you're suggesting, we need to hit multiple targets in order to have the same level of impact. We're sending a message that we're willing to be as blatant in our attacks as they are. We can be indiscriminate too."

"Can we at least do the hits at night in order to minimize casualties?" asked Gage.

"Sure," replied Livy. "But we need to hit them all at the same time so we're not allowing them time to check the mosques out between hits. We want to take all of them down."

"How are we going to do this?" asked Boston. "Are we looking at bombs with timers, or remote detonation? Or are we going to run around throwing grenades into the buildings?"

"I like the grenades." It was Glenn chiming in. "The reason why is because that is what they used here in Golden and then they would have no doubt about the source of the attacks."

"But we probably don't have enough people to have someone throwing a grenade into each of the mosques simultaneously," returned Lincoln. "Maybe a combination of bombs with timers and grenades would be appropriate."

Just then Livy received a message from Alvin. "Team, I have to jump off the call for a few minutes. I just received a message that Alvin may have an update for me. Let me find out what it is and then I'll get back on this call with you."

The Dragon Pit team continued their conversation debating whether it was appropriate to attack all the mosques and what approach they should be taking in the attack. It was less than five minutes and Livy was back on the call. "Here's the update," she started. "First off, Brian is safe. The Denver office of the FBI was able to take him away from the Air Force Security Forces claiming that he was some type of informant for them and they needed to get some specific information from him.

They took him directly to the safe house where his family is staying. The next thing that is happening is that Alvin has the new IDs ready and they are being sent out to Denver as well. They should be there tomorrow. Then Brian and family will quickly be escorted to Canada, and who knows where they go from there.

"Additionally, we now have specific information about which mosque we are talking about. So maybe we don't want to attack all the mosques. Maybe we should just attack the one in question and see if that quiets down these terrorist activities."

"Love it," replied Lincoln. "I like hitting directly at the source a lot better than random hits. It looks like this mission is my mission since I am a Ranger and sharp shooter. I'll go in there and see if he has any family and shoot out the knees of each of his family members. Then I'll paralyze the Imam. What do you think? Will that quiet him up?"

"I think the family hit is appropriate," suggested Gage, "since they attacked Brian's family. Then I think we need to leave it for a few days so that the Imam can share in their suffering. But then I think we need to take the Imam out, because even if he's paralyzed, he can still cause problems with his mouth. He sounds like the typical terrorist Imam in that he loves to get others radicalized and get them to be suicide bombers, but he doesn't have the guts to do anything himself. He's basically a chicken. We need to silence him so he doesn't send others out to do more damage."

"Agreed," inserted Livy. "You know the FBI won't touch him until they can actually prove that he was connected with the bombings, and by then it will be too late and there will be more deaths. We need to be more responsive if we're going to tie our hit with the hit on Brian's family."

"Will do," replied Lincoln. "I suppose I should get going as quickly as possible."

Then a new voice inserted itself into the phone conversation. It was a voice that everyone was familiar with but it was a voice no one was expecting to hear. "It's time for me to jump in and help out a little." It was the voice of Gene Wiseman, the Colorado Engineering School faculty member and mentor who led the Dragon Pit through their PhD program.

"How did you get on this call when you're not registered as a caller?" asked Livy.

"I have my ways. I've known what you've been doing all along and now that you're getting yourselves into trouble I think I need to help out a little. First off, Livy, tell Alvin that I will have my plane available for Brian and his family to fly out of Canada to whatever location they choose. I need you to let me know where and when in Canada I should be picking them up. I have some suggestions on where they can hide out and still lead a very nice life, but I'll wait and give those suggestions to Brian directly after we pick him up.

"The second way I can help is by getting Lincoln to Ann Arbor without being detected. He should leave all his credit cards, cell phone, and IDs at home so there's no chance of him being identified. I can fly him in my private jet to somewhere close to Ann Arbor. Then, if you or Alvin can personally arrange for a car for him so that he won't be connected with renting a vehicle he will be able to get around safely in the area. We can't have the larger arm of the FBI involved in renting this car because you're suspecting a mole. We need you or Alvin to do it directly yourselves.

"Lincoln can use my plane as his hotel room. We can falsify flight plans making it impossible to track us. Then we'll get him back home and no one will ever know that he ever left Golden. Lincoln, when will you be ready to go?"

"Yesterday," he eagerly replied. "I'm home now and can be ready in ten minutes, weapon and all."

"I'll have my driver come over to pick you up in thirty minutes and I'll have my pilot get the plane ready so that by the time you get to the airport it will be ready to go," replied Gene.

"Perfect."

Livy added, "I want Alvin to chime in on this as well. I'm going to update him on our plans and make sure he's comfortable with what we're doing and how we're doing it. Then, if he's okay with everything

I'll get you the details about the mosque and the Imam and have them forwarded on to you. Gene, how do I get him the information if he's leaving his phone here?"

"Text it to me," replied Gene, "and I'll forward it on to the airplane."

"Perfect," replied both Lincoln and Livy at the same time.

***

Lincoln was on his way. This time it would be his turn to show what he could do. He was impressed with what Brian had accomplished, and now he wanted to show that he was every bit as good. He had packed his collapsible high-powered rifle with infrared scope. His sharp shooter abilities would finally be put to good use.

During his drive to the airport, Lincoln had a conversation with Gene using the airplane's burner phone. Gene started, "I have sent the address of the mosque in question to your phone. The Imam has two wives. That may not be normal practice in the United States, but he is hiding his second wife so the authorities don't know about her. He also has four kids, two from each wife. He lives immediately behind the mosque. The family has a house and a yard and hopefully you will be able to spot them in the yard and take them out from one of the high buildings which surround the mosque. After you have made your hit, come back to the airport and I'll have you flown home. Then, in a few days, whenever you're ready, we'll repeat the routine and fly you back so you can take out the Imam. Does all that sound workable to you?"

"It sounds perfect," replied Lincoln. "Will they have a car for me?"

"Livy confirmed that a car will be waiting."

"I guess I'm ready to go."

"I guess you are," confirmed Gene.

Chapter Twenty-Three

The Escape
November, 2017, Denver, Colorado

Brian was picked up at the Air Force detention center by the FBI, not really having any idea what was going to happen. He assumed he was being transferred to a new location and they would be interrogating him there. So far he had revealed nothing, even though they had shown him the pictures and videos showing that he performed the exchange of the control box in the airplane. But he felt loyal to his friends and did not want to have anyone else share in the frustration and embarrassment he was suffering. He believed in what he had done and he knew most of the Air Force guys questioning him felt the same way. They were not brutal with him and some even indicated some level of sympathy. But they couldn't be openly sympathetic or they might also be labeled as traitors.

So it was a surprise to Brian when the FBI came in and took him out of the hands of the Air Force Security Forces. He wasn't sure he liked the change. He always felt it was better to be with the enemy you know than the enemy you don't know. But he really had no choice other than to go with them. He was convinced it wasn't going to be good.

Brian questioned what he guessed were two FBI agents that were doing the transfer, but they kept saying they didn't know what was going to happen to him. They said, "We are doing all this outside the auspices of the FBI. We are contractors especially hired to make this transfer. That's all we know. This type of clandestine operation usually occurs because someone suspects a mole within the FBI. They wanted to keep you safe."

Eventually Brian became convinced they did indeed know nothing other than that he was being transferred. He settled back in the seat of the vehicle and consigned himself to his unknown fate.

They arrived at the safe house and Brian was escorted inside. The shock of finding his wife and children in the house was overwhelming to him. He had feared it would be a long time before he would ever see them again, and seeing them so suddenly brought tears to his eyes. He was excited and thrilled.

Brian's wife was similarly thrilled as she ran and, without saying a word, literally jumped into his arms. Similarly his two boys came running and grabbed the happy couple's legs, one on each side. They didn't understand what was happening, but they could see from their parents' reaction that this was an exciting moment. The emotion of the moment caused the boys to cry as well. After a couple minutes of huddling and crying together, Brian's macho side kicked in and he tried to compose himself. But he wasn't very good at it. It was all just too exciting to him. He still didn't know his fate, but just being with his family made the world better.

The boys were the first to talk. The first boy said, "Daddy, you should have seen all the police and all the shooting." Then the other spoke up and said, "Daddy, our house is burned down. Where are we going to live?"

Brian looked questioningly at his wife and after she could compose herself enough to talk, she had to go through a detailed explanation of everything that had occurred. Brian became extremely upset. He kept apologizing to them for what he had gotten them into. It wasn't until that moment he finally realized he would never be able to return to his normal life. His family had become the target of the Muslim terrorists and they would never be completely safe again. All he could do was apologize.

His wife's comment was, "It doesn't matter. All that we've lost are just things. What's important is that we're all safe and together. It doesn't matter where we live or what we do so long as we're together. I didn't know how important all of that was until these last few hours when I nearly lost all of you. I would rather live in the remote jungles of Africa than to be separated again, and especially in such a scary way."

Once Brian had listened to the stories of his wife and the boys, he went to the FBI agent who was stationed inside the safe house and asked him what he knew about their situation. Brian quickly learned this agent also didn't know anything. All he said was "this information was only given out based on need-to-know" and he didn't need to know. Brian guessed that these must also be contractors working outside of the normal ranks of the FBI.

Knowing next to nothing about their future, only knowing they were not allowed to leave the safe house was frustrating. Brian realized it was better than being tortured and separated from his family. But he wished he knew more about the fate of his family. Would they be able to stay together or would they be separated again? Going home was out of the question but would his extended family ever be able to know what happened to him? There were so many unknowns and this frustrated him.

They passed the night not knowing any more. In the morning they had breakfast and after eating a van appeared at the safe house. Two additional contractor agents arrived with the van and they entered the house and sat down with the family at the kitchen table. One of the agents, an aggressive and focused lady in her thirties, started to explain, "Our orders are to get you out of the country by the safest route. We have new identities for each of you." She handed each of them new passports, driver's licenses, and social security cards. "These will get us across the border into Canada. Then we will be taking you to an airport. Beyond that, we don't know what will happen to you. We weren't given any information. The assignment for us is to get you safely out of the United States. All old IDs, cell phones, credit cards, etc. have to be destroyed. You will have a new life in a new home."

Looking at their papers they could see they were now the Plet family. Brian was now Gerd Plet and his wife was Jenny Plet. It would be challenging trying to get used to these new names. Their initial reaction was that these names were rather dorky. But they weren't in a position to be picky. The agent continued, "From now on you need to only use your new identities. You need to get used to using these names. You need to figure out where you came from and why you're going to Canada. And you all need to agree on the same story. So, during the drive, you need to discuss and rehearse your new roles."

Brian's wife jumped in, "Thank you for your help. I know you are doing what is best for us. It's too bad that we have to have our entire life destroyed, but if the impact of all of this is to get the message out that we're willing to fight fire with fire, and that this message may result in reducing terrorism, than it was all worthwhile."

The agent spoke up again, "Please do not tell us anything about what you've done or why you're here. We work strictly on a 'need-to-know' basis and the less you share the less chance there is of anything getting out. Please keep your conversations to the here and now and do not tell us anything about the past or about your future."

"Understood," replied Brian. Then, looking over at his wife, he said, "Thanks for being understanding."

"I'm part of this too," his wife responded. "It was my decision as much as yours."

"Thanks," was all Brian could think to say. Turning to the agent he asked, "When do we leave?"

"Now," responded the agent as she stood up from the table. "Go pack what little you have and let's get going."

"We stink and are in the same clothes we wore for the last couple days, but I guess that's trivial when compared to getting us to safety," replied Brian's wife.

"That's right," the agent responded. The FBI contract agent had a very businessey style and approach. She was abrupt and to the point. Her mannerisms indicated that she wanted to get going immediately.

"We'll get ready!" Brian responded. He knew the FBI was trying to get him to safety. He also realized this was most likely Livy's doing since she was in the FBI and he was thankful for her help. He wondered if he would ever see her again in order to be able to thank her. But today, none of that really mattered. The only thing that mattered was getting his family to safety and he trusted these FBI agents knew best how to accomplish that.

Once they were all tucked away in the van, the second FBI agent, a male of surprisingly small stature, acted as the driver. The female agent rode shotgun, and the new Plet family occupied the back seats. The van was a minivan with the side and back windows tinted not allowing anyone from the outside to see in. They were off.

Leaving Denver they headed north on a route that would take them to a safe border crossing with Canada. The FBI had contacts at some of the border crossings which would be able to help them. They headed toward Cheyenne, Wyoming on Highway 25. They crossed north through Wyoming and on to Casper. From there they continued north until they connected with Highway 95 which led then through Sheridan and on into Montana. In Montana they connected with Highway 94 east of Billings. On Highway 94 they headed east away from Billings and through Miles City until they were nearly at the Montana, North Dakota border. From there they headed north on State Highway 16, close to Glendive. Highway 16 took them through Sidney after which it took a left turn and continued on north toward the Canadian border. After Plentywood, Highway 16 took a right turn and finally came to Saskatchewan, Canada where it became Canada Highway 6. The border crossing at this location was one where the authorities had developed a long-term relationship and where the FBI knew they would have very little customs and immigration trouble. From there it was a straight northward run to Regina, which would have an international airport and a waiting plane.

They were on the road by eight in the morning. It was a long drive but they had several bathroom and fast food breaks. The boys in the back were getting squirmy and frustrated with the drive which was easily resolved with a little Dramamine, which quickly put them to sleep. Gerd and Jenny Plet had to come up with a story that fit their Wyoming driver's licenses. They decided they were ranchers from Cheyenne and they were on their way to visit some rancher friends in Regina, Saskatchewan, Canada. They rehearsed the story they invented for the border crossing with their agent friends and it seemed to resonate with them as well. The only question that remained was how do they explain the need for an escort by the two agents? If it wasn't for the need to return the vehicles back into the United States, the Plets could simply have finished the trip on their own. However, leaving a vehicle at the airport in Canada would have offered a give-away lead for anyone pursuing the Plets.

The FBI agents already had the border transfer covered. They were being met at the border by a second car. The Plets would cross on their own in the van. The second car would take the agents across. Once across, the two agents would return back into the van to finish the trip to the airport with the Plets, and the transfer vehicle would be returned to the United States when these agents returned from Regina.

The eight thirty at night border crossing from Montana to Canada went like clockwork. The Plet's looked legitimate in their minivan. With the agents back in the van they continued their travels to the Regina airport. So far the trip had taken twelve and a half hours and they still had two and a half hours to go before they made it to the airport.

Once they arrived at the airport they went directly to the area where private planes were hangered. The agents placed a call to their contact and were told what airplane was theirs. It was a Gulfstream G-400, private executive jet that belonged to Gene, the director of the Dragon Pit program. It was the same plane that would be used to help Lincoln accomplish his mission in Ann Arbor.

Once on board, the plane took off immediately. There was a pilot and co-pilot who also acted as the steward of the flight. Once they were in the air, the first item on the agenda was a discussion of where they were going. The co-pilot informed Gerd and Jenny Plet that they were on Gene's personal jet and that they had been instructed to take them somewhere safe, anywhere in the world they would like to go. Gene had recommended a couple possible options where he already had connections in place. One was in Costa Rica and a second was in Peru. Either location offered them isolation and anonymity which was what they would need for at least the next few years. After some conversation Costa Rica was selected because of its remoteness and its friendliness to Americans. The co-pilot went off to inform the pilot about their destination. Unknown to the Plets the co-pilot had also placed a call to Gene. Upon his return he informed them that Gene had set up a bank account for them with US $1,000,000 and that they had a hotel room waiting for their arrival.

The Plets were shown the on-board bedroom and bathroom and were told to shower and get cleaned up. That was followed by bed and a good night's sleep before the morning when a new life, with a new language, in a new country waited for them. It was exciting and scary all at the same time.

Chapter Twenty-Four

The Ann Arbor Hit

November, 2017, Ann Arbor, Michigan

Traveling in Gene's private jet made it easy for Lincoln to bring his high-powered sniper rifle with him. He had scored the bore to change the ballistic fingerprint of his weapon. He would do that again after he completed his mission so that his military issue rifle would not be tracked to this shooting. As a second precaution he selected soft copper hollow tipped ammunition that would self-destruct upon impact making ballistic tests nearly impossible.

He had learned the location of the mosque and after looking carefully on Google maps, he had identified the perfect location from which he would be able to observe the activities of the Muslim family of the Imam. It was on top of an office building across the street. The rooftop was one floor higher than the two-story home of the Imam. This allowed Lincoln a direct line of sight into the upper rooms, which of course included the bedroom. The trip from the Ann Arbor municipal airport was a short one and it wasn't long before he was in position on the roof of the building. He was wearing plastic gloves to avoid fingerprints. He had used a fire escape to get to the top. Once on the roof he assembled his rifle and scope. It was eleven at night when he was finally in position. He started watching to see what activity he could identify. Unfortunately the curtains were drawn, but the scope on his rifle allowed for infrared. He could see all the activity going on in the house, even if it meant seeing through walls.

The Imam had two wives and four children. Lincoln was able to make out the two wives and the Imam. Two of the four children were asleep, but the other two children must be on the other side of the house beyond the ability of his infrared sensors. He had difficulty locating them. He stayed in position, viewing the house, trying to determine how best to accomplish his goal. But then fate intervened and someone showed up at the door of the house. He could see a driver with two teenagers standing at the door. One of the wives from upstairs was moving down the stairs, apparently planning to answer the door.

The opportunity had presented itself. Everyone was in position for him to execute his mission. The Imam was sitting in a reclining position, apparently watching television. One wife was in what appeared to be the bathroom. The second wife was nearly at the front door. Lincoln decided to take a shot at the wife in the bathroom because she would be isolated and probably would not be heard over the noise of the TV. Lincoln took careful aim at the infrared image and pulled the trigger. Unfortunately, the infrared image was often slightly distorted in much the same way water distorts images underwater. Therefore, Lincoln needed to adjust his shot to compensate for the distortion. He just hoped he had made an appropriate adjustment for the target. He wasn't sure how far into the building the image was actually located.

He had to change his ammunition to bullets that would penetrate the walls of the building before hitting the target. The shot hit its target, but it looked like he had hit higher in her leg than he was aiming for. Rather than taking out the knee, it looked like he had hit the left leg high and on the backside. The woman crumbled to the floor and lay there unsuccessfully struggling to get up.

The Imam didn't move. He just sat there, continuing to watch his show. Either he didn't hear the woman, or he didn't want to hear, but either way he stayed detached from her struggle.

In the meantime the second wife had met the boys at the door and let them in. Apparently these were the Imams other two children. The three were on their way upstairs. Lincoln decided to take a shot at the person who was lowest on the staircase. This would be one of the sons. He had another successful hit, this time a little closer to target and directly in the knees.

This shot aroused the attention of the other teenager and the wife. Lincoln had to react quickly and fired off the third shot into the knees of the second son, and that son collapsed as well. By now the wife, who was on the stairs with the sons, was flaying her arms around and moving toward the two boys. Lincoln quickly fired off the fourth shot, but this time, because the wife was starting to kneel down toward the son, he hit her higher in the body. She immediately fell over on top of the sons. Lincoln feared that he must have ended her life since a shot in the upper body with these high-powered bullets was usually deadly.

That left the remaining two children. By now the Imam had heard the screaming and had moved toward the stairs to see what all the fuss was about. Lincoln knew he needed to react quickly. It wouldn't be long before the authorities were called. Lincoln had to get away from the area before they were notified.

One of the sleeping children was getting up out of his or her bed and as the child started to walk Lincoln took a fifth and final shot. This shot was true to its mark and hit the child in the leg. The last child did not wake up which was an indication that the child was very young, probably under three years old. The only shot Lincoln could fire at this youth was at the head, and he just didn't feel good about killing such a young child, so he decided his mission was completed.

Lincoln quickly but silently packed up, climbed down from the roof, climbed into his car, and avoiding any sign of being in a hurry he slowly drove off to the airport. As far as he was concerned, the mission had been successful even though one child was left untouched and at least one wife had been killed. Once on the plane, it took off immediately and Lincoln was soon safely back in Colorado. The entire mission had taken less than eight hours and it was all accomplished under the cover of the night.

Chapter Twenty-Five

The Fallout from the Ann Arbor Hit
November, 2017, Golden, Colorado

The following morning the news media was screaming about a racist attack. They were making the Imam and his family sound like martyrs. In the end both wives were killed in the attack and three sons were severely crippled. But according to the media the Imam had bravely survived the attack without a scratch by the mercy of Allah.

After returning, Lincoln used his burner phone to get on a conference call with Boston, Glenn, Carlos, and Gage. Livy wasn't available to take the impromptu last minute call because she was in meetings related to the Ann Arbor shooting. Lincoln started the conversation, "We can't let this ride. We can't let them think this was some kind of indiscriminate and random racist attack. We have to let the world know what's going on here."

"But how do we do that?" questioned Glenn. "They will be able to trace any message we post back to its source which would expose us and we don't want to end up living with Brian in some hideaway."

"I can do it," replied Boston. "I can post a message on U-Tube and make it look like it went viral. Then the news media will check into it to see what the story is. I can make it untraceable, or rather, I can make it so that when they trace it they will be led to a dead end."

"Good," continued Lincoln. "What should our message be?"

It was Carlos's turn to jump in, "We call ourselves the NERDS and we say that this is not a racist hit. We say that we have incontrovertible evidence that this Imam was behind the attacks in Orlando and North Dakota, and that he is now sending attacks against innocent families in Denver, and that we believe in an eye-for-an-eye just like the Koran teaches. We are delivering our response by directly attacking the individual that we know to be responsible for each of these attacks."

"Perfect," replied Lincoln. "Can you do that, Boston?"

"You bet," Boston replied. "I'll have it on U-Tube in an hour. Now, Carlos, you need to say all that again so I can write it down."

"I'm sure glad we have a techie on our team who knows how to do these things," replied Carlos as he repeated the entire message.

* * *

An hour later the news media message was flashing an interruption to regular programming with an update. The news reporter started by saying, "There has been a significant and shocking update on the attack on the Muslim family in Ann Arbor, Michigan. Apparently this wasn't a random racist attack. This was a targeted revenge attack by a group calling themselves the NERDS. Here is the message they placed on U-Tube just minutes ago." With that the reporter played the message Carlos had dictated along with a small add-on which Boston added which said, "Medina for Orlando, Ann Arbor for Denver, we're still thinking about North Dakota, and Mecca is looking pretty good. We're already on location and in place."

No one failed to recognize the threat. The news media and the Muslim world went ballistic. Sami, the Imam from Ann Arbor, was being interviewed on live television saying, "Why should the entire Muslim world suffer for the sins of a few Islamic radicals? They have attacked the wrong person. I am not in the Muslim Brotherhood. I am not behind these attacks. Why are the holy shrines of the Muslim world being attacked because of the actions of a few radicals? This is inhumane. The American government has a responsibility to stop these crazy idiots."

The news reporter who was interviewing Sami wasn't going to let this comment sit. He asked, "The Muslim world didn't seem to care when Americans were killed in Orlando. In fact we have videos showing Muslims in Saudi Arabia and Iran dancing in the streets after the attacks. If the Muslims really cared about what happened in Orlando and North Dakota, shouldn't they do a little house cleaning of their own? Saying that the Americans need to put a stop to the NERDS is the same as saying the Muslims need to put a stop to the Muslim Brotherhood, isn't it?"

Then the true colors of the Imam came out when he turned red and said, "The Americans started this by being so decadent and living such an extravagant and offensive life style. If your life style wasn't so offensive, these attacks wouldn't happen."

The reporter kept pushing, "So you're saying the attacks on Orlando and North Dakota were justified."

"Yes," replied the Imam before he realized what he was saying.

With that comment the reporter was left shocked and didn't know what to say next. After a pause the reporter said, "I really don't know what to add to that. I am too shocked. I'm going to return this broadcast back to the network," and with that the broadcast switched back.

*　*　*

Lincoln immediately called Boston and said, "Good work. But you really created a firestorm with that last little bit."

"Hang on," replied Boston, "Livy is trying to call in and I'll add her to this call." After a couple clicks Boston asked, "Livy, are you there? And, Lincoln, are you still there?"

After receiving an affirmative from both people on the phones, Livy started with, "First off let me say good work, Lincoln and Boston. The entire mission was executed perfectly. Alvin is running interference keeping the FBI investigation off your tail. But do you realize what kind of a firestorm you've created for me and my team? We have everyone in Washington on our case wanting to know who these NERDS are and how do we stop them. Originally they assumed Brian was working alone but now they're checking into his friends, colleagues, and associates. And they want constant eyes on that Imam in Ann Arbor who seems to be behind all these attacks because they now see him as a credible threat, but they have no evidence on which to arrest him except for your message and the recent interview that he blundered. We may end up using the Patriot Act just to get him off the street for his own protection. But then, why would we want to protect him? And the Saudi's are begging for our help to find what the threat is that is in place in Mecca. Everyone is screaming bloody murder around here. It's crazy!"

"What does Alvin have to say?" asked Lincoln.

"So far we've been too busy to have a private conversation, but he did give me a smile and a wink, so I think he is on board."

"What can we do to help?" asked Boston.

"Nothing," replied Livy. "Lay low. Don't make any mistakes by saying the wrong things to the wrong person. Boston, you did a good job of hiding your identity because they couldn't trace the message and they gave up on that angle. But don't put any more messages out there because they are watching for you in hopes that you will show your hand. So the best thing you guys can do right now is to do nothing. Resume your normal life with all the same routines you did before. Pass this word on to the rest of the team to do the same."

"Will do," responded Lincoln, and Boston agreed.

Chapter Twenty-Six

Sami's Frustration

November, 2017, Ann Arbor, Michigan

Sami wanted desperately to identify the infidels that had killed his wives. He resented these terrorist attacks against him. He was only trying to do Allah's will and they had no right to take this out on his innocent wives and children. This type of behavior could not go unpunished. He had to take action. But how was he going to weed out these NERDS?

He decided to broadcast his own message on U-Tube in the hope they would see it. His message was, "We know the NERDS are bluffing. We have searched every nook and cranny of Mecca and we found no bombs. All we found was a never-ending flow of believers. The NERDS should identify themselves. They should quit the cowardly attacks on a peaceful and God-fearing people. God will punish them. If they would quit their cowardly attacks and come out in the open, we will discuss this problem with them and find a solution."

He hoped this message would get a reaction. Maybe the NERDS would be dumb enough to send a message in reply and then they could be traced. Sami would just have to wait and see if there was a response. But the response he received was not immediate and not the one he hoped for.

Sami had to try to pick up the pieces of his family which had been torn apart. His children were inconsolable and comforting them was something he had never had to do in the past. That was always the role of his wives. He just didn't know how to be a father. His mind had always been consumed with his work at the mosque and he felt extremely uncomfortable in this new role. He wished he could delegate it to someone else, but with both wives gone there was no one else to pass these duties too. Three children were in the hospital and one, the youngest and the one that needed the most attention, was still at home. He tried to pass the youngster off to a sister, but she was out of town at the time, so he contacted one of the families in his congregation and they readily agreed to take care of the child so that Sami could spend time with the three that were in the hospital.

Sami didn't know how to talk to his children. Instead of giving them comfort he would go into one of his tirades about the evils of the American culture and how decadent this society was. He tried to explain how it bred violence. But the words coming out of his mouth were plagued with regret. He felt hypocritical in that his violence may have somehow triggered the attack on his family. Didn't Allah know he was doing his work? Didn't Allah know that in order for Sami to accomplish this work he needed his protection? Where was Allah when he needed him most? His pain, discouragement, and frustration were overwhelming. He had loved his wives and now they were gone. The infidels must pay!

He was sitting next to the bed of one of his sons when he received an unexpected call. "Hello," Sami answered the call trying to be quiet and not wake his son. At first he thought it must be someone in his congregation, but he didn't recognize the phone number.

"Is this the Imam Sami Abdulaziz?" asked a female voice on the other end of the line.

"Yes," replied Sami in a grouchy voice.

"I am Niran," said the voice. "I want to please Allah and do his wishes. I believe you are one of his servants. I saw your message on the television. I live in the same complex that Brian Pearson lived in. And I know you are looking for friends of his who may be involved in these attacks. I don't know who these NERDS are but I can tell you who many of his friends are and maybe you can learn more about these NERDS from them."

Sami's heart leapt. He was pessimistic about ever finding out who the NERDS were. Now his hope in finding them, and more importantly his trust in Allah, had been restored. He jumped up and went out into the hospital hallway so he could talk without disturbing his son. Excitedly he said, "You are the answer to Allah's wishes. Yes, I very much want to learn about the infidel's friends. I have four members of my team coming to Golden right now. Can they come and visit you and learn from you?"

"Of course."

"Then please text me your address and I will forward it on to them," requested Sami. "I have your phone number and they will be calling you when they get to town. Allah will be enormously grateful for any help that you give them."

"Of course," she replied. "I'll do that immediately."

Sami's depression had turned to a sudden flash of excitement. Maybe there was hope for revenge after all. Maybe he could repay these infidels for their brutal attack on his family.

The Imam immediately placed a call to the foursome, Abdul-Wadud, Fatih, Yusuf, and Husam, that were headed to Golden. He was excited to give them the good news. Now their journey was no longer a journey where they were searching for a lead. Now they would be able to formulate a plan. Sami suggested, "We need to have an approach. I'm sure the friends of Brian will know his whereabouts. I'm thinking that if we kidnap one of the families who are close friends of Brian Pearson, then we can use that to intimidate him into telling us about the NERDS. In fact, we may be kidnapping one of the NERDS without even knowing it. It would be good to apply a little pressure on these friends to see if they know anything. I will leave it to you. But, in order to facilitate a kidnapping, you first have to have a place to bring your victims. So find a location that is isolated and where you can hold the hostages. Then meet with Niran to find out who these friends are. And then capture the entire family. You may need a van or some larger vehicle for the kidnapping. You should steal it so the use of it can't be traced back to us. Any questions?"

"None," was the reply over the phone. "Thank you for giving us a mission. We were uncertain what we were going to do and now we have a plan."

"Praise be to Allah for giving us this plan," replied Sami.

After the call Sami returned to his son's hospital room feeling much better. Maybe this was Allah's plan all along. Maybe his wives were due to return to Allah's presence and Sami was supposed to find new wives to replace them. Maybe this attack on his family was necessary in order to weed out these infidels.

Chapter Twenty-Seven

Brian's Bold Statement
November, 2017, Monteverde, Costa Rica

Brian, now known as Gerd, and his family had settled into Monteverde, Costa Rica and were starting to get comfortable with their new life style. They found a home close to the bird park. The location was remote, even for Costa Rica. The roads were intentionally jagged and rocky because the citizens of this beautiful location wanted to discourage immigrants and tourism. The road had potholes often more than a foot deep, and jagged rocks sticking up over six inches as well. The fastest you could travel was five to ten miles per hour in order to avoid breaking an axle or blowing out a tire. Ironically, the remoteness was exactly what attracted Brian. If he was going to be hard to find, he was going to make it impossible.

They found a school which was bilingual, teaching both English and Spanish. They found that even in this remote location they could have the latest and greatest in technological capabilities including full high-speed internet access.

They enjoyed the local attractions, including the cloud rain forest, which was an adventure every time you entered it. They also enjoyed the tourist activities, like zip lines, rafting, and coffee plantation tours.

Financially they were taken care of. The FBI witness relocation program chipped in and gave them money for their travel, housing, and per diem expenses and Gene had left them a healthy endowment. Additionally Brian easily found a job managing one of the local hotels. He wasn't the type of person who could stay home all day and sit. He had to have something that would keep him busy. This wasn't his dream job, but it gave his family some spending money, and it kept him from going stir crazy with boredom.

One day, while at work, Brian was passing through the lobby of his hotel and a news bulletin caught his attention. It was an interview of Sami where he claimed Mecca was risk free and the "terrorists" who had attacked Medina had no chance of planting any type of bomb into Mecca. He claimed Mecca was safe and could not be penetrated.

Sami's arrogance annoyed Brian and his mind immediately went on a roll. What could be done to shut up this arrogant idiot? Contacting his Dragon Pit counterparts was way too dangerous. The FBI agents had made it abundantly clear that all international calls into the Denver area codes would be checked. He would end up having to uproot his family again and move to another location if information about his stay in Costa Rica was leaked.

He spent the next couple days mulling options around in his mind. He was no longer in a position to take over one of the Air Force drones. He lacked the software and computer equipment. Besides, he was sure security had been significantly increased since his hit on Medina. But he could easily take over a private drone. He could do an internet software download and use that software to take over one of these planes. He would just have to break through the password, which wasn't hard. These planes would not have a weapons load, but maybe he didn't need to destroy anything. Maybe all he needed to do was to show Sami that Mecca wasn't as invincible as he thought he was.

Brian didn't need the sophisticated military piloting software. He knew how to get access to the software for flying private drones off the internet. All he needed was special uplink equipment if he was going to take over one of the private drones. He would have to be able to communicate with a satellite and transmit the signal back to the drone he wanted to kidnap. Once he had access to the drone's computer systems he would reprogram the drone to respond only to his commands.

It took Brian some time, but eventually he figured out how he could use the satellite phone provided by the FBI for emergency communication, to uplink the instructions to the drone. Next he would need to identify which drone he wanted to steal. He wanted to find one that wasn't in use very often so it wouldn't be missed immediately. He wanted to complete the mission before anyone even realized there was a problem.

Finding an available drone turned out to be challenging. He had to search and discover who owned the non-military drones. He found that many were used for mapping and for weather and climate observations. After identifying the available drones he had to check them one by one to see which ones had the least amount of flight time for their age. This meant accessing the databases of each drone individually and calculating their weekly usage. Then he needed to check their current location and the fuel supply. Would the drone make it all the way to Saudi Arabia? This would obviously be a one-way trip.

Brian became obsessed with his idea. Everything else, including his work and home responsibilities and even sleep were suddenly put on hold. His wife understood what he was doing once he explained what his obsession was all about. She knew how frustrated Brian was to have his entire life thrown upside down.

Eventually Brian had a plan. He had located a ground-water mapping drone owned by the State of New York that was rarely used. It was parked at La Guardia airport. Since this was a busy airport there was a risk that his take-off would be noticed. He hoped no one would bother to check it out and they would assume it was an authorized mission. They wouldn't realize it had been hijacked until it was too late. The plane was fueled and would easily reach Mecca.

Everything was in place and Brian didn't want to miss his window of opportunity. If he waited too long to take off there was always the possibility that the State of New York would use the plane since it was fueled up and ready to go, and then the opportunity would be lost.

Brian waited until it was about three in the morning Washington, DC time, when activity at the airport was at a minimum. He took control of the airplane, rolled it out of the open hanger, and streaked it down the runway taking off. Once in the air he headed due east, straight for Saudi Arabia.

Brian was still a little uncertain about what he was going to do once he entered Saudi air space. But then an idea struck him and he formulated a plan. He took the drone straight down the middle of the Mediterranean. He didn't want to get too close to Israel because they were sure to detect him and they had already shot down drones in the past. Near the end of the Mediterranean, he banked south heading down the Suez Canal and over the Red Sea. At this point he started to climb. He climbed to the upper altitude limit of the drone, right on the edge of space.

When he was parallel with Mecca, he banked east and headed straight for the city. He hoped the Saudi radar tracking systems wouldn't be able to catch him so high up. He also hoped that by the time they sent a response squad after him, he would already be at Mecca.

His plan worked. The UAV was not detected and within minutes he found himself directly over Mecca. Using the on board cameras, he was able to see the Kaaba, the black box-like structure surrounding the sacred rock.

Brian sent the drone into a nosedive, heading straight for the Kaaba. He didn't want to do any damage. He only wanted to leave a warning message.

* * *

Pilgrims were surrounding the Kaaba, paying homage to the sacred shrine. Suddenly someone noticed something in the sky-streaking straight for them. They screamed, pointing upwards. Everyone in the area started screaming as well. They were pointing and running, not really knowing which way to run. If it was a bomb, they really had no chance for escape. But panic caused them to react randomly. They were convinced this was the day they were going to meet Allah.

Unexpectedly the UAV banked and started circling the Kaaba, flying a little lower with each rotation. On the sixth rotation it landed and parked, turning so as to point directly at the Kaaba.

The worshipers stared in stunned surprise. They were frozen, still not sure if the plane was going to explode. Then a crowd, who was screaming eariler, slowly started walking toward the drone. Eventually a group started to build up around the UAV still staying about five feet away as if there was a magical shield between them and the drone. Then someone kicked at it in anger. Another person kicked it as well. Someone else hit their fist on the wing. Before long a mob reaction took hold and everyone was attacking the plane. It was a reaction to the fear the plane had generated. But, at this point, they were still unsure of the significance of the landing.

Several of the worshipers recorded the descent of the UAV on their phones and sent it to their friends. Someone posted it on the internet and within hours the pictures went viral and were all over the news. The Saudis tried to spin it as a foiled attack that they had prevented, but everyone could see through the ruse. There were no Saudi military planes around. No one brought the plane down. The plane swooped in and landed completely uncontested, and could easily have contained an explosive device that would have left Mecca, the holiest place in the Muslim world, in ruins.

* * *

Sami and his Muslim Brotherhood contacts were furious. This stunt of landing a drone in Mecca made them look like idiots. Now everyone knew Mecca could be penetrated. Their holiest site was vulnerable to attack, and the entire Muslim world was in an uproar. Some of the accusations were directed against the West, but most were not. Rather it was directed against the individuals responsible for the attack in the first place. They had made the connection that the attack on Medina and the plane landing in Mecca were directly connected to the attacks in Orlando and North Dakota. The Islamic broadcast channels screamed out at the Islamic world to stop the insane attacks against the West. They realized that if the plane that landed in Mecca would have contained a bomb, the Kaaba would have been destroyed. The sacred shrines must be protected at all costs.

But the Muslim Brotherhood saw it differently. They felt that the team with the biggest hammer wins. They just needed to find a bigger hammer. Maybe the bombs that were used in Orlando and North Dakota weren't big enough. Maybe more was needed, not less.

The Brotherhood felt that for now the focus had to be on the source of the threat on Mecca. They were convinced it was the NERDS, because they had also used a drone for the attack on Medina. The NERDS had to be identified and eliminated at all costs.

Chapter Twenty-Eight

Traitors
November, 2017, Ann Arbor, Michigan

Abdullah and Kadeem had been boyhood friends since their youth. They were devoted to Allah and studied the teachings of the Prophet. They started attending Sami's mosque about three years back and were strongly influenced by his messages. They even supported the initial attacks on the Orlando theme park and North Dakota. They weren't bothered by the deaths of infidels. But when some of their own friends were killed in Golden, fear crept in. They didn't want to be sacrificed unnecessarily. They no longer wanted to be suicide bombers. They enjoyed life too much. Doubt started to enter their minds. Was this really the work of Allah? Or had Sami gone astray?

Doubt caused the two boys to decide to no longer attend Sami's one-on-one sessions with the exclusive team. They didn't want to be selected for one of these suicide efforts. They trusted Allah. But they found it confusing because when they attended a different mosque, they heard an entirely different message. The other Imam taught that bloodshed was not always the best course. He taught that jihad or holy war can't be declared by isolated individuals. There had to be some kind of consensus about the reason for the holy war and who they were fighting against. He taught that the only true jihad was a defensive one, not where you went on the attack. He said it was wrong for suicide bombers to be attacking civilians and not military combatants. This Imam taught that these murders were not the will of Allah. He taught that Allah proclaims jihad, not an Imam. The conflicting messages between Imams were extremely confusing to the two boys.

The boys wondered, if the Imams couldn't even agree amongst themselves on the teachings of the Koran, then how were they as students to know what was true and right? The boys didn't want any part of an effort that would someday be found out to be against Allah's wishes rather than supporting him.

Abdullah and Kadeem decided to not meet with Sami any longer. He was too extreme for them. They were after truth, not after blood. They wanted to support Allah, but in the right way, and it seemed to them that Sami was just after blood. It seemed like he would never have enough blood until the only individuals living on the earth were Muslims. Somehow that didn't seem reasonable. If the world contained nothing but Muslims, then where would the evil be? Where would Satan go? It just didn't make sense that everyone needed to be Muslim.

The two boys shared a dorm room at the university. Their Muslim heritage brought them together even though they were studying entirely different subjects. Abdullah was focused on construction engineering while Kadeem loved computers. They were both progressing reasonably well through their programs. The hardest part was staying away from all the distractions including dating. They enjoyed the university's culture where sex was readily available, and they wanted to take advantage of every opportunity that came up. This wasn't something that was available to them back home.

It was about nine on a Wednesday evening and they were both sitting at their dorm room desks focused on their assignments when there was a knock on the door. It was normal for there to be a knock. They had several friends who would regularly invite them to some party or bonfire. The boys took turns answering the door and it was Abdullah who went to the door to see who was there. As he started to open the door a shot was fired and Abdullah crumbled to the floor.

Kadeem didn't hesitate. He had quick reaction time. He immediately slipped off his desk chair, which was right next to his bed, and crawled under the bed to hide. Just then he heard the door push open. He listened to voices and he immediately recognized them as two of his fellow worshipers at Sami's mosque.

"Kadeem's not here," Kadeem heard one of the voices say. "Let's get out of here." Luckily they were in too big of a hurry to check under the bed.

The intruders were gone and were immediately replaced by a cluster of students at the door. "Abdullah's dead! Call the police."

At that point Kadeem crawled out from under the bed and said, "Did anyone see those guys?"

"Yes," replied the individual who had been checking Abdullah's life signs. "They were guys that had visited you several times. I remember seeing them here."

That eliminated any confusion for Kadeem. He knew who the attackers were and he also knew who had sent them. Kadeem didn't want to wait around. He knew the police would be here soon and they would want to question him. What would he do? Would he identify the attackers? Would he dare to turn Muslims over into the hands of infidels? Which was the worse crime: his friends killing Abdullah, or the betrayal of the Muslim Brotherhood to infidels?

The answer was obvious. He could never betray fellow Muslims no matter what they had done. They were brothers in belief, and he had to respect that. So he was left without a choice. He had to get away as quickly as possible. He had to escape the grasp of the local infidel police.

The crowd at the door barraged him with questions. "Who was that? What were they doing? Why did they kill Abdullah?" He quickly pushed his way past them without answering any of their questions. He headed to the common hallway bathroom, giving the impression he was going to throw up. But as he came close to the bathroom door he diverted his path and he made a break for the stairway. He decided to avoid the elevator. He would probably just encounter people or police that he really didn't want to talk to.

He jogged down the stairs. Once at the bottom he took the emergency exit door out of the building rather than returning into the building. Once outside, he could see a crowd was starting to form. He headed toward the parking lot in the hopes he would be able to get into his car and escape.

He crossed the grassy field which was spotted with the occasional oak tree, and was nearing the parking lot when he suddenly felt a surging pain in his left shoulder. He hadn't heard the shot fired, mostly because of the blood rush and his heart beating strongly and loudly into his ears.

He spun around to see where the shot was coming from just in time to feel a second surge of pain, this time in his lower left leg. The pain threw him to the ground. He knew he was doomed. The assassins would easily be able to catch up with him and then they would finish the job. He started to black out from the pain. He was quickly slipping into shock.

Shortly before he blacked out Kadeem heard a lot of shouting followed by more shooting. Then the lights went out completely for him.

* * *

When Kadeem finally regained consciousness he found himself lying in a hospital bed with bandages on his left shoulder and leg. He felt stupid. He was disgusted at how weak he was and that a couple small wounds were enough to cause him to crumble to the ground. He always thought he was a little stronger than that. He had disappointed himself.

Who had brought him to the hospital? Why hadn't his friends finished the job of executing him? But his questions were answered in a flash as he noticed a police officer standing watch at the door. He realized somehow the police had stopped the attackers and he was now in their care and custody.

He lay there for the next couple hours pretending to be unconscious, wondering what was going to happen to him. How much do the police know? Do they know about his involvement in Orlando and North Dakota?

He lay in the bed, afraid to get up because of all the wires and tubes he was connected to. Eventually, after a couple hours, a man entered his room. He quickly decided this was a police detective because he didn't wear any of the medical regalia the hospital staff wore.

The detective spoke first, "Welcome back to the land of the living."

"Happy to still be here," Kadeem replied. "Can you tell me what happened out there?"

"I was hoping you could tell me what happened. But I'll tell you as much as I know and let you fill in any blanks for me. First let me ask a few questions. The obvious one being, who were those guys and why were they shooting at you?"

Kadeem was surprised by this question. "You mean you don't know who those guys are? You weren't able to capture them?"

"After we saw them shooting you we came at them and told them to drop their weapons and instead of complying they turned their weapons on us and started shooting. We returned fire and they're both dead."

The officer continued, "We've identified them and we know they attended the same mosque as you, but we don't understand why they were targeting you. Can you explain their behavior?"

Kadeem was conflicted. If he didn't reveal the intentions of his attackers they may come after him again. But if he did reveal their intentions he wondered if he was betraying Allah. He didn't want to betray the Brotherhood, but he didn't want to die. He also didn't like Sami's interpretation of the Koran, especially if it meant he was now on the hit list.

The detective came up with an argument which scared Kadeem. The officer, seeing that Kadeem was conflicted and confused, decided to put on more pressure. "Think about your family. You know if the killers can't get at you they will try to draw you out by attacking your family. We can help protect your family while you are here recovering if you explain why you are being attacked. But first we have to know what is going on."

That was it. That was all Kadeem could handle. He asked, "Will you send someone out to protect my family?" The police officer nodded. With that confirmation Kadeem gave in to the officer and explained everything. He explained the role of Sami, the attacks on The Orlando theme park and North Dakota, and the events in Golden, Colorado.

* * *

The officer was frantically taking notes. What he was learning was more than unbelievable, it was outrageous. He had stumbled on a terrorist cell right here in his own backyard, and he knew he had to take immediate action. He continued questioning Kadeem, but soon realized Kadeem really didn't know a lot. Sami was the mastermind of this operation and the police would have to create a surveillance network that would monitor Sami's communications and activities. He needed hard evidence that would put Sami away for good, and he needed to know who Sami was communicating with in the Muslim Brotherhood network.

After a busy hour of note taking, the detective left the hospital and immediately called a meeting with his local law enforcement leadership and with the FBI. That meeting would run several hours as they strategized on next steps. He would also need to work on a warrant that would allow him to tap Sami's communication lines. He would immediately send someone over to Sami's mosque to start monitoring his activities. All this information would be tracked and relayed back to police and FBI headquarters as they attempted to learn more about the terrorism activities that were going on in Ann Arbor.

In the combined police and FBI meeting, the local officers learned the FBI had already installed monitoring equipment into Sami's mosque. They also learned that Sami had removed the monitoring equipment. The FBI admitted that since Sami knew exactly where to find the equipment and remove it, and because he successfully removed all of it, someone must have informed him where to look and what to do.

They agreed that replacing the monitoring equipment in the mosque would be a waste of time, since it would probably be removed again. They decided to place monitoring cameras at locations across the street from the mosque and they would monitor those cameras 24/7, hoping to gain some insight into Sami's activities.

The task force resisted the urge to bring Sami in for questioning, because that would just alert him to their active interest. They were sure there was a bigger fish behind all of these activities, and they wanted a chance to identify the top leadership.

Chapter Twenty-Nine

Niran

November, 2017, Golden, Colorado

The foursome, Abdul-Wadud, Fatih, Yusuf, and Husam, entered the Denver area about four hours after receiving the call from Sami. They had retraced the travel route of their Islamic revolutionary brothers that had come here a few days earlier. They had a mission and they were not going to fail like their brothers had failed. Failure had cost Imam Sami his wives and the health of his children, and they were not going to let something like that happen again. They immediately headed for Golden. They knew they had to locate a hiding place where they could stash their kidnap victims. Once they had that figured out, they would make contact with Niran and use her information to help track down their victims. After that it would be an easy task of stealing a van and executing the kidnapping.

They were excited. They had never been involved in something that would have such a significant impact on Allah's kingdom. They were thrilled that they could be of service in Allah's jihad against the infidel world. They could feel the adrenaline build-up in their bodies and they had trouble controlling their excitement. This experience was going to be both fun and rewarding.

Following the guidance of their team members who stayed behind in Ann Arbor, the foursome passed through Golden on Highway 58 and on the west side of the city they jumped on Highway 6 heading south. They turned right on Clear Creek Lane which was a small road that dead-ended into the forest. At the end of the road there were several old shacks which looked as if they hadn't been occupied for decades.

The foursome decided this was the perfect location for hiding the kidnapped infidels. They would need to purchase some chains and zip ties in order to restrain their victims, but that was the easy part. Now they could proceed with the planning of the kidnapping. The inexperience of the foursome caused them to select a hideout that only had one road in and out. They didn't realize they were trapping themselves in as well.

* * *

Niran received the call she knew was coming. It was from Imam Sami's allies who were the warriors sent out to do Allah's mission. The phone rang and Niran answered with, "Hello!"

"Is this Niran?" the warrior asked.

"Yes. Are you the messengers sent by the Imam Sami?"

"Yes, can we meet?"

"Yes. We can meet on the Colorado Engineering School campus in the park that is in front of the administration building. I am on campus now. I'll meet you there in thirty minutes." It would be inappropriate for Niran to meet with males that were not of her family unless it was in a very public place so she selected the park in the center of the university. The warriors knew this as well and did not question her choice of location even though a public meeting may result in their meeting being noticed and recorded. But Allah's law had to be obeyed.

"Yes," Abdul-Wadud specified. "Thank you for meeting with us."

* * *

The park in front of the Administration building was larger than the warriors expected. They thought of the Colorado Engineering School as a small school, not like the State University of Michigan where they attended. CES was smaller, but in many ways it had a stronger reputation in some specific areas of engineering and economics. It had a strong international following and received excellent support from the natural resources industry. One of its supporters was the Carters brewery that was very close to the school. The heating for many of the

CES buildings was supplied via underground piping from the brewery. It generated heat through the brewing process and this heat was recycled for the use of the university. However, it would often leave a residue brewery smell in the buildings. The student's didn't seem to mind.

The four warriors spotted Niran sitting on a bench in the middle of the park. She was easily identified because of the Abaya dress and Hijab on her head. She was the only one in the park in the traditional Muslim clothing. She didn't wear the face covering, which was not always required in Saudi Arabia.

The warriors walked directly to her and two sat on the beach next to her while the other two stood next to the bench. Niran gave the traditional Muslim greeting, *"as-salam alaykum,"* which was an Arabic greeting often used by Muslims around the world. It translates to "peace be upon you", but was often considered the equivalent to "hello" in English. The greeting was generally accompanied with a hand placed on the heart, which she did. She handed the warrior sitting next to her on the bench, a piece of paper.

The warriors replied with the traditional greeting, *"Wa alaykumu s-salam."* Then they looked at the piece of paper that Niran had supplied. It contained a list of names and addresses.

Niran explained, "These are the friends I have seen visit Brian Pearson's home. I looked up their address as well. I hope this information is helpful."

"This is incredible," explained Abdul-Wadud who was holding the piece of paper. "You have made the work of Allah so much easier. Thank you for your help."

The warriors stood up to leave, and with the same traditional greetings, they bid farewell and headed back to their vehicle. On the way, one of the warriors placed a call to his friends in Ann Arbor. He read off the addresses and asked them to identify their closest option. A few minutes later, before they had reached their parked vehicle, their smart phones received a text message with a map showing them where to go.

They were off. They weren't ready to do the kidnapping. They didn't have the van or the zip ties. They wanted to stake out the home of these infidels prior to the kidnapping. They wanted to determine when the best time would be to execute. They wanted to make sure they were able to get everyone in the family in one shot. So they would have to watch and see when everyone was home and then they would strike.

Ten minutes later they found the apartment complex where Glenn Pierre lived. He lived in the bottom right hand unit of a two story four-plex. The warriors parked across the street in a strip-mall parking lot which gave them an excellent view of Glenn's home. They continued their observation for several hours. During their surveillance they made small talk about the weather and what they were studying in school. These conversations were intermixed with long periods of silence. But no one minded the quiet. In many ways they preferred it rather than talking about topics that had no value.

They felt guilty for not saying their ritualistic daily prayers, but they felt the need to be inconspicuous and kneeling out on the parking lot was sure to draw attention to their presence. Eventually Abdul-Wadud spoke up, "This is a waste of time. Why don't we just go in during the night when they're asleep? Then everyone is sure to be at home and we can get them all in one swoop."

"I agree," said Husam. "Let's go get the van and the other materials we need so we can be ready for later tonight."

"Let's go," said Fatih. "I remember seeing a hardware store close by and we can get the twist ties there. But I would recommend that we get the van in the middle of the night because then no one will realize the van is missing until in the morning and by then it will be too late."

"Agreed," said Abdul-Wadud, and they drove off toward the hardware store.

Chapter Thirty

Glenn Pierre
November, 2017, Golden, Colorado

Glenn lived in a small two-bedroom apartment with his wife Cynthia. He had two children, a four-year-old boy from his wife's previous marriage and a two-year-old girl that they had together. They loved the Golden area for several reasons. They loved the way the seasons were well defined and they loved living right next to the mountains. They also loved how a hilly barrier buffered Golden from the larger Denver metropolis. With just a short drive through those hills they could take advantage of the benefits offered by living in a larger city. They also loved being a short drive from ski resorts and rock climbing, which they both loved. They had made a pact that after Glenn finished his twenty years with the Marines and retired, they would return to this area to live permanently.

Glenn and Cynthia were visiting the local shopping mall and had just pressed the up button on the elevator when their young daughter started to scream. She was riding in a stroller behind them. Glenn and Cynthia immediately turned their full attention to her to see what she was yelling about. In the meantime the elevator door opened and their older, four-year-old son stepped in the elevator without either of them noticing. Suddenly the elevator doors started to close. Cynthia let out a scream, seeing that her son was about to take a ride by himself in the elevator. Glenn jumped up and stuck his foot in the elevator door when it was about six inches from shutting. The door pressed against his foot and was stuck. It didn't reopen, as he expected it to do. Waving their hands in the open door slot in order to trigger a sensor also didn't work. Pushing the elevator button did nothing. Nothing would reopen the door. It just remained stuck against his foot. Glenn was able to pull his foot out, but then the elevator would leave and go to some random floor, and he had no idea where it would go. Then his son would be stranded on some other floor. That wasn't acceptable. So Glenn continued to stand there with his foot wedged in the elevator door. He quickly instructed his wife to get help.

Inside the elevator, his son was getting more and more frantic. He was on the verge of crying and kept saying, "I'm stuck in the alligator!" Glenn tried to reassure him by telling him that they were getting help and would have him out soon. But the only thing his son said was, "Tell mommy I'm stuck in the alligator!"

It was ten minutes before help arrived. The mall cops and a mall manager came to the elevator. The conclusion was that they were going to send a security guard to each of the floors. Then, when the guards were in place, Glenn was to take his foot out of the elevator. Glenn tried to explain the situation to his son but all his son could say was, "I don't want to be stuck in the alligator anymore!"

Everyone was in position. Glenn pulled his foot out and the doors finished closing, but the elevator didn't move. None of the floor buttons were pushed. The elevator just sat there. By now his son was crying and they could hear him through the doors, "I don't want to be stuck in the alligator ANYMORE!" He was too distraught to understand the instructions to push one of the floor buttons.

The mall manager suggested that the only option was to reset the elevator. This would require cutting the power on the elevator, which would put the boy into total darkness. Then, when the power came back on, the elevator should operate normally allowing them to push the elevator button on the outside and thereby open the elevator doors.

There was no choice. The power was cut off. The inside of the elevator went into total darkness for about sixty seconds, the longest sixty seconds in history. When the power was back on, Glenn pushed the elevator button and the elevator doors opened. His son was standing there and all he could say through his tears was, "I was stuck in the alligator!" He kept repeating this phrase over and over in spite of all the reassurances that Glenn and Cynthia could give him.

Cynthia was so excited she grabbed her son up in her arms. In her hands she was holding the car keys and as she stood there and hugged her son the car keys fell.

At the front of the elevator there was about a half inch slit between the elevator and the outside floor. It was so small a slit that no one ever recognizes it or pays any heed to it. However today the slit became important because Cynthia's falling keys managed to hit the slit perfectly and fell through. She could hear the keys hit the ground at the bottom of the elevator shaft. Today was not a good day.

The mall manager apologized. He had no way to get the keys out of the elevator shaft without the help of the elevator technician, who only comes once a month to service the elevator. She would either have to wait till the technician came out, or else pay for a special service call, which wasn't a possibility on a student's budget. It was turning out to be a really, really bad day. Glenn called Boston, who lived close to the mall, and asked him if he could give his family a ride home, and then bring him back with his extra set of keys so he could drive his car home.

Finally arriving at home, the routine for the rest of evening continued on as normal. Cynthia, having worked all day at a local bank, and then spending the last couple hours at the mall, made dinner at around seven. Glenn helped with the salad and kept his son occupied and on track with some early education workbooks they used. Some evenings went better than others and so far this one had started out strange. His son was still obsessed with saying, "I was stuck in the alligator!"

His wife could only say, "I can't believe I lost those keys. If I would have wanted to drop those keys in that slot I could have tried 100 times and not have hit it right. Today is just a frustrating day."

By seven fifteen they were all sitting together around the kitchen table. Glenn asked Cynthia's son to bless the food and after the blessing they had the option of making a chicken burrito or a chicken taco salad. Mexican food had become a family favorite.

By now it was seven thirty and the kids went off to take their baths and get ready for bed. Getting ready for bed included a bedtime story read by Glenn and by eight thirty the house was quiet. That give Glenn and Cynthia an hour to watch something they liked.

With the kids in bed Glenn and Cynthia finally had time to watch a recorded episode of a singing competition, jumping through the commercials and the judges' comments in order to make the show go faster. This was one of those seasons where the judges spent more time beating up on each other than offering anything of value to the contestants. But it was the singing that was the best part of the show. After the show, Glenn and Cynthia enjoyed debating who they thought did the best job with their song and who they would vote to keep on the show. After the show they watched a couple episodes of a comedy. This would end the evening on a happy note.

By eleven the lights were off and everyone was sound asleep, not realizing that in just a few hours they would be rudely awakened.

* * *

It was two in the morning when the Islamic warriors were back at Glenn's house. About one hour earlier they had stolen a van from an apartment complex parking lot. They had to find a van that didn't have windows on its sides or in the back, and it had to be empty. They didn't want to spend a lot of their time unloading the van. Finding the exact van that would satisfy their requirements turned out to be a bigger task than they originally expected. But luckily they found exactly what they needed, and it was even unlocked. After hot-wiring the ignition switch they took the short drive back to Glenn's house. They drove both vehicles away from the location of the stolen van because they feared that leaving the car behind might lead the police back to them.

After arriving close to the house, the four reconvened back into the car to discuss next steps. "What do we do now?" question Abdul-Wadud as they sat to the side of Glenn's apartment building.

"We go get them," replied Husam.

"How do we get in?" asked Abdul-Wadud.

"It's either through the front door or through the window," replied Fatih.

"Let's go," insisted Husam as he opened his car door. The rest followed his lead and exited the vehicle. By the time they were all out of the vehicle, Fatih had opened the trunk of the car and was loading a pistol. He was anxious to get the process started. The other three followed suit and each grabbed a weapon that they could use. Before they were done Fatih had arrived at the front door and was already trying the doorknob.

The door was locked so he put his shoulder to work slamming against the door as hard as he possibly could. The first hit had no result. Then Husam joined him and the two of them hit at the door together. The door gave way just a little and they could hear the cracking of the doorjamb as it started to break open. A third hit by the pair and the door broke through the jamb. They were in the apartment.

The loud crashing noise could be heard throughout the house and the intruders could hear Cynthia in the back bedroom say, "What was that?"

* * *

"Stay here!" yelled Glenn, his Marine instinct caused him to quickly retrieve a pistol from the nightstand drawer. He cocked it in preparation for what he might find. He hoped the noise from the pistol would be enough to scare anyone off. He heard no reaction so he assumed the noise didn't come from an intruder. Maybe it was one of the children. Nevertheless he still stayed ready, pistol pointed toward the ceiling, and moved toward the front room.

Unfortunately Glenn and Cynthia's comments caused the warriors to prepare themselves. They took positions on either side of the end of the hallway and waited. Then, when Glenn entered the front room they jumped him. One of the intruders held on to the pistol and kept it pointed away from them while the other started wrestling with Glenn. A third intruder joined in the fray. It was a struggle and Glenn nearly won the battle, but the three assailants finally were able to take Glenn down to the ground. Glenn's mouth was taped shut followed by having his hands twist tied behind his back. Two of the warriors started to drag him out of the apartment when they heard a shout from the back bedroom, "Glenn, are you all right? Is everything okay?"

* * *

Not hearing an answer spooked Cynthia, who could then be heard closing and locking the bedroom door. But Cynthia quickly realized that this was a bad move. What about the kids? Feeling a little self-conscious and guilty for ignoring the little ones, she quickly slipped on a pair of pants but her see-through nightshirt was a poor covering for the top half of her body. She felt a pang of urgency for her family. She decided she was going to sneak into the kids' bedroom and make sure they were okay. Then she would barricade herself and the kids into that room.

A second thought occurred to her. What about calling 9-1-1? She grabbed the cell phone and hit the keys as she slowly started to open the door. Suddenly, there was a strong hit on the bedroom door from the other side and she was pushed back into the room. She fell sprawling on the floor as the phone went flying. She saw the outline of someone surging into the room.

Someone grabbed Cynthia and started wrestling with her, dragging her out of the bedroom and into the living room. Cynthia kicked, screamed, and punched. But to no avail. Her captor held her to the ground, rolling her over face down. He intentionally grabbed her breast in the process so he could cop a feel. Once he had her face down, he sat on her to hold her down and he took her arms and zip tied them behind her. She screamed causing the warrior to cup a hand over her mouth and quickly apply duct tape. Once constrained, the Islamic warrior reached under her, once again grabbing her soft breast, and rolled her onto her back. He pulled out more duct tape and ran the tape around her head taping her mouth securely.

The same intruder continued to sit on her in order to hold her down, hoping to get a little more of a thrill from her. After groping a few more feels, this time with both hands on her two breasts, he decided to get up and move away from her. But Cynthia had other plans. As the warrior started standing up she jerked her knee up and gave him a rapid kick in the groin. The warrior screamed in pain and fell down to the floor next to her, grabbing at his crotch. Cynthia had made a direct hit on her target.

Cynthia started to get up but by then one of the warriors who had taken Glenn out to the van was just returning. He grabbed her and started to forcefully direct her to the van. He ignored his friend's screaming and cursing about the kick on his groin, thinking he deserved what he was getting. That guy had a perverted streak in him.

One warrior remained in the van with a gun trained on Glenn and Cynthia. The other two warriors went back into the house to round up the kids. The fourth warrior remained on the floor of the apartment massaging his testicles.

What no one realized was that the 9-1-1 call that Cynthia had tried to dial had gone through and an operator was listening to everything that was going on in the apartment. Sheriff's cruisers had been dispatched to the apartment. But would they get there soon enough?

The three warriors found two children huddling together on one of the beds, hugging each other in fear. The warriors quickly grabbed the children. As they exited the apartment they heard the sirens off in the distance. They hurriedly threw the children into the van, started the engine, and started rolling out of the parking lot just as the fourth warrior came screaming out of the apartment. They had almost driven off without him. The van stopped and he jumped in, just in time. The van drove off and was half-way down the block before they realized they had forgotten the car. It was still in the parking lot at the apartment building. The four started yelling and blaming each other for the mistake. It was all in Arabic so the Pierre family had no idea what they were talking about. They hoped it wasn't about how they were going to get killed.

This kidnapping had been a comedy of errors and now the warriors had left their car which was a clue that would allow the police to directly connect them back to Ann Arbor. They drove slowly and inconspicuously away heading toward the east, not wanting to draw any attention to themselves. Then they circled around on a side street and worked their way back toward their hideout where they would be stashing the family.

* * *

"You idiots," yelled Abdul-Wadud in Arabic, directing his comments at the other warriors. "What are we going to do now? We're driving around in a vehicle that we know they will be searching for. And by leaving that car we left them with a big sign to tell them who we are. How could you have been so stupid?"

"You're as much to blame as any of us!" yelled Fatih back. "Our mistake is your mistake."

Abdul-Wadud, who had apparently designated himself as the leader, continued, "First we stash these infidels. Then we get rid of this van and find ourselves another vehicle to get around in. We're going to need to get food and supplies. All of this may take a while. Afterwards we call Sami and see what he thinks we should do with these hostages now that we have them under our power."

"Great idea except that we left our phones in the car," replied Yusuf.

"Then I guess we have to purchase a throw-away phone for ourselves too," replied Abdul-Wadud. "I can't believe the screw-ups we have committed. Allah is really testing us this time to see if we will complete his mission."

By the time they had finished debating, the warriors had arrived at the location of the hideout. Glenn and his family were rudely yanked out of the van. Then they were roughly pushed toward the small shack that would be their temporary home. Once inside Glenn and Cynthia were pushed to the floor in one corner of the room. The children quickly followed and cuddled between their two parents. They kept asking them questions, but it was impossible for their parents to offer any answers with their mouths taped shut.

Then, in Arabic, Abdul-Wadud barked instructions at the kidnappers and he and Fatih rushed out the door of the shack. A few minutes later the van could be heard driving off.

The Pierres continued huddling in the corner, trying to keep themselves warm in their nightclothes. The children were scared and continued to cry, looking to their parents for comfort. One of the children reached up and started to pull the tape away from their mother's mouth, all the time watching to see if there would be a reaction from one of the Arabs. Yusuf looked over and saw what the child was doing. He then looked away, feeling that no one would hear them even if they yelled and screamed. The child finished pulling the tape off of his mother's mouth. She winched in pain as the tape also pulled out some of her hair which was caught on the tape as it was wrapped around her head. Seeing that their captors weren't going to do anything to stop the process, the other child did the same for her father. The children wanted to untie their hands as well, but the twist ties were too strong for them to break.

The parents tried to comfort and console the children, telling them everything was going to be all right. But they weren't sure of it themselves. They weren't sure they were going to make it out of this mess with their lives.

Glenn decided to speak up, "Can you tell us why we're here? Why did you kidnap us?"

Husam spun around and jumped up. Apparently he was still thinking that their mouths were taped shut and he was surprised. But Yusuf spoke up and in Arabic told him it was okay. Husam sat back down but continued to keep an eye on the hostages.

Yusuf responded, "Quiet you infidels. We brought you here for only one purpose. We need you to tell us who the NERDS are and to tell us where Brian has gone."

Glenn responded, acting ignorant of the situation, "What are you talking about? Are these NERDS a group of people? And, as for Brian, we were wondering what happened to him ourselves. The whole family disappeared. We're sure it has something to do with the destruction of their home. But we really have no idea where they are. We wish we could talk to them too. They were good friends and now they just disappeared. So it sounds like you've kidnapped the wrong people. We have no idea what you're talking about or how to help you."

"Quiet, you liars!" screamed Husam, shaking his fist at them as if to threaten them. "We know you are lying. Soon we will get the truth out of you." He was the same individual who had molested Cynthia earlier and he still felt the pain of her response. He would love to execute some form of revenge on the family but he knew it had to look legitimate or his fellow Islamists would never allow it.

There was some confusion in Islamic ideology. Sexual indiscretions were explicitly not allowed, but when it came to infidels, who in many ways were less than human, did this rule still apply, and with women who were already second-class citizens, was it really an indiscretion if the act was against an infidel female? Obviously Husam thought he was legitimately justified. In spite of the fact that his friends felt differently he would soon get his revenge against Glenn and Cynthia. But first he would have to make it look justified to the other warriors. Husam was angry and he looked forward to the opportunity to inflict his punishment.

Chapter Thirty-One

The Pierre Family Turmoil

November, 2017, Golden, Colorado; Ann Arbor, Michigan, Washington, DC

Within minutes of the first 9-1-1 call the home of the Pierre family was surrounded by sheriff's vehicles. But it was a few seconds too late. The front door was wide open and the family was gone, and there were the obvious signs of an intense struggle inside. But there was no blood, which probably meant, at least for now, everyone was still alive.

The police immediately canvassed the neighborhood asking questions about what they may have seen and heard. One renter was able to describe the vehicle that had been used for their get-away. She described the van and also mentioned that she thought they had arrived with two vehicles but only left with one since some of the kidnappers walked in from a different direction. She thought she saw five men but it was too dark and the lighting was poor so she couldn't describe them very well.

Immediately the police went on the hunt for any vehicles that didn't belong to the tenants. The search was a quick one because the Chevy with Michigan license plates was a quick give-away. It didn't take long to figure out that the vehicle was a rental from Ann Arbor. The cell phones inside the vehicle were also helpful in identifying who the kidnappers were. Digging a little deeper allowed the police to discover that the kidnappers were connected with Imam Sami and his mosque.

Within an hour, Imam Sami was sitting in an interrogation room in Ann Arbor being questioned about the kidnapping. He denied everything. He even denied knowing the kidnappers, even though they had his phone number in their cell phones and they were part of his congregation. Sami claimed he knew so many members of his congregation he didn't distinguish one from the other. They were a big blur to him and he didn't recognize the names they were questioning him about. He ended the interrogation by saying he would be sure to notify the police if he learned anything about the kidnapping. He would ask the members of his mosque to come forward and be helpful to the police.

The police found the interrogation of Sami extremely irritating. He had a personality that infuriated and frustrated the police. He was openly mocking them and making fun of their efforts. He was looking down on them as if they were inferior in some way. Sami acted as if he had the upper hand and everyone else was just stupid.

In the end, the police had to release Sami because they had nothing they could charge him with. But they knew there was more information he was hiding. They knew he had a role in the kidnapping, but at this point they couldn't tie him directly to it.

***

Livy was livid. First Brian and his family had to go into hiding and now Glenn and his family were in trouble. What was going on? What was the source of this obvious leak within the FBI? She sat down in Alvin's office and shut the door. Alvin immediately recognized the signs of her frustration by her mannerisms and facial expressions. He knew this wasn't good. Ironically, he enjoyed visits from Livy, even if it was bad news. He just liked being around her. "What's up?" he asked her.

"We have a leak somewhere and we need to get it plugged," Livy started off. "I thought the leak was in the Air Force when Brian was targeted and his family was hit. But how would anyone know that Glenn was a part of the NERDS? There has to be a leak, and I can't tell if it's in the FBI or within the NERDS themselves. I just don't get it. How much more secretive can we be?"

"I agree," responded Alvin. Now that he had become the de-facto leader of the NERDS he felt personally responsible for making sure their operations were successful, and this news was something he had also suspected. "The answer is in this Imam in Ann Arbor. How is he getting this information? How does he know to send one team of four students after Brian's family, and now he sent another team of four students after Glenn's family? Where is he getting this information from? Are you sure none of the NERDS are Muslims?"

"We could ask the same question about the FBI."

"Quite right. What do you propose we do?"

"I'm not sure of anything at this point," replied Livy. "The Ann Arbor police had to let the Imam go because they had nothing to hold him on. I guess it's not a crime to have your phone number listed in the contact list of the kidnappers. I'm shopping for ideas here. Do you have any suggestions or next step recommendations?"

Alvin responded, "I'm suggesting that someone needs to spend a little one-on-one time with the Imam and see if there is anything else he may know that he is not telling us. He's successfully avoided our phone taps. Apparently he has more than one phone and we don't have all the numbers he is using. But you may have someone who could have a more direct conversation with him and get him to share some information. As you know, the FBI can't engage in the type of behavior that I am suggesting. Do you have someone on the NERDS team that might be able to have this conversation with him?"

"You're right. We could spend a lot of time doing internal investigations within the FBI and elsewhere. We could keep doing this mole hunt and still end up with nothing. Or we could go directly to the person who is acting on this information and see where the source actually is. I'll get someone on it immediately."

"But we also need to simultaneously set a trap for our mole. I'm suggesting we leak some information about where Brian is located and see what happens. We can have someone waiting to see who shows up. Only problem is that it won't necessarily dig out the mole. It will just give us the guy tagged with the mission to find Brian."

"Let's do both," confirmed Livy. "I'll send someone after the Imam and you set up a mole trap. Let's only pass the information around the FBI first and not the NERDS. Then we can narrow down where the mole is located."

"I'm sure you're using burner phones and encrypted phones, aren't you?" added Alvin. "You never know who might be listening."

"Agreed," answered Livy as she stood up and started to walk toward the office door. "And yes we are."

Livy went even further. She went outside and took a walk before placing a call to Lincoln. He answered immediately, "What's up?"

Livy explained, "We have a mole and we don't know where it is. Somehow this Imam in Ann Arbor knew about Brian and now about Glenn and who knows what else he knows. Anyway, he seems to be the key to identifying this mole. And I'm thinking there is no one better than you to figure it out."

"Gage," replied Lincoln. "He's a Navy Seal, part of Seal Team Six that found Osama Bin Laden. How about the two of us go in together and do this. Does Alvin think we should go after this Imam?"

"Alvin is in complete support of the idea. And your idea is an excellent idea, but I want answers, not a corpse. Just one of you guys scares me but the two of you together – that's real fear. I just hope I never make the two of you mad at the same time."

"Quit worrying," replied Lincoln. "We'll get you both."

Livy was confused, "What do you mean both?"

"We'll get you the answers you need and we'll throw in the corpse as a bonus."

"I don't want to know about a corpse. I just need answers."

"I'll work it," replied Lincoln, and the phone connection went dead.

***

Lincoln, avoiding the phone, took a drive over to Gage's apartment in hopes that he would find him there. Luckily he was there. It took a total of about ten minutes for Lincoln to explain to Gage what he thought they needed to do and to get Gage's full agreement and commitment. The two of them drove off to visit Gene Wiseman to find out if he would allow them the use of his plane. Once again, the conversation lasted less than ten minutes.

The flight was set for an evening departure, just like last time when Lincoln put the hit on the Imam's family. Hopefully they would be back again by morning in time for breakfast, just like last time.

* * *

At six that evening, the plane lifted off from the Boulder municipal airport. They didn't want to leave from or arrive at the same airport twice. They wanted to keep their travels as "off the record" as possible. The flight plans were also falsified as to who and where the flight was going. The Dragon Pit / NERDS wanted it to be impossible to be traced. An hour and a half later they were landing at the Willow Run Airport near Ypsilanti, Michigan. As before, Livy had an FBI vehicle available at the airport. This time it was a large, windowless van with only a driver and passenger seat. Otherwise the van was empty.

Lincoln and Gage drove into the neighborhood of the mosque and parked close by. As before, Lincoln went up the fire escape from where he had previously shot up the Imam's house. He was going to observe the activity in the mosque and in the Imam's house while Gage waited in the van for next steps and directions. It didn't take long before Lincoln had the Imam located. He was just arriving home.

Lincoln gave Gage a heads-up that Sami had just arrived in the house and that he did not see any other activity in the house. Lincoln suggested, "I know we were planning on doing this in the van, but he's all alone in his house. It would be easier to get the information we need from him there and avoid dragging him out into the street. But remember, the local police and the FBI have placed cameras on the street watching everything that's going into and out of that house as well as his mosque."

"Agreed," replied Gage. "I'm going in. I have the ski mask ready and I've turned my coat inside out so there are no identifying markings. You keep watch."

"Perfect," responded Lincoln. He could see Gage get out of the van. A few minutes later he saw him going around the side of the house. It wasn't long after that when Lincoln could see Gage's heat signature inside the house.

"Where is he?" whispered Gage.

"Directly above you, one floor up," replied Lincoln.

"Thanks." Lincoln could follow Gage's movements up the staircase on to the next floor. He gave Gage a little more directional information, but he knew Gage would not be verbally responding in order to keep silence.

Lincoln watched Gage move in on Sami. Then suddenly, as if in a flash, the Imam was lying face down on the floor. His hands and legs were tied. It all happened so fast it reminded Lincoln of a rodeo event he had seen earlier where the cowboy rode up on a horse, lassoed the calf, and had him tied up in a fraction of a second. He couldn't help but smile at the thought that Gage would have made a good cowboy.

* * *

Sami's hands were tied behind his back and his feet were also tied together and hooked back up to his hands. Then Gage rolled Sami over and said, "I have only one question that I want answered. I won't ask the question again. I'll just count to ten and you'll see what happens. But I warn you, it will be painful. Here's the question: What is your source for the information about Brian or Glenn's family? I won't ask you again."

"You have no right to do this to me," screamed Sami. "This is a breach of my civil rights. Who are you and what do you think you're doing to me. Are you police? FBI? I'll sue you and make sure you never work again. Who are you and what do you want? You can't treat an American citizen like this."

Gage wasn't going to get sucked into the ironically stupid argument Sami was implying. Apparently the Imam doesn't want his rights abused, but he cares very little about the rights of the Americans he has already killed or injured. With that Gage started to slowly count to ten. All the time the Imam kept screaming, "What are you going to do? Why do you keep counting? What is it you want? Get away from me you fiend from Satan. I am a religious leader and this torture is racist prejudice and will be published in every news program in the world. I recommend you stop it now before you go too far and there is no return."

The Imam's ranting went on and on but Gage continued his slow count to ten. At ten, Gage pulled out a pointed hunting knife and slowly, while simultaneously twisting the knife back and forth, dug a hole into the front upper leg muscle of Sami's left leg. Gage made it painful and slow. Sami screamed at the pain. "How can you do this?" he complained. "This is uncivilized. This type of torture does not happen in civilized culture."

Gage re-started the count at one. "Let's try this again," he said matter-of-factly.

* * *

When the count reached four, Sami realized that he wasn't going to get out of this situation by complaining. Either he gave up what he knew or he would be hurt again. But in his mind he thought, *Maybe that was the only pain he is going to inflict on me. Maybe this infidel will realize that I don't know anything or that torture isn't going to get information out of me. I will wait out another count and see what happens.*

When the count reached nine the Imam couldn't control himself and he yelled out, "I don't know anything. I can't give you something I don't know."

The complaints fell on deaf ears as the count reached ten and Gage unceremoniously took the knife and dug a matching hole into the top of Sami's right leg. Sami screamed in agony.

Sami feared dying. He believed in the Koran and in the Allah's teachings, but there was that little twinge of doubt that something may be slightly off in these teachings. There were some inconsistencies he was afraid to voice. He couldn't be seen as anything but a true and complete believer. Islam did not have room for even the slightest bit of doubt. His small doubts were enough to make him fear death. He wished he had the faith and devotion his students seemed to possess.

But he questioned if they truly had faith, or if they were just pulled along by the social intimidation of it all. He just didn't know what was right. He felt frustrated by his lack of faith. All he knew was that he wasn't ready to die until he figured out what the truth really was.

Gage had started the count again a third time. As the count reached five Sami decided it wasn't worth it. He realized he wasn't going to get any help. There wasn't any rescue coming. Besides, he didn't owe anything to the girl who informed on Brian's friends. He would give up her name and location and maybe this torture and threat would end. He would sacrifice her. She was small potatoes and had little else to offer the cause.

"Stop," Sami screamed as Gage said eight.

"Tell me," was all Gage said.

"I know her as Niran. She is a neighbor of the infidel who insulted Islam by attacking Medina. She told us about the friends of the family and we hoped that if we attacked the friends then we would be able to draw Brian out and get a reaction from him. That was the way the four warriors in Golden hoped they would be able to find Brian."

"How do I find Niran?" asked Gage. "And how did she help you find Brian in the first place?"

"We found Brian through the Muslim Brotherhood," explained the Imam. "They have a contact in the Air Force who has a prominent position and who is a Muslim. I received my information about Brian from my Muslim Brotherhood contacts in Egypt. I don't know who this guy in the Air Force is. They will never share that information with me. It was decided that this was information I did not need to know."

"And Niran?"

"Her number is in my phone. I don't know any more other than she is a neighbor of Brian's and she called me to let me know the information about his friends. I can't give you any more than that."

Gage checked the phone and quickly found a telephone number with the correct area code. He decided to keep the phone. He may need to call Niran directly and it would be better if she thought the call was coming from Sami. There would be a better chance of her answering his call. He also found the text message that gave her address.

"Thanks," responded Gage. Then, acting as if he was walking off, he walked behind Sami and unceremoniously slit his throat in halal fashion. He walked around to the side of Sami and gave him a swift kick knocking his body to the ground. "For nothing," was Gage's parting comment.

* * *

Using infrared, Lincoln was able to watch everything Gage was doing. He could only hear Gage's side of the conversation through the earpiece, but it wasn't too hard to figure out what was being said by Sami. When he saw Gage's kick followed by Sami rolling over he knew it was finished and it was now time to return to the van and head back to the airport.

"I guess we decided to kill him after all," said Lincoln as he packed up his rifle and scope and headed down the fire escape.

Chapter Thirty-Two

The Kidnapped Family

November, 2017, Provo, Utah and Golden, Colorado

Alvin decided to set up a trap for any potential informants. He personally traveled to Provo, Utah in order to set up the trap. He started by acquiring a fully furnished house which looked like something Brian and his family would like to live in. He found the perfect two-story house with a big fenced yard on 25 West 4200 North in Provo. He bought the place under the name of Brian Colter.

Next he plastered hidden cameras and recording devices throughout the inside and outside of the house. He set it up so he could monitor, record, and play back any of these recordings through the internet on his computer. To complete the picture, he left a car parked in the driveway. He did all of this in one day and then returned to his base in Washington, DC.

Back in the FBI offices Alvin leaked the information that Brian and his family were still in the United States and they had never left, that the entire run to Canada was to throw off any potential attackers. He suggested that Brain had been relocated to Provo, Utah somewhere along the Wasatch Front. Alvin also suggested that he had been placed in the witness protection program under protective custody and given a new identity. He even hinted at the identity, saying he was still called Brian but had only changed his last name. Alvin felt this information should be enough for anyone to find the house he had set up as a trap. Now he just had to wait and see what happened.

***

The two warriors, Abdul-Wadud and Fatih, had been given the mission of swapping out the van they had used for the kidnapping, replacing it with a new stolen vehicle, and picking up some supplies. They left the hideout and drove into the Golden area. The "old town" area was just a few minutes away and it included a grocery store. That's where they originally planned to get the food they needed. But since they also needed some additional supplies, like more tape and zip ties they changed their mind and decided to drive to Superstore Mart. Superstore Mart was a bit further, about a fifteen minute drive to Applewood, a suburb of Denver. The two planned to use the quickest route which would put them on Highway 58 heading east to Interstate 90. This turned out to be a big mistake. As they drove through the town of Golden heading for Highway 58, the owner of the van was walking down the street and recognized his stolen van moving through the town. The owner quickly called 9-1-1 on his cell phone.

The sheriff was immediately notified. A couple police units were posted at the east end of Golden and watched for the van as it traveled in their direction. As the van drove by on Highway 58 one of the units successfully identified the stolen vehicle and jumped into action. He pulled out behind the kidnappers, blasted the siren, and started flashing the red and blue lights.

The warriors became scared. They didn't know what to do. They thought they were immune from being identified since Allah would surely protect them, and the possibility of them being discovered wasn't even considered. Now what do they do?

"Pull over," yelled Abdul-Wadud.

"I can't," responded Fatih, the driver. "If I pull over then they will arrest us and we will leave our team stranded. I can't outrun them in this van. I don't know what to do."

"We have to split up," suggested Abdul-Wadud. "You have to pull over long enough to drop me off. I'll jump out and run off. Then you need to make a run for it and try to get away from them."

"That does not sound desirable, but it might work. At least that way if you escape you can get another vehicle and get what supplies we need in order to help out our brothers."

"But I don't know how to steal a car. That's something that only you know how to do."

"Fine," replied Fatih. "Let's switch seats and you can find a good place to drop me off."

"While we're driving?" questioned the Abdul-Wadud. By now the van was racing at about eighty miles per hour, and there was a trail of three sheriff's vehicles in pursuit.

"Get over here," commanded Fatih, pointing to the floor behind the driver's seat.

There wasn't a middle divider in the van, just two-bucket seats, so the passenger was able to stand up and move into position behind the driver's seat. The driver put the vehicle on cruise control and started to slide off the seat, holding on to the steering wheel with only one hand. He stood as far away as possible from the driver's seat, making room for Abdul-Wadud to slip in.

As Abdul-Wadud pulled on to the seat he accidently bumped the steering wheel. The van jerked and started swaying back and forth across the freeway, side swiping a small Toyota Corolla which he was just starting to pass. The Toyota rebounded from the hit and was driven off the road, bouncing and kicking up dust as it hit the shoulder and raced into the bushes.

Scrambling Abdul-Wadud grabbed the wheel and overcompensated in the other direction, hitting the rumble strips along the side of the road. The van swayed back and forth, running on two wheels part of the time and nearly tipping over.

Fatih hadn't been able to sit down on his seat and he was brutally thrown back and forth from one side of the van to the other. He hit his head hard and put a large gash into it. Then he fell to the floor and just lay there, hoping his companion would get the vehicle under control.

After a few more waves back and forth Abdul-Wadud finally regained control of the vehicle and accelerated back up to nearly ninety. Fatih was now able to get up and settle into the passenger seat. He gave his companion a look that would kill. Then he pulled off his shirt and used it to tie a bandage around his head, hoping to stop the flow of blood.

"How are we going to get you out?" questioned Abdul-Wadud.

"Pull over to the side of the road somewhere where I can make a run for it," Fatih responded. "Then I'll jump out and you take off. You lead the police away from me to continue the chase."

"Do I have to stop?" asked Abdul-Wadud.

The companion looked over at him as if to ask if he had gone insane. Then he asked, "Is it your goal to kill me?"

The van was already slowing down in anticipation of the grand escape attempt. There were a lot of houses in the area with minimal fencing and it looked like an area where Fatih would easily be able to hide for a time. The van was still rolling forward when Abdul-Wadud yelled, "Jump for it."

Seeing that Abdul-Wadud had no intention of coming to a full stop, Fatih opened the passenger door and dove out of the van, trying to roll. The van had slowed to twenty miles per hour but it was still traveling dangerously fast for a stunt of this type. After the jump the driver accelerated causing the van passenger door to slam shut.

The jump wasn't very successful. About the only thing that was successful was Fatih was out of the van. Unfortunately he was skinned up pretty badly on his arms and legs. Now he was bleeding all over his body, and if that wasn't enough punishment, after he finished rolling, he found himself face down in a nest of brown recluse spiders. The brown recluse was the most poisonous spider in North America and their bite was known to leave large holes on skin tissue resulting in scars. They live in nests, and before he realized what was happening, he received a rash of bites directly to his face.

Fatih screamed in pain and jumped up just in time to see that one of the sheriff's vehicles had stopped. Two cops were getting out and were already in hot pursuit. He started running, tripping several times. He wasn't sure which was worse: his face bitten up, the gashes to his head from being bounced around in the van, the cuts and scrapes from diving out of the van, or being arrested. None of these were desirable. At this point he had lost all concern about his friends. They could fend for themselves. He just didn't want to end up in prison.

He jumped a fence and continued running through an open field. He noticed a cluster of bushes off in the distance and headed in that direction. He ran past the bushes but then circled back and hid himself in the bushes.

The ruse worked. The cops ran past the bushes and continued onward between a series of small farm outbuildings. The kidnapper stayed in the bushes for another fifteen minutes until the cops returned and headed back toward their patrol vehicle. He thought they had given up the search but then he heard one of the officers get on the radio and say, "Get the dogs out here so we can track him."

At that moment he was not actively being chased so he knew he needed to act fast before the dogs arrived. Fatih stepped out of his hiding place, still laying low so he wouldn't be seen over the bushes. He headed for a group of houses located a short distance away. He hoped he would be able to find a vehicle that he could quickly steal. He would have looked pretty scary, if anyone had seen him, dusty and dirty, clothes ripped, shirt tied around his head and soaked in blood, arm and leg chewed up and bloody, and his face marked with welts. He could easily have come out of a Hollywood zombie movie.

The task of finding a car to steal turned out to be harder than anticipated. Most people kept their cars in the garage, and the old clunkers he saw outside of the garages concerned him because he didn't want to spend time breaking into a vehicle that ended up not working. He continued walking down the road passing several houses until he found a new Toyota Corolla that wasn't locked. It was on the far side of a garage so no one would be able to see him from the house. The house was in a location where no one was around. He climbed into the driver's seat and went to work hotwiring the car. It was just a matter of a few minutes and the car was running.

The timing turned out to be perfect. Just as he started pulling away he could hear a helicopter overhead. It was starting to circle so it was obviously a police helicopter looking for him. He drove cautiously so as not to draw attention.

Fatih drove off, not really knowing what to do next. He just knew he had to get away. He decided to stop off at a corner gas station so that he could use the bathroom and get himself cleaned up. As he entered the small convenience store connected with the gas station the attendant looked at him and asked if he needed help. He responded by asking for the bathroom.

Once in the bathroom he tried to wash out the three wounds in his arm, leg, and head. It was excruciatingly painful and he nearly yelled out several times. After cleaning himself as best he could he went into the store and found some bandages and triple antibiotic ointment that he hoped would help keep the sores from becoming infected. After purchasing the medical supplies he returned to the car and went to work patching himself up.

Next Fatih headed to the Superstore Mart in Applewood. Luckily it was one that included groceries. He picked up a shirt and pants to replace the ones he had damaged. He purchased a bigger set of bandages and some wraps so he could do a better job of patching himself up. Then he went to the store's bathroom where he redressed and rebandaged himself.

Feeling almost human again, he went to work acquiring the items he was originally sent out to get. These items included a propane space heater, food, water, and throwaway phones.

Having accomplished his mission, he headed back to the kidnapper hideout. He wondered what had happened to Abdul-Wadud and if he had survived the onslaught of police that were chasing him.

Chapter Thirty-Three

The Mole Hunt
November, 2017, Denver, Colorado

Looking back in the rear view mirror, Abdul-Wadud saw his companion hitting the ground hard and rolling over and over in the dust. He also saw one of the cop vehicles pulling over to chase him.

"Guess he's been caught," grumbled Abdul-Wadud out loud.

What concerned him more were the three sheriff's vehicles that were still pursuing him, and because he had to slow down they were getting way too close for comfort. What was he going to do next? Abdul-Wadud couldn't out run them. He could ditch the vehicle and run but like his friend, he would probably get caught in short order. He was sure they would torture him in order to find out where the kidnapped victims were being held, and the thought of being tortured scared him worse than death. He feared he would probably give in and tell these infidels everything. That would be disgraceful. He preferred death. Maybe the best thing for him to do was to meet Allah. He had done all he could. He had completed his portion of the mission and now it was up to his friends to complete the remainder of the mission.

Abdul-Wadud had resigned himself to ending his life. But why should he go alone. Maybe he can do Allah a favor and take some of the infidels with him. Up ahead he saw a school bus. It looked like it was full of children, and as he raced at high speed toward the bus, he saw the bus was loaded. It was most likely on a field trip of some type. He decided that taking out this bus was probably the most damage he would be able to inflict. But what was he going to do? How was he going to cause the bus to wreak? All he could think of was that he needed to run the bus off the road and cause it to overturn. Maybe a disaster like that would even get the cops to quit their pursuit.

"Praise be to Allah for the inspiration and guidance," he yelled out.

The freeway had three lanes. He was traveling in the far left lane and the bus was in the far right lane. As he approached the front end of the bus, he made a sharp right turn causing him to diagonally cut across the three lanes and crash with full force into the front left corner of the bus. The hit was hard and unexpected. It occurred just as the bus driver was starting to slow down because of the sirens and flashing lights of the cop cars.

Upon impact the bus jerked to the right and within a fraction of a second it was over the curb and surging into the dirt. Then the inevitable happened. The bus flipped on to its side and slid another twenty feet in the dirt. Children screamed as they were hurled out of their seats and smashed together on the side of the bus that was now on the bottom.

The Islamist's van was badly damaged on the passenger side, but it was still drivable and the warrior decided to continue his flight. He felt excited by his success. Maybe there would be another target he could take out before his inevitable demise.

For the cops the race was over. They were no longer going to just follow this idiot. They had to take him out now that he was using his vehicle as a weapon. Several additional cop cars had joined the chase and it had become a parade of flashing red and blue lights racing down the freeway. A couple of the pursuit vehicles pulled over to help with the bus while the others continued the chase. They knew what they had to do. One of the patrol vehicles raced along the right side of the van to the front of it and immediately swung left. The terrorist was expecting the hit, but it was more forceful than he could manage and he was immediately pushed off the road.

Abdul-Wadud didn't want to be captured. His van had slowed but it was still drivable and he surged back onto the freeway, this time behind the cop vehicle that had pushed him and he accelerated into the back of the cop car. The hit was hard, but didn't have a significant impact. The cop car was slowing down, hoping it would be able to slow the van to a stop. The warrior decided the chase was over but he wasn't going to turn himself in to the cops. He swung around the cop car. He accelerated the van to go as fast as possible. Steam started spewing out of the front of the van. He had apparently damaged the cooling system when he crashed into the back of the cop car. But he didn't want to be arrested and interrogated.

Up ahead he saw an overpass over the freeway. There was a middle support post between the two sides of the freeway. Abdul-Wadud accelerated the van, driving it as fast as possible. Then he crashed headlong into the center post.

The van was obliterated. It was a glob of unrecognizable metal. But no one seemed sad about the accident.

* * *

It wasn't long before Alvin received a message to his cell phone that there had been activity at the Provo house. He immediately went to his computer and brought up the web site for the surveillance system at the house. The intruders were still in the house. There were two of them and they were going through the house room by room to see if they could find anyone. Unfortunately for the intruders the house was quite large. It had two separate kitchens and living quarters. It had a total of eleven bedrooms which were serviced by three air conditioners and four furnaces. So it took them a long time to search out the entire building. In the meantime Alvin had dispatched a local FBI unit to the house. This FBI team had previously been alerted to be ready. They were told that they would need to jump into action at a moment's notice if called on. They arrived at the house just as the intruders were about the leave. They didn't make their escape in time. Two FBI vehicles had their vehicle boxed in.

The two intruders jumped out of their vehicle and tried to run for it. But it was too little too late. The FBI was quick to react. One of the intruders who refused to stop was immediately shot in the leg and the other, upon seeing what had happened to his friend, stopped immediately. The FBI had them captured.

Rather than taking the intruders to FBI headquarters, they took them back into the house. Why not interrogate them there? They escorted them to separate rooms. They took one individual in the living room and the second downstairs in the basement. The two teams of FBI agents each started their own interrogations. The plan was that after the interviews they would compare notes.

Both individuals were Arabs. There was no question that they were Muslim. The first interrogation felt like a waste of time. This individual was in his early twenties and didn't seem to know why he was there except that his friend had asked him to come along. He seemed extremely scared. He stressed several times that he didn't want to be tortured. He acted like he would be willing to tell them anything. But he didn't know anything.

The second interrogation, the one in the basement, went a little better. This Arab was in his late thirties and was obviously the lead in the mission. Similar to the first interview, he wasn't completely sure what his mission was except that he was supposed to learn the whereabouts of a family. He handed the FBI a picture of the family he was supposed to find. It was Brian's family.

"Who are they?" questioned the FBI agent, trying to see how much the intruder knew.

"I have no idea," he replied.

"What were you supposed to do once you found them?" asked the interrogator.

"Report back that we had located them," replied the intruder.

"Who are you reporting to?" asked the FBI agent. With this question, the Arab became squirmy and was reluctant to respond. The agent didn't give up and asked, "How were you supposed to report back?"

"By phone," replied the intruder. Then he realized that admitting to the use of the phone was a big mistake.

"Give me your phone," demanded the FBI agent.

The intruder complied, knowing that if he didn't give up the phone it would just be taken away from him anyway.

A quick scan of recent phone numbers showed a call from the Washington, DC area which didn't have an ID attached to it. It was obviously not one of his close friends. The immediate conclusion was that it was the intruder's contact and since it had a Washington interchange it would be reasonable to assume that the call came from someone within the FBI.

* * *

The FBI agent immediately placed a call to Alvin and informed him of what he had found out and gave him the phone number. Alvin put a trace on the number and found it to be not only out of state but out of country. The phone was currently in Toronto, Canada. This added confusion to his mole hunt. How did an FBI agent in Toronto know about the Provo, Utah location for Brian?

Alvin instructed his Provo FBI agent, "Arrest them on a breaking and entering charge. That will allow you to hold them for a while and it should give me enough time to check out these leads. I'll get back to you as soon as I know anything."

Alvin searched for all the agents that were in the Toronto area. He found fourteen. None of them had anything to do with Alvin and his team. Additionally, looking at their names he found none of them to be Arabic, and their phone numbers didn't match the one he had received. Alvin came to the conclusion that there had to be another middleman. Perhaps the phone call from Toronto was actually from an al-Qaeda, ISIS, or Muslim Brotherhood member and not from an FBI agent. Perhaps there was an additional layer of contacts.

Alvin did a search on all communication to and from the contact phone number that was in Toronto. Apparently it was a burner phone because there were very few calls made from that phone, and none of them had the Washington, DC exchange. He cross-referenced the phone number on the phone against all known FBI phone numbers, both official phones and private phones, and there were no matches. He concluded that the person making the call must have used a different phone for communication with the FBI mole.

Alvin wasn't ready to give up. He contacted two of the FBI agents in Toronto and sent them to the location of the mystery cell phone. Alvin had triangulated a position using the phone's GPS and he dispatched the agents to that location.

Ten minutes after he sent out the agents, and five minutes before they arrived at the Toronto location of the burner phone, the phone went dead. The user of that phone must have learned that the two Muslim intruders in Provo had been captured. Now, since the phone was turned off, the connection back to the user of the phone was broken.

Alvin placed a call to the Provo agents and asked them to keep trying to get more information from the two intruders. He informed them that all the previous leads had been failures and he needed more information. He didn't have a lot of hope that they would come up with any more information but he thought they should try. He didn't know where else to turn. He had chased every lead he could think of during this mole hunt. Probably, the only thing he accomplished was to let the mole know that he was getting close and now the mole would be more careful and would become even harder to catch.

Chapter Thirty-Four

The Imam
November, 2017, Ann Arbor, Michigan

One of the three Imam's sons that were hospitalized was anticipating the arrival of his father. His leg was in a cast, but he was being released by the doctor. He was being allowed to return home. But his father didn't come and the son was becoming increasingly concerned. It was unusual for his father to not come and take him home. Initially the son just assumed that something had disrupted his father's schedule. But as it became later and later in the evening and it was starting to grow dark, he knew something was terribly wrong. Had his father gotten into an accident?

The son tried to call his father, but couldn't get an answer. Next he called his uncle Shihab and told him about his concern. The uncle, who only lived a few houses away from the mosque, listened to his nephew and also became concerned. He had noticed that Sami had not been present at the last couple prayer sessions in the mosque, which was also unusual. He had assumed Sami was at the hospital.

The uncle went to the Imam's house and knocked on the door. There was no response. He took out an extra key he had for the house and tried to unlock the door but found it unlocked. He opened the door and entered. He yelled out but there was no response. Searching the first floor, he found nothing. He went to the stairs and yelled out again before going upstairs. Again he heard nothing. He went upstairs and there, lying on the floor, he found Sami in a large pool of blood. His throat had been cut. The uncle knew enough not to touch anything. Sami was dead. He could only hope the police might be able to find a clue from what was now a crime scene.

Shihab called 9-1-1 and twenty minutes later the entire house was buzzing with police. They took a statement from Shihab who afterwards proceeded to go to the hospital and finish the assignment Sami could no longer take care of. He picked his nephew up from the hospital and, after giving him the bad news drove to his own home. He knew it would be days before the police had finished their investigation and anyone could go back into the Imam's house. Besides, it would be too depressing a place for the young boy to be by himself. It would be hard to be alone in the house where his mother and father had recently been killed.

Shihab was infuriated. There was only one thing he could think of: revenge! These infidels had just gone too far. It was time for Shihab to step in and take over.

* * *

Shihab knew Sami had been priming some of the local youth as Islamic warriors. He thought Sami was always a bit on the radical side, but now that his brother had been brutally executed, he wanted revenge. He knew who the local youth were. Sami had kept him updated on all the activities of his cell. Shihab contacted one of the youths and asked him to get everyone together for a meeting. An hour later they met with him in the Imam's chambers at the mosque.

"What?" questioned Shihab. "There are only four of you?"

The four warriors explained what had happened to the two teams of four. They had been sent to Golden, Colorado on a mission. One of those teams was in Golden right now executing Sami's plans. They also explained that there were two members of their group which had backed out of the program and Sami had wanted them eliminated. Sami didn't want to risk exposure. But as far as they knew, only one of the two traitors had been executed. The whereabouts of the second traitor was unknown.

Shihab was disturbed. He sat for a moment taking in the news. He had been thrown in the middle of a mess which included traitors, failed missions, and executions. This was not what he had signed up for. But regardless he could not let the execution of his brother go unpunished.

After a few minutes of silence, Shihab spoke up, "I need to get help. I am going to talk with the leaders of the Muslim Brotherhood and see what they recommend we do. Then I will get back in touch with each of you and give you further instructions."

"Understood," replied the four warriors in unison.

"For now, go out and see what you can learn about the second traitor," Shihab stressed. "We can't just let this slide. We can't have our efforts for Allah be betrayed. For all we know this traitor has turned informant to the infidels. He may have been a spy for them all along. This behavior cannot be allowed and must be punished."

* * *

Shihab waited till all the student warriors left. He shut and locked the door for privacy. Then, using his cell phone he called his Muslim Brotherhood friends in Egypt for support. What he didn't realize was that even though all the internal taps had been removed, Sami's cell phone lines had also been tapped. Shihab considered everything within the walls of the mosque as a holy sanctum. This area should be above reproach. He didn't realize that his conversation was now being recorded.

The call went through and was answered with the traditional Muslim greeting, *"As-salam alaykum,"* to which Shihab responded, *"Wa alaykumu s-salam"* followed by the code name that was used for identification purposes, *"Nu'man,"* which means blood in Arabic.

"Explain the purpose of your call?" came a cross sounding voice. It was an intimidating voice which sounded more like a scolding than a question.

Shihab explained the situation. "Sami and his wives have been killed. Sami had indoctrinated sixteen warriors. One of the warriors had successfully executed the Orlando theme park attack. Another was successful at the North Dakota oil fields. But since then things have not gone so good. Someone sent a drone to Medina and attacked the sacred mosque. The team had used Islamic heroes and patriots inside the U.S. Air Force and the FBI to discover the true source of the attack.

It wasn't a direct attack from the military. It was someone stealing military equipment and using it for their own form of revenge. Sami used this information and sent four of his warriors to Golden, Colorado to attack the family of the infidel who had initiated the attack on Medina. Unfortunately, these four heroes have been killed and the attacker and his family have gone into hiding. In an attempt to draw out the attacker, Sami sent four more warriors to Golden to kidnap friends of the attacker. The kidnapping has occurred, but it looks like this effort may also be going wrong. One of the warriors has already been killed and I'm concerned that the other three may bungle the mission."

Shihab continued his explanation in a stressed and concerned voice, "In addition to this problem, there have been two traitors. One of them has been killed, but the second one was missing and was probably under the protection of the police or the FBI. I am down to four warriors left out of the original sixteen, and these were the weakest of the bunch because the strong ones had already been utilized."

The voice over the phone reviewed what he just heard, "So, out of the original sixteen, you have eight dead, three at risk in a poorly planned kidnapping in Colorado, one traitor whose whereabouts are unknown, and four that you don't have a lot of confidence in. And, in addition to that your leader has been assassinated. What do you expect us to do?"

"I want you to take over the kidnapping mission," explained Shihab. "I want you to send someone to Golden who knows what they are doing. That's the most important. Secondarily, I need your help in locating and eliminating the remaining traitor."

The voice on the phone responded with, "And you don't think you can handle it?"

"No. Unlike my foolish brother, I do not pretend to be an expert at these things. I don't know how to execute a kidnapping so I wouldn't know where to start in helping them. This was Sami's project, not mine."

"Are you saying you are not willing to avenge the execution of your brother?"

"Actually I am very interested in avenging his death, but I want it to be successful and not a bungled up mess. That is why I'm asking for your help."

"Understood, but we may need you to do more than just make a phone call. We may need you to be involved."

"Agreed," responded Shihab. "I am willing to help, but not to lead something I know nothing about."

"We'll have a couple people travel to you and then on to Golden today. Tell the current kidnapping team to do nothing until we arrive. I will send my men to Ann Arbor to meet with you first to see how they can help with the traitor. We can't have a traitor running around and sharing information with the police about our operations."

"Allah be praised. Now I can feel confident that my brother's death will not be wasted."

The voice from Egypt continued, "In addition to that, I am greatly offended by the attack on our mosque and on an Imam. This is sacred ground. I feel that we need to retaliate in some way."

"What do you have in mind?"

"Something local. I want there to be a direct connection between the attack of the mosque and our proposed target. Think of something Christian in the Ann Arbor area that would be symbolic of Christianity. We want the connection between the mosque attack and the attack on the Christian site to be unquestionable."

"But they've demonstrated that they can retaliate with an attack on Mecca," expressed Shihab with concern.

"That's okay," replied the Brotherhood spokesman.

"How is that okay? We're talking about Mecca. The holiest site in the Muslim world. How can you be all right with an attack on Mecca?" Sami's brother thought this was going too far. How could an attack on Mecca be acceptable to any Muslim? It's unheard of.

"Just think what will happen. If these infidels dare to attack Mecca, either Allah will stop it, since he is all powerful, or he will allow it to happen in order to unite the Muslim family around the world. It will ignite one great and glorious Jihad uniting the world's Muslims against the evil empires of America and Israel. We will finally have a chance for a great victory. But no matter what happens, Allah knows what is happening and what he allows to happen is just a stepping-stone for his kingdom and its on-going growth. The only question we need to answer now is, 'Are you willing to work towards a Jihad? Are you willing to do your part? Will you be ready with your mission? Will you hit a Christian target and follow the teachings of the Koran which require an eye for an eye?'"

"And a tooth for a tooth," replied Shihab. "I'm just worried we'll all end up being eyeless and toothless. But yes, I will do my part. I'll start looking into it right away."

The two finished their call by sharing a few comments about the weather and then disconnected. Shihab felt confident he had done the right thing. He felt confident his brother's kidnapping mission would be a success now that he had expert help. He unlocked the door to the chambers and left the mosque.

* * *

Shihab didn't realize it but the FBI now felt confident too. By listening in on the conversation they had just learned the details of an on-going terrorist cell and its plot. They have now been alerted and would be on the lookout. They would track the arriving Muslim Brotherhood members and use them to lead the FBI to the kidnappers. It was a perfect opportunity to put an end to the kidnapping.

Chapter Thirty-Five

The Informant

November, 2017, Golden, Colorado

Lincoln and Gage returned to Golden safely after their visit to Ann Arbor. They were careful not to leave any fingerprints by using plastic gloves and wiping everything down. Before they drove to their own homes, they had a mission to complete. In spite of the fact it was the middle of the night, they were going to visit Niran, the informant that had been identified by Sami.

During their flight, Gage had contacted Livy to see if she could track the location of the cell phone number on Sami's phone. That was an easy task and she quickly came back with an address where the phone was currently located. It matched the address on Sami's cell phone. She also informed them they needed to break the phone SIM card immediately because the police would also be using it to track their location.

Back on the ground, they jumped into the car that had been provided along with the plane, and headed directly to Niran's location. They wanted to tie off this loose end before there were any more problems.

They arrived at Niran's apartment, which was very close to the previously destroyed apartment where Brian and his family had lived. Lincoln and Gage weren't really sure what they would find. They both had a small handgun and silencers and they took it with them as they left the car and headed to the door. They put on thick, tight fitting plastic gloves which would shield any fingerprints. Lincoln quickly picked the front door lock and they were inside the apartment in minutes. They could hear snoring sounds coming from the back of the apartment. Using night vision goggles, they worked their way down the hallway to the back. They found two bedrooms, one on each side of the hallway. They noticed there was one girl in each of the bedrooms. One of the girls, the one in the right bedroom, had the covers thrown off and she lay in her bed naked except for her underpants. The other girl had a sheet pulled over her, but she was probably dressed the same.

***

The girl on the left was Nadia. She was in the United States on a student visa and was attending the Colorado Engineering School working on an Engineering degree. Back home in Chechnya there was a lot of mining going on and a mining engineer would have a comfortable life. She was Muslim and had roomed with Niran because they were both of the same faith. They had the same prayer and diet rituals which made sharing an apartment much easier. Nadia was a tall five foot nine with pitch-black hair and dark eyes. She had a mystical appearance.

Across the hall, in the other bedroom was Niran. She was from Saudi Arabia and was also in the United States on a student visa. Her family had sponsored her education at CES in hopes she would bring back a degree in International Oil Economics. She was extremely committed to her Islamic faith which took priority over everything else. She was shorter than Nadia, being only five foot four. She also had black hair and eyes. She was darker skinned and had the down-to-business appearance of someone who wasn't ready for a social life or boyfriends. She was here to do her job and was happy and willing to leave the identification of her future mate to her parents.

Both girls took pride in their heritage and religion. They would do anything for Allah without question. They trusted their Imam completely to interpret the word of God for them.

***

Lincoln put his two arms up and shrugged his shoulders, indicating he didn't know which girl was the one they were after. Gage pointed to Lincoln and then pointed to the room on the left. Then he pointed to himself and pointed to the room on the right. Lincoln glared at Gage and mouthed the word, "Sure! You want the naked one."

Gage mouthed the words, "You bet," and he nodded his head in the affirmative.

They each went into their respective bedrooms, put one hand around the girl's neck in a potential strangle hold, and with the other hand they held a gun to the girl's head. They timed their attacks so precisely that both girls screamed and tried to get up at exactly the same time.

"Quiet down," commanded Gage in an authoritative and aggressive voice.

"What are you going to do?" asked the naked girl. She was obviously in shock and fear, not knowing the intentions of her captor. "Are you going to rape me? Please don't rape me. I'm still a virgin and if I lose my virginity, no one will marry me."

"I'm not here to rape you," Gage instructed the girl he was holding down. "What's your name?"

"Nadia," replied the girl.

"And what's the name of your friend?"

"Niran."

"Looks like you found the girl we're after," yelled Gage to Lincoln. Then he continued questioning the girl, "Are you Muslim?"

"No," she replied, thinking that the denial may give her some advantage but she really wasn't sure what.

"Why are you rooming with a Muslim if you're not a Muslim yourself?"

"The university just assigned us to live together."

* * *

Meanwhile, Lincoln had thrown the sheet off Niran, also exposing her naked body. He pulled her over so she was no longer on her side and pushed her on her back. Then he sat on top of her stomach, the whole time keeping his pistol pointed at her head. "Well, Niran," he started talking to the extremely frightened girl. "I understand we have a problem. Apparently you have a big mouth. You think that the lives of

Americans are expendable. Apparently you are part of a Muslim terrorist cell and have been giving out information about Brian and his family."

Even though the girls were in different rooms, with the doors open it was easy for them to hear what the other was saying. "What are you talking about?" asked Nadia, jumping into the conversation. "Are you kidding me? Niran is part of a terrorist cell? That's ridiculous. If something was going on here I would know about it and I would be long gone. You have to be mistaken."

"Tell her, Niran" Lincoln commanded. "Tell her what a naughty girl you have been."

Niran glared at Lincoln as if she wished to kill him. But she said nothing.

"I guess Niran has decided to become a deaf-mute," continued Lincoln. "But she better get her tongue back quickly or I'm going to have to do something drastic." Then, moving his head closer to hers and looking directly into her eyes he said, "What do you know about the kidnapping of my friends? Who are the kidnappers and where have they taken them?"

No response. But the closeness gave her the opportunity to spit in Lincoln's face. Lincoln ignored the act. "One last time," Lincoln threatened. "Who are they and where are they?"

Still no response.

With the silencer mounted on his pistol Lincoln turned slightly from his position of sitting on top of her. He side-saddled her, swung his arm around and quickly shot her in the foot. He was hoping this would encourage her to talk but instead she screamed and started slapping and kicking violently at him. She made several hard kicks to his back and a couple good punches to his face. Lincoln used his pistol to whip her on the side of the head which left her bleeding from a small cut but calmed her slightly. Then Lincoln, who had been sitting on her stomach, slid up on her chest and pushed her arms under each of his knees. She kept screaming and squirming but was no longer a danger to him.

***

The commotion temporarily distracted Gage who had turned around to watch the activity. This gave Nadia the opportunity to grab a pen from her nightstand. She jabbed the pen into Gage's upper left arm. Then she started wildly kicking and slugging Gage as if she was suddenly possessed.

Gage was both surprised and angry. He had become complacent since Nadia wasn't acting like the threat. Now he paid the price. Gage felt the surge of pain and his immediate reaction was to crack Nadia in the forehead with the pistol handle. This left a large gash on her head which started bleeding heavily. But, rather than calming her down, she became even wilder in her actions.

Gage still had his left hand around her throat, but his right hand, which held the pistol, swung around and hit her again, this time on the side of the skull. Nadia did not let up. She yelled out, "You infidel! You pervert! Who sneaks into a girl's room in the middle of the night just to question her? You have us here naked and all you do is ask stupid questions. You don't even take advantage of us in the way any normal infidel man would do. You must be either stupid or crazy or both. I'll show you what a real man would do." With that she took a series of strong punches at Gage's groin, hitting pay dirt several times. Then she grabbed his balls and starting squeezing with all her strength.

Gage was beside himself. Obviously she was a Muslim or she wouldn't be calling him an infidel and apparently she wasn't going to offer any useful information. Additionally, now that she had seen the two of them she would be able to identify them. In desperation, seeing that hitting her on the head hadn't helped, not knowing what to do next and feeling that his balls were about to pop, he pulled the trigger of his pistol. The bullet went through her left breast and into her heart and she dropped back on the bed in a heap of naked female flesh.

Gage slowly pulled the pen out of his arm and put the pen into his pocket. It hurt like crazy. He didn't want to leave anything behind that had his blood on it. He didn't want to risk being identified. Once it was out he yanked the pillow out from under Nadia, took off the pillowcase, and tied a small tourniquet on his arm to stop the flow of blood.

With Nadia out of the picture, Gage turned to see how he could help Lincoln. Lincoln still had his hands full with Niran. He was still sitting on her with one hand around her throat and his other hand holding the pistol. Lincoln was asking again, "Who are the guys from Sami's cell and where are they holding the hostages?"

"You shot me, you idiot. My foot is killing me," was all Niran would say as she kicked and tried to break free. She had become increasingly violent.

"Answer the question," insisted Lincoln.

"I wouldn't tell you even if I knew, and I don't know. I have no idea. I gave the information to Sami and I don't know where it went from there," screamed Niran in a loud and angry voice.

"Then we have no use for you," replied Lincoln as he turned and shot a hole into her other foot.

* * *

Lincoln had calmed down slightly and started to use his better judgment. He remembered how Sami's cell phone had found Niran. Maybe Niran's cell phone could help him find the kidnappers. Finding her phone was easy. It was lying next to her on her headboard. Flipping through her recent calls, he found a couple calls which used the 734 Ann Arbor, Michigan area code. He immediately recognized the first of the numbers as the number of Sami's phone. The obvious conclusion was that the other phone number must be the one used by the kidnappers.

Using his secure phone, Lincoln immediately called Livy, who was still at FBI headquarters on the East Coast. She immediately picked up the phone saying, "What's up? I had to step out of a meeting to take this call. I knew you wouldn't use this phone unless it was urgent. I knew you guys were in the middle of something and I didn't want to miss the call."

Niran's screaming made it hard to hear. Lincoln responded, "I'll fill you in later but for now I just wanted to know if you could put a trace on a phone number that I have here and find out where it's located. What's the safest way for me to get the number to you?"

Livy thought for a moment, then suggested, "Use Brian's favorite book and text me the number using our encryption method. I'll decipher the code and check it out. I'll get back to you as soon as possible."

"Will do," replied Lincoln. He disconnected the call and turned to Gage and said, "We need to go. She's not going to give us anything anyway."

"What do we do with her?" asked Gage.

* * *

As she heard the conversation Niran was convinced she was about to receive the same fate as Nadia. She let loose, kicking and screaming with all her strength. She slapped, as best she could, hit and bit Lincoln. She felt she had nothing to lose. She worked one hand loose and grabbed Lincoln's gun and tried to fight it away from him. She was unrelenting. She pulled hard on the barrel of his pistol, not realizing that he had his finger on the trigger. Suddenly the gun went off. Niran fell backwards onto the bed, a circular spot of read forming on her forehead.

* * *

"These girls were feisty," commented Gage. "They weren't going to give up easily. Let's get this place cleaned up and get out of here."

"We need to find a copy of the Book of Mormon so I can send Livy a message," replied Lincoln.

"We're not going to find it in this Muslim home. Let's get out of here and find one. Let's do it."

Lincoln checked for a pulse on both girls and finding none, he said, "They're both gone. Let's make sure we didn't leave anything behind and let's get going." After writing down the phone number he took the SIM card out of her phone and broke it.

In spite of their gloves, they wiped down anything they might have touched. They wanted to make sure there was no record of their having been there. They took away anything that had Gage's blood on it. Then they were off.

Chapter Thirty-Six

Livy and Jonathan
November, 2017, Golden, Colorado

Jonathan was feeling guilty. His relationship with Livy wasn't very good and he felt the need to make it better. He wasn't ready to lose her just yet. Her heavy travel schedule didn't mix well with his extra-curricular sporting activities and the only time they seemed to spend together was in bed and that didn't develop a meaningful long-term relationship. He needed to spend more time with her. He needed to be interested in her work and her schooling. He needed to go with her to her boring Dragon Pit social gatherings, even though they seemed stupid at times. He remembered the last time he went to one. They went to some bar that offered free finger foods. The Dragon Pit team made dinner out of the finger foods just to save a few bucks. Then they spent the whole evening discussing how geometric programming proves that the intersection of two lines pinpoints the minimum point of the curve which was the sum of the lines. To this day he had no idea what geometric programming was or what they were talking about. He had no idea why any of this should be important to anyone. He suspected there were very few people out in the world who even knew what geometric programming was or cared what it was. But regardless, he needed to join in if he was going to be part of Livy's world.

He sent her a text message, "Can we talk?"

"Sure," she typed. "I have a few minutes. Call me."

Jonathan placed the call and Livy answered with a question, "What's up?"

"I just wanted to talk," started Jonathan. "I'm feeling like I'm not doing our relationship justice and I wanted to see if I can make it better."

"Wow. That's not a five minute conversation. I've been feeling the same way. It's almost like we have to schedule time on our calendar just to be together. We haven't done anything meaningful for a long time. Like, right now I have no idea what you're doing or what you're working on. And I doubt that you know much about me either."

"That's how I feel too. What can we do to make it better?"

"To me, the first question is; 'Do we want to make it better?' What will we get if we make it better? Do we even like each other enough to want to make it better? Sometimes I feel so distant from you in interests and goals that I don't feel any connection at all."

"I think that's my fault," replied Jonathan. "I really haven't been connected. I'm jealous that you have a better job than me. I've been interested in making sure my life is connected and fun and haven't really cared much about your life. I'm really sorry about that. I want to give our relationship a serious shot and see if there is something there. Are you willing to try?"

"Of course I'm willing to try," replied Livy. "That's what I've been trying to do for the last couple years. But sometimes it seems like we're going downhill faster than we're going uphill. So what are you suggesting that we do differently?"

"Let's start by spending some meaningful time together. Let's start with a detailed conversation about each other's lives. Let's share our work, our interests, our goals, and what we see our future looking like. Let's talk either in person or on the phone each night before we go to sleep and share our day. Let's start with that. And maybe next time you're in town we can hang out together. I'll go with you to some of your Dragon Pit meetings and I'll even try to be sociable. Are you willing to give that a shot?"

"Of course. Let's start with a phone call tonight. Whoever goes to bed first needs to call the other."

"Perfect," replied Jonathan. "I'll let you get back to work." They shared goodbyes and disconnected the phone.

* * *

Livy was confused. This was very uncharacteristic of Jonathan. It sounded fishy. He loved being alone and being wrapped up in his own world except for his sports and he was consumed with that. He hated going to the Dragon Pit gatherings. She concluded that he must really be trying hard to make the relationship work if he was willing to go through so much trouble.

Chapter Thirty-Seven

The Hostages
November, 2017, Golden, Colorado

It had been a couple hours when Fatih, the warrior who had been sent out on a mission for food and supplies, finally returned with his arms full. He returned in a white Toyota Corolla which was about as generic a car as you can get. There were so many of these cars on the road that if anyone wanted to chase one down, they would have a hard time distinguishing the vehicle.

"What happened to you? Where is our friend?" questioned Husam, one of the kidnappers who had stayed behind to watch the hostages. He was wondering about all the bandages and welts that Fatih had over his face and body. He was also referring to Abdul-Wadud but they had decided to not use names and always speak in Arabic in case the hostages were eventually freed.

"I have no idea what happened to him," explained the exasperated Fatih, ignoring the question about his own wounds. He really didn't feel like talking about how he was injured. He went on to discuss the details of how the two of them were being chased and how he was dropped off. Abdul-Wadud drove off, hoping to pull the police off of Fatih's trail.

"What a disaster," responded Yusuf, the third remaining kidnapper.

"I acquired the supplies that we needed! You should be happy about that. We'll just have to wait to see if our friend returns. But with all the cops that were chasing him, it didn't look good."

A shouting match ensued. The three remaining kidnappers started shouting at each other, each blaming the other for a lack of insight. The entire kidnapping had been a botched job and now the police probably have one of their team members. They were worried that Abdul-Wadud might be spilling the story of the kidnapping to the police and they may all be surrounded any minute.

"We need to get out of here as soon as possible," declared Yusuf.

"Where are we going to go?" asked Fatih. "This is the only place we scouted out. Are we just going to go out driving around until we find something convenient? We don't even have a vehicle large enough to transport everyone. We'll need to get another van."

"Maybe that's what we need to do," replied Husam. "What choice do we have?"

Just then Yusuf's phone rang. "Hello?" he said, more as a question than a greeting. He listened for a while then he said, "Yes. We have a vehicle. We can pick you up. We'll be there." Then he pushed the "end" button on the phone to finish the call.

Turning to the others, Yusuf said, "Our problem just went away. The Muslim Brotherhood is sending a pair of individuals here to help us out. They will be landing soon and we are to pick them up and bring them back here. They will be taking charge of the kidnapping. We won't have to worry about these hostages any longer. The Brotherhood will take care of the situation."

"Excellent," said the other two warriors simultaneously.

Then Husam turned to Fatih and said, "Go get them." The airport was located at the opposite end of Denver, about as far away from Golden as possible and still be in the Denver area.

"Will do," he replied. "Let me know what airlines they are arriving on next time you talk to them. I need to know where to pick them up."

"We'll keep you informed," replied Yusuf.

In the meantime, while everyone seemed deeply distracted and concerned, Glenn had worked the ropes loose on his wrists. The three terrorists had stepped outside to talk and he took this opportunity to try to sneak out of a back window. As he swung up and started climbing out, he was spotted and a cry went out, "He's getting away! Stop him!"

One of the warriors ran back into the house while the other two ran around each side of the shack hoping to head Glenn off no matter which direction he ran. By the time they made it to the back of the shack Glenn was already in a full sprint, heading straight out and away from the shack. The two warriors that had run around the side of the shack were just starting to fall in behind him when a shot rang out. Husam, the warrior in the house had fired a shot intended for Glenn, but instead Yusuf, his own companion, fell to the ground and screamed out in pain. "You shot me in the leg, you idiot!" Yusuf screamed. Fatih stopped to check on his condition but Yusuf screamed again, "Don't worry about me. Go get that infidel! We can't let him get away!"

Husam had now come out and was heading to the teammate he had shot. Yusuf wasn't very grateful for his help. He slugged him as hard as he could in the chest. Then, the two of them stood up and started to hobble back to the shack.

In the meantime Fatih continued his chase and eventually was close enough to Glenn to take a shot. The shot hit Glenn in the lower leg muscle and caused him to stumble and fall to the ground. The fall gave the Muslim warrior enough time to catch up with him and train his weapon on him. "Get up," he commanded.

Glenn had no choice but to comply. But first he took off his shirt and tied a tourniquet around his wound in order to stop the bleeding. Luckily no bones were broken so he was able to stand. He stood up and hobbled along until they were both back in the shack.

"What the heck was that?" yelled one of the warriors at Glenn. "What do you think you're doing? If you do that again we'll kill off the rest of your family, and you'll have no one but yourself to blame. Now get back over where you were sitting."

Glenn went back and sat down next to his wife. Fortunately his wound was only a slight flesh wound and not very serious. Husam went and retied his hands together.

"I better get going if I'm going to pick those guys up," said Fatih as he headed for the door. A couple minutes later the car could be heard driving off.

The other warrior worked on the leg of the fallen warrior, trying to stop the blood flow. "Do either of you know anything about medicine?"

The wound on Yusuf's leg was serious. A major chunk of the side of his leg was blown off and the loss of blood was great.

Glenn and Cynthia both shook their head but Husam wasn't ready to accept that answer. "We need some clean cloth to tie down the wound," he said, looking over at Cynthia. He noticed that she was still in her soft cotton nightgown and he decided that this would be perfect for a bandage. "Take off that nightgown so I can use it to tie off the wound."

"You can't be serious," yelled Glenn. "She's naked underneath that nightgown."

The Muslim looked back at him and said, "Are you trying to talk me out of it or into it. What do I care if she's naked? That makes it even better." Then, with an even sterner voice he said, "If you don't take it off and give it to me I'll take it off of you myself."

Cynthia could see a fight ensuing between Glenn and the terrorists and fearing that Glenn would get hurt even more, or possibly even killed, she went over to Husam who cut her hands free. Then she proceeded to quickly take off the nightgown and throw it over at the captors.

"Cute boobs," came the sarcastic comment from Husam as he smirked. Then he proceeded to use the nightgown to tie off the wound on his friend's leg.

Unfortunately Husam was now aroused by the sight of Cynthia's breasts and he wanted more. After tying Yusuf's leg as best he could with the nightgown he decided to go over to her and started feeling around on her. First he rubbed her legs, working his way up her thighs.

This become more than Glenn was willing to tolerate and he jumped up and gave the Muslim molester as sharp kick in the ribs, making him scream out in pain.

The children, who were scared anyway, now cried out in fear. They yelled, "NO! NO! NO!"

"You'll pay for that," the kidnapper yelled. He grabbed his gun and shot at Glenn's groin. Luckily Glenn saw it coming and successfully jumped before the shot was fired. The kidnapper tried to take a second

shot, but this time the gun misfired. He slammed the gun to the ground. Giving up on the gun, he kicked Glenn in the crotch as hard as possible. Then he kicked him in the leg wound causing Glenn to scream in pain. After that he took ropes and tied Glenn's legs together. Then he tied the hands to the legs behind Glenn's back. This left Glenn lying on the ground completely incapacitated.

"Now I'm going to turn you so you can watch," the pervert said in a sadistic voice.

He pulled Glenn around so that he was looking directly at Cynthia. With Glenn in position Husam returned to Cynthia and started reaching toward her breasts. Cynthia, whose hands were still free from when she removed her nightgown, slapped him as hard as possible across the face, causing a loud smack. The warrior was even more infuriated than before. He proceeded to retie her hands together, this time behind her back, and then he tied her legs up behind her similar to how he had tied Glenn. Then he sneered at her, "What are you going to do now?"

He returned his focus to her breasts, and this time he was not going to be gentle. He grabbed her breasts, one in each hand, and fondled and yanked. Then he moved his head in close to take her breast into his mouth and bite on it. Cynthia took the opportunity to strike out. She crashed the top of her head as hard as possible against his forehead. The sound of the two skulls hitting sounded like both skulls were cracking. Husam fell backwards. He was obviously stunned by the hit and he stumbled briefly and then sat down on the floor, trying to recover his bearings.

The hit had placed a gash on Cynthia's head, and it slowly started dripping blood onto her nose. But the position of the hit had apparently done considerably more damage to Husam than to her. Husam was stunned and hurt and Cynthia only ended up with the gash.

"You pervert!" screamed Yusuf. "Are you about through trying to molest her? You better quit before they kill you. It doesn't look like you're winning." Yusuf was feeling weak from the loss of blood, and it was all he could do to yell at Husam, but he felt he needed to do it.

"I'm going to kill the whole bunch of them," screamed Husam in anger, fully committed to carrying out the execution immediately.

"That's not a smart idea now that the Muslim Brotherhood is involved," commented Yusuf.

"I don't care what they think," he screamed. But Husam discontinued his attempt to molest Cynthia. He also backed off of his intent to kill everyone. He decided he wanted to get his senses back before he tried anything else. He picked up his pistol and sat next to his friend. Then he worked on the pistol, which had jammed earlier, trying to get it back into working order.

There was silence in the shack for the next hour. Everyone was left to their thoughts and frustrations. Glenn was thrilled with Cynthia's attack on the Muslim. He felt regret that he couldn't do more. Cynthia had a killer headache and she wished she could see the cut on her head. She didn't want it to turn into a scar because that would be embarrassing. The children were just scared. They didn't understand what was happening to their family. They didn't understand why they were being attacked. They crawled up and cuddled against their mother, looking for comfort. Cynthia was glad to have them next to her because it helped her to stay warm.

The Muslims were angry. The one because he had been shot in the leg by his idiot companion, and the other because he had been defeated and embarrassed by an infidel woman. Both looked forward to the arrival of their Muslim Brotherhood saviors. Then maybe they would be able to depart and head back to Ann Arbor where they felt safe.

* * *

Fatih, the Muslim warrior who was heading off to the airport, ended up in an enormous traffic jam. He correctly guessed it was probably because of an accident on the freeway, but he didn't realize it was because his friend Abdul-Wadud who had decided to crash his vehicle into a freeway post.

In the meantime Fatih slowly plugged along in the traffic jam, hoping it would soon break free. He decided to indulge in a little decadence of his own. He turned on the car radio so that it was really loud, found a country channel, and started bopping his head to the latest Scotty McCreery hit. He knew he probably looked ridiculous but he didn't really care what the infidels thought of him. Only Allah's opinion mattered. The traffic jam was going to cause him to be late in getting to the airport. Since there wasn't anything he could do about it, he decided not to get stressed out.

All three lanes of traffic were merged together into one lane. After an hour of traffic that was barely moving along, he finally arrived at the scene of the accident. At first he didn't make a connection with the mass of metal that was wrapped around the freeway pillar. But as he came closer, recognition started to kick in. That mess of metal he was looking at was the only thing left of his warrior friend Abdul-Wadud. His mind reeled. Was his friend forced into the pillar? Was he shot and therefore lost control of the vehicle? Or had he committed suicide? In the end it didn't matter. He had been on a mission for Allah and now he had returned to Allah's presence.

Fatih was a mixture of emotions. He felt sorry for his friend, but he also felt jealous that his friend was now surrounded by virgins. He hoped he would soon be enjoying the same pleasures. He also felt anger at the idea that the infidels had forced his friend to be sacrificed.

After passing the accident, the traffic started to pick up and he started moving faster. Now he had to pay attention to the moving traffic. But his emotions were still reeling.

A half hour later he was pulling into the airport arrival section just as his phone started ringing. He answered the phone with, "Yes?"

"Where are you?" asked the agitated voice at the other end of the line. "We've been waiting here for an hour."

"Bad traffic accident. I'm just pulling in. Where are you? I'm in a white Toyota Corolla so watch for me." Just then, off in the distance he could see a man with his phone to his ear waving his hand in the air. "I see you," Fatih curtly responded as he disconnected the phone call.

Quick introductions were exchanged as the two Muslim Brotherhood threw their bags into the trunk of the car. "Let's go," commanded

Nawwaf, who presented himself as the leader of the two new arrivals. Nawwaf was a five foot eight Kuwaiti, dark skinned and seemed to have a permanent scowl on his face. His companion, Rasil was a couple inches shorter, slightly darker skinned, and Egyptian. They made it obvious that they were here to take control and Fatih was now their servant.

Once inside the car and as they were pulling out of the airport Nawwaf spoke up again, "How long is it going to take for us to get there?"

"About one hour."

"So what is the situation?" Nawwaf continued. "You have four prisoners, two of them children, and there are four of you holding them captive. Is that correct?"

"Only three of us now," Fatih corrected as he began to explain how one of their team members had been killed. "You'll be seeing what's left of him shortly." He went on to explain that the earlier delay was caused by a traffic jam related to the crash of his companion.

Traffic slowed as they came closer to the point of the collision. But this time it wasn't because of a lane closure. This time it was because of the gawkers who wanted to take a look at the accident site. It wasn't long before the traffic was once again up to full speed.

In an attempt to generate conversation and to find out why the Muslim Brotherhood was now involved, Sami's warrior asked, "Why has Sami sent you out here? To help out with the kidnapping?"

"Sami's dead," replied Rasil.

"What? How did that happen?"

"He was assassinated. His family was attacked. His wives were killed. His boys were shot. And now he has been executed. It was Shihab who contacted us."

This put everyone deep into thought and the car went quiet for the remainder of the journey.

* * *

The international news media broadcast the headline, "Racially motivated attack on two Muslim students in Golden Colorado." The details of the story continued with, "Two Islamic students were attacked and raped in the middle of the night by what was obviously a racially motivated assault."

The Muslim community screamed in protest. The uproar was heard around the world. Reporters asked questions like, "What would cause such a brutal and offensive attack? The two were obviously singled out because of their cultural and religious background. Something must be done to bring the attackers to justice and to make sure this type of thing never happens again. We need to be a country of religious and racial tolerance."

Even the president of the United States became involved and made a public statement condemning the behavior. Cries for justice came from countries all over the world, and the Middle East Arab countries demanded the assailants be executed immediately. They stressed that they would consider any delay in the punishment as an insult to their culture and religion.

Chapter Thirty-Eight

Another Attack
November, 2017, Ann Arbor, Michigan

Shihab was enraged. In the past he had seen Sami's activities as extremist. But now that Sami and his family had been brutally attacked, and all the adults had been killed by these infidels, he saw it as his personal mission to follow the teachings of Allah in the Koran. He had to avenge these attacks on his family. It had become his job to avenge the cruel death of his brother.

Bringing in the Muslim Brotherhood was a bold and necessary move. Sami had used them to acquire the bombs. But Sami hadn't involved them directly in his activities and plans. Shihab wondered why Sami hadn't done this long ago. Probably because he wanted to be a silent version of Osama bin Laden. Sami wanted to be recognized around the world as one of Allah's heroes. But Shihab wasn't as proud. He preferred to be successful and bringing in the Brotherhood who was more experienced, and using them to help run these operations offered him a much greater opportunity for success.

The Brotherhood had assigned him with the task of doing something local that would retaliate for the attack on Sami's family and on the mosque. He flipped open the internet and searched for prominent Christian buildings in the Ann Arbor area. He wasn't impressed with anything he found. He wanted something big and he wanted to hit the biggest of the Christian Whores, the biggest religious organization in the world, the Roman Catholic Church.

Broadening his search area, he found the Cathedral of the Most Blessed Sacrament in Detroit. This was the perfect example of Christian decadence that he was looking for. It was a heavily decorated Gothic church which was the seat of the archbishop of the archdiocese of Detroit. It was located at 9844 Woodward Avenue adjacent to Detroit's historic district. It would be the perfect symbol of decadence and would work well as the symbol of revenge that Shihab was looking for.

With the target selected, Shihab called for his remaining four warriors to come to a prayer meeting. After the short meeting he challenged them with a rallying speech about Allah's need to avenge the death of Sami. "We cannot allow the murder of Sami and his wives to go unrecognized and unpunished. We are commanded by the Koran to strike back. And we must strike back in a way that will be recognized and remembered."

He continued, "The Muslim Brotherhood has asked us to select a target close to home so there would be no question that our retaliatory strike was because of Sami's death. I have found an excellent target in Detroit and this target will raise the awareness that we will not tolerate our Islamic brothers, especially an Imam, to be abused in this way. I need a volunteer. Who will dedicate themselves to this cause? Who will avenge Sami? Who will make Allah proud?"

All four immediately raised their hands. That was exactly what Shihab was hoping for. But he had already selected the individual he wished to sacrifice. He wanted to use the least talented of the team members. He wanted to keep the ones that were the most computer technology savvy for later missions.

Pointing to Akil, the warrior he had targeted, he said, "Allah wants you to do this mission. Are you willing?"

"Yes," he responded.

"Are you brave enough to walk into the location that we have selected and destroy it?"

"Yes!"

"Will you be Allah's warrior?"

"Yes! Yes! Yes!" Akil replied.

Shihab dismissed the remaining three warriors, explaining only the warrior involved will know any information about his mission. Once the other three had departed, he beckoned the remaining individual to a seat and sat down next to him. He explained, "Our target is a Christian religious symbol in Detroit. We no longer have any of the nuclear bombs that were used in Orlando or North Dakota, but we have enough destructive power to take down the structure and possibly it's surrounding buildings. Are you ready to give your life as a warrior in Allah's jihad?"

"Yes! I am ready. When can I go?" questioned Akil.

"Today." He walked over to a nearby closet, opened the door, and pulled out a bomb-loaded vest. The vest had C-4 explosives wrapped around it with detonators already inserted. The vest was armed and ready to go.

Attached to the vest was a wire and a switch. "Don't hit this switch until you are in position," he instructed. "Your target is the Christian Cathedral in the heart of Detroit. I want you to go inside, get positioned centrally near something structural like a pillar, and push the switch. Can you do this mission for Allah?"

"Yes," replied Akil, a little exasperated for being repeatedly asked the same question. "I am Allah's slave and if this is what he wants me to do then I am honored to serve."

"Yes. This is what Allah wants. He wants revenge on the infidels that have brutally attacked Sami and his holy mosque. Take this belt and go now." He gave the warrior the address of the Cathedral of the Most Blessed Sacrament in Detroit and sent him on his way.

Akil took off his jacket and put on the explosive vest. Then he put his own jacket back on in order to hide the vest. He gave the traditional farewell greeting to Shihab, and departed.

* * *

The vest was cumbersome to wear. Even with the seat of his car pushed back as far as it could go it was a tight squeeze between the seat and the steering wheel. But Akil did not want to take off his vest in case anyone saw what he was doing. He wanted to be successful and that's all that mattered. He wanted to be a hero to Islam. He wanted to win Allah's favor. He wanted to make his family proud.

The drive from the mosque in Ann Arbor to the cathedral in Detroit took about forty-five minutes. Akil decided to take highway M-14 E because he felt safer on this route rather than taking the main freeway along I-94 E. His GPS routed him on Davison West onto the Davison Expressway. A right turn on Woodward Avenue led him directly to the cathedral.

He turned on Glynn Court realizing too late that it was a one-way street in the wrong direction. He had been too distracted by his thoughts to realize what he was doing. There was no traffic so he quickly flipped the car around in the opposite direction and found a parking space. He exited his car and started walking toward the cathedral. He felt a little stupid when he realized he had searched for a parking spot that offered at least two hour parking. Obviously it really didn't matter what happened to the car. He was done with cars in this life.

Akil walked up to the front door of the Cathedral and tried to open the door. It was locked. "Why would anyone lock a place of worship in the middle of the day?" he asked no one in particular. It seemed strange to him that people had to schedule their worship around the availability of the cathedral. He decided to walk around the side of the church to see if he could find another entrance. There weren't a lot of options, but eventually he found a doorway that led to a basement souvenir shop. He decided this would have to do. He was on a mission and he wasn't going to wait around for someone to open the doors of the cathedral. He could cause just as much damage from this basement location, maybe even more since it was under the main structure.

The clerk at the store greeted Akil with, "Welcome. Can I help you find anything?"

"No thanks."

Akil felt out of place. He knew he didn't look like someone who belonged there. He worried that the store clerk was growing suspicious. He became uncomfortable and confused.

Akil tried to hide himself from the attendant by walking between several rows of book shelves but the attendant came walking over and she seemed to look strangely and suspiciously at Akil's oversized upper body area. Akil knew he had been discovered. He knew she realized that he was hiding something under his jacket.

"Can I help you?" was the clerk's attempt at getting some interaction.

Akil tried to avoid eye contact. He was non-responsive and walked off in a different direction. This seemed to cause the attendant to become even more suspicions and, rather than confront him herself, she returned to her spot behind the counter. Akil could hear her calling security. Akil decided to not wait any longer.

The eruption was like an earthquake that started in the basement and then tore its way up through the center of the cathedral all the way to the ceiling. The center of the cathedral quickly became a ball of dust and debris, and then, as if the explosion had caused a vacuum. The outer walls of the cathedral immediately collapsed inward.

What just a few moments earlier had been a beautiful place of worship had within seconds been turned into a pile of collapsed rubble. Portions of the end walls still stood, but the remainder of the structure was no longer recognizable.

Akil had been successful. He was now with Allah and had earned his place with his private harem of virgins, which was the reward given to all of Allah's warriors who had sacrificed their lives for his glory.

Off in the distance, in a completely Islamic community, children could be seen cheering and jumping up and down clapping their hands. They were excited to see the destruction of another symbol of infidel obsessiveness. This was their own little 9-11 victory. The children screamed, "Death to the infidels. Allah has spoken."

* * *

It was another bad day for the FBI. They had been monitoring Sami's mosque from across the street and had seen people coming and going all day. They regretted their failure to pay close attention to Akil and his bulky coat which was obviously hiding something. Unfortunately they didn't notice anything unusual about Akil's departure. He left the mosque and went directly to his car and drove off, just like everyone else who had come to the mosque. There weren't enough agents for the FBI to follow everyone who came and went to the mosque and Akil didn't stand out as someone that needed to be followed. This time the FBI would pay the price for their mistake.

Later, as they reviewed the tapes, they noticed a bulge in Akil's coat. But by then it was too late. The deed had already been done.

Chapter Thirty-Nine

Another Retaliation

November, 2017, Golden, Colorado

Livy had just arrived at the Denver airport when she heard the news on the overhead television set. She hadn't let Jonathan know that she was coming back. Her return was last minute and she thought she would surprise him. But listening to the news told her that she would be leaving immediately.

The destruction of the Detroit cathedral was national news. There was no question in Livy's mind the reason behind the destruction of the cathedral. Even though the method of operation was different for this attack in that a nuclear bomb wasn't used, she was convinced it was a retaliatory attack for the hit on Sami. The question that plagued her was, who is now leading the attack? Could it be that the Muslim Brotherhood was taking over?

The FBI knew from their tap on the cell phone that Shihab had taken over the reins for Sami and that he was now in communication with the Muslim Brotherhood. She was sure that if the team on the ground in Detroit was able to determine who the attacker was then he would be tied back to Shihab. But the question in her mind was whether Shihab was now in charge or if the Brotherhood had taken over.

Livy knew she would be receiving instructions to go to Detroit on the next available flight, so she decided to not even leave the airport. Instead she placed a call to Lincoln using the secure phone number.

"Hi there," Lincoln answered. "Where are you today?"

"Sitting at the Denver airport waiting to be told to go to Detroit," Livy replied.

"Good for you. I'm glad to see you're building up your airline mileage."

"Not very funny when you realize why I'm building up mileage. Anyway, let's get down to business before I have to drop off. I traced that phone number you sent me and apparently the number is to a phone which was involved in a deadly car crash right here along the freeway. It's now been impounded by the police. But by looking at the phone records of that phone I was able to get a list of phone numbers which may be helpful. I'm just not sure what numbers to trace."

"Probably the most recent calls."

"It's not that easy. Apparently nearly all the recent calls were to Sami or to other individuals back in Ann Arbor. He probably had no reason to call the phones of the cell members that he was traveling with. So I'm not sure which, if any, of the 100 numbers that are in this phone are relevant. I was going to get you the list but that was before this attack in Detroit. I'm not sure how to get the information to you at this point, but I think we now have a higher priority."

"Yes," came back Lincoln. "Like an attack on Mecca."

"Can't do that," said Livy followed by an explanation about the phone call the FBI had tapped and how the Muslim Brotherhood had said they welcomed an attack on Mecca because it would unify the Muslim world. An attack on Mecca would trigger a holy war against the western infidels. "I think we need to find a local target, the same as what they did with the cathedral. We need to respond in-kind so they know we understand their message and we're willing to play ball in the same way. I'm thinking of a mosque. What do you think?"

"I understand your logic and I think you're right. But there really aren't any local Islamic targets that would be considered a comparable 'eye for an eye' attack. They destroyed a cathedral. That's like a dozen churches rolled into one."

"How about multiple targets?"

"That works," responded Lincoln. "I'll get the Dragon Pit together and we'll figure out what makes sense."

"We need to do this quickly so there is no question about the connection," suggested Livy.

"Agreed!"

"The call I was expecting is coming in and I have to take it," stated Livy, referring to a call from her boss Alvin Foller.

"No problem. I'll take care of this," he said.

Livy switched over to the incoming call and answered, "Hello!"

As expected it was Alvin on the call. "Where are you?"

"Still at the Denver airport," replied Livy. "I just arrived and I have a feeling that I'm going to be leaving this airport the same way I arrived."

"You're right about that," he responded. "Apparently there were surveillance cameras at various points around the cathedral and hopefully something of value was captured. I need you to dig into that as soon as you arrive."

"Will do."

"That's not all. But first encrypt your phone and I'll do the same on my end." A few clicks could be heard and then Alvin continued, "Are you ready?"

"Yes."

"Apparently Sami's brother has taken over leadership of Sami's cell and he is bringing in the Muslim Brotherhood to help out. We learned the kidnapping in Golden is now being taken over by the Brotherhood from Egypt and we also learned the Ann Arbor cell was instructed to execute some kind of retaliatory response for the killing of Sami. I would assume the destruction of the cathedral in Detroit was that response."

"Wow. Interesting. Our enemy just became tougher to deal with," Livy responded. "I guess that confirms our suspicions about who is behind the attack in Detroit."

"One more thing that may interest you and our Dragon Pit team," suggested Alvin.

"What's that?"

"Apparently there were a couple of defectors to Sami's cell and he had placed a kill order on them. We've learned who the defectors are, but unfortunately one of them has already been executed. The local police have picked up the second defector and have him contained in a local hospital. I'm going to travel there to interrogate him. Maybe we can get some information about the Brotherhood or specifically about the kidnapping from him."

"That would be great," confirmed Livy. "How can I help?"

"You can help by figuring out who executed the blast in Detroit and tying it to our cell," replied Alvin. "I assume it was a suicide bomber, but if not, we need to know."

"I'm on my way. Also, I wanted to check with you about the need for a response to the cathedral attack. I talked with Lincoln from the team and we discussed the need for an appropriate response. We're thinking about multiple mosque targets in the Ann Arbor and Detroit area. What are your thoughts?"

"I'm in agreement. Mosques would probably be the best because there would be no confusion about the connection to the cathedral bombing. How are you planning on executing the attack?"

"I left Lincoln working with the rest of the team to try and figure out the logistics of the attack. I'll check with you when we have a plan and get your approval."

"Sounds perfect," replied Alvin as the two of them wrapped up the call.

* * *

Using the burner phones, Lincoln called Gage and set up a meeting with him in the central lawn area of the Colorado Engineering School. He had become concerned about all the surveillance equipment that was getting set up. He no longer trusted his home or the insides of any building. He wasn't sure what area was safe for a conversation. He only contacted Gage because he knew this next operation would be a military strike at several targeted mosques in the Detroit or Ann Arbor area. The other Dragon Pit members that were military were Glenn and Brian. One had been kidnapped and the other was out of the country hiding somewhere. But Lincoln was sure he and Gage could successfully execute this mission.

Before the meeting Lincoln did a little research and had discovered a mosque in Dearborn that was the largest in the United States. That would have to be one of the first targets they hit.

Gage was already waiting for Lincoln as he arrived. "What's up?" was his short and to-the-point welcome.

"We have a mission," Lincoln responded.

"What do we need to do?" asked Gage, not questioning the reason behind the mission. He already knew it had something to do with the explosion in Detroit.

"We need to hit mosques in the Detroit area."

"We're going to have to hit quite a few if we're going to equal the damage that they did to the cathedral. I'm good with that. Let's do it."

"I made up a list of the mosques in the Detroit area," Lincoln started with his explanation. "There are thirteen of them and the largest is the one in Dearborn which is the largest in the United States. So we have to hit that one for sure."

"How are we going to hit thirteen targets at once? If we do them one at a time they'll catch on to us and be watching for us."

"We're going to plant bombs at each location. We'll use timers and set them all to the same time. They will all go up at once. I've already contacted Gene and he's going to let us use his plane so we can assemble all the bombs here and take them with us. Then it's just a matter of us placing the bombs at each location. I suggested we fly out tonight and get the deed accomplished ASAP so there is no doubt about the connection to the cathedral bombing."

"Love it," replied Gage. "Where are the bombs we're assembling?"

"We have to assemble them. I think we should rent a storage unit, bring all the bomb making materials there, build the bombs, take them directly to the airport, and go," suggested Lincoln.

"Let's do it. You've dragged me into some of the weirdest missions and I have a feeling this is another weird one. But let's get it done."

"I suspect this one is going to be easier than dealing with a couple of naked, screaming women."

"No doubt," replied Gage as he stood up and the two of them started walking away from the area. "What do we need to get?"

Lincoln laid out a list of bomb components that they would need and gave Gage his portion of the list. The list also had disguises which included hats and ski masks. "You get the storage shed and let me know where we're meeting for our bomb building exercise. I'll map out directions for each of the mosques we're going to hit when we're on the plane and maybe we can each go off in different directions to get the bombs planted. We'll set them to explode sometime after we depart Detroit. I have no interest in being a suicide bomber. I'm more interested in living to fight again another day. I'll have you get all the bomb components including backpacks for storing the bombs, and I'll head to the Army Depot in Pueblo to get the C-4 and the detonators. I have connections down there which will allow me access to whatever I need. Hopefully no one will stop me for any vehicle inspections when I leave the depot. That drive will take about five hours. Then I'll meet you at the storage shed and we can wrap up these bombs. It would be best to only use cash and not leave any purchase trail. Additionally, don't get everything from the same location. Go to four or five locations when you buy this stuff."

"Good enough. But don't you think the ski masks will raise suspicions? I think we should get things like fake wigs, mustaches, and beards. That will be less suspicious in the event that we're spotted."

"You're right. I'll leave it to you to figure out what will work. We have to assume we will be under suspicion now that two members of our team are connected to the terrorists. That means we need to work extra hard to cover our tracks and not leave any evidence. Make sure you are not being followed. Do everything you can to stay low."

* * *

Lincoln, the Army Ranger, set out immediately for Pueblo. The drive from Golden to the Army Depot in Pueblo took about two hours each way. He knew timing was of the essence, and a hit on the mosques within twenty-four hours of the hit on the cathedral would demonstrate the power of the Dragon Pit team to reek the same type of revenge that had become the trademark of the Muslim Brotherhood. As far as Lincoln was concerned, this was the only way to put an end to the terrorist attacks. Sometimes you just have to fight fire with fire and this was the type of fire these guys understood the best.

Getting on the depot grounds was easy for Lincoln. He had been there many times and was extremely familiar with the facility. During the time of his studies in Golden, he had been temporarily assigned to the depot and it was home base for him. His assignment at the depot was to oversee some of the munitions movement. He knew how to get at the C-4. He also knew how to fix the paperwork to make it look like the missing C-4 was tagged to a specific allocation.

Lincoln went into the storage facility containing the C-4 plastic explosives. Fortunately no one was around, as was often the case this time of day. There were guards outside, but the inside of the facility was empty. He grabbed a case of the C-4 along with a case of the detonators and took it to one of the redistribution locations. He also pulled a case-labeled "Water Bottles" out of the break room, removed the bottles, and put them in the fridge. Then he packed the C-4 and detonators into the water bottle case. He crushed up the C-4 and detonator cases and put these into the same water bottle box. He re-sealed the "Water Bottle" case to make it look unopened and headed out of the building. He would take care of the paperwork for the missing C-4 during one of his normal assignment days. That way he wouldn't draw suspicion by logging on to the inventory tracking system during a non-work day.

As he exited the building, a guard stopped him and asked, "What do you have there?"

The guard was a longtime friend of Lincoln's and he knew he would let him pass. "Water for a meeting in one of the other buildings. I knew we had plenty here so I volunteered to go get them a case. How are you doing anyway?" Lincoln knew changing the subject would get the guard away from thinking about the carton.

"The family's great. How about yours?" Lincoln continued the chitchat with the guard. He didn't want to seem rushed because that might raise suspicion. Eventually they bid farewell and Lincoln headed for his car with the box. He placed the box in his trunk so the guards at the gate wouldn't see it, and headed off the depot grounds. He breathed a sigh of relief when the guard at the gate peeked into the side window of the car and waved him on.

Lincoln felt as though he was home free, as he jumped on the freeway heading back to Golden. During the drive, he received a text from Gage indicating that he had all the supplies. He also indicated which storage shed had been rented. Lincoln responded he was on his way.

Working together at the storage shed the bombs were quickly assembled. The timers Gage had acquired were installed in short order. Then each bomb was packed into a backpack to keep it as inconspicuous as possible. The backpacks were placed into the trunk of Lincoln's car.

Gage drove his vehicle off a short distance and parked it in a shopping center parking lot. He then joined Lincoln in his car and they rode together to the airport. A quick phone call to Gene confirmed the plane was ready for them at the airport.

Another quick call to Livy using the secure phones allowed them to confirm their activities with her and keep her in the loop. "We need two cars at the airport in Detroit," requested Gage. "We're each going off to plant presents in different locations. We thought that by doing double duty we can get this completed a lot quicker and leave the area." He knew better than to use terms like "bomb" over the phone lines in case there was any automated monitoring of calls.

"Sounds like a plan," responded Livy. "I'll communicate with Alvin and see if he has any reservations to what you're doing. Assuming there are no issues, we'll have the cars waiting for you. Do you know which airport you're flying into?"

"Not yet. But I know it will be a different one than last time."

* * *

Livy always played the middleman in communications between the Dragon Pit team and Alvin. Even though Alvin was now the leader, he didn't have one of the burner phones the rest of the team had. His communication with Livy used the encrypted FBI phone. So Livy was constantly switching between phones. For now the system worked, but each time Livy had to repeat a conversation she swore she was going to get Alvin a burner phone and program the rest of the team into that phone so that he could be directly connected to any conversations.

"Alvin here," was the response Livy received as she called Alvin on her encrypted line. Livy went on to explain the plan to bomb several mosques in the Detroit area. "That seems like an appropriate response," replied Alvin, "but I would be concerned about the large number of visits that need to be made. Each time the guys go to one of the mosques they run the risk of being caught on video. They don't exactly look like one of the believers who would be seen at a mosque."

"I understand," agreed Livy. "But I don't see what other options we have. This seemed like a very appropriate 'in kind' response."

"You're right. But just tell the guys to wear hats and be really weary of cameras. And they don't want to have any conversations with anyone or allow anyone to remember their faces."

"Understood. They'll need a couple of cars at the airport to complete the mission. I'll let you know what airport they're arriving at as soon as I know."

Alvin continued, "On a separate note. Our investigation has logically turned to investigating the friends of Brian. I can't block this investigation without seeming too obvious. I have to let it go forward. What it means is that you will probably be pulled off of the investigation because of your association with Brian. You and I will obviously continue communicating, but don't be surprised if someone comes in and tells you you're off this case."

"Got it. I expected something like that to happen."

She proceeded to contact Gage and give him Alvin's response and concerns. Gage and Lincoln were just beginning to circle the airport getting ready to land when she called. The mission was a go.

Chapter Forty

The Death of the Mosque
November, 2017, Detroit, Michigan

During the flight to Detroit, Lincoln used the on-board computer system to pull up maps of each of the mosques in the Detroit area. He mapped out a route for each of them which would allow them to visit each of the mosques in the shortest amount of time.

The timers were set to three in the morning to minimize casualties. The execution of the entire plan was expected to take about two hours. The goal was for them to be finished and on their way by one. That would give them plenty of time to leave the area before the explosions started.

The plane landed at an airport that was again different from the ones where they had landed during their two previous visits to the area. They didn't want anyone to see a pattern in their activities. They were ready, complete with makeup and disguises.

Alvin had two cars waiting for them and Lincoln and Gage quickly transferred the bombs, now wrapped in backpacks, into the trunks of the two cars and took off. There wasn't a lot of conversation between them. They were both solemn and deep in their thoughts. They were wearing their concentrated business faces. They had a mission to complete and they were focused on doing the best job possible.

Lincoln took the route that would lead him to six mosques in Detroit and Dearborn. Gage would travel to ones in Dearborn, Detroit, and Hamtramck.

The procedure was simple. Park somewhere close by. Get a backpack out of the trunk. Place it somewhere strategic to maximize the structural damage but place it in a location that would not stand out and would not be noticeable. In a couple instances, where the mosque roof was low enough, throw the backpacks on the roof. On other occasions they would hide it behind an air conditioner enclosure or in a stairwell. They were successful in placing all the bombs within the two hours and were back on-board the plane shortly before one in the morning. The mission was on schedule and executed as planned. The plane departed the airport without mishap.

Upon arriving back in Denver, Lincoln and Gage checked the television monitors expecting to see news reports about the explosions in Detroit, but there was nothing. It was past three Detroit time and the explosions should have occurred.

"You know what's wrong?" asked Gage, saying the question more like a statement than a question. "We set the clocks to Denver time. The bombs aren't going to go off for another two hours."

"Rats," responded Lincoln in frustrated disgust. "You're right. What a bone-headed mistake. I guess we'll have to check back on the news in a couple hours."

"Correct. So we may as well leave and head home."

"Agreed."

The drive from the airport to Golden took close to an hour. They went directly to Gage's bachelor pad and flipped on the television. By the time they were settled in they only had about twenty more minutes to wait before the anticipated fireworks would begin.

It began on queue. About ten minutes after three there was a news flash on the television, "Largest mosque in the United States has been attacked and almost completely destroyed. It is unknown if there were any casualties related to the blast."

Without a word, Lincoln and Gage high-fived each other. Then Gage said, "The message has been sent. Let's see how it's received."

Ten minutes later the news flash was broadcast, "Three more mosques were attacked in the Detroit area. There is still no estimate of casualties. We will be broadcasting videos of the blast locations as soon as possible. It has been suggested that these attacks are in retaliation for the attacks on the cathedral in Detroit. No one has claimed responsibility for the attacks at this time."

"They made the connection," commented Lincoln. "They know why the mosques were attacked. Let's see how they react."

The two of them couldn't get their eyes off the TV. "This is more exciting than the Super Bowl," commented Gage. "I can't wait for the next touchdown."

After about an hour, the television crew was finally able to transmit videos of the explosion sites. The newscaster announced, "There have been a total of twelve mosques in the Detroit area that have either been entirely destroyed or at least seriously damaged. Apparently it was executed by a lone individual who was seen going near one of the mosques with a backpack around midnight. We're not one hundred percent certain that this individual was the reason for the explosion. FBI sources on the scene are investigating the possibility of a connection." Then the announcers went into their repeat mode of saying the same things over and over again because they had no new information to add.

After a few minutes there was another reporter who announced, "Apparently there was a backpack bomb set at a thirteenth mosque which did not go off. They found the bomb and are investigating the backpack and its contents to see if they can find a clue as to who the bombers might be."

"Oops," commented Gage. "That's not good. I'm glad we wore gloves. And all the components were from Superstore Mart, which is about a generic as you can get. So we should be okay."

"I hope so," replied Lincoln, "or we may soon be vacationing with Brian. Hopefully our disguises worked."

"Ending up with Brian wouldn't be so bad either."

Just then another news flash came in, "Tragedy has struck. As the FBI was removing the thirteenth bomb it detonated killing several agents and a dozen bystanders. And we now have a thirteenth mosque that was seriously damaged. We are getting word from all over the country that people are fleeing from the mosques in fear that there will be more mosques attacked. Daily prayers for the Islamic community have been devastated. Muslims are staying away from their mosques and doing their prayers at home."

The broadcast was switched to a reporter who was interviewing an Islamic leader from the Detroit area. The Islamist said, "Detroit is a center for the Islamic faith in the United States. This is where the largest concentration of Muslims in the United States live. This racist attack has been devastating to our community. Unfortunately I know that the destruction of the Roman Catholic Cathedral was also an unfortunate terrorist activity. But does that justify the destruction of thirteen of our religious centers? I plead with the individuals who are behind the attacks on the mosques to stop these attacks immediately."

"How about the terrorists who attacked the cathedral?" asked the reporter. "Shouldn't we also plead with them to stop?"

"Of course," replied the Islamist. "All terrorism should end immediately."

"It sounded like you think the attacks on the mosques are worse than the attacks on the cathedral?" asked the reporter.

The Islamist showed his anger and said, "Of course not. Don't put words in my mouth. All terrorism is evil. It's just that the attacks on the mosques are more personal to me. But all terrorism is evil."

The reporter continued, "Then wouldn't it make more sense for us to stress that the terrorist attacks that are executed by Muslim extremists should stop so that the retaliatory strikes against mosques would also stop?"

The Islamist leader was outraged, "How can you connect the two? The attacks on the mosques are unprecedented and uncalled for. There is no justification for these attacks. How dare you try to blame the attacks on the mosques on the Muslim people. This is an outrage." With that he turned around and walked away, refusing to be interviewed any further.

* * *

The Muslim community was grieved, both for the loss of their mosques, and for the loss of the people who were killed at the blast sites. A cry went out from the Islamic community that defied the Muslim leadership. The cry was that the news reporter was correct and that Muslim terrorism must stop. The back and forth retaliation had gotten out of hand. The message from the larger community was that the Muslim people want the bloodshed to end. There were public speeches, radio advertisements, articles in newspapers, and billboard postings all encouraging an end to the Muslim retaliation. Ironically, one of the Muslim posted billboards supporting an end to the attacks displayed a modified quote from a Jewish individual taken from the movie "Fiddler on the Roof" which said, "Following the principle of an eye for an eye and a tooth for a tooth we will all end up eye-less and tooth-less."

In spite of several Imams' cry for revenge, stressing that the Koran insists on revenge against the infidels, the general Islamic population wanted an end to the destruction and manslaughter. They didn't want any more destruction and death. However, in spite of the general outcry, there were still Imams that preached the Koran's version of revenge and insisted that action must be taken.

Shihab was one of those who preached revenge. In his home he was sharing his frustration about the attacks on the mosques with his wife. He had two wives but only the senior wife was home at the time. But she wouldn't listen. "How many people need to die before we stop this senseless killing," she screamed. "I don't want our sons to end up like Sami and his sons. I don't want to end up dead like his wives. Enough is enough! Stop your terrorism talk. You're being stupid."

Shihab was incensed. Wives have no business reprimanding their husbands. It was not right. He reacted without thinking and slapped her as hard as possible across the face. She fell backwards and unexpectedly hit her head hard against a sharp corner of the kitchen counter as she was falling. The hit put an enormous gash in the back of her head and immediately knocked her unconscious.

Shihab didn't even bend down to check on her. "Stupid woman," he said as he turned and walked away. He left the house and headed over to the mosque to pray, hoping Allah would give him some ideas on what he should do about these brutal attacks against the mosques. He behaved as if he was obsessed. Revenge had to be taken. But what form that revenge should take was still a mystery.

After spending a couple hours in the mosque in Sami's old office he heard a siren outside. Wondering what the commotion was all about he went out into the main prayer area of the mosque. He was quickly surrounded by the police and handcuffed.

"What is the meaning of this?" Shihab questioned. "Do you dare to desecrate this holy mosque by coming in here without even taking your shoes off? How dare you manhandle me in a brutal manner? How dare you!"

The police responded, "You are under arrest for the murder of your wife. You have the right to remain silent. Anything you say . . ." The entire Miranda rights were read off to him as he was escorted to the backseat of the police cruiser which was waiting outside. It would be a long while before Shihab would once again be in a position to share his beliefs with Sami's congregation. Or would it?

Chapter Forty-One

The Kidnappers
November, 2017, Detroit, Michigan

Livy, now working on the cathedral bombing in Detroit, was given the additional duty of investigating the mosque bombings. Alvin, realizing there might be videos of Livy's friends, felt she needed to be involved in viewing these videos as soon as possible. Ironically, she already knew what had happened. Rather than seeing her role as one of the primary investigators of what happened at the mosques, her role became one of filtering the incoming information making sure there was nothing that would incriminate any Dragon Pit members. In this role she requested all video recordings around any of the bombing sites be sent to her first. She would do a preliminary review and then send them on for further processing if something meaningful was identified. She gave the mosque bombing videos priority so she could perform the screening. Fortunately there wasn't much to screen. It was night and the lighting was bad on most of the videos. Those that were viewable showed little or no activity. However, there was one shot which looked a lot like Gage walking toward one of the mosques. In spite of the disguise, his walk and body structure may have given him away. Livy made sure that this video disappeared.

Moments after Livy had eliminated the video of Gage at the mosque, two FBI agents walked into the taping room and confronted Livy. One spoke up saying, "Livy, we have identified you as one of Brian's close friends and because of that you need to disqualify yourself from any investigation that would be connected with the bombing of Muslim sites. You should have already done that. Please disqualify yourself immediately or we'll have to force the issue."

"Understood," replied Livy, thankful she had had sufficient time to go through the mosque bombing tapes and hopeful no more would turn up. "I was just trying to help. But I understand the need to take me off these investigations. I assume I am still on the Orlando, North Dakota, and Cathedral investigations."

"Correct. We discussed this with Alvin and he wants you to continue on those investigations. But you need to disassociate yourself with the mosque bombings and the Medina bombing."

"I will comply immediately." She needed to appear agreeable so there would be no additional suspicion.

The cathedral videos proved to be extremely useful. It didn't take long to identify an individual who was obviously wearing something under his jacket, which must have been the bomb vest. Livy was also fortunate in getting a picture of the face of the bomber. It didn't take much effort to connect him to Sami's mosque, since that was the first place she looked. Several people at the mosque easily identified him off the video picture.

Livy passed this information on to her Dragon Pit team members using the burner phone network. She also explained that the Dragon Pit team was being monitored because everything around Brian was being monitored including all his friends. She mentioned she had been pulled off of all activities associated with Brian. She stressed that the arrest of Shihab was directly related to the monitoring process. She commanded it would be smart for everyone to replace their burner phones. It wouldn't do any good if only some of them replaced their phones. All of them had to be replaced simultaneously or else any one phone could connect and link all the others. Everyone readily agreed.

* * *

Alvin traveled to Detroit to lead up the two investigations. He knew what Livy was doing and why she requested all the videos come to her first. He didn't have to confront her directly and ask what was going on. He already knew, and was somewhat impressed with the Dragon Pit team's ability to carry out such an elaborate plan without leaving a trace. But he was extremely unhappy about the loss of three agents who were killed when the thirteenth bomb accidently exploded in spite of them using a bomb robot and the bomb squad. It exploded so unexpectedly the team wasn't able to get all the equipment in place in time.

Upon arrival Alvin's first order of business was to get the investigations rolling and on track. His second task was to talk to Kadeem, the Sami team member who had deserted the pack. He hoped Kadeem would be able to work as an agent inside the cell that was behind the cathedral, Orlando, and the North Dakota bombings. He hoped to learn two things; the first being if there were any future bombings planned, which he doubted Kadeem would know because the bombings seemed to be last minute and need-to-know. The second being the location of the kidnapped victims.

Alvin knew Kadeem had been moved from the hospital and was under arrest at the local Ann Arbor police station. He had already admitted to being involved in Sami's cell and explained he didn't want to be part of that effort any more. Alvin sent a couple agents to pick him up and bring him to an interrogation room of the FBI branch in downtown Detroit on Michigan Avenue.

Alvin wanted to personally do the interrogation. With video cameras rolling, Alvin entered the room. "Kadeem, correct?" he asked, trying to initiate conversation.

Kadeem was nonresponsive. He didn't say anything. He didn't even make eye contact.

Alvin did not back down. "I know your friend Abdullah was killed by members of Sami's cell. You've admitted being involved as a member of that same cell. That makes you as responsible for Abdullah's death as if you pulled the trigger yourself. We have other members of the cell who have identified you and are willing to testify against you." He lied in order to send Kadeem off guard. "So, as I see it you have one of two choices: either you tell us what we want to know and we make a recommendation for leniency with the DA, or your second option is we arrest you today and charge you with murder." Alvin used Satan's trick of mixing truth with lies. You give the suspect just enough truth so they conclude everything you are saying was true. And you mix in enough lies to shake the suspect's foundation.

Kadeem spoke up, "I already made a statement explaining my involvement with Sami and the rest of the group. But I haven't heard anything about my family. Your agent promised that if I give you this information you will protect my family. When is that going to happen? If you don't keep your promise, then I don't see any reason why I should give you any additional information. You're just a bunch of liars."

"Don't worry. Your family will be taken care of. Look, I have fourteen bombings to investigate here in Detroit, and I'm not going to waste time with you if you're not willing to cooperate. So I'm going to ask you one more time if you are willing to talk to me. If I walk out of this room then I will instruct my agents to charge you with murder and lock you up. We'll put you in a cell with some of your other Sami cell buddies so you will have lots of company. You can share good times with Shihab." This was another bluff since Alvin really had no chance of convicting Kadeem for the murder of Abdullah. The evidence showed him as a victim, not as a killer.

* * *

"What have you done to protect my family? You know they are at risk, but so far you have done nothing." Kadeem's mind was reeling. He didn't want to be released from police custody because he knew the assassination squad would be out there looking for him and he didn't want to be put in a cell with Shihab. He knew Shihab was more dangerous to him than the FBI. Maybe he could work a deal with the FBI.

Alvin abruptly stood up. That was enough to trigger a reaction from Kadeem. "I have some conditions," burst out Kadeem, hoping he could negotiate for his safety.

Alvin remained standing, "Like what?"

"I don't want to be placed in the same prison or the same cell as any Muslims," continued Kadeem. "They will have no problem killing me in the name of Allah. They see me as a traitor. I can't be anywhere close to them."

"Okay. So are you willing to talk to us?"

Kadeem felt as though he was betraying Allah, but he feared death even more. He was extremely conflicted and confused. He left Sami's terrorist cell because he didn't want to become a suicide bomber like his friends had become. He didn't want to die. Now this same cell was trying to kill him. Why did he have to kill in order to be loyal to Allah? Why did he have to die? Why did his family have to be at risk when he knew what he was doing was the right thing? He had committed his life to Allah, but would Allah really expect him to end it by killing others and himself, even if they were infidels? After all, infidels often believed in the same God as he believed. Wasn't there the possibility that they could also learn the truth that was restored to Mohammed? What if he killed someone right before they joined Islam? Wouldn't that have been unfair? Wouldn't that be an unjustified killing? Wouldn't that be offensive to Allah? Kadeem was so confused about what he believed. He believed in Allah because Allah had often answered his prayers. Allah had been very good to him. Would the same Allah who helped him to find his keys this morning want him to kill someone this afternoon? It just didn't make sense.

"Yes," spoke up Kadeem. "You need to take care of my family. But I really don't know what I can tell you beyond what I've already told you. Sami only explained the plan to the individuals directly involved. What do you want to know?"

Alvin sat back down, took his pad of blank paper that he had brought into the room, turned it around, handed Kadeem a pen, and said, "Let's start with a list of all the individuals who are in the cell."

Kadeem again felt a surge of guilt. Was he betraying his "friends" who were trying to kill him, or was he betraying Allah? He reflected for a couple minutes, but in the end he started writing. Once finished he pushed the pad back across the table to Alvin.

Alvin pushed the pad back and asked, "Next to each name I want you to tell me what each individual's role is. I want to know about everyone, including those who were killed in the bombings."

Kadeem pulled the pad back in front of him and started identifying the roles of each of the individuals. He indicated who each of the suicide bombers were including the one for the Orlando bombing and for the North Dakota bombing. He indicated who the individuals were that went on the first mission to Golden, Colorado and he indicated which kidnappers were sent out on the second mission to Golden. He also indicated which team members were still alive and ready to be activated.

The list was passed back to Alvin without a word and Alvin studied it for a few minutes. "Excellent," Alvin commented. "Where are the kidnappers and their hostages?" Alvin didn't expect Kadeem to know, but he thought he should at least ask the question.

"I don't know," responded Kadeem.

"Is there someone who would know?" continued Alvin in his questioning. "Is there a member of this team who would know where the kidnap victims are being held?" Alvin was pointing at the tablet lying on the table.

"I don't think that even Shihab knows their location," Kadeem replied. "Not because it's a secret, but because no one knows what those guys are up to out there. They're like a loose cannon. They were sent out by Sami before Shihab was involved and they've been on their own ever since."

"Do you know any of their phone numbers so we can try to trace them?" asked Alvin.

"If you give me my cell phone I can give you their numbers," replied Kadeem.

Alvin, not speaking to Kadeem and seeming to speak to no one specifically, said, "Someone come in here and bring me Kadeem's phone."

Almost immediately an agent entered the room and tried to hand the phone to Alvin. Speaking to the agent Alvin said, pointing to four names on the list, "See if you can find these individuals in the phone."

"If you give me the phone I can find them for you," Kadeem volunteered.

"We can't give you the phone just yet," replied Alvin, sticking to FBI protocol which suggested that the suspect might tamper with the phone while it was in his possession,

The agent started writing phone numbers down on the pad next to each of the four names. Once that process was completed, Alvin ordered the agent, "Now go and try to locate each of those phones and put a tap on them."

"Yes, sir," replied the agent as he took the pad of paper and left the room.

Turning back to Kadeem, Alvin asked, "Now, what do I do with you?'

"Protect me like you promised," replied Kadeem.

"The question is, what's the best way to do that?" Alvin responded.

"A private cell would be nice," suggested Kadeem, still thinking he was going to be arrested for murder.

"Actually that won't be necessary," replied Alvin. "I was thinking more about one of our safe houses. I want to keep you close in case there is another way you may be able to help me. But I have no intention of charging you with murder at this point."

Kadeem was ecstatic. The FBI was going to help him hide out, and it wasn't going to be in an uncomfortable prison cell. Life was going to be good after all.

The transfer to the safe house went like clockwork. Less than an hour after the interview Kadeem was safely tucked away in what he imagined would be a life of lazy luxury. The guardian of the safe house had stocked it with all types of food and treats. The television had more channels than anyone could reasonably watch, including a few Arabic channels.

It was five in the afternoon and Kadeem was settling in front of the TV with a bag of potato chips and a diet coke when there was a loud bang on the front door. The resident safe house agent went to the door and looked through the surveillance camera to see who was there. But before he had a chance to look there was a loud explosion blowing the front door off of its hinges and into the room. The stunned guard was quick to draw his weapon, but it was too late. His body was suddenly riddled with automatic weapons fire and he crumpled to the ground.

Kadeem knew it was him they were after. He jumped up and ran toward the kitchen, hoping to make an escape out the back door of the house. As he ran through the back door he was greeted by a second barrage of automatic weapons fire. Kadeem's life of protected luxury had lasted less than two hours.

Chapter Forty-Two

The Kidnapping
November, 2017, Golden, Colorado

Livy was in a panic. She didn't want any more members of the Dragon Pit to be kidnapped or forced to move. She had to meet with the Dragon Pit team but she could no longer trust electronics. The meeting had to be in person and it would be best if Jonathan didn't know she was in town because he would want to join in the meeting and that was a complication Livy didn't want to deal with. She just wanted to pop into town, share the information she had, get the new burner phones activated so each team member had the other's phone number programmed into their phones, get rid of the old burner phones, and get out of town and to work.

Livy texted Lincoln, Gage, Carlos, and Boston and had all of them meet her at the local Golden fast food hamburger stand. It was a strange place to meet but Livy was concerned about being monitored. She had become convinced there was a mole in the FBI and the mole was the cause of the numerous information leaks, including the most recent one where Kadeem was targeted at the safe house. That attack occurred so quickly, the only reasonable explanation was an FBI internal informant. Additionally, Livy was convinced the leak had to be coming from a closet Muslim within the FBI. It had to be someone who was sharing secrets with their Muslim counterparts. It had to be someone who didn't want to openly profess his religion, but who secretly supported the belief that the infidels could not be allowed to corrupt pure Islam. But this was a challenge. Rights of privacy disallowed any connection between an agent and his religious convictions. It would be inappropriate to ask someone their religion at work. Human rights policy also discouraged religious symbolism in the workplace. This made it nearly impossible to identify anyone who might be a Muslim informant based on their desk decorations.

The Dragon Pit members sat down together off to one corner of the restaurant. No one referred to themselves as the NERDS. That title seemed to have fallen into disfavor. Additionally, since the news media had picked up on the label, it was no longer a good idea for anyone anywhere to be referred to as NERDS. It would immediately raise suspicions.

Livy started the conversation, "It seems like forever since we last met. A lot has happened since then. The worst of which is we already lost two Dragon Pit members and their families. Brian had to flee for his life and the life of his family. And Glenn and his family have been kidnapped, which is even worse. And the agency is pretty upset about the three agents that were killed by that faulty bomb."

"That was terrible," chimed in Lincoln. "Thank God it wasn't worse."

"Guess you're right about that." Livy had become the impromptu leader of the group now that Brian was out of the picture. But Alvin, although behind the scenes, was considered to be the CEO and funding support of the group. Nevertheless each of the team members saw themselves as equals. Each focused on their personal specialty. Livy continued, "But even though Brian's not directly part of the team anymore, he's still out there somewhere giving us his support. Wasn't it cool the way he landed that plane in the middle of Mecca right after those braggarts said it couldn't be done?"

"That was the coolest thing I've ever seen," responded Boston.

Livy continued sharing information with the Dragon Pit, "I don't know if you realize it, but there are 157 known terrorist organizations out there and our FBI, CIA, Secret Service, and military are desperately trying to keep tabs on all of them. And these are only the known organizations. Who knows how many unknown ones are out there. And then there are those that are not listed, which are these small, self-radicalized groups like the Boston Marathon bombers or Sami's cell in Ann Arbor which pop up and bite us in the butt. It's next to impossible to keep track of them all. We'd love to have surveillance equipment in every mosque in the country, but the legal system won't allow it. It's an infringement of their civil rights of free speech. We can't even maintain monitoring equipment in Sami's mosque because someone warned him about the devices. We are successfully able to tap into the phone system and record phone conversations, but we have no equipment on-site. Additionally their lawyers are all over us and are trying to get us to stay away. These radicals even have judges in their pocket. I'm not sure if they are Muslim judges, or if they're just getting paid well. It doesn't matter because for us in the FBI, the results are the same. It's frustrating. That's why our group is getting such strong support from inside the FBI from Alvin. He sees our little Robin Hood Dragon Pit band as a group that's not hamstrung by the legal system. We can do things that the FBI can't."

"You're scaring me," responded Lincoln. "If there are 157 known organizations out there, and we're just fighting one, and the one we're fighting isn't even one of the known ones, what kind of terrorism nightmare is out there? Does anyone really have a chance of making a difference?"

"We make a difference if we attack the foundation of terrorism. We need to attack the basic belief system which says that revenge is acceptable. We need to continue your approach of fighting revenge with revenge. We won't win this war on terror by attacking these organizations one at a time. We need to focus on the big picture and hit them in a way that hurts all of them at once. Maybe that way we can make enough people realize revenge only succeeds in leaving us all eyeless and toothless, as Tevye, the milkman in 'Fiddler on the Roof' said."

Lincoln continued, "Well we know the after-the-fact approach of attacking the terrorists hasn't worked. In fact it seems to have generated more terrorist groups. Maybe our frontal attack against the foundational beliefs of these terrorists will make a difference."

"Totally agree," commented Gage. "Revenge is never the solution. But right now that seems to be the only thing these terrorists understand. So we need to change their understanding."

Livy, bringing the conversation back around to the reason for calling the meeting in the first place, said, "I wanted to update you with what I know and maybe you can update me with what you've been working on. First off, there is a mole in the FBI and someone is trying to figure out who we are. They probably already have a pretty good idea just based on Brian's network of friends. I recommend we have only person-to-person communication using the new burner phones we're distributing today, or like we're doing now by meeting at a neutral location. It's becoming too dangerous to trust even the homes we live in, as you can see by the kidnapping of Glenn and his family. We need to make our conversations sound like they're related to a study session or something to do with the school. As far as the bombings go, you all know about the cell in Ann Arbor headed by Imam Sami. That cell, which is now run by his brother, sent out the suicide bombers that hit Orlando, North Dakota, and the cathedral in Detroit. They're also behind the kidnapping of Glenn and the attack on Brian's home. But we don't know how he's getting his information. We also know the brother that took over the cell is now in prison for killing his wife."

"Another peach of a guy," commented Lincoln.

"I wish that was the end of it," responded Livy. "We had an informant who was previously in the cell tell us who its members were. We were hoping he could direct us to the kidnappers and their location. But other than giving us the names of the kidnappers and their cell phone numbers, he really didn't have a lot of information for us. Sadly, two hours after we moved him to a safe house, he was attacked and killed. That is how we know beyond a doubt we have a mole."

"Guess that safe house wasn't very safe," replied Gage.

"Actually we're more upset about the agent that was killed with him," answered Livy. "And, talking about agents getting killed, my boss Alvin is really upset about the agents killed in the Detroit mosque bombing."

Lincoln apologized, "We are too. We have no idea why that bomb didn't go off at the same time as the rest. Everything was set to go off at once."

"Sadly the agents are also partially to blame. They were being a little sloppy by assuming the bomb was disarmed or dead. They should have been more careful. But the bottom line is that they're dead and we're to blame. And that's not good. The good news is the Muslim community is screaming to end this back and forth retaliation. They didn't mind when it was just us getting hurt. We even have video clips of them cheering the destructions in Orlando, Dakota, and the cathedral. But they don't seem to like it as much when it's in their own backyard. However, the radical Imams are not buying it and are screaming for even greater retaliations. Unfortunately, it only takes one crazy to escalate this feud."

"And we can't stop now; not when we've gone this far," suggested Boston.

"No we can't," replied Lincoln matter-of-factly.

Livy continued with her update, "The phone numbers we received from the informant were traced. We're trying to follow-up on the four that are involved in the kidnapping. One is dead. Apparently that big crash on the freeway the other day was one of the kidnappers. The other phone numbers cannot be traced until they are used. The phones were turned off or destroyed. We're monitoring them, but we don't have any information right now. I'll get you the information as soon as I receive it, but you know the FBI will also be after these kidnappers as soon as they get any information on their location."

"Just let us know how we can help," suggested Gage. "We had a little conversation with Sami but it didn't gain us any information either. It's scary. The kidnapping of Glenn and his family could have been any of us."

"I understand," replied Livy. "But we also don't want to give away our little group by getting involved too quickly and showing our hand. Besides the FBI is trained for recovering kidnappings so they're better at it than we are."

"Thanks for the update," replied Lincoln. "We're terribly sorry about the FBI agents who were killed. That obviously wasn't part of the plan."

"I'll keep you informed," replied Livy. "Just minimize the use of electronic communications and when needed use the burner phones or meet in neutral locations. We need to be extremely cautions until all of this blows over. I came back to Golden just to meet with you guys and to talk this over. And I wanted to get these new phones activated. But now I have to hurry back to Detroit. By the way, one of the videos, which I 'accidentally' erased, showed Gage walking toward one of the mosques a few hours before it blew up."

"Hopefully there aren't any more of those," suggested Gage.

"I do too," replied Livy. "Especially now since I've been pulled off of that assignment because I knew Brian." With that she stood up and started to leave.

* * *

Livy had a two hour wait for her flight to Detroit. She sat at her gate in the Denver airport listening to the latest news updates. The news turned out to be a steady barrage of criticism for what they called the "targeting of the Muslim minorities." She became infuriated by the liberal news media that pretended to be open minded and receptive to various viewpoints while simultaneously criticizing anyone who disagreed with them. To her this was just another example of biased reporting.

The news media interviewed one Muslim after another asking them about the mosque bombings. Everyone condemned those attacks as racist by unjustly targeting Muslims. Some even went so far as to suggest that the attacks were an attempt to drive the Muslims out of the United States, or to commit genocide on their religion.

The news media also hinted at a government conspiracy that was trying to unjustly blame Islam for the attacks on Orlando and North Dakota. They suggested the FBI was extremely efficient in finding the bombers at the Boston marathon, but were unbelievably slow at finding the bombers of the Muslim mosques. It had to be a conspiracy of some type, even though it had been less than one day since the bombings. It seemed everyone was looking for a scapegoat and an excuse that would win sympathy to their side.

The Arab news median broadcasted news reports which tried to draw a connection between all the attacks on the Islamic community. They claimed the attacks in Detroit and Medina, and the landing of the remote plane in Mecca were all connected. They then went on to say these attacks had caused Muslim countries like Saudi Arabia to go into full national alert. Security around Mecca had been increased dramatically. People who even mildly looked suspicious were getting strip searched before they were allowed into Mecca. Armed soldiers were everywhere. The logistics of going to Mecca had become extremely complicated. An atmosphere of fear had taken over.

The Arab news media condemned the Arab world for letting fear dominate their religion. They suggested Muslims should never have fear. That Allah would always protect them. That this fear came from Satan. Then they went on to connect Satan to what they called "the great Satan" of Western society. They claimed, "Mecca has become an island of fear because the Arab world has allowed the corruption of the West to creep in. Islam is being openly attacked by the West. We must unite to drive out this evil."

Livy chuckled slightly, thinking it was about time they felt a little of the terrorism fear the West has had to live under since the 9-11 bombings of the Twin Towers. But she was also frustrated. The liberal media pretended to defend the rights of the Muslim community while the cathedral bombing seemed to be completely forgotten even though it had only occurred one day earlier. It all had a sad irony. The Old Testament from the Bible and the Koran both talked about and eye-for-an-eye but the Islamists only saw it as one sided. Now they were experiencing an eye-for-an-eye retaliation in their own backyard, and they didn't like it.

* * *

Fatih, the warrior from Ann Arbor who had made the pickup at the Denver airport, arrived at the kidnapping hideout with his two Muslim Brotherhood passengers Nawwaf and Rasil. As they entered the building there was no question about who was taking charge. Nawwaf's aggressive demeanor by walking out in front and center told everyone that he was now in charge.

Nawwaf looked around the room and barked questions, "What's the matter with him?" he asked pointing at Yusuf.

"He was shot and has lost lots of blood. We need to get him to a hospital quickly or he will die," replied Husam.

Nawwaf went to Yusuf to take a closer look. He saw that Yusuf was extremely pale and there was a lot of blood around him. "How do you feel?" Nawwaf asked.

No answer. Then Husam answered for him, "He's been passing in and out of consciousness. He's really bad off and we need to get him to a hospital immediately."

Nawwaf, without the slightest sign of emotion, walked over to his checked baggage, pulled out his pistol, walked back over to Yusuf, and shot him in the head. Then, still without emotion, he said, "We can't afford to be seen in a hospital full of cameras. That would give us all away. And he didn't have long to live. I just sped up his journey to Allah."

Nawwaf next directed his attention to the hostages. "Why is that woman naked? Who has been raping her?"

Husam immediately pointed to the now dead Yusuf in an attempt to turn attention away from himself. At the same time he gave an evil eye stare at Fatih, giving him the message to keep quiet.

Nawwaf was not fooled, but he did not let on that he could see through the lie. "If I hear of any of you having sex with an infidel cow I will treat you the way I treated Yusuf." He glared first at Husam and next at Fatih. "Untie her and give her some clothes," Nawwaf commanded.

Husam jumped to attention and rushed to obey the instructions. Nawwaf's gruff demeanor was scaring everyone else in the room.

With that settled Nawwaf continued his dominance by saying, "This place is a dump. I have no intention of staying here. Where do you guys sleep? This is pathetic. I want to move to a new location tonight. Additionally, this is the dumbest place in the world for you to hold out. There is only one road in or out of here. If the cops come in here we'd be completely trapped. We need to find a safer hideout than this." Turning to Fatih and Rasil, he commanded, "Go out and find us a place to stay. Rent a furnished house that is in a somewhat remote location, nothing with close or connected neighbors, and get us moved in immediately. Make sure we have nice mattresses so we can sleep more comfortably."

Looking back at Husam and Fatih, Nawwaf continued, "Do you have cell phones?"

"Yes," they replied simultaneously.

"Are they the ones you used to talk to Sami and Shihab?" he continued.

"Yes. But we keep them turned off."

"You idiots," blurted Nawwaf. "Don't you know that they are probably tracking you right now? Immediately take your phones out of your pockets and remove the batteries. Don't ever use those phones again." Turning to Rasil he said, "Pick up a couple new throw-away phones when you're out. Now go!"

Rasil and Fatih headed for the front door of the shack leaving Nawwaf and Husam behind to stay with the captives.

Chapter Forty-Three

Shihab

November, 2017, Ann Arbor, Michigan

The police station in Ann Arbor became the meeting place for four men in flashy new high-priced suits. After they were all together they approached the desk attended by the sergeant in charge. "What can I do for you?" the sergeant asked.

"We're here to see our client, Imam Shihab," demanded one of the four lawyers who had designated himself as the leader of the group.

"Can't see him now," responded the sergeant. "He's in the interrogation room."

"You can't interrogate him without us present," insisted the lawyer.

"He didn't request your presence."

"That's because you haven't given him a choice."

"He's been read his rights. If he didn't pay attention, it's not our fault."

"Get me your captain," demanded the lawyer. "You obviously aren't familiar with the law in these matters. I demand to speak to your captain immediately."

The sergeant was thoroughly irritated at this point. He showed his irritation by getting up from his desk extra slowly and moving across the office in an exaggeratedly slow pace. When he finally arrived at the captain's office he entered the office and said, "There are four lawyers at the front desk that insist they're here to speak to Shihab. I told them he didn't request any lawyers but they don't seem to care. They're mad at me for refusing them and they insist on speaking to you."

"I don't want to speak to the lawyers of a terrorist," replied the captain. "They're going to try to get him released and we have to try to come up with a reason to continue holding him here. I'll work on that while you take them back to Interview Room Four and then bring Shihab in there as well. We'll have to let them talk to him. There's not much we can do to stop them short of getting ourselves into a lot of trouble. Go ahead and do it."

The sergeant wasn't happy but he already knew this was going to be the result. The lawyers have a way of winning even if it's not in the best interest of the public and in this case it definitely wasn't in the best interest of American citizens.

The sergeant returned to his desk and told the lawyers to follow him. He brought them to Interview Room Four as instructed by his captain and informed them he would get Shihab. Then he left them in the room for over twenty minutes, just because he was irritated with their attitude. After twenty minutes he brought Shihab into the room.

"What took so long?" challenged the lead lawyer.

"Are you telling me how to do my job?" asked the sergeant

"You're obviously stonewalling us. I know it doesn't take that long to bring a prisoner to an interview room," demanded the lawyer.

"You're not the only people I'm taking care of you know. And you're definitely not the favorite."

"Has he been charged with a crime?"

"Yes," was the abrupt response.

"What is the crime," asked the irritated attorney who expected a more detailed response.

"Murder."

Then the irritated attorney barked out, "Get out of here. We need to be left alone with our client."

"Gladly," replied the sergeant as he exited the interview room.

*　*　*

He waited till the sergeant was gone. Then turning to Shihab the lawyer said, "What are they holding you on?"

"They think I killed my wife," replied Shihab.

"Did you?"

"Of course not."

"Don't lie to me. I need the truth so I know what I'm dealing with. Tell me what happened and give me every detail."

"First tell me of your allegiance to Allah."

"We are all Islamists. We are all believers in the Prophet Mohammed as the mouthpiece of Allah." The lead lawyer was speaking but all four of the lawyers were nodding their head in agreement. "Now tell us the truth and don't leave anything out."

Shihab explained, "My wife was giving in to the hype of the masses. She was angry at me for insisting revenge was the only option. She wanted me to give up my fight for Allah. I couldn't have that type of talk in my house. I had to stop it so I slapped her. Apparently it was enough to make her stumble and she fell hitting her head against a corner of the counter. It was Allah's will that she die. Apparently he was upset with her as well. I am just the instrument. Allah decided that she needed to go. I am disappointed because she was a good wife and also a good mother. But if Allah is angry with her and decided to take her, who am I to disagree."

The lawyer spoke up, "This sounds like an accident. It wasn't murder. What evidence do they have to convict you?"

"Nothing. I was the last to leave the house before she was found dead and so they're trying to pin this on me. But in reality they don't have anything that would stick in court."

One of the other lawyers started on a rant, "This is ridiculous. That's why we need our own Islamic legal system and our own courts separate from the U.S. court system. We shouldn't be subjected to these inferior infidel legal constraints. If a wife or child insults Allah it is the responsibility of the husband to deal with the insult. If he does not deal with it then he becomes a participant in the insult. It's just part of the sharia legislation system which is the Islamic moral and religious law as set down by the prophet."

The lead lawyer joined in. "Sharia deals with all the areas of life and many of these topics are addressed by secular law which the government feels they have priority over, like crime, politics, economics, or in this case what they consider to be spouse or child abuse. That's what makes it hard. I agree that sharia law is the higher law and cannot be superseded by secular laws. But we are in an infidel country and we have to manipulate our way around their legal nightmare. The only part of the sharia law that these infidels will allow us to obey are those related to personal behavior such as sexual relations, hygiene, diet, prayer, fasting, etc."

"Sharia is the infallible law of Allah," responded the lawyer who started this rant. "His law is not open to interpretation by man!"

"I agree, but let's get back to the problem at hand. It should be easy to get Shihab out," said the lead lawyer to the other three lawyers. "They have nothing, and even if they did, how can they prove that Shihab did anything. She might have slipped after he left?" Then turning to Shihab he said, "We'll get you out of here in a couple hours. We need to talk to a judge and get bail set. Then we'll be back and come get you out of here."

"Thanks," replied Shihab. "I need to get back to leading prayers at the mosque and to taking care of my family. Can you do one more favor for me?"

"What's that?"

"Can you make sure there is no one doing surveillance in Sami's mosque? I'm sure they have been keeping tabs on me and I don't like it. I want to be able to hold prayer meetings without a lot of infidel cameras staring at me?"

"That's easy enough to do," replied the attorney. "We have a judge who will gladly issue a restraining order against any government surveillance. Then they will have to go to court if they want to reestablish it. We'll have that accomplished for you today."

With that everyone gave the customary farewell greeting and separated; Shihab to his jail cell and the lawyers to their legal duties.

***

Two hours became three, but eventually one of the lawyers came back with the bail money and the court order allowing Shihab to be released. They also informed him they made sure all the surveillance equipment had been removed from around the mosque.

Shihab was irritated. If he had mildly considered revenge in the past, he was now totally committed to it. How dare these infidels reprimand him for following Allah's sharia laws. His wife had committed sacrilege. She had defied the rule of her husband. She needed to die. Shihab felt no sorrow or loss. If she couldn't be obedient, then he didn't want her around.

Shihab's mind reeled in frustration. He wanted to strike back but he didn't know how. He wanted to make a big display that the infidels would never forget. He didn't ever want to be imprisoned by these infidels again. As he drove off he decided he would talk to his congregation and to the Muslim Brotherhood and see what they thought he should do.

Chapter Forty-Four

Does Revenge Work?
November, 2017, Ann Arbor, Michigan

The mosque was jammed with people, and they didn't appear to be very happy. It was Sami's mosque and Shihab had called a meeting of what he referred to as "the warriors of Allah." He started the meeting with the normal prayer ritual. Afterwards he turned to face the congregation in order to give his sermon. He started with a loud commanding voice, "The infidels have risen up against us. Allah requires that we retaliate."

Someone yelled out, "Muslims struck the first blow!"

"The infidels struck the first blow by perverting the ways of Allah. Muslims are required to cleanse the earth of all infidels and their influence!" another voice in the crowd yelled out.

"Don't be surprised if they don't like it and fight back," responded the first voice.

"We must strike back," demanded Shihab, taking control of the conversation in a loud overpowering voice. "The Koran clearly states that we must cleanse the earth of all infidels. The world must be purified of all pollution. The infidels are prostituting our sacred beliefs. Their behavior can no longer be tolerated. And now they are trying to prevent us from performing the cleansing that is required. They have killed Sami and his wives. And my wife is dead and they unjustly threw me in prison for that as well. They are attacking our community. They are attacking our mosques. Soon our mosque will be destroyed just like the mosques in Detroit have been destroyed. We can't sit around and wait for it to happen. We must fight back. And we must fight back now!"

"You're an idiot," blurted out the first heckler. "The Koran also speaks of tolerance and patience. If we take your approach we will see Mecca and every other Islamic holy site in the world destroyed. Enough is enough! No more retaliations!"

"How can you be so blind?" questioned another member of the audience. "Allah requires an eye for an eye."

"But we have killed many more than they have. All we have gained is a lot of destroyed mosques and Medina annihilated. What have we really gained?"

"Silence," blurted out an angry Shihab. "Allah has spoken and we must retaliate."

"Then you be the suicide bomber this time," yelled out the first heckler. "Rather than sacrificing our youth, let's see you put your life on the line for a change."

"Who are you?" demanded an ever-angrier Shihab. "You're probably not even a Muslim. You're probably an infiltrator who is trying to disrupt the harmony of our meeting. Grab him! He is a traitor. He is an infidel."

No one reacted. No one around the heckler made any moves to restrain him.

"What's the matter with you? Grab him and bring him up here."

The heckler continued, "You are a coward! You want everyone to do your dirty work for you. Come down here yourself if you want to see me. Strap on a bomb yourself if you want to blow something up. Quit expecting everyone else to do your dirty work for you, you coward!"

Shihab could see he had lost control. In his mind he raged with the thought, *That's why I didn't want to become an Imam. These people are idiots. They don't understand Allah or the Koran. They are imbeciles.* With that he turned around and stomped out of the auditorium area, heading back to Sami's chambers.

The remainder of the congregation stood there in surprise and shock. This was an extremely unusual turn of events. It was unheard of to challenge the Imam in such a public way. It simply was not done and for the Imam to give up in the middle of the debate was also unusual. The congregation stared at each other in confusion. Then, after a few minutes, they started to disperse, each heading off out of the mosque. It was as if they had lost their direction in life. They didn't know which way to go without the direction given to them by the Imam. Should they try to comfort him? Should they ignore him? But more importantly, was he right? Should they trust his radicalism? Did they really want more destruction, both within the Islamic community and without?

It was as though the Muslim community had developed a rift. There were those who still looked forward to revenge and thought it was the right thing to do, and there were those who no longer thought it was Allah's plan. The Imam of one mosque would often disagree with the Imam of the next mosque. So who was truly speaking the will of Allah? Maybe none of them were. Unfortunately there was no higher Islamic authority to turn to who could resolve this confusion. Mohammed was the last prophet and there would not be any additional revelation to clear up the confusion.

The destruction of mosques in Detroit, along with the destruction in Medina, had stopped many of the Muslim extremists in their tracks. They didn't think Allah would allow this type of an attack. They thought they were protected. They expected an all-powerful Allah to be able to prevent hits on his own worship centers.

But then maybe Allah wanted these places destroyed. Maybe Allah wanted everyone to have a wake-up call. Maybe there was too much divergence and the Muslim believers needed to be shocked into looking for a way to realign their beliefs. There was nothing but maybes. Maybe the true believers were just tired of the destruction and deaths.

A new group started to organize itself in the larger Muslim community. They called themselves Muslim Friends, to differentiate themselves from the Muslim Brotherhood. Their charter was to "stop the deaths of all the children." They saw the Muslim Brotherhood as a threat to Allah's vision for the world. They believed in world unification and world harmony. This would be created by sharing Islam with the infidels, rather than killing them. Their first effort focused on sending out the message on radio, television, in the newspapers, and on billboards that Islam wants peace. Billboards would be made that said

"See what the Koran says about Christ." They wanted to show that Islam was tired of the terrorists who are causing so much death and destruction around the world. They believed it was Islam's responsibility to put an end to the terrorism that their fellow believers were causing in the world. Their campaign message also included a plea for no more retaliatory strikes to occur on either side. They pled for a truce on both sides.

Unfortunately, they knew the message of peace wouldn't convince everyone. The hardest individuals to convince were the Imams within their own community. But they felt they had to try. They didn't want any more mosques destroyed. They didn't want any more believers sacrificed for no good purpose. They wanted the terrorism war to end.

The Muslim Friends were convinced of one thing, that if there were any more strikes against Western targets, there would be retaliation. This terrorism now had two sides to it. The new enemy was willing to indiscriminately attack Islamic targets just the way Islamic radicals had in the past been indiscriminate about their attacks on Western targets.

The only way to stop the attacks on Islam was to have no more attacks against the West. The Muslim Friends knew it and they needed to figure out how to convince the Muslim world to put an end to the violence. But the Muslim Brotherhood had a different view of how the world should look.

Chapter Forty-Five

The Kidnapping Exposed
November, 2017, Golden, Colorado

Rasil and Fatih left the kidnapper's shack and headed to the car. "Is he always like that?" questioned Fatih.

"What do you mean?" asked Rasil in a bit of a grumpy tone indicating he didn't like what Fatih was implying.

"Is it so easy for him to kill someone?"

"Are you not a child of Allah? Death is nothing. He did that guy a favor. He sent him to Allah without going through any more suffering. Allah's warriors should not be afraid. Are you afraid of death?"

"I am not afraid of death. But Nawwaf shot him so easily as though he was nothing."

"He WAS nothing," insisted Rasil. "As a warrior of Allah we must be willing to sacrifice even our lives for the greater good of Allah. No hesitation. No regrets. I see you still have a lot to learn."

"We are always learning," replied Fatih, trying to assure Rasil so he didn't sound so angry.

But Rasil wasn't finished. He used this opportunity to ask, "Whose stupid idea was it to kidnap these infidels? I don't understand why we're going through all this?"

"We were instructed to kidnap one of the close friends of Brian in the hope it would draw Brian out. Or maybe these close friends might even know where he is. But they keep insisting they have no idea where he is. Then we thought these guys may even be part of the NERDS who are behind all these attacks against our Islamic holy sites. But again we didn't have any luck pulling any information out of them."

"Then why are we still holding these hostages?"

"Because we're planning to send out a message to Brian that if he doesn't identify himself to us we'll execute our hostages," explained Fatih.

"This whole kidnapping circus is a nightmare if you ask me," responded Rasil. "We're just going to waste a lot of time at it and still end up with nothing. But we were sent out here to help and so we're going to help. It seems like a horrendous waste of time to me."

Once on the main road the two of them headed further away from Golden, hoping to spot a "for rent" sign on the way. It didn't take them too long before they spotted a "seasonal rental." They called the phone number on the sign and learned that the house was available. They were told to go to a rental office in town. They would need to go there to finalize the paperwork on the rental and to get the keys. They were convinced that Allah was with them or this wouldn't have been so easy. It was a perfect location, slightly isolated so no one would see them, and available immediately.

They headed off into the old town of Golden where the real estate rental office was located. The first order of business was to finalize a new location. After they wrapped that up they would go to the local Superstore Mart where Fatih had already visited earlier in the day and pick up some throwaway phones and food. Next they would need to hijack a van that could be used to transport the hostages.

Having completed the rental process using the fake ID and credit cards that Rasil had available, the two headed to downtown Golden where they found a grocery store which was reasonably busy. The parking lot had a couple full sized vans. Rasil was an expert at breaking into vehicles and hot-wiring them so the switch in vehicles took less than five minutes. They were off again, taking both vehicles so as not to leave the car behind for the police to find. They dropped it off on a remote side-street as they headed to the Superstore Mart.

Superstore Mart shopping was quick and easy. They knew what they wanted: three throwaway cell phones and food which was primarily a collection of snacks. So far they had only been gone a little over an hour. They were ready to head back to the shack.

Their next stop was back to their newly rented house where they off-loaded all their supplies. Then they were ready to pick up their partners and the kidnapped infidels and bring them to this new location. Fatih thought it was a bit extravagant to rent a house just for these infidels, but he knew he would appreciate a good night's sleep so he didn't argue and he knew Nawwaf would insist on better quarters. Nawwaf always felt he deserved a little luxury when he was in the service of Allah.

* * *

"Special Agent Gerick Johannes," was the answer Livy received on her call to the Denver FBI office.

"Hello," responded Livy. "This is Special Agent Livy Cobar from the Washington office." Gerick perked up in his seat. The Washington office never calls. They usually send their messages using e-mail. So anytime the Washington office called it was urgent.

After going through the customary ID checks and password validations, he switched to a secure encrypted line. Then Livy continued, "I'm calling for Alvin, who I'm sure you're familiar with. We have an urgent assignment for your team. This is in relation to the kidnapping of the family of four in Golden. We identified the phone numbers of the kidnappers and we traced their cell phones. We have their location and we need you to get out there quickly. The kidnappers are located in a field on the west end of Golden. I will send you a map showing the specifics. I need you to urgently round up your best team and head out there. Hopefully we can catch them by surprise."

"We're on it," responded Gerick. "Send me the information and we'll get there within the hour. I'll organize my team immediately."

"The map is on the way," replied Livy. "Go and free those hostages!"

Gerick called for an emergency gathering of all available resources. Fifteen minutes later they had all gathered together in a large situation room to get briefed. Gerick described the location of the kidnapping and stressed the need to organize approaches on several fronts. There would need to be a frontal assault as well as a team covering the kidnapper's location from the back in case they tried to escape.

"We don't know if the victims are actually there," explained Gerick. "We have the kidnappers pinpointed in a wilderness area at the west end of Golden. All we know is that their cell phones are at this location. We have to assume the kidnappers and their victims are there as well. I have already sent a pair of agents out to spy the location, but they are not on site yet so we don't have any more information than what I just told you. But we need to get out there and be ready for anything. I'll request the helicopters to come out there for support after we are in position, but I don't want to spook the kidnappers by having helicopters flying around until everything is in place."

With those instructions Gerick organized the teams, gave them their assignments, and sent them off to the kidnappers' location.

* * *

As they traveled back toward Golden using Interstate 70, and connecting with Colorado Highway 58 Fatih and Rasil noticed and overabundance of black Suburbans intermixed with police vehicles heading east. Without a word Rasil immediately picked up his phone and called Nawwaf.

"Yes," Nawwaf curtly responded.

"We have trouble," said Rasil. "There's a wave of cops, I'm guessing FBI, heading your way. Get out of there now!"

Fatih jumped into the conversation and Rasil held the phone over for him to talk, "If you go out the back way there's a bridge that goes over Clear Creek and leads to Highway 6 right above the bike trail. We can pick you up there on the highway rather than coming back to the shack the usual way. There are some wooded areas along that road where we can ditch everyone and hide them out for a few hours until all of this blows over. While they're hiding I'll ditch this van and find a new vehicle. Then we can circle back and pick everyone up."

"Hurry! We'll meet you across the bridge," was all Nawwaf had to say, and Rasil passed the message on to Fatih who was driving.

Fatih accelerated as much as reasonably possible, not wanting to be stopped by highway patrol. Once on Highway 6 they noticed the parade of Suburbans had turned south toward Clear Creek Road. They were convinced the parade was after them. Fatih passed a small parking lot on the left which was used by individuals exercising on the bike trail. Shortly after the parking lot he pulled off the main road, waiting for Nawwaf's arrival.

* * *

Nawwaf was quick to start yelling out commands. "Everybody get up on your feet! We need to leave immediately!" Then to Husam he yelled, "Untie them quickly and you carry the smallest child!"

"I'm not a babysitter!" complained Husam.

"Kill the child if anyone tries to escape," commanded Nawwaf, making sure his instructions were loud enough for his prisoners to hear. "Now let's go!"

"What about him?" asked Husam, pointing at the dead body of Yusuf.

"He is with Allah now."

"But he must be buried as soon as possible," comment Husam, referring to the Muslim requirement of a quick burial.

"We're going to have to let the infidels do it for us."

Everyone responded quickly to Nawwaf's aggressive commands. The threat to kill the child had registered harshly with Glenn and Cynthia. Husam untied the two captives and grabbed the smallest child. They were all quick to respond. They were out the door in seconds.

"Where's the bridge?" Nawwaf asked Husam who shrugged his shoulders.

"In that direction," jumped in Glenn, pointing toward the northwest. He was familiar with the bike trail and had been in this area in the past. His concern for his family had encouraged him to help. He didn't want to be caught in the middle of a shootout.

"Hurry!" urged Nawwaf aggressively.

Everyone started jogging in the direction Glenn had pointed. It wasn't long before they found themselves crossing the bridge. Luckily it was abandoned. There was very little bike traffic in the middle of the workday.

Once on the bridge the brush and undergrowth helped them to be hidden from the shack they had just left. As they crossed the bridge they heard several vehicles arriving at the shack they had just vacated. Someone with a megaphone was yelling, "You are surrounded. Throw out your weapons and come out with your hands up."

The kidnappers and their hostages knew the FBI was close behind them. After they were across the bridge they could hear dogs barking. Apparently the FBI had dogs and they were now tracking them. They could hear the dogs getting closer and closer.

"Get behind these bushes and keep out of sight until the car gets here!" barked Nawwaf. He saw a van coming his way and didn't realize it was his compatriots so he ducked behind a tree. Just then his phone rang.

"We are here," commented Rasil. "We are driving a white van. Where are you?"

Nawwaf, realizing the van was the vehicle for their escape, jumped out from his hiding spot and started waving his hands. The van came to a stop next to Nawwaf and the sliding doors on the side of the van opened.

"Hurry and get in!" yelled Nawwaf. The hostages and Husam jumped in the van and sat on the floor around the exterior of the van.

"Stop or we'll shoot!" the FBI chasing them yelled at them. But Nawwaf was not interested in yielding to the command.

"Move it!" yelled Nawwaf at the driver as he struggled to close the sliding van door when the vehicle jerked forward.

Several shots were fired, one striking the driver side window and going out through the front window. But no shots were fired at the body of the van itself for fear that one of the hostages would get hit.

The kidnappers and their victims had made their escape, just in the nick of time.

Chapter Forty-Six

Reconciliation
November, 2017, Golden, Colorado

Livy arrived in Golden feeling she had successfully suppressed any videos of the Dragon Pit members visiting the mosques. Now that she was taken off of that part of the investigation there was little else she could do. She also felt she had successfully identified the terrorist who destroyed the cathedral. It was time to get back to her studies at the Colorado Engineering School. She also felt an obligation to Jonathan who seemed to be trying hard to improve their relationship. He would call every night and talk to her about her day. He would even act interested in how her day went and he would ask her questions about her investigations and her findings.

Livy felt comfortable sharing with Jonathan because he was sworn to secrecy in the FBI just like she was. She didn't want to squash his enthusiasm by holding back. If he really thought their relationship could work, she should at least give it a reasonable try.

After landing at the Denver airport Livy called Jonathan but ended up talking to an answering machine. "Let me know if you want to meet for lunch," was Livy's short and to-the-point message.

Then she placed a call to Alvin. Livy and Alvin had just learned about the failed rescue attempt. They were upset when they learned that their Denver on-the-ground team had missed the kidnappers and their hostages by just seconds. But they were relieved to learn that the family was still alive. "So what do we do next?" asked Livy.

"We do what we can," replied Alvin. "We managed to pull a partial on the license plate and we know what type of vehicle it was. It shouldn't take too long to track down the vehicle and see where that leads us."

"And who was the dead person in the shack?"

"It was one of the guys that Sami sent from Ann Arbor. It looks like he was executed. He had a bad leg wound and had lost a lot of blood so I think they just executed him so they would not need to be bothered with him any longer."

"That's horrific. Those guys never fail to surprise me."

"It didn't surprise me. Those guys have been brutal since day one."

"Since I'm on the ground here in Denver now please keep me posted in case there is something I can do to help," suggested Livy. "As you already know, I have a personal interest in this case."

"I understand and will do," agreed Alvin. "Talk to you later."

During the conversation with Alvin, Livy had received a phone message from Jonathan. Listening to the message she learned he had recommended a restaurant in the Golden area near her home. He stated he was still at the site of the kidnapping which was west of Golden but he was wrapping up his part of the activities and she should let him know when she arrived in Golden so they could meet for lunch.

* * *

As Livy entered the Golden area using Highway 58 she texted Jonathan and told him she would be arriving at the Old Capital Grill on Washington Street in Old Town Golden in about ten minutes.

Jonathan replied with a text, "I'm on my way."

She arrived first and went to a table to wait for him. She ordered a diet Coke and ordered him a beer. He arrived a few minutes later and greeted her with a hug.

"How was your trip?" he asked her.

"I'm numb and wore out," she replied. "Flying has become part of my daily routine and there really isn't a good or bad about my trips anymore. They just happen, like driving down the street."

"Well then, what's new in DC? Have they identified any of the attackers?"

Livy went on to explain how each of the three attacks, the one in Orlando, the one in North Dakota, and the one on the Detroit cathedral, were all suicide bombers coming from the same mosque in Ann Arbor. She also broke down and shared a little more than she had planned to share. "You have to keep this totally a secret but the attacks on the mosques in Detroit were carried out by the Dragon Pit."

"What?" exclaimed Jonathan. "Are you saying that those geeks that you go to school with actually carried out all those bombings on the mosques and on Medina? That's outrageous! They should be arrested immediately. They killed several people including some FBI agents. Why aren't we going after them? I was wondering what the story was behind Brian going missing like that. I knew there had to be a story behind it. But this is too much. Which side are these guys on anyway? They are becoming their own version of vigilante terrorists? Let's go get them immediately."

"I can't go after them. I'm one of them."

Jonathan was dumbfounded. He sat back in his chair and just stared at her. He was at a loss for words. "Are you telling me that my girlfriend is a terrorist?"

"I prefer freedom fighter. Or possibly avenger. We only execute attacks if there is an attack on us."

"But that doesn't make it right! Muslims are people too, even if you don't like how they think."

Livy was dumbstruck. Up to now Jonathan had always made statements that were supportive of finding a way to end the terrorist attacks. But now he was sounding as if he was more concerned about the welfare of the Muslim community. She pulled back and wished she hadn't exposed this information to him. She suddenly felt uncertain about how he would react. Having already opened the door, she pushed him further to test his loyalties and identify where he stood. She invented a story to test his resolve. "They're planning another attack on the mosques in Ann Arbor and they could use your help. Would you like to join them?"

"What?" Jonathan's emotion showed in his voice. "You want me to be a terrorist too? Do you really believe this fighting fire with fire nonsense is going to do anything but get more people killed? This is unbelievable. I should report you right now."

"Go ahead," challenged Livy, picking up her phone and calling his bluff. "Do you want me to dial the number for you?"

Jonathan stood up as if to leave. "I have to think this over. I'm not sure what I should do. I'm supposed to be fighting terrorists, not living with one. I suppose your guys had something to do with the execution of the two Muslim girls here in Golden."

"No idea what you're talking about," Livy claimed innocence. She was certain she had already given out too much information. This wasn't turning out the way she had imagined. Something was terribly wrong here.

"The two girls that were brutally killed in their own beds! You can't tell me you don't know anything about that. Was it your guys?"

"What would that have to do with anything?" Livy responded, trying to throw Jonathan off that line of thinking. "That doesn't sound like a fighting-fire-with-fire type response."

"Whatever," snorted Jonathan as he turned away and headed for the door.

"So much for fixing up this relationship," mumbled Livy to herself. Then, apologizing to the waiter she said, "Guess we won't be eating after all. Sorry."

Livy was struck with a thought and made a quick call to her FBI team in the DC area. Edward answered the phone and she explained her concern about Jonathan's loyalties without giving away any information about the Dragon Pit. Edward asked, "Are you telling me that you were playing house with our mole and that you were the primary leak? What are you thinking we should do?" he asked her.

"No comment! But can you have someone track his cell phone," she replied. "Let's see where he goes and who he talks to."

"I'll have to get Alvin's approval first. I'll have him let you know if we see something unusual."

"That's fine," responded Livy, wishing she had gone directly to Alvin to begin with. Working with Edward just complicated the process.

During their conversation Livy received a message that she needed to go back to Detroit. New videos of the cathedral bombing had been discovered and she needed to do a review of the tapes. She left and directly headed for the airport, all the time feeling frustrated and confused over her conversation with Jonathan.

Chapter Forty-Seven

The Van
November, 2017, Golden, Colorado

The van was bare bones and had been used for construction. There were bits of gravel and debris on the floor. For Cynthia, who wore nothing but a blood soaked nightshirt and pajama pants, the rocks felt like knife pricks into her legs and butt. The children were uncomfortable as well and they decided to sit on the comfort of Cynthia's lap, which made her even more uncomfortable. Their weight pushed her down on the pebbles in the van and added to the pain. But she didn't want to complain. If she made a fuss then their captors might remember that they hadn't tied up their hostages. If they decided to tie them up again then it would be even more uncomfortable.

Glenn had on a pair of jeans and the pain for him wasn't as poignant. He tried to get at least one of the children to come sit on him and thereby ease the pain on Cynthia, but they would have none of it. They insisted on having the comfort of their mom. Somehow moms generated more comfort and reassurance than dads.

Fatih was driving and Rasil was in the passenger seat. Husam and Nawwaf sat in the back of the cargo van on the floor with the hostages. Husam wished he could be the one snuggling up against Cynthia's breasts but he knew these Muslim Brotherhood guys were too straight laced to allow him to have any fun.

"Where are we going?" yelled Nawwaf at the two in the front. He had to be loud enough to be heard over the street noise.

"We have a slight problem," replied Rasil. "We were heading up into the mountains when we picked you up, but unfortunately the place we rented is in the other direction. And we don't dare go back the way we

Gerhard Plenert

came, so we need to find another way to circle around and head back to our new hide out."

"Have you figured it out yet?" yelled Husam. "It's not very comfortable back here."

"It looks like there's no quick way around this," responded Rasil. "We still have a long drive ahead of us. Highway 6 circles left up here and connects with Interstate 70, which will take us back into the Denver area. That's really our only option if we're going to avoid meeting up with the FBI."

"We don't want all the details," barked Husam, "we just want to get there."

"Watch your mouth," challenged Rasil, "or I may have to do something about it."

"Lay off you two," ordered Nawwaf. "Just get us to this place you set up."

The place they had rented was on Pine Ridge Road north of Golden. The shortest route would take them directly through the area where the FBI was now searching and where the previous hideout was located. That would be a very risky move so the team decided it would be better to spend an extra hour of travel time just to avoid the area. They traveled on Interstate 70 until it connected with Highway 58. At that point they headed west toward Golden and took Highway 15 north. West 60th Ave became West 58th Ave and connected with Highway 93. Taking this highway south they jumped on West 56th Ave which finally connected them to Pine Ridge Road. Heading south a short distance they were able to arrive at the newly rented hideout. The entire trip had tripled the travel time, but they were safe.

Using the garage door opener provided by the rental agency, they opened the garage door as soon as they hit the driveway. They drove the van into the garage and quickly shut the garage door behind them. Then it was finally time for all the travel-weary passengers to unload.

The back corner bedroom, which had the smallest window, became the new prison for the hostages. Husam went to work tying the hands and legs of the two adults. He left the door open so he could keep watch on them.

In the meantime Rasil and Fatih were busy in the kitchen trying to assemble something worth eating. It was mostly snacks, but they were quite happy having a bag of chips and calling it dinner. Rasil threw a couple bags of Lays potato chips on the bed with the hostages and told the children to feed their parents. Then the four kidnappers huddled in the living room to strategize.

Nawwaf, the alpha male leader of the group, started the conversation. "Tell me again. Why are we holding these hostages?"

Husam, who decided he was superior to Fatih, responded, "We were trying to get information about one of their close friends, a guy named Brian, who was behind the bombing of Medina. We're not one hundred percent sure but we think he is also the one who dropped that plane in Mecca."

"And did you get the information?" barked Nawwaf.

"I don't think they know anything," responded Husam. "Then we thought maybe we would be able to draw Brian out if he knew we were holding them as hostages."

"Who told you that these individuals would know anything?" asked Nawwaf.

"We had a Muslim sister who lived close to Brian and who had seen them together regularly with our hostages," explained Husam. "Unfortunately she was one of the two girls who were brutally executed a few days back. She is the one who put us on the trail of these guys. After determining that these guys really don't know anything, we decided to hold them as ransom for information, insisting that if we don't hear from Brian or from someone who can tell us his whereabouts we'll execute them."

"Did that get you any results?"

"We haven't tried it yet. We were about to do that when you guys showed up and took over."

"Do we know who any of the other members of this group are?" asked Nawwaf.

"No," responded Husam. "We have a list of Brian's friends, but we don't know if any of them are part of this terrorist group. We don't even know for sure if these guys are connected with the terrorists that are attacking us. All we know is that they're close friends of Brian and we're using that knowledge to try to get at the ringleader. Brian is the only guy that we know for sure is involved and so we're trying desperately to get in contact with him."

"How do you plan to get the message out there to let Brian know?"

Husam looked stumped so Fatih suggested, "By posting a message on U-Tube and then letting the media know about the message."

"This is the stupidest operation ever. It doesn't make sense that we spend all these resources and get two people killed just to kidnap a family that might be able to get somebody to come and help them. This is ridiculous! There are a lot of better ways to go about this but at this point we're stuck with these hostages. Here is what we're going to do," commanded Nawwaf. "We're going to place a call to one of the local news stations using one of these throw-away phones. We're going to disguise our voice with a rag. We're going to tell them that unless we hear from Brian within twenty-four hours we're going to kill the hostages."

"Can't hurt to try," confirmed Rasil. "What if we do get access to Brian? Then what are we going to do? Of course kill him, but then what? Is there a bigger objective here, like showing these attackers that we've outsmarted them and that they better not try anything again? What is the big goal here? Killing Brian seems trivial. That's just one infidel. We need the whole cell."

"My point exactly," responded Nawwaf. "What are we doing here? We have bigger problems in the world to solve than getting you university idiots out of the mess you created for yourselves. We have these hostages and we know there is a connection with this group that is terrorizing us, which has to be bigger than just this Brian who flies planes. The mosque bombings in Detroit took at least two people to execute, and it's highly unlikely that Brian was one of them since he is in hiding somewhere. The same is true of the execution of our brave sisters here in Golden. So let's make our demand bigger than Brian. Let's make it something that will get us at the heart of this terrorist group which is terrorizing Allah and subverting his will."

"So what do you suggest?" asked Fatih.

"I want revenge. I want confirmation that these guys were the terrorists that destroyed Median and our mosques. I want confirmation that this was a CIA plot. I want an apology from the President of the United States that this should not have happened. And I want the United States to compensate the families of the dead and rebuild Medina. I want a commitment that the United States will control its citizens and not allow this type of terrorism in the future."

"So let's script our message," suggested Rasil. "What are we going to say in our message to the media?"

Nawwaf repeated, "We'll say that we have a list of demands which includes information about the location of Brian and his family, information about the other members of this American terrorist cell that Brian was a part of, confirmation that the CIA and FBI are behind the attacks in Medina and Detroit, an apology from the President of the United States, remuneration to the families of the dead in Detroit and Medina, and reconstruction of Medina. What do you think? Does that seem like a reasonable list of demands? And our threat will be that if they do not meet these demands we will start killing the members of this family, starting with the youngest."

"Understood," assured Rasil who was frantically taking notes as Nawwaf spoke. "I'll craft the message and then make the call to the media. We'll see how they react to the message."

Rasil wrote out the message, then took a phone and went into one of the bedrooms to relay his message. He covered the phone with a cloth and then placed the call. He placed his first call to the ABC newsroom and read off his demands. Then he decided to also send the message to a conservative news station like the FOX network where he did the same. After the calls he disassembled the phone and removed the SIM card. The phone was now dead and the demands had been made.

Rasil returned to the living room where his companions were watching television. He had them switch to ABC to see how long it would take them to broadcast the headline news they had just received.

His wait wasn't too long. Networks like ABC loved saying they had an "exclusive" that no one else had. They were still living in the dark ages thinking that someone actually cared who was first with a story. But this time they were first and they made sure everyone knew it. They also used one of their favorite words, "shocking", about twenty times in the news clip. The headline said the kidnappers had given the FBI a series of demands, and if these demands weren't met they would kill the hostages. Then they switched to their "experts" who analyzed the message and who spent ten times more time giving their opinions about the message than was spent actually sharing the message. There wasn't a lot of confusion in the message. But by the time the experts were done with it a great deal of confusion had set in.

The news reported that the FBI refused to comment when they were asked about the report. The news media knew the FBI hadn't even heard about the demands so it was a little difficult to expect them to comment. Nevertheless the news reporter made it sound like the FBI was incompetent or that they were hiding something.

Nawwaf high-fived Rasil. "Success!" Nawwaf exclaimed. "The message has been received. Now let's see how they react to the message."

"And if they don't react?" questioned Rasil.

"Then we kill the hostages and our two worthless Muslim brothers and get the heck out of here," whispered Nawwaf so that the college students didn't hear. "This is small potatoes and we're not going to waste our time here any longer."

"You have my agreement on that."

Chapter Forty-Eight

A Crisis
November, 2017, Golden, Colorado

Livy was on an encrypted conference call with Alvin and several members of his team including Edward. "These demands are ludicrous," stressed Alvin emphatically. "They want confirmation of guilt from all the agencies and from the White House. That will never happen. And then they want us to give up the people that executed these counterattacks. Again that's something we won't do, even if we knew who they were, and we don't." Alvin was pretending to not know about the Dragon Pit team because there were FBI agents on the phone who had no business knowing about the team. "We'll broadcast a message that we would like to sit down and talk to them about their demands. We'll suggest that some of them are within our ability to comply, but some of them are beyond our ability to comply and therefore we can't commit to them. But we're open to negotiating a compromise."

"I just hope they're willing to have a conversation," responded Livy. "These guys are crazy and are capable of doing anything."

Edward chimed in, "They are setting their demands high in the hopes that they will get something from us. There is probably only one of those demands that they really want, probably the one about who the members of this retaliatory hit squad are."

"Either way, we can't tell them something we don't know," stressed Alvin.

"But can't we find out who they are? If we focused on identifying that team we should be able to negotiate a deal with these terrorists. I can't believe we don't have at least one video showing these guys." Edward aimed the comment at Livy who was the video screener.

"Even if we had the video, we're not going to give up one set of Americans for another," jumped in Livy. "We don't negotiate with terrorists. And that's final." Since she was one of the members of the team, she had a special interest in not giving up their names. It wouldn't be reasonable to give up one member of the NERDS team in order to free a different member of the team. "That wouldn't make any sense. As for the videos, we were assuming these were going to be westerners dressed in western clothes. What if the guys that blew up the mosques were dressed as Muslims? What if they were Muslims?"

"That's nuts," barked Edward. "Why would Muslims blow up their own places of worship?"

"To ignite a holy war," jumped in Alvin. "It wouldn't be the first time something like that happened. There are several examples in Syria and Egypt where revolutionaries blew up their own people so they could blame it on the incumbents. In Syria they even used chemical and biological weapons on their own people and then blamed it on the administration just to get world sympathy. The Muslims don't value life in the same way that we do."

"I don't buy it," chimed in a resistant Edward. "The whole thing doesn't make sense to me. Are you suggesting they also bombed Medina?"

"The Saudi's already destroyed it once and rebuilt it in order to avoid idolatry. I'm just throwing out an alternative scenario which I think we must realistically consider," responded Livy. "But back to the demands. I think we should do as Alvin suggested and post a message that would open up some form of negotiation."

"Good enough," replied Alvin. "I'll post the message by contacting the same news media people they used for their post and hopefully they are watching for the reactions to their post. By the way, Livy, did you learn anything new in Detroit?"

"Nothing," was her response. "Coming out here was a waste of time. I'm done here and heading back to Denver. Maybe I can help find the hostages and do some good there."

* * *

Alvin posted a message on U-Tube and called the ABC and FOX news stations stating he would like to negotiate a truce with the kidnappers. After several hours of monitoring the site, he still had not received a response. This process continued on through the night, anxiously waiting for a response.

The following morning started a day filled with jittery nerves. Alvin and his entire team were worried that the message had not been received or was being ignored.

Alvin crafted a second message and stressed that he wanted desperately to talk to the kidnappers. Again there was no response.

Finally, at about eleven a response was posted which said, "Time is running out and we have no patience for negotiating anything. Our demands are final and if they cannot be met, you won't be seeing our hostages alive again."

An FBI team was in place at both of the news stations that had previously received the message in the hope that they could somehow trace the call back to its source. But the attempt was futile. The call was too quick and the cell phone they had used for the call was immediately disconnected after the call. The call lasted long enough to confirm that it originated in the Denver area, but that was all they had time for. There would be no lead coming from that source.

The message was scary for everyone, especially for Livy and Alvin and the remainder of the Dragon Pit team. However, there was no chance that the requirements could be met so Alvin placed a final and desperate post which said, "We cannot give you something we do not have. Please communicate with us so we can come up with an equitable solution. We need you to request things we have access to and we would willingly work with you to identify what you need and what we are capable of supplying. Please contact us at 999-999-9999."

Alvin suspected this was a futile attempt to negotiate a reasonable outcome. He was desperate to find a solution to the problem. But he was at a loss as to how to come up with a solution without a conversation with the kidnappers. All he could do was wait and see what would happen.

* * *

Nawwaf received a phone call which he answered immediately, "Hello."

"This is a friend to the Brotherhood," answered the voice at the other end of the line. "They gave me this phone number so I could talk to you directly. I am faithful to Allah and I work within the FBI. I'm calling to let you know that the FBI is doing nothing to satisfy your demands. They are waiting for you to cave in. They think you really don't want everything you are demanding."

"What do you know about Brian or any of the other members of this NERD group?" asked Nawwaf. "Can you get any inside information about them?"

"I don't think the FBI knows who the NERDS are," replied the caller. "And they don't know Brian's location. Or else they have been extremely successful in hiding the information, which is very unusual within the FBI. Usually they like to brag about information like that."

"Thank you friend for this information," replied Nawwaf. "I suspected as much. I will quit wasting my time here and move on to other things." With that he disconnected the phone call.

Nawwaf grabbed one of the automatic weapons that was lying on the kitchen table and went into the bedroom where the hostages were assembled. Without a word he aimed the rifle at the hostages, starting with the father, and put several rounds into each of them over the screams of the children who had to suffer through the horror of watching their parents executed before they were also killed.

Nawwaf walked toward each of the four bodies to make sure they were dead. Then he left the bedroom and shut the door. He walked back into the kitchen where he found several questioning faces. "What just happened?" asked Rasil.

"We have an informant within the FBI and he told me the FBI was not taking us seriously," replied Nawwaf. "I have no wish to hold out here for days just to learn that we're not going to get any information on this band of terrorist renegades we are searching for, so I just accelerated the inevitable. Now we can leave this United States hell hole of iniquity and go home."

But Nawwaf wasn't finished. He was still holding the automatic rifle and he quickly aimed it at Fatih and Husam, firing several rounds into each of their chests as they looked on in total surprise. Then he said to Rasil, "Now we don't have to worry about any leaks. We've cleaned up the mess here. We're just going to leave everyone laying here and in a few weeks someone will come around and notice the rent isn't getting paid or whatever, and then it will be too late for them to react. Let's get going."

"But we owe them a burial within twenty-four hours of their death," objected Rasil, referring to Fatih and Husam.

"We'll leave the infidels to take care of that." He was selective in what pieces of the doctrine he chose to follow. Some aspects of the Koran he took very seriously, but other parts he tended to ignore, like the requirement to bury believers within twenty-four hours. His passion for the Koran also had an element of convenience connected with it. He followed those elements that were convenient at the time.

Rasil knew better than to make a fuss. He knew Nawwaf would have no problem leaving him lying on the ground next to his Muslim friends. A few minutes later they were pulling out of the driveway and heading back to the airport, again avoiding the area near the original hideout shack where they knew the FBI would still be active.

They remembered that the earlier van had been spotted during the previous escape from the shack and by now every police officer in the area would have been notified to be on the lookout for the one they were in now. So they knew they would need to switch out their current vehicle and find another mode of transportation to take them to the airport. "Let's do the unexpected," suggested Rasil. "They're going to expect us to steal another vehicle. What if we took a taxi to the airport? I think that would completely throw everyone off. They wouldn't expect that. In fact they would probably think we stayed in the area and they would continue searching Denver."

"I like that," responded Nawwaf, "I remember seeing a train station not far from here. I think it was in the 58th and Broadway area. That would be a perfect place to pick up a taxi."

It wasn't long before Nawwaf and Rasil were sitting in an ironically named Freedom Cab on their way to the airport.

* * *

The twenty-four hour deadline came and went, and there was no additional communication from the kidnappers. Livy was frantic, but she had no alternative except to wait. She contacted the Denver office to see if their search of the kidnapper's hideout had revealed anything. It was a waste of time. They had nothing but the body of one dead Arab from the shack. They knew the hostages had been there which gave everyone the reassurance that the hostages should still be alive. But beyond that there was nothing useful.

A helicopter had been dispatched to chase the van which was spotted leaving the area with what seemed to be the hostages and the kidnappers. But a delay in getting the helicopter off the ground meant they were too late and never found anything. Roadblocks had also been set up in the immediate area surrounding the escape. But these were also too little, too late. It began to seem like the bad guys were always ten seconds ahead of the FBI and the good guys just could not catch a break.

Chapter Forty-Nine

Turmoil
November, 2017, Golden, Colorado

With Alvin's approval, Livy headed back to Denver to take over the kidnapping investigation and the search for her friends. She wasn't sure she would be able to do anything any better than what was already being done, but she just needed to be in the middle of the action. She felt guilty for not being more involved. She felt personally responsible for each of the tragedies that had befallen the Dragon Pit team. Brian and his family were now in hiding somewhere and Glenn and his family were prisoners to a terrorist group. This wasn't the way any of this was expected to go down. But unfortunately it was the situation they now had to deal with.

The other tragedy in Livy's life was Jonathan. He refused to answer her calls or text messages. She needed to know his feelings, but he wasn't willing to share, which caused her to be depressed. She had mixed feelings about his rejection. It was more than just the loss of a close friend. She worried that he would somehow betray the Dragon Pit. She feared that somehow the bad guys would get the names of the members and they would all be subject to kidnapping or worse. She needed to talk to him and try to win him over to her line of thinking. She never expected him to be so strongly opposed to what she was doing that it would put the entire Dragon Pit members at risk. She would go out of her way to make sure she had a conversation with him and returning to Denver would hopefully give her that chance.

Flying from Detroit she landed in the Denver airport and headed toward the airport-parking garage where she had left her car. As she walked along the airport lobby she passed two Arabic looking individuals. It wasn't unusual to encounter Arabs, but something about these two seemed different. One caught her eye and gave her a smile and a wink. "Pervert," was the thought that popped into Livy's mind.

In the parking garage she quickly found her car. She had lost it in the parking lot enough times that now she always parked in approximately the same spot. She had a similar problem with her keys at home and a multitude of other things. She was now creating a discipline of always putting things into the same place and it was saving her a lot of time.

Once in the car she drove off heading directly to the Denver FBI office. Along the way she sent a text to the lead agent in the Denver office, Gerick Johannes. His response indicated that he was just returning from the kidnapper's shack and he would meet her at the office. Without the two of them specifically stating it, Gerick already knew what the focus of the conversation was going to be.

After parking in the parking garage under the FBI building Livy headed for the elevator and went up. She departed the elevator and headed straight to Gerick's office. The door was open and she entered the office, closed the door, and approached his desk.

Gerick jumped up and put out his hand to greet her, "It's good to finally meet you. We've talked on the phone several times but now we meet in person." Gerick had been transferred to this office a few months earlier and had not crossed paths with Livy even though he had heard a lot about her. He also knew she was connected to Jonathan. He wasn't sure how that mixed with office politics so he wanted to feel her out before he passed judgment.

"Same here," Livy responded. She was also a little uncertain on how the relationship with Jonathan was going to influence her work with Gerick. But she had no intention of letting Jonathan's recent tantrum affect her focus on recovering the hostages which she hoped were still alive.

"How can I help?" asked Gerick.

"Start with an update on what you learned from the kidnap site."

"Not as much as you would hope," started Gerick. "The hostages were definitely there and they were seen entering a white van which escaped. It was on the other side of a river across a small footbridge and our vehicles couldn't get around the river quick enough to chase them. We deployed a helicopter but we didn't want it to come too early and spook the kidnappers, and by the time it finally did arrive, it was too late and they never found their tail. Roadblocks weren't successful either. They produced nothing. We didn't have all our avenues covered when we dove into this and so they escaped. It all just happened too quickly. Our invasion of the kidnap site was not well planned. It happened at the last minute in a rush.

"We thought there were four kidnappers, but the numbers aren't adding up. One was killed in a freeway crash, and one was shot in the shack, apparently by another one of the kidnappers, and left there in the shack. But one of my agents saw two individuals he identified as kidnappers enter the van, and there was another one driving. What concerns us is that they must be getting reinforcements somewhere. The two dead kidnappers were definitely part of the terrorist cell that was connected with Sami, the Imam in Ann Arbor, Michigan. And we suspect that two of the other three were connected to them was well based on the information we received from our informant in Ann Arbor, the individual who came to us from the cell but was later killed. That covers all the guys we saw climbing into the van. But there was someone in the driver's seat of the van. Who was the guy in the van? We're not sure. And are there more? Were there still others in the van that we did not see?"

"What have you used to locate the hostages?" questioned Livy.

"Mostly cell phone tracking. We don't have much else. We found the location of this shack by cell phone tracking as you know, but apparently someone was smart enough to kill all the phones and now we have nothing. We've put out an APB so we have every cop in the Denver area looking for this van, but it's a needle in a haystack. There are a lot of white vans in Denver. We're not even sure they're still in this area. All we know is that the phones they used for their communications with the news media places them in this area. But that doesn't necessarily mean that the hostages are still in this area."

Just then Gerick's desk phone rang and he decided to answer the call, "Yes?"

After listening for a short period of time Gerick said, "Thanks for the update." Then, turning to Livy he said, "They found the van at a train station. It's empty but there are definite signs it was used to transfer the hostages. We also went to the homes of the two remaining Sami cell terrorists in Ann Arbor. They wouldn't talk to us or give us pictures so we went to the Department of Motor Vehicles and to the university. From there we picked up ID pictures of the two individuals and we're going to see if anyone recognizes these two individuals, but again it's a long shot."

"Are there video cameras outside the train station that may have photographed the arrival of the van?" asked Livy.

"Good thought. I'll put someone on that right away." He picked up the phone and made a quick call giving instructions to collect any recordings of the outside of the train station.

"I want to become an integral part of this process. I have no interest in interfering with your job, I'm sure you know what you're doing, but I have certain areas of expertise that may be able to help. For example, I am really good at video analysis and if you can get me those videos I'd like to take a quick first shot at them."

"Excellent. That's an area where we're not all that well staffed so it would really help. And don't feel like you're interfering. We can use all the help we can get. This is a frustrating case for us. It's the first time our office has had to deal with terrorists from a terrorist cell. But I could use your help in giving me a little more information in one area, and I hope you don't think I'm intruding, but I need to understand your relationship with Jonathan. Is that going to be a problem with you working here?"

"Quite honestly, I don't know," replied Livy. "We parted on bad terms the last time we were together. I'm not sure where his head is at right now. I personally don't have a problem in working with him, but he might. I wish I could give you some assurances that there won't be a problem, but I feel I must be honest with you. I really don't know how

this will affect his work performance. As for me, I am focused on resolving this kidnapping and nothing is going to interfere with that."

"Well that doesn't leave me all warm and fuzzy," responded a disappointed Gerick. "I was hoping for a different message. But I appreciate your honesty. That way I now know better what I'm dealing with. In the meantime, let me introduce you to our lab where you'll hopefully find all the equipment you need in order to analyze any videos that should be coming across."

"Perfect," responded Livy as they both stood up and exited Gerick's office.

* * *

Livy sat at a desk provided by Gerick and checked e-mails and other messages waiting for some videos to come her way. After about an hour she received the message that several video recordings were in route to the Denver office and that she should be getting them within the next thirty minutes. The videos had come from several locations including office buildings across the street.

She placed a call to Alvin in the Washington office to see if there were any updates from that end. Unfortunately he had nothing useful to add. Then there was Jonathan. How was she going to handle his obvious rejection? She decided she would start by pretending that nothing had happened, that nothing was wrong. His reaction to a neutral message would tell her a lot. She sent a text message that said, "I am back in town at the Denver office." She hoped he would react in some way indicating whether there was anything to be concerned about. He didn't answer right away. So she waited.

The videos arrived and Livy immediately took them to the lab and went to work. They were from security cameras outside the train station and from some of the shops across the street. She used pictures that were taken of the "crime scene" where the van was left in an attempt to zero in on any activities surrounding the van.

She found that one of the cameras pointed directly at the location of the van. Then it became a matter of just backing up the video to find the spot when the van arrived on the scene. It didn't take long before she had a clear picture of the van arriving and two individuals getting out of the van. She could see the driver clearly. The passenger was a little harder to see because he was on the opposite side of the van from where she was looking.

She zoomed in on the driver in hopes that she would be able to get a picture that was clear enough to distribute. As the picture encrypted itself she said, "Oh my gosh! I just saw this guy at the airport."

She immediately charged into Gerick's office to tell him what she had found. "These guys were trying to throw us off track. They want us to think they took the train. But instead I see them getting out of their van and getting into a taxi. And I saw them at the airport, probably ctching a flight, not more than two hours ago. They may still be at the airport now waiting for a flight. Can you get agents and the airport police to go search for them?"

"Absolutely," responded Gerick emphatically. "I'll get them going on it right away. Can you tell me where you saw them?"

"It was near gate B21. They were heading in the direction where the gate numbers increased."

"Excellent. That will narrow the search considerably. Hopefully they aren't on a flight that already took off."

Gerick went to work making calls to the airport police and to agents in the area. He transmitted the picture of the terrorist to all these individuals and the picture started popping up on their phones immediately.

Then Gerick turned to Livy and said, "Even though we didn't get a clear picture of the second individual, I can tell from the profile and from his stature that neither of these guys are the guys from the cell in Ann Arbor. Where did they come from? How are they involved? And what happened to the two guys that we know about and that come from the Ann Arbor cell? I have more questions than I have answers."

"Interesting," responded Livy. "I would assume the other two kidnappers are still with the hostages. This gets messier by the minute. Let's try to get IDs on these guys."

Chapter Fifty

The Flight
November, 2017, Denver to Detroit

Airport police were quick to react. They cordoned off the exits beyond Gate B21 and sent several agents on a waiting room seat-by-seat search looking at each of the passengers from B21 upwards. Next they contacted each of the airline desk agents for any flights that had left in the last hour, showing them the picture and asking if they had boarded these individuals. Initially they seemed to be wasting their time. But at one of the terminal desks they were referred to an agent that was still on the gangway. The police waited for her to come through the security door and, when asked if she recognized the individuals in the picture she informed them she had boarded them on a plane that left about thirty minutes earlier headed for Detroit.

The airport police notified the FBI and the FBI rushed to the gate to also talk to the agent. In the meantime the agent had located the passenger manifest and had pulled up the name of the individuals. "I remember these guys because they looked so creepy. It was as if they looked right through you," said the airline agent.

"So there were two of them. Describe them as best you can," requested the FBI.

The gate agent went on to describe them in as much detail as she could remember, which turned out to be quite a lot. Then the FBI agent contacted Livy and Gerick to inform them that the kidnappers were already in the air. They learned what flight they were on and contacted the Air Marshal's office to find out if there was a marshal on board the flight. After learning that there was a marshal on board, they sent a text to him with a picture and description informing him that he had kidnapping suspects on the flight.

The Air Marshal indicated that he would walk around on the plane and see if he could spot them. About fifteen minutes later Livy received a text from the marshal indicating that he had identified the suspects. He asked how he should proceed.

"Don't confront them or raise their suspicions," recommended Livy. "There's very little you can do on the plane anyway. Just keep an eye on them and keep us informed if anything unusual happens."

"Are they a threat to this flight?" asked the marshal.

"I don't think so. Their target was the kidnap victims, not the plane."

"I'll keep a close watch and let you know if I see anything suspicious."

By this time the flight from Denver to Detroit was already over half way to its destination so the decision was made to complete the journey. There would be a contingent of airport police and FBI waiting for the plane's arrival and they would stop it while it was still on the taxiway before allowing it to arrive at the gate thereby not endangering even more people within the airport.

The Air Marshal found a seat conveniently behind the kidnappers, a couple rows behind them and across the aisle. There weren't a lot of empty seats on the plane, but luckily he found one that was available. From there he could keep a reasonably good watch on their activities.

*　*　*

"I think we've been discovered," whispered Nawwaf to Rasil.

"What makes you think that," whispered Rasil in return.

"There's a guy a couple rows back who conveniently took a seat right next to someone else, rather than taking one of the seats near the back where he wouldn't have anyone beside him. That's a little strange. Why would he sit right there in a cramped seat? I think he's watching us."

"How would he have found out so quickly?"

"I'm not sure but we need to be careful."

"What do we do?" asked Rasil.

"Nothing for now," suggested Nawwaf. "But when we get off the plane we need to lose him quickly. I wish we had something we could use to blow up the plane and end this right now. I'm tired of constantly feeling like these infidels are staring at my back. But since we don't have anything that we can use to blow up the plane, we'll just have to escape when we arrive. I still have big plans that I want to execute. But now is not the time to discuss any of that with so many ears all around us."

The conversation went quiet but both Nawwaf and Rasil kept an eye on the guy they believed was monitoring them to see if they spotted anything suspicions.

* * *

The plane landed safely and on time at the Detroit airport, and started to taxi toward the gate. While it was still taxing Nawwaf stood up and took his belongings out of the overhead compartment. The stewardess reprimanded him several times over the loud speaker, but he paid no attention to her remarks. He wanted to be ready to make a dash for the door as soon as the plane pulled up to the gate. But then something unexpected happened. After the plane had taxied off the runway and was on the taxiway, it stopped. It was still a long distance from the gate. Nawwaf knew this wasn't good. Over the loud speaker the captain said, "We have to wait here temporarily until our gate opens up. It should only be a few minutes."

Nawwaf waited a few minutes to see if the plane would start moving again, but then through the window he saw a ladder car pulling up to the side of the plane and several police officers coming up to the ladder car. They were coming on board the plane. Obviously the two had been discovered.

Just then the Air Marshal stood up and started cautiously moving toward them. He pulled out a pistol which had been hidden in a shoulder holster inside his coat. Just as he was about to point it at the kidnappers, Nawwaf jumped up out of his seat and grabbed the nose of the pistol and yanked it sideways, jerking it out of the Air Marshal's hands, but not before a shot rang off. Everyone in the plane quickly slipped down in their seats, hiding behind the seat back in front of them as if that seat had the power to shield them from bullets.

Neither Nawwaf nor the marshal paid much attention to the shot that was fired. Rather, they concentrated on controlling the pistol. The marshal slammed his right fist into Nawwaf's jaw causing him to stumble a few steps backward. But Nawwaf didn't release his grip on the pistol. Nawwaf, a lover of kickboxing, swung his right foot up into the crotch of the marshal, causing him to buckle up in pain. Nawwaf was about to win control of the pistol, when he felt a crushing blow to the back of his head. One of the passengers had decided to get involved and had used his laptop as a weapon, smashing it on the top of the kidnapper. Nawwaf immediately went unconscious and fell to the ground.

In spite of his pain from the kick, the Air Marshal quickly retrieved his pistol and snapped it back into his shoulder holster. Then he grabbed a set of handcuffs, rolled Nawwaf over, and snapped them on his hands behind his back.

During the struggle Rasil had started to jump up to try to help his friend. Unfortunately, just as he was about to get involved, the shot that rang out found its way into Rasil's left chest and into his heart. He immediately collapsed to the floor in front of his and Nawwaf's seats. For him the struggle was over before it even started.

The FBI and airport police arrived on the plane and quickly took Nawwaf and Rasil off the plane. Everyone on the plane applauded as the two were carried off the flight. There was no question in anyone's mind that they had just experienced a close call. After they were removed the Air Marshal took the microphone and explained, "The two individuals that were just taken off the plane were suspects in a kidnapping that occurred in the Golden, Colorado a couple days ago. We are still in search of the victims. A family of four was kidnapped including two small children. We're hoping that the remaining suspect will be able to supply us with information that will help us find the victims."

After his comments, there was another round of applause. He also announced that the FBI would need to take statements from some of the individuals closest to the event. He explained that since someone was shot and killed, and the Air Marshal's gun was used in the killing, the event needed to be carefully documented. Everyone else would be allowed to leave the plane. A bus would take them to their arriving gate so they could continue on in their travels. The people in the two rows behind and the one row in front of the event were taken off to different parts of the plane and interviewed by agents. Then, when the agent had a signed statement from each of them, they were allowed to leave the airplane.

Some people were frustrated about missing their flights, but everyone understood this was a necessary part of the process. It was critical that the Air Marshal did not get blamed for the shooting.

As they arrived at the gate and life returned back to normal for everyone, the passengers looked around at the other people in the airport and it was as if nothing had happened. However, the people on the plane never forgot the feeling of fear they felt when the gun went off in their airplane. As soon as possible, everyone dialed their cell phones as they departed the plane. They wanted to share their experience. Everyone's immediate reaction was to contact someone close to them and tell them what happened. They all felt a need to be connected with someone they loved. Life seemed very fragile at that point in time and they wanted to make sure they weren't alone.

One elderly lady in her seventies was so shaken up she refused to get on her connecting flight. The airlines worked with her and ended up helping her get to a train station so she could finish her travels by rail. The experience scared her enough to where she would never again travel by plane.

* * *

Rasil's body was sent off to a coroner. There wasn't much question about the cause of death, but protocol required that the bullet be removed and identified as having come from the gun of the Air Marshal. The Air Marshal would automatically be put on leave until all the details were verified. There was no question that he would be cleared and be back to work in a week.

Nawwaf wasn't as lucky. His problems started with a bad headache from the hit over the head. But that would turn out to be the least of his problems. He was given cursory medical attention by the airport medics, and then carted off in the back of an FBI cruiser to the downtown FBI detention center in the middle of Detroit.

* * *

Livy and Alvin electronically high-fived each other when they learned that Nawwaf had been captured. Livy was still in Denver and Alvin in the DC area. Alvin decided to proceed directly to Detroit to act on any information they might receive from Nawwaf. Livy stayed in Denver looking for the kidnappers and their victims. They would have preferred that Rasil hadn't been shot. That would give them two kidnappers to play off of each other. But at least they had captured one of them.

They shared the information with their Denver and DC teams, which caused everyone to congratulate each other. But it would be short lived. Fifteen minutes after Nawwaf was brought into the Detroit FBI offices a team of three lawyers appeared at these same offices. It was three of the same lawyers that had helped Shihab get his freedom just hours earlier. They demanded to be allowed to talk to Nawwaf immediately. The Patriot Act allowed the detention of terrorists, but the evidence didn't support the idea that Nawwaf was a terrorist. In fact, there was little evidence that he was one of the kidnappers. The only evidence linking him to the kidnapping was the van, and that was a fuzzy link. Even though they found evidence that the victims were in the van, they couldn't prove that Nawwaf was actually involved in the kidnapping. Nawwaf claimed that Rasil must have stolen the van somewhere after the kidnapping and that the connection with the kidnapping was strictly coincidental. He claimed he had no idea where the van came from or that it was stolen. He claimed he thought Rasil had rented it. The only charges they could place on Nawwaf were his attack on the Air Marshal on the plane and that he was in possession of a stolen vehicle.

Livy, Alvin, and the entire FBI team were frustrated by how quickly the lawyers had found out about Nawwaf's capture. Unfortunately Alvin's mole hunt in Provo, Utah didn't give him the information that he needed.

The entire story that Nawwaf created for the FBI agents made very little sense to anyone listening. But without evidence to the contrary, there was little to hold him. His lawyers twisted the air marshal attack into an attack by the air marshal on Nawwaf and Nawwaf was the one who had to defend himself. The entire event on the plane was explained by Nawwaf claiming he was in fear for his life when he saw someone coming at him with a gun which caused him to fight back. So after several rounds of questioning which was often blocked by the lawyers, the FBI was forced to release him on bail which had magically been set in record time through one of the local judges.

The FBI put a tail on him. Unfortunately after some car swapping and maneuvering through some building parking lots it wasn't long before they lost him. They had also planted a tracking device on him, but that was thrown out of the car window very early in the chase. The lawyers must have had a bug detection device with them.

* * *

Nawwaf was free. His Muslim Brotherhood lawyers helped him get a vehicle and he headed off to Ann Arbor planning to meet up with Shihab. He laughed out loud at how easily the lawyers were able to get him away from his FBI captors. He had learned that Rasil was dead. He didn't mourn the death. Rather, he envied it. He was going to avenge it, along with all the other deaths these infidels had caused. He was going to go out in a blaze of glory, and no one was going to be able to stop him now that he was free.

* * *

Alvin was extremely upset at how quickly Nawwaf was released. He was upset at how quickly the lawyers knew he had been captured. The information had to have come from a mole. Alvin's first attempt at a mole hunt had been a complete failure and had only resulted in warning the mole he was being hunted. He decided he was going to try a slightly different tactic. He was going to clone the phones of all of his agents and have all their phone calls tracked. This would be an elaborate and expensive undertaking, and would require more resources than what he could do by himself. He had avoided these techniques previously because he didn't want anyone involved in this mole hunt except himself and possibly Livy. But he needed to dig out the mole, and he needed to do it quickly.

Tracking the desk phones in the hope of identifying the mole wasn't a problem. Alvin started the process immediately with the push of a few buttons on his computer. But he didn't have any hope at catching anyone from that source. His agents were smart enough to not use anything that obvious.

Tracking the known cell phones of each of the agents was also not too difficult. He knew what those numbers were. He set up a monitoring and tracking process for each of those phones. He would record all the messages and phone calls and he would use the phone's GPS to track the location of the agent. This was routine and was used when agents were on missions so they could be tracked by the control unit. The existing software already had systems that were in place to do the tracking.

Cloning the unknown cell phones would be the most difficult and the most productive. The phone cloning process would require someone to be in close proximity to the phone being cloned. If the phone was turned off then the phone wouldn't be identified and couldn't be tracked. However if the phone was turned on then the cloning could occur and the phone number would be identified. Then, with that phone number, Alvin could set up a surveillance mechanism which would record all calls and text messages that came through the phone.

He decided to also GPS the unknown cells because its close proximity to any known cell phones would show him who was using the phone.

Alvin needed two things. He already had the software and recording mechanisms in place. That was standard equipment at the FBI. But he needed someone to do the cloning of the unknown cells and he needed someone to review and go through the tapes. He knew he would be the best person for the first role. In a conversation with Livy he was able to convince her to take on the role of reviewing the tapes. She was good at that anyway, and that would keep the mole hunt limited to as few people as possible.

Chapter Fifty-One

Planning for Revenge
November, 2017, Ann Arbor, Michigan

Nawwaf was wise to the surveillance tricks and went out of his way to avoid them. He didn't want to be spotted on someone's security camera again. He correctly assumed they had monitored him when he dropped off his vehicle at the railroad station in Denver. The area was too public. He also didn't want the FBI listening in on his conversations. So he set up a meeting at a park outside of Ann Arbor, far enough away from the city to avoid any form of surveillance. He traveled on Interstate 94, going past the Detroit airport, and headed toward Ann Arbor. Using his car's GPS system he spotted Van Buren park right next to the freeway. He called Shihab and told him to get a throwaway phone at the local Superstore Mart and that he should bring that phone with him. Shihab was instructed to travel on Interstate 94 toward Detroit and text his current location to Nawwaf on the throwaway phone, and he would receive further instructions as needed.

Nawwaf did the same. He stopped in a local Superstore Mart and picked up a couple throwaway phones. These would be the "clean" phones that would only be used to call each other. No other calls would be made from these two phones. That way the FBI would never be able to track the phones.

Following the designated procedure, Shihab headed East on 94, texting the exits as he passed them. As he approached exit 186 Nawwaf told him to exit and turn right on Rawsonville Road and then immediately turn left on the I-94 South Service Road. From there he was instructed to pull into the large shopping mall parking lot. Nawwaf knew what car Shihab was driving. He had received a description of the car from Shihab earlier. He was watching for the car as it pulled in.

Nawwaf pulled up next to Shihab's car, rolled down the window, handed him his phone, and instructed, "Leave your phones in that vehicle and put mine in that vehicle too. The FBI will think we are sitting in this parking lot talking. We'll keep using our personal phones as tools to divert the FBI's attention, but I have new burner phones that we'll use for communication between each other. Then jump in with me and we're going to drive to a nearby park."

Shihab obeyed and joined Nawwaf. Shihab started to talk but Nawwaf shushed him and said, "We will talk in a few minutes when we are out of the vehicle."

They continued on the service road until they arrived at the park entrance where they turned right into the park and stopped at the first hiking trail. Both stepped out of the car and started walking on the trail. Nawwaf started the conversation, "Now we can talk safely. I have two new phones here, one for you and one for me. We will use these phones to only call each other. Never call any other number or the number will be known and identified."

"What is the urgency and all the secrecy?" inquired Shihab.

"The FBI has killed your warriors and they have also killed my companion. I am the only one left of the entire kidnapping team. The infidels are on a campaign to wipe out Muslims in the United States. And we cannot allow them to do that. These infidels cannot be allowed to commit genocide on the followers and believers of Allah. We must stop them. And I think it requires drastic and immediate action."

"But what can we do? We are a small force. What can we do against a force as strong as the United States FBI?"

"We have Allah on our side. The reason I wanted this meeting with you was so we could lay out a plan of attack. What can we do? What resources do we need to do it? And how soon can we execute?"

"Are you looking for something even bigger than Orlando or North Dakota?" questioned a concerned Shihab. "Those were pretty dramatic.

To me, it seems like we should be doing something that targets the people that have been causing so many problems."

"According to our FBI friend and hero it is a small renegade group that is not directly connected with the FBI or any other government organization," explained Nawwaf. "Apparently it has been difficult to tie down exactly who is a part of this team. Even the FBI has no idea who they are. Our last attempt was in Denver. The kidnapping you promoted earned us a couple hostages, but they really didn't seem to know much about this group of renegades. Anyway, these individuals have now been eliminated. We need to try some other method for identifying these infidels. I agree that we need to stomp them out. We want to discourage this type of behavior in the future. It's just not appropriate for them to attack Allah and his holy sites like Medina or Mecca. But even though we're having so much trouble tying them down, I think we still need to show we are serious. We need some kind of dramatic display and we need to make sure that everyone recognizes that it is in retaliation for the activities of these renegades. First off I need to know if you have any more bombs of the type you used in Orlando and Dakota."

"Not as far as I know. Sami didn't confide in me about everything he did, but I have searched and have been unsuccessful in finding any nuclear bomb materials. I'm convinced that he only had the two nuclear bombs and a couple smaller bombs, one of which we used on the Detroit cathedral. So, either he has it hidden really well, or there just isn't anything else here."

"Not a problem. We can come up with the materials. Let's concentrate on the target. I would like something dramatic, something unexpected. Something big like planes hitting the Twin Towers in New York. What do we have that can give us a big bang and which will shake the very foundations of this decadent society?"

"Let's focus on what they cherish. What do they love the most? These infidels build their entire lives around the three P's: Pennies, Pleasure, and Power. They love money, and they make heroes out of the people that have lots of money. They idolize Bill Gates and Warren Buffett. If we're going to hit their pocket books, then we hit lower Manhattan and Wall Street.

"Or we could go after their pleasure, which is Hollywood, where the movie industry lives with its perverted morality and false idols, or Las Vegas, the sex capital of the world. And then there's power, which is centered in Washington, DC and all the power brokers that have their personal decadent influences."

"Is there a way to hit all three of these P's at once?" asked Nawwaf.

"Getting at Washington, DC or New York has become nearly impossible since the strikes on the Twin Towers and the Pentagon," explained Shihab. "They have constructed a security perimeter around these areas that will make it hard to do a strike there. But that also makes it more challenging and therefore more fun. Especially the DC area where the power brokers huddle."

Ignoring Shihab's leaning toward DC, Nawwaf said, "Then that leaves us with Hollywood or Las Vegas. Which target do you like the best?"

"I guess I would pick Hollywood. Both locations are the seeds of decadence, but the damage inflicted in Hollywood would be more significant. There are more people and it will take a lot of years for the industry to recover." What he didn't say was that he liked going to Las Vegas once in a while. He enjoyed an occasional fling in sin city.

"Good enough. We'll destroy the film industry structure that is leading so many of our Muslim youth astray."

The two continued making plans for their proposed attack on Hollywood when Nawwaf unexpectedly decided to go on one of his anti-American rants. "I'll tell you what really bothers me about these infidels. I really don't understand a society that allows the murder of children, like late term abortions and now they're even allowing post birth abortions in some places. Isn't that murder? And in some European countries they have euthanasia of kids. How crazy is that? And of course most of these western countries have euthanasia of old people. At the same time they let murderers walk free amongst them. And they claim it's inhuman to execute murders. How stupid is that. Their morality is completely backwards. I can't understand a society that will throw you in jail for spanking your kids, but has no problem with killing them. These infidels are idiots. If they would just listen to themselves they would see how stupid they sound. Allah must be extremely upset. We need to do something to help. We need to make Allah proud."

"I don't think anything these infidels do makes any sense," Shihab sneered in agreement. "They apparently don't read history books. Every time a dominant culture rises to power, similar to the way the Americans have come to be a world power, the same things happen. It has happened so often, it's become predictable. The first thing that happens is they ignore and eventually reject their God. They come up with this idea that smarter people are too smart to believe in a God. They think science somehow trumps God. But in reality, they're just trying to ignore what they can't see with their senses. It doesn't mean that God doesn't exist. But what really irks me is that the atheists say they don't like the religionists to stuff their beliefs down their throat. But when you drive down the street you can see billboards where atheists are doing exactly what they don't like religionists to do. They advertise their belief that there is no God. And they're offended when the religionists do the same thing." The two slowly meandered along one of the parks trails. To anyone observing them they appeared to be enjoying the scenery.

Nawwaf continued, "But that's just the first step in the failure of a society that claims to be advanced. The next step is the destruction of the family. They start having less and less kids because kids are an inconvenience. They want to spend more time at work or in entertainment. And I would argue that for a lot of these infidels, their work is their entertainment. So the result is that with fewer kids, they end up with a labor resource shortage. And to make up for the shortage they bring in slaves or foreigners to make up for the lack of their own labor force. And these immigrants have no problem having lots of babies because they haven't caught on to the spirit of this supposedly advanced life style. And then, before long, you have the laborers outnumbering the original citizens. Then you get a take-over by the new citizenry. Then an internal strife occurs and the country starts tearing itself apart from the inside out. The original citizens try to hold control of the country, but the majority of the population wants to make their mark as well. You see this happening in many of the European countries as well.

"But that's not what bothers me the most. What bothers me more is the decay of morality. What was considered to be immoral just ten or twenty years ago in this country is considered acceptable behavior today. What they do is to redefine morality. For example, murder, like you mentioned, becomes more acceptable. Or homosexuality, which is actually a moral issue, gets redefined as if it was a reborn race issue and you have people defending it based on a belief that it's the same as racial discrimination. But it's not! It's a morality issue. Labeling it a 'new morality' doesn't somehow eliminate traditional authentic morality. It's just a play on words. Traditional morality is still the morality of today and cannot be arbitrarily redefined because it isn't convenient anymore.

"This society is so obsessed by moral relativism. They believe in the idea that the rights of the individual are more important than the morality of society as a whole. They believe that each individual has the right to define their own morality. This concept is destroying this Western society. They can't figure out what is moral because there are so many versions of it. Morality has become meaningless and undefined." Nawwaf stopped, bent over, and picked one of the flowers along the trail. It seemed so innocent, as if he was admiring nature, when all along he was plotting suicide attacks.

Then Nawwaf continued, "And what they're doing to the family is horrible. They criticize us for having multiple wives, but what they do is marry one woman, cast that wife away like she's dirt, marry another, and cast her away when she's no longer good in bed, and so on. How is that better than being loyal to multiple wives at the same time? I don't understand how it's acceptable to be bisexual, having free sex with either males or females, but it's against the law to be a polygamist. How does that make sense? Where is the logic of that type of morality?

"These infidels can't wait to ship their old people away to some rest home or care facility. They think they're rich, but they get those riches at the expense of both getting rid of their kids, by reducing the family size, and secondly by getting rid of their elderly by shipping them off somewhere and letting the government pay for their care. And then when they die they fight over the scraps that their parents leave behind like hungry wolves. It's absolutely obscene.

"Then, what you see next in this so-call advanced society is a major internal rift. You see that now in the United States. The Democrats and Republicans are nearly at blows with each other over this liberal belief in the right to redefine religion and morality, and the conservative belief in both a strong religion and a strong traditional morality. This same cycle has repeated itself time and time again. You see countries like Nazi Germany redefining morality as the right to eliminate what they consider to be an inferior race and creating their own Aryan superior race. Or Pol Pot in Cambodia deciding that anyone with an education is corrupting the world of the masses and should be eliminated. He killed people who were wearing glasses because he thought they must be too intellectual. Or in Africa where you have never ending tribal extermination wars. And you've seen the same in Stalin's Communist Russia, or the Soviet Union. Religion and morality are redefined to allow for a looser, more immoral society. I wouldn't be surprised if the Americans don't tear themselves apart from the inside out in the next twenty years or so thereby destroying their imperialistic superiority and world domination. I've given up trying to make sense of it a long time ago.

"These infidels have so few children that most families don't have sons. My sons are my whole reason for living. Everything I do is for my sons and their heritage. I look for the opportunity to leave them a legacy. If I don't leave a progeny behind, where my children, especially my sons, are proud of me, than I've achieved nothing. Having fun now means nothing. Being successful and leaving that legacy for your family is everything. But how can you expect a godless people to understand the importance of leaving a legacy. They think there is nothing beyond this life. They have lost their reason for living. They are wrapped up in this moral relativism. And so they live for the here and now and end up destroying their hereafter."

There was a quiet pause in Nawwaf's rant and after a couple minutes of silence Shihab asked, "Back to our current problem; what are we going do in Hollywood?"

"No idea," responded Nawwaf. "I'm going to get in touch with some Muslim Brotherhood friends and see what they recommend. They may have a different suggestion for a target. I'll call you on that new phone after I've had that conversation. Right now it's the middle of the night for them so I can't call them, but I can call them this evening. Then I'll get back to you. What I need from you is to see if there is anyone that would be willing to sacrifice their life for Allah. Can you identify some heroes who are willing to help us?"

"I can definitely do that. If I understand you correctly, my four warriors that were sent to Golden to do the kidnapping are all dead. And the FBI killed them all. What about the hostages?"

"Also dead," replied Nawwaf. Then he lied about what had happened in order to explain his escaping with no injury, "I was lucky enough to be able to hide in the backyard and waited till the FBI terrorists disappeared. Then I was able to escape."

"And what about your partner?" asked Shihab. He knew Nawwaf was lying. The story didn't make sense. Why wouldn't the FBI check the backyard? And where was his partner hiding? But he didn't challenge Nawwaf on the story. He didn't want to hear the truth.

"He was killed on the plane by the Air Marshal who attacked us there," replied Nawwaf. "Luckily I was able to escape uninjured."

Shihab could see that the story was full of holes. It just didn't make sense. But he didn't dare ask any questions because he knew Nawwaf was a killer and would have no trouble leaving Shihab dead lying there in the park.

Nawwaf and Shihab returned to Nawwaf's car, and he drove Shihab back to his vehicle. Nawwaf took his phone back and recommended, "Continue using your regular phone so the FBI thinks it is your only communication tool. Only use the new phone for conversations between the two of us." Then the two departed ways. Shihab returning to his mosque and Nawwaf looking for a hotel where he could spend the evening and make a few critical phone calls.

* * *

It was nearly midnight when Nawwaf finally connected with his Muslim Brotherhood comrades in Egypt using his new burner phone. He had to work around the eight-hour time difference. After the mandatory Muslim / Arab greetings Nawwaf jumped right to the reason for his call. "Here is the situation. There is a group of infidel terrorists that have taken it upon themselves to get revenge against Allah. They are the ones who attacked Medina and who destroyed the mosques in Detroit. They have also killed several isolated Islamic heroes. We have unsuccessfully attempted to identify who the members of this cell are with our FBI contact. We've identified one, and he disappeared completely. When we tried to draw him out by kidnapping some of his best friends, it ended in the deaths of several more Islamic heroes. At this point we don't know who these guys are. So what we thought we should do is to design some form of revenge that is so atrocious, the infidel community will have a large uproar and force these evil assassins out in the open. We thought a strike on one of the richest industries in America, the movie industry, would make such a statement. It would take out several of the American movie industry heroes as well as cripple a major source of income. And because the population density in the area is so large, it may also take a significant toll in eliminating a large number of infidels."

The voice at the other end of the line spoke up, "You have thought this through and we are proud of you. Never discuss the details of what you are doing over the phone. Go ahead and work as an isolated cell and successfully execute your plan."

"What I need is your agreement and support. I need a contact in the Los Angeles area that can help me there. I also need someone else to be my partner. These idiots over here don't know what they're doing.

They executed some small attacks, but this is much bigger and I need experienced support. And last of all I need a weapon that is large enough to have the impact that I'm after. Can you help?"

"I have the perfect person that can help you out," replied the Egyptian. "I will have him leave immediately to join you. Where should he come?"

"Detroit," responded Nawwaf. "Send me the details of his travel plans and I will pick him up at the airport when he arrives. Then we can travel to Los Angeles together."

"We'll do a search on available weapons and get back to you with a recommendation."

The call ended with the traditional farewell greetings and disconnected.

Chapter Fifty-Two

Organizing Revenge
November, 2017, Ann Arbor, Michigan

Alvin went to each of the offices of his agents and pretended to sit down with them to discuss their progress in various on-going investigations. While in the office he pretended to check his phone for a text message but in reality he was triggering a cloning process for any phones within a ten-foot radius. On several occasions the only additional phone that was picked up was the agent's cell phone that Alvin already knew about. But there were also several occasions where he cloned a cell phone that was not on the list of personal phones. He immediately set up tracking for these newly identified phones.

In the meantime Livy had started going through the phone text messages and recorded phone calls. It was a needle in a haystack and consumed a large amount of her time. But she knew the importance of the mole hunt and wanted to put an end to the deaths, injuries, and frustration this mole had caused. Seeing that Livy was somewhat overwhelmed and falling behind in going through the recordings, Alvin picked up a couple of the numbers and started listening in on those calls as well. They both put priority on the unknown cell phone numbers, guessing that any mole calls would most likely have been made on these phones.

* * *

Nawwaf wasn't as smart as he thought he was. As soon as he was released from FBI detention, the FBI had used all the resources at their disposal to keep an eye on him. APBs were placed everywhere, especially at travel centers. They had a lucky break when a rental car company informed them that a car had been rented a few hours earlier by someone who looked like Nawwaf and his lawyers. Luckily the car had GPS, which Nawwaf had requested so that he wouldn't get lost. This same system was used to follow the car's movements. For all his effort to avoid the use of cell phones and credit cards, Nawwaf had missed the fact that a car's GPS could be used to track him down. He had stupidly assumed the FBI would never be able to trace him to the rental car dealership and so his use of a car with GPS didn't matter.

The FBI didn't want to arrest him. That would just make him aware that they knew where he was. His lawyers would help him escape their grasp just as quickly as he had done earlier in the day. What the FBI wanted was to keep an eye on him. They hoped to find some grounds for an arrest, or, even better, they wanted to find who he was working for or working with so they could capture the entire cell in one stroke.

On GPS they saw Nawwaf arrive at Van Buren Park and they saw that someone was with him. But they were not sure who it was. They took telescopic pictures of the meeting, but it wasn't until later that they identified his accomplice as Shihab. Knowing that these two were working together confirmed the fact that Nawwaf had somehow been involved in the kidnapping which had originated with Sami and Shihab's cell.

The FBI continued monitoring Nawwaf and saw him take refuge at a nearby hotel. That turned out to be Nawwaf's second mistake. The phone call he placed to the Middle East was quickly identified. All calls coming out of that area were tracked at the local cell tower, and his was the only one calling that region of the world, so it was easy to track and listen in on the conversation. As far as the FBI was concerned, Nawwaf was a terrorist and therefore surveillance of a terrorist was authorized as part of the Patriot Act.

Earlier in the day, with Livy taking the lead on the mole hunt, Alvin had hopped on a plane for Detroit when he learned that Nawwaf was going to be detained, arrested and taken off of the airplane there. He knew that Detroit was where the action was and he wanted to help get as much information as possible from Nawwaf. Unfortunately, by the time he arrived, Nawwaf had already been released. So instead of doing the interviews Alvin became involved in the monitoring of Nawwaf's movements.

When Alvin saw the transcript of the recent call to Egypt he was horrified. Nawwaf had been careful to not identify the location, but it was pretty obvious what his target was. The movie industry was in the LA / Hollywood area and that was the large population density that he was talking about. These idiots were planning to hit on Hollywood. His FBI team had to stop them.

But it wasn't going to be accomplished as easily as arresting Nawwaf. Who was at the other end of the phone call and was mastermind of this operation? Who was going to execute it? Were they already in place in Hollywood? How much did Nawwaf really know about the operation? Where was the kidnapped family? Re-arresting Nawwaf would just put the rest of the cell on alert without preventing anything. What was Shihab's role? Were members of his mosque involved? There were more questions than there were answers. Therefore arresting Nawwaf was out of the question. They needed him to lead them to the rest of the operatives.

Alvin made a call to Livy and explained what they had learned about Nawwaf. Her first question was, "Did you learn anything about the kidnapping?"

"Sorry, no," replied Alvin. "The lawyers swooped in here so fast and gagged him that we couldn't learn anything. We're still a little stunned by how fast they found out about his arrest. And the phone call to Egypt didn't discuss the kidnapping."

"You couldn't make any of the charges about the attack on the plane stick?"

"No. He and his lawyers made it sound like the Air Marshal was the aggressive one and Nawwaf was scared for his life. It's a crock but our case was too weak to hold him."

"Even using the Patriot Act?"

"We had no specific evidence that justified claiming he was a terrorist."

"So we're nowhere," Livy complained in a discouraged voice. "We know they're planning another attack, but we don't know anything about it. And we still don't know anything about the kidnapping. The news couldn't be worse. Can we go after Shihab on the kidnapping and try to get some information from him without giving up the information that we have about Nawwaf?"

"We could try," replied Alvin. "But you know he's going to deny any knowledge of anything. Maybe we can shake something loose. I'll go right now myself with a couple agents and see what I learn. I understand the urgency of the situation. I just wish I could be more optimistic. However, there is one optimistic note to all of this. As long as we have Nawwaf under watch we have a better chance of learning where the bomb is going to be detonated. And ultimately that has to be our goal; avoiding the explosion."

"I would greatly appreciate your trying anything you can to find out more about the kidnapping too," pleaded Livy, her concern showing in her voice. "Call me as soon as you're done visiting Shihab in case there is something I can follow-up on here. I'm worried because the deadline has passed and we haven't heard anything. I'm getting worried that the worst has already happened."

"Will do."

The line went dead and Alvin rounded up a couple agents including Edward who had come with him from DC. They went to the parking garage, jumped into an FBI squad car, and headed for Ann Arbor.

Finding Shihab turned out to be a bit of a problem. He wasn't at his house or at the mosque. No one at the home or the mosque knew where he was, or at least wouldn't tell the FBI where he was. After about an hour of monitoring both locations, Shihab was finally spotted driving up to his home. It was as if he had been warned that the FBI was looking for him because he climbed out of his car and waited for them to swoop in on him. He had apparently resigned himself to the fact they would be talking to him, but he also knew they would have no cause to arrest him.

***

"Hello, gentlemen," Shihab sarcastically remarked. "What can I do for you?"

"Tell us about the kidnapping," responded Alvin.

"What kidnapping?" Shihab replied with a smug snicker. Nawwaf had told him that the FBI had captured the hostages and had killed all the kidnappers. So he wondered what game these FBI agents were playing. If they killed everyone then they should know about it. Shihab knew that Nawwaf had lied to him, but these FBI agents were even bigger liars, and he would still take Nawwaf's lies over their lies any time.

"You know what kidnapping I'm talking about. Your followers are the ones that executed the kidnapping and it's no use you trying to pretend you don't know what we're talking about. Tell me about the kidnapping."

"I'm sorry. I wish I could help you, but I really have no idea what you're talking about."

* * *

Alvin felt like pistol-whipping him but he knew that what he would probably get was more lies in the hope that they would get the FBI to leave him alone. After another half hour of threats and accusations, Alvin gave up and allowed Shihab to enter his home.

"Livy?" Alvin asked, responding to the ringing cell phone.

"How did it go?" asked Livy.

"We just finished up with him and it was a waste of time." He didn't realize that all he accomplished was to alert Nawwaf that the FBI was watching.

"How irritating," came back Livy, the frustration showing in her voice. "Where do we go from here?"

"Not sure we can do much about the kidnapping," said Alvin, the frustration and irritation also showing in his voice.

"What about Shihab?" asked Livy.

"Don't touch him for now," replied Alvin, knowing what she was thinking. "We're hoping he and Nawwaf will lead us to something bigger. And I honestly believe he doesn't know anything about the kidnapping. I think he came into the process too late and wasn't informed. Regardless, after we're done, your Dragon Pit team can have at him all you want and see what you can get out of him. I surely won't try to stop you."

"What's next?"

"On this end we're going to watch for the arrival of the additional Muslim Brotherhood that Nawwaf discussed on his phone call. For you I guess you keep pursuing the mole hunt and looking for the kidnapping. But be ready in a heartbeat to go to LA and help us prevent an enormous disaster from occurring."

"Understood," Livy said. "I'll keep you posted if anything changes on our end. At this point I really haven't found anything incriminating in my mole hunt going through all the tapes and recordings. And the search for the kidnappers has stalled out as well. It's enormously frustrating."

"Same here," answered Alvin and he disconnected the call.

* * *

Livy went back to work listening to recordings of phone calls and reviewing text messages. As a distraction from the boredom she would occasionally try to identify some clue that would lead her to the kidnappers and their victims. She decided to travel to the location of the shack to see if there was anything that might help. She was confident that her team had done a thorough job, but a second pair of eyes often saw something that was previously missed and she wanted to try. She would feel terrible if she could have made a difference but failed to try.

Chapter Fifty-Three

Anticipating Revenge
November, 2017, Ann Arbor, Michigan

Shihab convened his revenge cell in a nearby park. He learned the lesson Nawwaf had taught him that all things were trackable and traceable. He feared his home and the mosque were bugged in spite of what his lawyers had told him. He wanted to be extra safe. He didn't want to make any of the same mistakes that Sami had made. His only place of safety was somewhere neutral, like a park. He also wondered if he should not have used his phone to set up the meeting, but by the time he thought of not using the phone and getting another throwaway phone for these calls it was already too late. He was angry with himself for not thinking of it earlier and he swore to himself that in the future he wouldn't make the same mistake.

The FBI was grateful for his little oversight. They were able to listen in to his calls. They had observers staked out at the park even before Shihab and any of his warriors arrived.

The conversation in the park between Shihab and his cell was spotty and hard to hear. There were only three individuals in the cell, which surprised the FBI. Two of the members of the cell were the remnants of Sami's cell, and there was one new recruit. They were expecting a much larger group. They overheard words like "Hollywood" and "bomb" and they quickly made the connection that this was the group who was executing the attack, but beyond that they heard very little. However, what was valuable was that they now knew who the members of the attack cell would be. They would assign agents to track each of the cell members. Additionally, thanks to Shihab's phone calls, they now knew each of the members' phone numbers and they were able to track their calls and get their phone history.

But then a surprise unfolded, one they did not anticipate and one which disappointed them significantly. Shihab pulled out a Superstore Mart bag and out of the bag he took limited-use burner cell phones, handing one phone to each of the cell members. Apparently he had learned a new trick from Nawwaf. He had learned that cell phones were traceable and it was best to keep all their communications on a phone that would not be used for any other purpose.

Unheard by the FBI, Shihab, who was talking in a quieter than normal voice, instructed his team, "These phones are only to be used for calls amongst ourselves. You need to program all the phone numbers of each member of the cell into your phones. Your regular phones are traceable and when you are on a mission for Allah, you are to leave your regular phones at home. Remember, the FBI probably knows your regular number and is listening in on your calls. And they will use cell tower triangulation or the GPS system of your phones to track you. As long as you are living your normal lives, that's not a problem, but when you go on a mission you need to either leave your personal phones at home or better yet, put them somewhere, like in someone else's car, where it looks like you are still local and traveling around town."

Then Shihab went into an even softer whisper. "I want to send the three of you on a mission to Los Angeles. I need you to travel separately, one of you will go by train, one by plane, and one by car. After you get there, you will use these new phones to contact me and I will instruct you further. But for now that is all you need to know. Are you all ready to serve Allah?"

In unison they replied, "Yes," and one of the members continued, "All we want is to get a chance to prove our commitment to Allah. We look forward to our mission. We will leave immediately."

Another of the team members spoke up, "Who travels by which route?"

Shihab quickly made the assignments. Najid would go by plane. He would catch the first direct flight from Detroit to Los Angeles, rent a car, drive to Hollywood, book a hotel for the night, and call. Taqiy would travel by train. Amtrak traveled from Detroit to Portland, Oregon, where he would switch trains and then travel on to Los Angeles. He would similarly rent a car and travel to Hollywood. Uthal would go by car. He would travel to the airport with Najid, rent a car, and start driving toward Los Angeles. He would travel to Salt Lake City following a route similar to the one previously traveled by the warriors who had gone to Golden. Then he would connect with Interstate 15 heading directly to the Los Angeles area. He would also book himself into a hotel before contacting Shihab.

Then Shihab explained, "Najid will obviously arrive there first and will receive the first assignment. Then when the other two of you arrive you will each receive your assignments. We have prioritized these activities so that the most critical activity goes first, and so on. We specifically want you traveling separately so we can get as much accomplished as possible. If you travel together and something happens like a car accident, then we lose all three of you and that would be a disaster. Going separately is also a buffer. If one of you is discovered, we will still be able to complete the mission."

"Understood," replied the warrior who had originally asked the question.

"Now, give me your regular phones. I'll take care of them and send them off in different directions in order to confuse anyone that may be spying on you. Go now and book your tickets, and get going on your travels."

The FBI, still hiding in the shadows, saw the four members of the cell disperse. They were disappointed in their listening devices. They had no idea what had happened during the last part of the conversation. They had hoped to learn more. Fortunately they had enough agents on site so they could immediately start tailing the four cell members as they each went their separate ways.

Najid and Uthal went off together to Najid's vehicle. They immediately started their journey to the airport with two FBI agents in tow. Similarly Taqiy took off heading for the train station. Shihab headed off toward the mosque where he would then place the personal cell phones under the seats of the cars of three worshipers. He hoped this would keep anyone from tracking the real whereabouts of the warriors.

After the three warriors had departed, Shihab placed a call to Nawwaf using the secure phone to inform him that the warriors had departed and were on their way to Los Angeles.

* * *

A call came through to Nawwaf, who was still sitting at the hotel waiting for the arrival of his Muslim Brotherhood companions. He planned to meet them at the airport when they arrived. He had tried to intercept them by calling his contacts in Egypt, and tell them to go directly to Los Angeles, but he had been too late. They were already on their way. So he decided to meet them at the airport and then they could travel on to Los Angeles together. But he did learn one important fact from the Egyptians. He learned there were already several Muslim Brotherhood sleeper agents in the LA area and he was supplied with their contact information.

Nawwaf decided he couldn't leave such an important mission in the hands of three college kids who weren't smart enough to wipe their own noses. He remembered all the mistakes that were made by the kidnap team in Golden and he didn't want a similar comedy of errors. He wanted to take control to assure the mission's success.

Shihab called in to give Nawwaf an update. While talking to Shihab, Nawwaf complemented him on giving the warriors new phones and he asked for each of their phone numbers. Then he informed Shihab that as they arrived in Los Angeles they were to contact him directly. He would give them instructions on what their missions were and how they were to carry them out. It was better if Shihab was out of the loop on the details of each of the three warriors' missions. This would be a need to know activity from this point forward.

Nawwaf's next call was to the Muslim Brotherhood cell that was in the LA area. "Hello," was the response at the other end of the line. The voice sounded completely American. There was no hint of an Arab accent. The voice slightly confused Nawwaf and he wondered if he had received the correct phone number.

"I am Nawwaf and my Egyptian contact told me this would be a safe number to call if I needed any help," responded a cautious Nawwaf.

"I have to confirm that you are who you say you are," replied the voice. "I don't want to be talking to the FBI. I will call you back shortly as soon as you check out. I see your number here on my phone."

"No problem," replied Nawwaf as he disconnected the call.

About ten minutes later Nawwaf's secure phone rang and it was Uday, the same individual he had talked with earlier. "We've confirmed your identity. What do you want?" The individual talking was abrupt and bordered on being rude.

"I need three bombs," responded Nawwaf. "I have three warrior heroes on their way to the LA area and they need bombs."

"What's the target?"

"Can't tell you. But it's critical we get the bombs quickly. What can you do to help?"

"How big of an explosion do you want?"

"Two of them should be bigger than the ones used in Boston at the marathon, but not as big as what we did in Orlando," Nawwaf explained. "We don't necessarily want nukes, but we want to at least take the building down. The third one should be the biggest bomb you have available. We want the third one to cause maximum destruction." He didn't expect the LA cell to have access to nuclear weapons.

"Well, I think it's rude you won't share the target with us," criticized Uday. "But since the Brotherhood in Egypt confirmed the level of importance of your mission I'll do my best. We do have one nuke bigger than the one you used in Orlando if you want it, but the other two would have to be C-4 bombs. We can pack enough together in a backpack to take down a pretty large building. When do you need them?"

"We need the first one, one of the smaller ones, tomorrow and the other two in a couple days," responded Nawwaf. He was excited about the prospect of having access to a nuke and this went to the top of his priority list. "How soon can you have the nuke ready?"

"It can be ready in a couple days. We can have a C-4 bomb ready for you in a couple hours."

"Excellent," replied Nawwaf. He was excited and his mind was rattling, thinking of what the target should be. He was going to have a bigger impact than he had previously imagined. This was going to be a glorious day for Allah. Now that he had all the tools in place it became his responsibility to make sure the revenge demonstrations were successful.

* * *

Nawwaf relaxed for a few hours in the airport-waiting lounge for the arrival of his Muslim Brotherhood friends from Egypt. In his last communication with Egypt he was told that two were on their way and he was excited to share the good news with them.

It wasn't long before they came in. After the traditional formal greetings, the three found a secluded place in the airport waiting area. Nawwaf shared the news that the targets for the revenge attacks would be in the Los Angeles and Hollywood area. He also informed them that the suicide warriors and the bombs were all in process.

The three purchased air tickets for the next available flight to Los Angeles. Then they made their way through security and headed out to the gate for the journey west. This would be a glorious time for Allah.

Chapter Fifty-Four

Tracking Revenge

November, 2017, Los Angeles, CA

"Los Angeles," was the anxious report from the FBI agent who had been listening in on Shihab as he organized and sent the suicide bombers on their missions. "I'm sure the target is Los Angeles. They mentioned Hollywood and LA several times. I'm sure that wasn't a coincidence." The agent was on a conference call with all the involved FBI agents on a secure line.

"That makes sense since they were hinting at that location on some of our previous wire taps," responded one of the agents who had been tracking Najid and Uthal. "The two guys I was following went to the airport and then separated. One caught a flight to LA and the other went to the car rental place. I'm there now trying to figure out what he's up to." The agent supplied the travel details of Najid.

Alvin cut in, "I'll have agents in LA meet the flight and keep track of Najid. What about Taqiy? Do we have a report on him?"

"We lost him," chimed in a third agent. "Not sure what he's up to."

Livy jumped in, "I think it's obvious. The three are working toward some mission and they are taking different routes and modes of travel to get there. I would suspect Taqiy probably rented another car at a different location and is on his way to LA too."

"Or train," responded Alvin. "Can someone check out all the travel options to see if either of these possibilities check out?"

"Will do," responded the agent who had lost Taqiy. "I'll work all the travel options other than the airport to see if I can find anything."

Alvin continued his instruction, "I think we may have misread this situation. Instead of containing it I think we lost control. My read is we have at least three suicide bombers headed for the LA area and we have no one in place to stop them. I'll alert the LA FBI offices to try and intercept the three we know about, but we have to assume the worst. We have to assume we've lost them and we need to get as many of us there on the ground as soon as possible. I need as many of you as possible in LA. I'm going to pack up here in Detroit and take my team down there immediately and only leave a skeleton crew behind. Livy, Jonathan, and Gerick, I need you to do the same in Denver. I'll get a group of agents sent out from our DC office as well and we'll pull in agents from the areas surrounding LA too. We can't have another Orlando or North Dakota in Los Angeles. The death toll would be horrendous."

Livy chimed in, "What about the kidnapping?" She didn't want to mention the mole hunt over a conference call. But Alvin could easily read between the lines.

"Your skeleton crew will have to work on that and maybe some of the local police. And anything else you're working on will just have to wait. You're not making any headway anyway. You're more critical right now on site in LA and I need all of you there now. We can resume the work on the kidnapping after we return." By the sound of his voice it was obvious that Alvin had lost hope in ever finding the kidnap victims alive. The long time that had passed since the last communication from the kidnappers made it painfully obvious.

Livy wasn't ready to give up on the kidnap victims, but she knew Alvin was right. There just wasn't enough to go on. The skeleton crew would have to maintain the search effort.

* * *

Before leaving, Livy convened a meeting with her Dragon Pit team in a local park. As usual, they were all on time and eager to get her updates.

"We've encountered a major setback," Livy started. "We still haven't heard from the kidnappers and we don't have any clues or inspirations to work with. The search for the kidnappers has stalled out."

"What about the cell in Ann Arbor," asked Lincoln. "Can't we get anything from them?"

"They don't know anything," continued Livy. "Shihab, who is now running the cell, isn't the one who sent the kidnappers out. Additionally, two Muslim Brotherhood team members have joined the operation and, from what we can gather, they have taken it over. We tried to arrest them but one was killed and the second one was rescued by a team of lawyers. It was crazy. The lawyers almost beat us to the police station. We have no idea how they found out about the arrest. Bottom line is we haven't been able to get any information from anyone. And not hearing from the kidnappers is an enormous concern. Normally that's not a very good sign.

"And now we have a second and possibly even bigger problem. The Muslim Brotherhood member that I was just talking about, his name is Nawwaf, met up with Shihab, and they're planning some kind of attack on LA. We're afraid it's going to be another Orlando or North Dakota, but with a lot more bodies. What we know is that Shihab and Nawwaf had the meeting. Following the meeting Shihab immediately dispatched three of his followers to LA. We're guessing they are going to be the suicide bombers. We're not sure how Nawwaf fits into all of this but he's been making calls to Egypt, we assume to the Muslim Brotherhood. We suspect the instructions for this attack are all coming from Egypt."

"So what are we doing?" asked a concerned Gage.

"I'm going with the FBI team down to LA in mass," replied Livy. "That's why I wanted to meet with you quickly. I have to go to LA to try and stop this disaster. But I need you guys to continue looking for Glenn and his family here in the Golden area."

"The common thread in all of this is Shihab," suggested Lincoln. "Why don't we just go after him?"

"Because we can't touch him. After the death of his brother and the brother's family, everyone is screaming discrimination and the FBI says we must 'tread lightly' which is another way of saying hands off or you may lose your job over this. He's manipulated himself into an untouchable situation. We hauled him in for questioning, but, as I already mentioned, the lawyers were able to get him released. And we really have nothing to hold him on. So the only thing we can do with him is to watch and see if he makes any mistakes or if he leads us to any more cell members. And besides, like I already said, I think it would be a waste of time. He's small potatoes and really doesn't know anything."

"But that doesn't include us," suggested Boston matter-of-factly. "We don't have to adhere to FBI rules. Maybe we can have a talk with him. Maybe we can learn something about LA or about the kidnapping."

"You're right," added Lincoln.

"Tread carefully," cautioned Livy. "Don't let him know we have connected him to Nawwaf. I'm sure you realize they have surveillance and guards all over the place at the mosque and at his house trying to catch you guys. I'm not sure this is the right time for cowboy diplomacy."

"But if we can learn more about the kidnapping and about what they're planning in LA, wouldn't it be worth it?" asked Carlos.

"Of course. But we don't want to lose any more Dragon Pit members just because we became careless. That wouldn't be good either."

"But worth the risk," replied Lincoln and several others nodded in agreement.

"Well, I'll let you guys figure out what you want to do there, but I warned you to be careful. Alvin and I discussed this option and we really think that the risk is greater than the benefit. I'll leave it to you and we'll support you, but be extremely cautious. If you learn anything please let me know ASAP. It can have a definite impact on what we're trying to do."

"What else is there for us to do?" expressed Lincoln with concern. "That could be my family out there instead of Glenn's. I would sure hope everyone didn't give up on us too quickly."

"We're not giving up," stated Livy emphatically. "We're just chasing the devil we know best. Everyone wishes we had more information, more leads on the kidnappers, but we just don't so we're stuck."

"Livy, don't worry about us. If we learn anything about the kidnappers or LA we'll let you know right away," Gage jumped in, switching the conversation away from the idea of Livy giving up on Glenn. He knew it wasn't true and he didn't want an internal war to begin between the Dragon Pit members. They had accomplished a lot as a cohesive group, and he didn't want the cohesion to be lost.

Gage turned to Lincoln and said, "I think we know what we need to do."

"You're right about that," responded Lincoln. "I'll touch base with Gene and see if we can borrow his plane one more time."

"And I'll have a car waiting for you if you let me know when and where you need it," replied Livy.

The meeting between the Dragon Pit members broke up and they all went their separate ways. Livy headed toward the airport. Lincoln and Gage huddled to discuss a trip to Detroit. The rest of the team members headed to their homes.

Chapter Fifty-Five

Anticipating Reverse Revenge
November, 2017, Ann Arbor, MI

Shihab knew it was coming and he was scared. He would never let on that he feared death because that would be taken as a lack of faith. He was supposed to be the leader replacing his brother Sami. He needed to be the strong one. Ironically, he had no problem sending off other members of the cell to their deaths, but he could never see himself as someone who was brave enough to do something so stupid. At least he saw it as stupid for himself. He had a greater purpose. These stupid kids weren't that important. The thought of being attacked by this mystery group who called themselves the NERDS and who had killed Sami scared him so badly he shivered.

Shihab knew these infidels would be returning to attack him and possibly his family. He had become the target and they would probably try something similar to what happened to Sami. He knew the local police weren't trustworthy enough to protect him. In fact, for all he knew, they may be the ones who were doing the attacks. He called upon the key supportive members of Sami's mosque to meet with him in the mosque for a short, critical meeting. He didn't want any of the naysayers that were in the previous meeting.

The meeting occurred as planned and Shihab began, "My family and I are at the same level of risk as my brother, your beloved Imam was in when he was killed. I keep getting tormented by the FBI, and now I'm hearing that the NERDS are after me too. I need your help. Many of you have weapons. I fear we must turn this mosque into a holdout. I will bring the remainder of my family here and we will hide out. But I fear we need guards to protect my family and I would appreciate your help protecting us from the onslaught that is coming. We know the police won't protect us. They think we're some kind of terrorist cell," Shihab lied about knowing that the NERDS were after him because he hoped it would increase the level of sympathy.

One of the group's self-appointed spokesman said, "We will protect you. We are your humble servants. We will go in shifts and get our weapons and return to make sure you are safe. If you, as our leader, are at risk, then we, as a community, are all at risk. We will make sure you are safe."

Another, less convinced individual said, "That's nonsense. No one is trying to attack you."

"Doesn't matter," replied the spokesman. "If our Imam fears for his life we need to take it seriously and protect him. If nothing happens, all the better. But we have an obligation to make sure that nothing happens. As they say 'better safe than sorry.'"

The spokesman took over as leader of the protection detail, sending one group of men for their weapons while Shihab, protected by a small contingent of men, went to his house to get his family and bring them to the mosque.

After everyone who was going to be involved in the protection detail had arrived with their weapons, the mosque was closed up. All the doors were sealed and the windows were locked. Mats were thrown on the floor for sleeping. Food and supplies were brought in to support an extended stay. Assignments were made for a rotation of protection detail shifts. They were hunkered in as if they were expecting a big fight.

* * *

Lincoln and Gage were on Gene's plane within an hour. They were planning on arriving into the Detroit area, once again using a different airport in order to avoid detection. Livy made arrangements for a car to be available upon their arrival. They had mapped out the location of Shihab's house, which was close to the mosque. They had brought the same set of weapons they had used for the Sami operation, but this time they had added a grenade launcher to their arsenal. They weren't sure why they brought the grenade launcher. It just felt right to bring it along.

They arrived at Shihab's house within an hour after landing in the Detroit area. They did their usual stakeout of the house on a roof across the street and used their infrared tools to search for signs of life. They found no one in the house. This disappointed them. Had Shihab traveled somewhere? But if he traveled, would he have taken his entire family? It just didn't make sense. Someone should have been in the house.

"Let's go to Sami's house," suggested Lincoln. "Maybe they are holding up there. I wouldn't know why, but we're here now and we should check out all the possibilities."

"Agreed," replied Gage.

Sami's house was another disappointment. They found a couple people in the house by using the infrared scanners, but not enough to account for Shihab's entire family. "That must be the remaining children of Sami along with a caretaker of some type," suggested Gage and Lincoln nodded. "What do we do now?"

"How about the mosque?" suggested Lincoln.

"Probably nothing but it doesn't hurt to check. It looks like this trip may have been a big waste of time."

The mosque was close to Sami's house and as they drove by they noticed it was closed up and looked deserted. They were about to give up when Gage said, "That's strange. The place is boxed up but I thought I saw light through one of the cracks. Let's turn on the infrared and see what that tells us."

Infrared showed close to fifty people in the mosque. But that didn't make sense to Lincoln and Gage. If they were holding worship services, why would they lock up the building so tightly? Worship services normally left the doors wide open inviting everyone, even late comers. So what was going on?

A closer look at the infrared images showed that they were nearly entirely men. Off to a room in the back was a woman and a few children. But in the main worship area of the mosque were only males.

"We need to take a closer look," suggested Lincoln. "This is really fishy. I don't think they are having normal worship services. They are not even lined up the way they would be during worship. They are all mingling around."

Gage interjected, "I would be really careful. To Livy's point, I'll bet they have security cameras all around the place. I'll bet they are just itching to catch us in the act. We need to keep ourselves masked if we're going to go anywhere close to the building. And the other problem is that they may be speaking Arabic and not English. So we'll basically learn nothing. I wish we still had the FBI surveillance in there, but those lawyers forced all the surveillance equipment to be taken out. Now we're running blind."

"Then what do we do? This is definitely suspicious. We have to find out what is going on."

"Let's get into a better position. Let's find a rooftop where we can watch the action and use our infrared to get a more accurate look at what's going on. Then let's call in some help."

"What the heck are you talking about?" questioned Lincoln.

"Let's call in a fire alarm on the building and watch what happens," responded Gage. "Let's see who comes out of the building."

"Excellent idea." The two searched out and found a three story building nearby with a fire escape. They parked the vehicle, grabbed their hand weapons, put on tight fitting plastic gloves to avoid leaving fingerprints, and quickly scaled the fire escape so they could set up position on the top of the building. Once they were ready and in position, Lincoln started dialing his phone. He called 9-1-1 stating they were in the building and they smelled gas and smoke. The pair had also brought their cameras and small weapons including a scoped rifle, but they didn't bring up the larger automatic weapons or the grenade launcher. Once in position they waited to see what was going to happen.

It was just a matter of minutes before the fire truck sirens could be heard and the blinking red lights could be seen off in the distance. Two trucks quickly appeared and parked in front of the mosque. The firemen charged to the building and were pounding at the doors of the mosque demanding they be let in to investigate a reported gas line leak. But they were denied access. Without engaging in a lengthy debate, the firemen took their axes and started hacking at one of the exterior doors of the mosque.

Chapter Fifty-Six

Planning Revenge Details
November, 2017, Los Angeles, CA

Najid arrived at the Los Angeles airport thirty minutes late. It irritated him when planes weren't on time. But he knew it really didn't make a big difference. He was here on an assignment that would not require a minute-by-minute timetable. Nevertheless, it was still an irritation.

Unknown to Najid, an FBI agent was watching for him as he exited the plane. The agent immediately fell in behind him and followed him out of the airport and to the car rental location. The agent hung back so as to not be noticed. When he saw that Najid was going to rent a car, he placed a call to the manager of the local rental location and instructed him, "This is the FBI and I need your help on a critical matter of national security. Make sure your desk agent rents a car that has a GPS tracking device to the Arab looking man standing at your counter."

The manager called his agent back to give him instructions about the rental given to Najid. "Upgrade him if necessary, but make sure the car has GPS without him knowing that's what you're doing."

* * *

Following Shihab's instructions Najid drove to Hollywood, found a Courtland hotel along the way on West Olympic Boulevard, and checked in. Then he placed a call to Shihab using the secured cell phone he had given him.

"Hello."

"This is Najid. What are my instructions?"

"You are to call Nawwaf. He will take over the leadership of this part of your mission. I will text you the phone number shortly. He may still be on a flight but he should be there soon. Please forward this information on to your fellow warriors and also let them know where you are staying."

Najid immediately placed the call after receiving the text. Unfortunately, to his disappointment, Nawwaf's phone went directly to a message machine. Najid left the message saying he had arrived and was waiting for further instructions.

* * *

After landing, as Nawwaf taxied off the runway in LA and the plane headed toward the gate, he turned on his phone and checked for messages. Najid's message was the only one on the phone. He was glad to see Najid had arrived safely and was tucked away in his hotel. That was a good sign to Nawwaf. He interpreted it to mean that the FBI wasn't clued into his activities. He wasn't going to make contact with Najid until he had worked out all the details of the plan. He needed to firm up that the bomb was ready, how he would get the bomb, what the target would be, and how he would get the bomb to Najid. Once all the details were in place, he would update Najid and let him know what his role would be. It was going to be a glorious day for Allah.

Departing the plane, Nawwaf and his new Egyptian Muslim Brotherhood companions Qasim and Kahil became somewhat uncomfortable. They felt as though they were being watched. But they couldn't explain why. It wasn't anything specific, just a feeling they wrote off to nerves. They didn't say anything to each other because it would be considered a sign of weakness, and they didn't want to seem weak to their brothers. So they just shrugged it off.

But they were in fact being watched. Not by anyone, but by a series of cameras. The airport cameras were everywhere and the FBI was able to track and record every movement of the three Muslim brothers. They also had agents on the ground that could be called in if anything looked suspicious. But they were specifically instructed not to do anything that would make it look like they were watching. The cameras would be used for that.

Nawwaf and his companions were observed going directly to the car rental location where they rented a luxury car. They wanted to make sure they had the best of what America had to offer. Then they sped off to the Ritz Hotel on Olympic Blvd in LA. Only the best would do for the warriors of Allah.

After arriving at their three bedroom suite, Nawwaf called Uday, the Muslim brother from LA who had committed to making the bombs and asked him to come to the hotel to meet. He also called Najid to find out what hotel he was at and what his room number was. About an hour later the four Brotherhood members were together in Nawwaf's suite. After the traditional greetings and introductions Nawwaf immediately wanted to discuss the mission at hand. Looking at Uday, he asked, "Where do we stand with the bombs?"

Pulling a backpack off his back, Uday said, "Here's the first one you asked for. It's packed with enough C-4 to take down this hotel. I'll have the other two bombs for you the day after tomorrow."

"Including the nuclear device?" questioned Qasim.

"You bet," Uday replied.

"I need you to deliver this first bomb to the Courtland Hotel on West Olympia Boulevard," commanded Nawwaf, pointing at the backpack. He provided an address and a room number. "The individual you will be handing this bomb off to is Najid. He will be the one delivering the bomb to its destination."

"But you won't tell me the target?" questioned Uday.

"You should know better than to ask."

"Understood," responded the warrior as he slung the backpack containing the bomb back over his shoulder, left the room, and headed for the elevator.

"Well, the first part of our mission is under way," Nawwaf reported to his two companions. "Tomorrow morning I will give the target location to Najid and by tomorrow evening we should be hearing about it on the news."

"And what have you selected as the first target?" questioned Kahil.

"The symbol of Hollywood of course, the Japanese Theatre on Hollywood Boulevard," responded Nawwaf. "Don't you think that would be an excellent target?"

"That would be a perfect target," replied Kahil. "That will receive worldwide attention, just like your hit on the Orlando theme park."

"Actually that wasn't my hit," responded Nawwaf, "but since the guys who did it are all gone I don't mind taking credit for it."

"Go ahead and take credit for it," replied Kahil. "Everybody already thinks you were the one behind it anyway."

"Good enough," replied Nawwaf as he headed for the mini bar in the hotel room. "Anybody want to join me for a celebration drink?"

* * *

An FBI shadow team had followed the three Muslim Brotherhood to the Ritz Hotel. A separate team was also on site at the Courtland Hotel watching Najid's location. But they had missed the connection with the LA Muslim Brotherhood bomb maker. They falsely assumed that the next step on the agenda was for the Najid to meet up with the Brotherhood and get instructions. The FBI had once again misread their queues. They had missed the visit by the LA bomb maker to the Ritz Hotel, and they similarly missed his visit to the Courtland. They were not expecting a third party to be involved. They thought tracking Najid's car would be sufficient.

Instead of watching Najid's room, they watched his car, assuming that if he was making contact with anyone he would need to leave using the same vehicle. Instead the LA Brotherhood member came to the hotel and went directly to Najid's room. He knocked on the door.

Najid answered with the traditional greeting and then Uday barged his way into the room. He took off his backpack, showed Najid the bomb, and instructed him on how the detonator should work.

"Where am I going?" asked Najid. "And is there a specific time that I'm supposed to be there?"

"I have no idea," replied Uday. "My job was only to deliver this to you. You will probably be getting a call giving you further instructions." With that the Brother abruptly turned and left the hotel room.

Najid was slightly unnerved by this visit. He always knew he wanted to commit his life to Allah. But it had suddenly become all too real. He wondered if he would actually have the strength and stamina to carry it through. Would he be able to blow himself up along with everyone else around him? "Of course he could," he told himself out loud.

At this point, all he could do was wait. Everything was in motion and he had to do his part. He had to make Allah proud.

* * *

It was a restless night. Najid couldn't sleep. He was tangled up in a mixture of emotions. He was excited, but also scared. He was nervous and anxious. He feared he would make a mistake, and this wasn't the type of mistake he would be able to recover from. He had one chance and one chance only to do it right.

He was anxious for the phone call that would give him further instructions. He feared that call, but he also wanted to get it over with. He wanted to know what his mission was going to be. But it wasn't until a little after ten in the morning when he finally received that long awaited call.

"Hello," he barked into the phone.

"This is Nawwaf," was the response from the other end of the line. "Did you get it?"

"Yes. I am ready to deliver it. Where do you want me to go and when?"

"Go to German's Japanese Theatre on Hollywood Boulevard. Stand as close to the building as you can. If you can go inside, do it. Sometimes it's open for tourists and sometimes it isn't. Anyway, stand as close as possible and detonate."

"That's it? Go to a movie theater and blow it up? That's the mission?" Najid sounded disappointed.

"That's what we need done," replied Nawwaf. "The theatre is a symbol of Hollywood decadence. Bringing it down would be a shot heard round the world. And your name will forever be inscribed in the cement out front as the one who did the deed. You should be proud to get such a glorious mission."

"Large or small, I will do the will of Allah. When do I go?"

"Right away. Go as soon as you're ready. I will be watching the news to hear that it has happened." With that he disconnected the call.

Najid was excited. He knew his mission. His future was clearly defined and he knew what he needed to do. After reflecting on his mission he agreed with Nawwaf. The theatre would be an excellent target. It was indeed recognized as an international symbol of Western Hollywood decadence. His family would be so proud when they heard what he had accomplished. His name will be heard around the world as a warrior for Allah.

Najid threw on the backpack and left the room. He didn't bother to collect his belongings. He wouldn't be needing any of that any more. All he needed was the backpack and what was inside. He was ready.

Chapter Fifty-Seven

The Showdown

November, 2017, Ann Arbor, Michigan

The fire department made quick work of the front door. They had no idea what they would find once they had broken their way inside. It was hard to understand why a group of men would barricade themselves inside a mosque, and then call 9-1-1 for assistance. Was this some kind of suicide pact?

As the first fireman broke through the door and was about to step inside the building, several shots rang out. It was the sound of automatic weapons fire. The fireman fell backwards to the ground bleeding from several spots in his chest. He had been shot. One of the other firemen jumped to his side and gave the unfortunate verdict. He was dead.

The remaining firemen hurried back to the shelter of their trucks. They didn't want to receive the same fate. This situation was obviously beyond their jurisdiction. It was now a police matter. A message was quickly relayed to the local police department.

The dead fireman was quickly transferred to an emergency fire department ambulance that was standing by. The ambulance rushed from the scene and the remaining firemen returned to their trucks to wait for the arrival of the police. It was just a matter of a couple minutes when the police department came flying to scene with a parade of police cruisers. They arrived rhythmically, one right after another. Soon there were over twenty cruisers on the scene and one of their first instructions was to move the fire trucks out of harm's way. Then a SWAT van pulled into replace them. It wasn't long before the SWAT captain had taken over the scene and was strategically placing his team of expert crime fighters at various locations around the mosque.

Then came the announcement over the loudspeakers. "You are surrounded by the police. Put down your weapons and come out with your hands raised."

There was no response. A couple minutes later the message was repeated. Again no answer. Then it came a third time but this time it included a threat, "If you don't come out we will be forced to fire on you." It was a hollow threat. The police would never fire into a crowd of this type not knowing whether there were hostages or possibly even children. But the captain thought he would try the threat anyway.

Again there was no response. After ten minutes the captain thought he would try a different approach, "We want to avoid a bloodbath. We would like to talk. We will meet you at the front door. Please have a spokesman meet us there."

No response. A volunteer negotiator was dressed in a bulletproof vest and approached the door as promised. He yelled out, "Can I speak with the leader of your group?" Instead of a verbal response, he received a barrage of four bullets to the chest. A bulletproof vest would have protected him if the shots were small rounds fire. But these were shot from an AK-47 and these bullets, rather than being stopped by the vest, were flattened and spread so that by the time it made it through the vest and to his chest it was nearly the size of a silver dollar, and the damage to the chest was devastating. The negotiator was taken completely by surprise. His face was in shock. He collapsed instantly to the ground dead.

As bad as he wanted to, the captain was unable to give the command to shoot back. They really didn't know any more than they did before. Were there hostages? What was the situation? Were there any demands? Without knowing more, it was unsafe to randomly shoot into this large group of people. For all they knew, it was just one individual putting on the whole show. They could potentially kill dozens of people unnecessarily. There had to be another alternative.

All this time, Lincoln and Gage were watching from the top of a nearby building. For them there was no question what was going on. This was some kind of standoff. Shihab had convinced his congregation that he was in trouble and they had gathered together to protect him. "He must be scared out of his mind," explained Gage. "Else why this elaborate protection plan?"

"I think you're right," replied Lincoln. "But these guys are going to play at this game for days. There is no way they're going to give in. They will just continue to pick off our guys one at a time. They have no fear of dying. They think they're doing some kind of great and wonderful thing here. They actually think they are making God proud. It's insane."

"What are we going to do? Sit here and watch? I can't stand seeing this butchery."

"That doesn't make sense either. We have our high powered rifles here and we have the advantage of having our infrared scopes which show us the location of everyone in the building. I suggest we silence our weapons and start picking them off one at a time. Let's start with the people they are trying to protect? Maybe that will shake something loose? Maybe, if these crazies don't have anyone to protect they will give up on this suicide watch. I'll go get our rifles." Lincoln departed and Gage continued to keep watch.

"I agree," replied Gage. When Lincoln returned with the weapons they mounted the silencer on the tip of their high-powered rifles. They set up the weapons on tripods for stability, and loaded them with armor piercing bullets which should easily go through the cement block walls and go on to strike their target.

The infrared scopes showed four people in a back room. In the front prayer room was where the nearly fifty men were situated. They were obviously the protection detail that had barricaded themselves into the building.

"I'm ready," informed Gage.

"So am I," replied Lincoln.

"The four in the back room look like two adults and two smaller children," offered Gage.

"Looking at their body structure, I would guess we have the mom, a teenager, and two smaller children," suggested Lincoln.

"You're probably right. So which one do you want?"

"You do the mom and I'll do the teenager. Then we need to watch to see who comes running into the room. That will probably be Shihab. We need to be ready to take a second shot. If more than one person comes in, you take the one on the left and I'll take the one on the right."

"You have it. On the count of three. One. Two. Three." The two shots rang out simultaneously. It sounded like one silenced shot. Through the infrared they could see that their shots had been on target. The two people that they were targeting instantly dropped to the ground.

Lincoln and Gage both continued to stare through their scopes, hoping Shihab would come running into the room. They released and reengaged their rifle bolts, ejecting the old cartridge and putting a new bullet in the chamber. They assumed the two remaining children would be screaming and their screams would cause a reaction.

The reaction wasn't immediate, but it finally came. Two men entered the room to see what was going on and Gage and Lincoln immediately pulled their triggers, not waiting for a count to three. Again their shots were successful and the two additional individuals could be seen dropping to the ground.

No one else dared to enter the back room. The smaller children could be seen sitting on the floor. There was no doubt that they were in shock. But they had no idea what to do next.

No one else seemed to be brave enough to come in to help the children. The two were just left to their own fears and trauma.

The SWAT team was surprised when after another five minutes someone could be seen at the front door waving a white flag through the hole in the door that the fire department had made earlier. Lincoln and Gage could barely hear what was being yelled. It sounded like, "Stop shooting. We want to talk."

* * *

Inside the mosque, Shihab was the first to hear the screams of the children. But, rather than go himself, he sent a couple of his bodyguards to the back room to see what had happened. He watched from a distance and when he saw the two bodyguards also hit the ground, he knew he was in trouble.

Shihab had sworn he would not negotiate with these infidels, but in his fear he decided he would try talking after all. He grabbed a white flag and went to the front door. He was desperate. He was in fear for his life, but he didn't know which route would be safer. Would it be safer to give in and let the police protect him? Or would it be safer to stay in the mosque where they were all being picked off one at a time? What should he do? So he decided to talk. What could it hurt?

Shihab stood at the front door waving the flag.

The police were extra cautious. They didn't want another casualty. The captain went directly to the loud speaker and told Shihab to call him on his cell phone and he gave him the phone number to call. Then everything was quiet while Shihab found a phone.

"Hello," said the captain when the call came in.

"Hello," responded Shihab. "Why are you shooting us? You are killing innocent women and children. How can you be so senseless and cruel?"

"What are you talking about? You have killed two of our men. We haven't killed anyone. How stupid do you think we are anyway?"

"Lies!" blurted out Shihab. "How dare you lie to me? You have killed my wife and my son and a couple of my warriors, and now you blatantly deny it. How dare you be so cruel?" Shihab was enraged. Shihab decided there would be no negotiating with the police. They would have to fight their way in. He wasn't going to sacrifice his life unnecessarily. Besides he was afraid to die. He had more work to do. He had to follow in the footsteps of his brother. He would now declare his own kind of jihad. He would declare his own holy war.

* * *

Lincoln and Gage stared at the individual with the white flag. He looked familiar, but they weren't sure what was familiar about him. Then Gage pulled out his Smartphone and looked at the picture of Shihab. "That was Shihab," he whispered to Lincoln with disappointment in his voice. "I don't know who we shot in that back room, but we apparently hit the wrong guys."

"Then I guess our job still isn't done," replied Lincoln. "How are we going to pull him out of that crowd?"

"We need to do something that will draw him out? If we can get him to come to the door again, we'll be ready for him next time."

"What are you suggesting?"

"Last time he came to the door because he was afraid we were taking him out one person at a time," suggested Gage. "Maybe we need to continue doing that until he comes to the door again."

"Good enough," replied Lincoln. "I'm a little nervous about the size of this group. They are a force to be reckoned with. Maybe a little culling would be a good idea anyway. Let's take out two at random. Then wait five minutes. Then take out two more at random. And so on. Let's see how long it takes for someone to start screaming and waving the flag."

"I'm ready when you are. Let's hit the first pair at the count of three. One. Two. Three." The two shots were again simultaneous, but instead of two individuals dropping, three fell to the ground. Apparently one of the shots had been powerful enough to pass through the first target and take out a second as well.

Five minutes went by and there was no white flag. But Lincoln and Gage could see a lot of turmoil in the mosque. The shots hadn't gone unnoticed. People were looking down at the three that had been hit. There was no sign of anyone trying to help them so they were obviously killed by the shots. But there was still no white flag.

Lincoln and Gage waited an extra two minutes. But when they saw there was no sign of anyone even preparing to come forth with a flag, they decided to try again. "I guess we do it again," suggested Gage.

"One. Two. Three." Again a simultaneous pair of shots rang out and two bodies fell in the mosque.

This time the reaction was obvious, but not what was expected or desired. Instead their infrared scopes showed the Shihab protection detail lining up along the walls of the mosque as if they were preparing to have a major gun battle, barrels pointing outward. This was becoming a shoot-out at the OK corral. This was turning into an all-out war.

Chapter Fifty-Eight

The First Step
November, 2017, Los Angeles, CA

Najid drove up and down Hollywood Blvd, frustrated he wasn't able to find a parking space near the target. Eventually he gave up and parked on a side street several blocks away from the Japanese Theatre. He was excited because he was getting close to successfully executing his piece of the much larger pie.

He swung on the backpack and checked his pocket for the detonator. It was still there, tucked safely away. All he needed to do was to get into position, open the safety cover over the detonator switch, and push the magic button. With that act he would become a hero to Allah and his virgins would be waiting to greet him on the other side. What a glorious day this would be.

* * *

The FBI had relaxed their patrol on Najid. They assumed he hadn't made contact with the Muslim Brotherhood and therefore didn't have any instructions telling him what to do. The FBI assumed Najid was spending the day seeing the Hollywood sights, which often started with the Japanese Theatre and then moved on to one of the tour busses. They didn't take note of the fact that the backpack he carried seemed to be stuffed fuller than what would make sense for someone just being a tourist. It was a similar mistake to the one made at the Boston Marathon bombing. The FBI was proving that even the sophisticated organization that they were can easily make the same mistake more than once.

The FBI agents kept an eye on Najid from a distance. They watched as he walked along Hollywood Boulevard, stopping to look at the stars along the street, occasionally showing that he recognized one of the names. He didn't seem to be in a rush. There was no urgency in what he was doing, which fooled the FBI agents even more. It all appeared as if Najid was just out there being a tourist. He didn't appear to be a threat to anyone.

* * *

Najid was having fun. He had always wanted to see these stars and the handprints in the sidewalk around the Japanese Theatre. He had seen this in pictures many times. He wanted to see if he could find any of his favorite stars. Most of all he wanted to find Elvis Presley and Sandra Bullock. Finding those two would make his day complete. So he took his time, taking in the scenery as many of the other tourists were doing. He was having fun. He hadn't forgotten his mission. That would be the culmination of the perfect day. But he wanted to enjoy this piece of it too.

Once he arrived at the theatre he looked at each of the impressions in the cement. It didn't take long for him to find Jack Nicholson and Jimmy Stewart, two of his favorites. He also found John Wayne. Eventually he found his two heroes. He noted that Sandra's prints were fairly recent, which surprised him because he thought she should have been recognized as a star years earlier. In his opinion she was an incredible actress.

Eventually the time had come for him to complete the mission he was sent to do. He walked toward the theatre, getting as close as possible. Off to the right side, against the wall, he pretended to be looking at one of the footprints. It didn't matter that he was looking at the prints of a person he had never heard of before. It just mattered that he executed his mission. Then he set the backpack down next to the building.

* * *

The FBI agents observing him suddenly realized their blunder. Najid was taking off his backpack. That wasn't a good sign. This drew their attention to the size and the weight of the backpack. It was obviously quite heavy and bulky. That wasn't normal for a tourist. Something was wrong here. In a panic the FBI agents started running across Hollywood Boulevard toward the theatre. One of the agents stayed behind and started screaming into his telephone that they were in a mayday situation. A bomb had been planted and detonation was imminent.

The agents that were crossing the street started screaming at all the tourists in the area, "Get away. Bomb! Get away! Hurry!"

Some made it away safely, but for many of them it was too late. As Najid saw the agents running toward him, he knew he needed to hurry. He quickly pulled the trigger out of his pocket, flipped open the protective covering, and just as one of the agents was about to make a grab for the detonator, Najid pushed the button.

* * *

Qasim, Kahil, and Nawwaf sat comfortably in their Ritz Hotel room watching the movie "The Proposal." They especially like the scene where Sandra Bullock was coming out of the shower and was walking across the room butt naked. Just as the movie was about to get to the scene they had been anxiously waiting for, the news broadcast cut away to a special report. The broadcast announcer said, "We have a special report. There has been a bombing at German's Japanese Theater on Hollywood Boulevard. Initial indications are that it was a suicide terrorist bombing. Observers noted that there were police or FBI agents running around trying to get people away from the site just seconds before the bomb went off. It was an enormous explosion which leveled the entire theatre. Cars that were driving by on Hollywood Boulevard were ripped off the roadway and thrown into the building across the street. There are no initial estimates of the casualties, but it looks to be in the hundreds."

Nawwaf was angry and blurted out, "Why did he have to blow up that bomb right then? He messed up the whole movie for us."

But Kahil brought him back to reality, "We had a successful detonation. We should be proud. I'll let our Brotherhood in Egypt know about the success and they can post pictures of Najid so everyone can recognize him as our latest hero."

With that the three Brotherhood members high-fived each other. "This is a great day for Allah," spoke up Qasim. "This day will be remembered for many years to come as the day we made a mark against the decadence of Hollywood."

Nawwaf commented, "Now that we have made our mark and gotten their attention, we are ready for both the second and third part of our mission. The bombs and the heroes for both missions will be available tomorrow. Let's focus on the third part of our mission, which will be the biggest part. We need to plant our nuclear device somewhere in the Los Angeles area. Any suggestions on where we should place the bomb?"

"I say we finish off Hollywood," suggested Kahil. "Maybe we hit Beverly Hills or one of the studios."

"Shouldn't we maximize the casualties?" asked Qasim. "I think we can make this the biggest strike that ever happened, all with one quick bomb."

"How about we take out the LA airport?" asked Nawwaf. "That would shut down a major traffic center; especially one that impacts interactions with all of Asia."

"All these ideas sound good," responded Kahil. "I guess we need to ask ourselves if we're trying to impact the financial structure or the population."

"Can't we hit both?" asked Nawwaf. "If we pick our target appropriately I think we can have an impact in both of these areas. I think we can hit two birds with one stone. If we hit central LA we will disrupt both the population and we'll also force a shutdown of the LA airport."

"Where in LA do you suggest we make the hit?" asked Kahil.

"How about right here?" suggested Qasim. "How about right here in this hotel room? We are close enough to the airport to disrupt air traffic. And we're definitely going to impact the LA population from this location."

"Then it's settled," responded Nawwaf. "I will have the bomb delivered to this room and I will ask our hero to come to this room and detonate the bomb here. But that will mean that we will need to get out of here. We need to get to Las Vegas or on the other end of the grapevine if we're going to avoid the blast. I'll get everything set up and then we need to get out of here fast. Let's plan to leave as soon as the bomb and our hero are in place."

"I vote we go to Las Vegas," commented Qasim. "I love that town."

"Las Vegas it is."

"Let's worry about the second part of our mission later. I don't really care where we set off the second backpack bomb. It's the third part, the nuclear part, that has to go off without a hitch."

Chapter Fifty-Nine

The Second Step
November, 2017, Los Angeles, CA

Taqiy's train arrived close to midnight. He had exchanged text messages with Najid. Najid had made a reservation for him at the same Courtland Hotel he was staying in. All Taqiy had to do was to catch a taxi and travel directly to the hotel. During the taxi ride he interacted with the taxi driver. He informally asked the driver if there was any news. Taqiy knew Najid was scheduled to perform his piece of the revenge puzzle soon after he arrived, but he had no idea what it was. He hoped the taxi driver would be able to give him an update.

"I guess you haven't heard," the taxi driver started. He was one of these guys that after you get him started talking it is hard to shut him down. He would go on and on for hours if you let him. "I guess you don't hear much on a train. There was a big explosion at the Japanese Theatre in Hollywood. They think it was a suicide bomber. They think it was one of these idiot Muslim terrorists who think killing themselves is the way to make a difference. All they're doing is making everyone mad. I can't believe they really expect to have a bunch of virgins waiting for them. I can't understand why they think that killing a bunch of innocent people should be rewarded. Now we have these vigilantes out there going after these terrorist idiots. I hope they blow Mecca back into history. It would serve these idiots right to lose their holy shrine. Their Allah must be an idiot if he thinks all this killing is for some holy purpose. These heathens don't have a clue what they're worshiping anyway. They can't even draw a picture of it. It's just nuts."

Taqiy's blood was boiling. How could anyone be so stupid? How could he tolerate this blasphemy? It's no wonder Allah wants all these infidels destroyed. They are sinners and infidels of the worst kind. They need to be destroyed. How dare they blaspheme against Allah. This was unheard of. If there was ever any doubt whether what he was doing was right, that doubt was gone now. There would be no second thoughts or hesitation for him when it came time to pushing that button.

The taxi driver continued on his rant, "The Old Testament says 'Thou shalt not kill' in several places. I guess these Islamic terrorists think they're somehow above the commandments of the book they claim to believe in. That's really twisted. They say they believe one thing and then they do the exact opposite. I'll never understand how anyone can kill themselves along with a bunch of other innocent people and think that they're doing a good deed. Can anyone really be that stupid?"

Taqiy couldn't take any more. He always thought of himself as tolerant. But today, when he was so close to achieving his goal and making his mark, his tolerance level had achieved its maximum.

"Stop the car immediately," he yelled out.

"I can't stop here," complained the taxi driver. "I'm in the center lane."

"I don't care. Pull over and stop the car immediately."

The taxi driver followed his instructions, made his way over to the side of the road, and stopped the car. Taqiy jumped out of the car followed by the driver who yelled out, "Don't tell me you're one of those idiots?" The taxi driver was worried that he was going to lose a fare.

Taqiy yelled at him, "You are the idiot. You don't understand what you're talking about. People like you should be erased from the earth. You are the reason why this is such an evil place. People like you destroy the faith of the believers. People like you are the cause of an infinite amount of grief and pain in Allah."

"People like me? Its people like me that give people like you a world to criticize. We make the world a success and you terrorize it claiming that killing people like me makes it a better place. Do you ever listen to yourself? Do you realize how stupid you really sound?"

"Go away and leave me alone," commanded Taqiy as he turned to walk off.

"Not till you pay your fare," ordered the taxi driver.

Taqiy started walking away but the taxi driver would have none of it. He ran after him and grabbed him on the left shoulder with his right hand. "You owe me for the fare, you crazy ignoramus."

Taqiy was even more enraged. He turned around rapidly and punched the taxi driver in the nose. The taxi driver took a step backwards and put his right hand to his face but grabbed Taqiy with his left hand. He wasn't going to let this thief get away. So he swung back with his right hand formed into a fist throwing an uppercut, striking Taqiy under the chin and causing him to collapse to his knees. "Pay up, you pervert," commanded the taxi driver.

Taqiy was a little groggy, and used that to his advantage to pretend he was too dazed to respond. Then he remembered a trick he had seen on one of the crime shows on TV. He grabbed a ball-point-pen he had in his shirt pocket, jumped up, maneuvered himself behind the taxi driver, put one hand around the driver's neck, and with the other hand he stuck the pen into the taxi driver's neck.

To the surprise of both the taxi driver and Taqiy, at the instance that the pen went into the driver's throat, a bullet went into Taqiy's forehead. No one tried to figure out where the shot came from. They were both too surprised to realize what had just happened. The driver was only concerned about his neck, and Taqiy was too dead to care. He had gone to visit his virgins earlier than expected.

* * *

The driver went into shock. He couldn't believe what just happened. He struggled for breath and groped at the pen, uncertain if he should pull it out or not. But as he struggled for breath, the decision became obvious. He yanked at the pen and pulled it from his neck. As he did, he was suddenly surrounded by several FBI agents. They just seemed to appear out of nowhere. They immediately went to work trying to save his life. In the distance a siren was blaring. It would be the ambulance that would come to the taxi driver's aid and save his life.

The FBI agents had been on the train having joined it a few stops after Detroit and they were tracking Taqiy. Seeing the taxi driver get stabbed forced them into action. They would have preferred to keep an eye on Taqiy, but his attack on the taxi driver forced a response.

The agents performed first aid until the ambulance arrived. The taxi driver would be all right. But phase two of the three-phase attack on Hollywood would be skipped and phase three would have to wait for the arrival of a third warrior.

Chapter Sixty

The Second Step Repeated
November, 2017, Las Vegas, Nevada

Uthal was thrilled to be chosen to drive a car to Los Angeles. He always wanted to see the scenery across the United States and he decided he wasn't about to rush his life's final journey. This was going to be fun. He followed the exact same route as the previous warriors who had traveled to Golden, Colorado. He made it to Denver and gave them a call on their cell. He wanted to pay them a short visit and see how their kidnapping was going while he was in town. Since he didn't receive a response to several call attempts he continued on, crossing the Rockies using Interstate 70. He entered Utah and jumped on Interstate 15 some distance below Provo. He would stay on 15 all the way to the Los Angeles area. But he couldn't resist the temptation to take a few deviations.

His first divergence was to see Cedar Breaks National Monument just outside of Cedar City. It was just as beautiful as he had always heard. The colorful mountain crags were unbelievable. It was the most beautiful thing he had ever seen.

Now he was on a roll. His next divergence was to travel along Highway 9 and then along 89 heading through Zion National Park and on toward the Grand Canyon. He would be crazy not to visit the Grand Canyon when he was so close. Besides, the mission in LA wasn't going to go away just because he was a day or two late.

After the Grand Canyon he went on to Flagstaff, Arizona, and then headed west on Interstate 40. At this point he remembered one of his favorite movies, "Fools Rush In," and he decided he wanted to throw a coin off the Hoover Dam into the reservoir. He hoped it would make him lucky and he would be able to successfully complete his mission for Allah.

At Kingman he jumped on Highway 93 and, as he crossed the dam on the Arizona-Nevada border he threw a coin from the car window, aiming for the reservoir below. But it didn't make it. In the movie it had seemed so easy for the girl to throw the coin into the reservoir. He opened the driver side window and whirled the coin out. But the distance was further than he thought. His coin fell to the street near the edge of the embankment.

This frustrated Uthal. In anger, and not really caring if he received a ticket, he stopped his vehicle, jumped out, and retrieved the coin. He immediately threw the coin again. He ran to the side to watch it hit the water, but there wasn't any water there. He had thrown the coin over the wrong side of the dam. The coin fell away to nothing, toward the deep abyss that was the far side of the dam.

Loud speakers were blaring at him ordering him to get back into his car and drive on. But he paid no heed. He searched his pockets for another coin but couldn't find one. Now what was he going to do? In desperation and frustration he jumped back into the car and drove on eventually crossing over the dam. But he wasn't going to be deterred. He drove on to the visitor's center and purchased something from them so he could come up with a few coins. Then he set out again, driving over the dam this time coming from Nevada and crossing over to the Arizona side. This time he was going to be a little smarter. He opened the passenger side window and threw the coin out the window. Almost at the instant he released the coin, he realized he had again tossed the coin over the wrong side of the dam into the deep abyss. He was driving the opposite direction on the dam and he should have been throwing the coin out of the opposite side of the car.

Uthal became so angry he punched the steering wheel with his fist. Normally that would have made him feel better. However, this time he had his hand slightly twisted and when he hit the wheel he ended up breaking his index finger. He screamed in pain and frustration, wondering what else could possibly go wrong. Luckily he had more coins so he rolled down the driver side window, took all three of his remaining coins, and hurled them as high as possible toward the edge of the embankment. But his luck had turned and this time two of the coins made it over the edge of the dam and fell into the reservoir. The third coin fell hopelessly on the pavement.

Once he arrived on the Arizona side of the dam, Uthal pulled into a lookout point. His finger throbbed and he desperately looked for some tape so he could tape two of his fingers together. He hoped this would ease the pain and give some stability to the broken finger. He obviously wasn't going to get the finger set. That would be a ridiculous waste of time considering his short-term future. He wanted to get on with his mission and a broken finger wasn't going to delay him.

Uthal turned around and once again crossed over the dam to the Nevada side of the border. Then he returned to Highway 93 and headed on to Las Vegas. He had always wanted to get a close look at "Sin City." He could see the Strip from a long way off and drove into town heading directly for the tallest building there, which was the Stratosphere tower. After arriving on the Strip he cruised back and forth for over an hour just to check out all the sites. Then he pulled into the Winningers Hotel parking lot. He had always wanted to stay in that hotel. He had heard a lot about the entertainment and rides in the hotel and he wanted to check it out.

Before going to the hotel, Uthal's first stop was to a pharmacy where he picked up some bandaging tape and a splint. Then he wrapped his broken finger into the splint and against the finger next to it. Almost immediately it felt better. It still hurt, but the limited movement kept it from throbbing.

He checked into the hotel. Uthal no sooner was settled into his room when his phone rang. "Where are you?" It was Nawwaf checking up on him.

"Las Vegas," replied Uthal. He wasn't about to lie.

"Why aren't you in LA?"

"I had some car trouble and this is as far as I was able to go." He lied anyway. "I should be there late tomorrow."

"Good. Don't waste your time getting distracted in that city. Get down here as quickly as possible. We have a critical mission for you to accomplish. We need you right away."

"I'll be there," was all Uthal said, and then he disconnected the phone. But he had no intention of missing out on the fun he had planned for tonight, broken finger or not. He proceeded to the entertainment floor of the hotel and spent the rest of the evening playing games. He also threw a few dollars into the slot machines. He convinced himself this was just an experiment. He wanted to see what it felt like to gamble. He never intended to really gamble. He figured he was doing this for Allah. He wanted to be able to better understand why Allah hated it so much. But when he won a few coins, he was just as excited as any gambler. He ended up spending hours playing the slot machines.

It was a late night for Uthal. He didn't get to bed until four in the morning. But he never had as much fun. He realized that part of the reason this was so much fun was because he had noone watching over his shoulder. He wasn't accountable to anyone.

The city never seemed to sleep. The following morning it was ten-thirty before he finally woke up and then it was with a splitting headache. He knew this migraine was punishment from Allah for being so decadent. But it was fun anyway. He wondered what Allah would consider as punishment for his sins of the night before. But he knew he would be completely forgiven once he carried out his mission. He knew he had to repent if he was going to serve Allah. He wanted to be as pure as possible before his deliverance. Only then would his mission be pleasing to Allah. He would say his prayers to Allah and afterwards ask for forgiveness.

It wasn't until two in the afternoon before Uthal finally hit the road toward LA. He didn't really want to leave, but he knew he had to finish his mission. In earlier communications with Najid, he made arrangements for a room in the same Courtland hotel his friends were using. He had received driving directions so he knew how to get there.

But he wasn't going to let Nawwaf rush him too much. He still wanted to see the countryside before he arrived.

He followed Interstate 15 into the Los Angeles area, and then switched to Highway 210 for the remainder of the trip to the Hollywood area. Finding the hotel was easy. He had received good directions from Najid. Once he was settled into the hotel he placed a call to Nawwaf. After the customary greetings, he said, "I'm here. What do I do now?"

Nawwaf gave him instructions to come to the Ritz Hotel in the center of town in the morning where he would be instructed on how to operate the bomb. "We need you here exactly at ten and you will be taught by the bomb's manufacturer how to detonate the bomb. After that, we will set a precise time for the execution of your mission. Understand?"

"Understood," replied Uthal. "I will be there at ten."

* * *

After disconnecting the call with Uthal, Nawwaf immediately placed a call to Uday. "We are set for ten tomorrow morning. Can you deliver the nuclear bomb at that time?"

"That's a little rushed," replied Uday. "But I think I can make it."

"Excellent. We'll have the warrior here at that time and you'll need to teach him how to detonate the bomb. As it turns out, we won't be needing the second C-4 bomb. We saw on the news report that we lost the warrior that was supposed to use that bomb. Aparently he was shot after a confrontation with the police."

"Understood. How stupid of him. He should have been more careful. It's pretty simple to fire off the nuclear bomb so it shouldn't be a problem."

After the call was completed Qasim questioned, "Can we trust these guys? Who is this Uthal anyway? I am worried that there may be an information leak after the disaster we had with Taqiy."

"I understand your concern," responded Nawwaf. "But these are the resources we have at our disposal and I think we need to do the best we can with what we have available."

"That's not very comforting," responded Qasim, but he didn't press the issue any further because he knew it would be no use. He didn't have any other options to offer.

Chapter Sixty-One

Shootout at the OK Corral
November, 2017, Ann Arbor, Michigan

A white flag was being waved through the hole in the front door of the mosque. This drove Lincoln into a panic. He could see the entire group inside of the mosque lined up along the outer wall ready to fire. Referring to the police and the SWAT team, he said, "We have to warn them. The guys in the mosque are setting up a trap. This is going to be a slaughter."

"What can we do?" asked Gage. But his question was too late. Lincoln had already acted. He had taken a shot. He had killed the flag bearer and the flag fell to the ground. This act spooked the police who had started to approach the white flag, and they quickly moved back behind the protection of their vehicles.

"Good job," complemented Gage. "And it looks like the police haven't figured out where the shots are coming from yet. These silenced sniper rifles are really quiet. Did you see that the cops were all looking at the mosque like they think the flag bearer was somehow stopped by someone inside the mosque? They don't even suspect us yet. But we better be careful because that may change any minute."

"That was a desperation shot, but we needed to do something bigger to warn them," responded Lincoln who was uncomfortable receiving a complement from Gage. It rarely happened so he didn't know how to react. "I think I should go down and get the grenade gun and bring it up here," suggested Lincoln. "We may need it before all this is over. Obviously everyone in that building is ready to shoot at our police. We know there aren't any hostages. But our police can't go with that assumption. So we may need to help the process."

"You're right. But you're going to have to be extremely careful getting that rifle with all the cops crawling around down there."

"Agreed," commented Lincoln as he stood up and headed for the building's fire escape.

Gage remained behind. Lincoln's mission didn't require both of them. Down below he observed the police in turmoil. They were afraid to approach. They laid back and waited. Then the captain in charge used the loud speaker to announce, "What's going on in there? Call me on the phone so we can talk."

The response from the mosque was immediate and unexpected. Rifles could be seen protruding from around the edges of the numerous doorways, and this was immediately followed by a barrage of weapons fire aimed at the vehicle behind which the captain was taking cover. Over two dozen shots were fired. The captain could be seen collapsing to the ground. Contrary to the hype that Hollywood movies portray, cars don't offer much protection from heavy weapons fire. Most of the shots from the high-powered rifles went through both sides of the car is if it was cardboard. The captain didn't stand a chance.

But there wasn't any return fire from the SWAT team. No one ordered return fire. The captain could no longer do it. They were in a dilemma. They had lost their leader, and the second in command was hampered with the thought that there might be hostages. There were no clear shots at the shooters in the mosque. The second in command called his headquarters to report the situation and to ask for recommendations. He was told that the only option was for a standoff. They would simply have to wait out the terrorists in the mosque. There were to be no more announcements made. No more calls for a phone conversation. Just a dead silent wait. The police settled in for a long standoff.

Unfortunately, the individuals in the mosque had different plans. After about a fifteen minute wait, they repeated their barrage of shots, this time firing at another of the vehicles behind which three cops were sheltered. Sadly, the result was the same. Two more cops were down and the third cop was fortunate enough to have dropped to the ground when the shooting started. He escaped without a wound. But the other two lost their lives.

The second in command called for a strategic retreat. They weren't going to leave the area. But they decided to find better protection by putting a second layer of cars between themselves and the shooters in the mosque.

All of this activity kept the police occupied as Lincoln snuck his way to his car, retrieved his grenade launcher which was packed in its carrying case, and worked his way back to his hideout with Gage. After his return to the roof he approached Gage and handed him the carrying case containing the launcher. "You're the better shot with these things. Can you lay one through that hole in the front door?"

"Sure," replied Gage. "But we'll be spotted. A grenade missile isn't quite as inconspicuous as a bullet. I think the police will see the shot. They will spot us."

"Do we really have a choice?"

"No, but we better have an escape plan in our back pocket. The real danger is that we don't want to be connected with anything here or they'll start tying us to the Sami assassination as well, and maybe even the mosque bombings."

"Here's what we'll do. I'll take all our weapons to the car except for the launcher. I'll drive the car around to the bottom of the fire escape, and text you when I'm ready. When you get my signal, take the shot. Leave the launcher behind and get to the car as quickly as possible. And then we'll get the heck out of here and leave the rest of the standoff to the SWAT team."

"Sounds like a plan," replied Gage. "But if we get caught we're going to be in deep muck."

"We won't get caught," assured Lincoln. He grabbed the rifles they had been using earlier and headed for the fire escape. "Be ready for my message."

"Roger that." Gage started assembling the launcher as Lincoln went to retrieve the car.

Gage was an expert at this type of launcher. In Iraq he had become the master of the double load. He could fire a rocket grenade, and within two seconds he could launch a second grenade. The second grenade would be in the air at about the same time the first one exploded. However, after that second launch the launcher was too hot for a third grenade and the heat of the launcher could explode the rocket in the launcher before it was launched. But two grenades fired back to back allowed for the increased possibility of a successful mission. This was a time when a successful mission was needed.

Gage and Lincoln always wore the tight fitting latex gloves. These felt like skin but were thick enough to not leave any fingerprint impression. But, out of habit, Gage also wiped down the launcher and the launcher case to make sure there were no fingerprints from before he put on the gloves. The launcher itself had already been sanitized of any serial numbers and was untraceable. He was ready to fire by the time Lincoln's text arrived.

Gage took aim at the hole in the front door and then fired. The first shot was slightly left, hitting a piece of the broken door, and dropped to the ground in front of the door. Reloading was smooth and Gage was able to compensate for the inaccuracy of the sighting by aiming the second grenade slightly to the right. The compensation placed the grenade on target and it flew directly through the hole in the door less than a second before the first gernade exploded.

Now the chase was on. Gage dropped the launcher and ran to the fire escape stairs. He placed one foot on each side of the outside of the stairs and rapidly slid down. The latex gloves weren't as smooth as his hands would have been but he couldn't risk leaving any fingerprints. This was dangerous because of the height of the stairs, and the risk was that he would hit the ground dangerously hard. But he decided to risk it in order to make his escape as quickly as possible.

Gage did hit the ground too hard. His right ankle twisted slightly, just enough to sprain it. Lincoln saw the hit and reached over to throw open the passenger door. Gage fought through the pain and quickly jumped into the car. Lincoln was already driving off before Gage had a chance to shut the door.

* * *

As the door of the car closed, the second explosion could be heard. The first had been the explosion at the front of the mosque. The front door of the mosque was now replaced by a large gaping hole over twenty feet across and fifteen feet high. Access to the mosque was no longer blocked. The defenders of the mosque who had foolishly taken cover in the area of the explosion were now either killed or badly injured. Unfortunately for Shihab, he was trying to peek out the hole in the front door as the explosion occurred and he ended up being one of the causalities of the first blast.

The second explosion occurred when Lincoln and Gage were pulling away. This explosion was more devastating to the warriors then to the mosque. The concussion of the blast killed several dozen defenders and injured a dozen more. Those who weren't killed or injured were knocked unconscious and at a minimum were temporarily deafened.

The reaction of the police was initially one of surprise. They saw the first grenade hit the ground and weren't sure what to make of it. Then they saw the second grenade fly through the opening. Several police looked in the direction where the grenade had been fired from, but the edge of the building kept them from seeing anything. Luckily for Lincoln and Gage, the police initially assumed some other agency, like the FBI, had directed the attack and they didn't immediately react. The confusion in their change of leadership left them unsure about what to do next. They didn't investigate who or why the grenades were launched. They assumed it was all a part of some master plan. Since the captain was dead, and his second in command was inexperienced, the delayed reaction of the police gave Lincoln and Gage plenty of time to make their escape.

The mosque was no longer under siege. In spite of the surprise and delayed reaction of the police, the SWAT team was able to quickly sweep into the mosque and take the remaining defenders hostage. It wasn't long before all the defenders were either in handcuffs, on emergency gurneys, or in body bags.

* * *

Lincoln and Gage were amazed at the ease with which they had made their escape. There weren't any cops chasing them on the ground, and there weren't any helicopters in the air. Helicopters weren't dispatched because of the risk of being shot at from the mosque. Their escape had been easier than expected. They anticipated some kind of fight or at least a chase, but nothing happened.

The two headed back to the airport but took the long way around by driving a scattered route in order to avoid any potential trackers they might have missed. After arriving at the airport they quickly made their way on board the plane, Lincoln helping Gage because of his sprained ankle. They were off within the next fifteen minutes. The fast getaway was important. They assumed the quick escape would avoid any suspicion. In the event that any of their movement was tracked, they hoped the police would assume they would have departed too quickly to have been involved.

Lincoln and Gage felt successful. Once on board the plane Lincoln spoke up, "I'd declare this day successful even though we still don't know if we eliminated our target Shihab."

Gage jumped in, "At the very least we increased everyone's awareness of the dangers of the Islamic Jihad community and the Muslim Brotherhood. When it came to these groups, it isn't a matter of free religious expression. It's an issue of direct attacks against the American way of life. And these attacks cannot be stopped by Liberalist understandings and tolerance. They require an eye-for-an-eye approach. However, I am disappointed we didn't learn more about the kidnappings."

"Well I think we shared that revenge message today. I feel we were successful in delivering this message by showing how the Muslim community would even attack our police. They were willing to damage the United States which is the country they depend upon for their existence. Most of them are probably United States citizens. It just doesn't make any sense."

"It's pretty sad, but you're right. Nothing is as important to the Muslim community as the Muslim community; even if it comes to killing your non-Muslim neighbor."

It wouldn't be until several days later that they finally found out they had completed their mission. Shihab, the leader of the cell in Ann Arbor who had taken over after the death of Sami, was killed in the blast by the first grenade. His wife was also killed. She had been shot by an unknown assailant, assumed to be one of the individuals in the mosque because the grenade blast had hidden any trace of the shots fired by Lincoln and Gage into the building.

Chapter Sixty-Two

The Second Step Executed
November, 2017, Los Angeles, California

Alvin Foller, along with his FBI team which included Livy Cobar, Jonathan Lusere, Edward Colton, Gerick Johannes, and over a dozen additional agents, arrived in Los Angeles and headed directly for their respective hotels. They decided to spread out, not knowing exactly where their efforts would be needed. They did this because travel time in the LA area was so slow Alvin felt it was important to keep his assets at locations which could respond quickly to threats in any part of the city.

Alvin went to a hotel located close to the Hollywood hotel that Najid had stayed in. His hope was that there was some additional strategic reason for selecting this hotel and those other Muslim Brotherhood team members would also select this area.

Livy and Jonathan headed for the Ritz Hotel in downtown LA. They knew the Arab community had a tendency toward extravagance, and there was nothing more extravagant than the Ritz. However, the tension between the two of them had not subsided. They hardly spoke a word the entire time they traveled from Denver to LA. Once they arrived at the hotel, Jonathan took it upon himself to book a separate room away from Livy, explaining he needed time to think.

Edward and Gerick headed for the Anaheim area, suspicious that the Islamists may be planning another hit, this time on a Los Angeles theme park.

Alvin was frustrated. His team had failed in recognizing the threat presented by Uthal, and he realized they may have had a near miss with Taqiy. He knew there were possibly others out there. He knew of one more, Najid, who was the third of the threesome coming from Ann Arbor. But he didn't know who and how many more were out there beyond that. He wished he had someone on the inside who could keep him informed.

What frustrated Alvin even more was the realization that the Muslim Brotherhood had an informant inside the FBI. The tables had been turned. Rather than the FBI being the super sleuths, they were the ones being spied upon. His first item of business after saving LA was to continue to dig out the internal mole.

But then his thoughts returned to the business at hand. He knew about Uthal and using the GPS of the car, the FBI was successfully able to track him to the same hotel that his friends had used earlier. Alvin and a couple of his agents found a location close to the entrance of the hotel so they could observe any of Uthal's activities. They were convinced that he was here to perform a mission similar to Najid. This time they paid more attention to the hotel room and not just to the car. They had someone else monitor the car using the GPS tracker. They also booked a room next to his which allowed them to put monitoring equipment against the wall. That gave them the ability to listen in on any conversations. They took turns in shifts watching for any activity, but nothing happened until the following morning. They would be extremely careful this time. They weren't about to again make more foolish assumptions which would result in casualties.

* * *

Uday, the Muslim Brother in the LA area, was on time. He arrived at the Ritz Hotel, ready to deliver the bomb. The bomb fit nicely into a large suitcase, and no one was suspicious about a suitcase in a hotel. He went directly up to Nawwaf's room and knocked. After the traditional greetings, Uday was informed that Uthal had not yet arrived and they would need to wait for him. He joined Nawwaf, Qasim, and Kahil on the couch where they were listening to a news report about a standoff at a mosque in Ann Arbor, Michigan.

"Isn't that Sami and Shihab's mosque?" asked Nawwaf, realizing he had answered his own question. He was in a frenzy, jumping up from the couch and throwing his hands up in the air. "What the heck is going on? Have the infidels declared out right war on us? Are they now attacking us in our mosques? How can the police just invade and explode one of Allah's places of worship? This is another mosque in the Detroit area. How many are they planning on destroying? And look at the number of dead. This is open Jihad."

"I always knew it would come to this," responded Qasim. "Satan's influence over the infidels is strong. These infidels are the spawn of Satan and he is using them to do his dirty work, all with the excuse that power makes right. They think that just because they're bigger that they have a right to suppress and maybe even eliminate us. This is a Zionist attempt to bring Muslims into subjection."

The four of them had their hearts racing as they watched fellow warriors for Allah being escorted out of the mosque and placed into the back of a police truck-holding cell. Uday ranted, "Are we going to allow these Zionist infidels to place our Muslim brothers into concentration camps? Are they trying to send all of us away to Guantanamo Bay? This is an unprecedented level of torture, even for these infidels."

Uthal arrived at the Ritz Hotel about thirty minutes late. He wasn't worried about being on time because he assumed that the Muslim Brotherhood he was meeting with were on Middle Eastern time anyway, which meant anything within a couple hours was close enough. But Nawwaf had a different sense of time and he was both frustrated and irritated by Uthal's lateness.

After the knock on the door, Nawwaf, still frustrated by what he had just seen on the television, yelled at Uthal, "Where in the heck were you? What took you so long?" He didn't even allow for the traditional greeting to occur before he started barking. "We have been waiting for you all morning. I can't believe you are so rude as to keep Allah waiting."

"I didn't keep anyone waiting," Uthal uncaringly replied. "I'm here now and let's get this going. What is my mission? What am I supposed to be doing?"

"Have you heard about what's been happening at your mosque back in Ann Arbor?"

"No. What has happened?"

* * *

Nawwaf gave Uthal his version of the events in Ann Arbor, making sure it sounded powerful enough to make Uthal feel the urge for revenge. Uthal was in shock. His entire world seemed to be crumbling around him. These were close friends and possibly even family members who were attacked and killed in that mosque. He even recognized the faces of some of the people as they were escorted out of the mosque as the scene kept replaying on the television. Now his mission for revenge was definitely going to happen. Now there was no question whether he was going to detonate the bomb or not. All doubt had been removed. He wanted his day of revenge.

Nawwaf continued, "Uday will teach you about the bomb. You are to stay here in the hotel room and allow no one to enter. Keep it double locked and push furniture in front of the door if needed. Then, at two, you are to detonate the bomb. We have determined this would be the ideal time for the maximum effect." He turned to Qasim and Kahil and said, "Let's go. These guys can finish up here. We've done what we need to do."

The three Muslim Brotherhood departed and left Uday instructing Uthal about how to detonate the bomb. Uday explained the procedure, and then departed.

Uthal was left on his own. As instructed he locked the hotel room door and barricaded it with some furniture. Then he walked to the big window and threw open the curtains. He wanted to see the world that would soon be reduced to shambles. He wanted to see the decadent, capitalistic world which would soon feel the wrath of Allah. He felt proud as he stood in front of his window, and he knew his parents would be proud too. Then the thought hit him. How would his parents, or anyone else for that matter, know he was the one who detonated the big bomb in LA? He knew Allah would know and Allah would praise him for his work. But he wanted the approval and acceptance of his parents as well, assuming they had lived through the attack on their mosque. How was he going to get their acceptance if they didn't know anything about his accomplishments? He had to do something. He had to get a message out somehow.

* * *

Livy decided to do a late breakfast down in the hotel cafeteria. She was just finishing up when she noticed something strange. Three Muslims were rushing through the lobby of the hotel in what appeared to be a panic. They didn't stop at the front desk. They just wanted to leave the building. What made it even worse was that one of the three seemed strangely familiar, as if she had seen his face somewhere on a poster.

Livy immediately placed a call to Alvin. "I just saw three Muslims streaking out of here as if they had fire on their tail."

Alvin responded with, "And I just learned Uthal arrived at your hotel about fifteen minutes ago. The team at his hotel overheard him say something about meeting someone and then they followed him to your location. Then they lost him when he jumped on the elevator. There must be some kind of connection."

"Thanks for the update. There has to be a connection. What do you suggest?"

"I have guys on the street that had followed Uthal and I'm going to alert them to keep an eye on your friends that were leaving the hotel and try to follow them. I'm going to turn control of Uthal over to you. Hold on this phone line for a second while I alert my team on the ground." The phone went dead on Livy's side while Alvin communicated with his team. Then he returned to the phone call with Livy, "They have eyes on the guys you were talking about. They spotted them coming out of the hotel and were wondering about them as well. Our assets are now on their tail."

"Can you send me a picture of Uthal," requested Livy.

"I'll do it right now," responded Alvin.

"I'm going to stay here in the lobby to see if I spot him at the elevators. And I'll check at the front desk to see if he is a registered guest, which seems unlikely since he is already registered at the Courtland. But it's worth asking the question. Maybe they know a room number. I'll also try to get access to the hotel's surveillance cameras and see if I can find out where he went. I'll let you know if I see him, or anything else suspicions."

"I'll keep you informed as well if anything new happens at this end," responded Alvin as he disconnected the call.

Chapter Sixty-Three

Escape

November, 2017, Los Angeles, California

Nawwaf, Qasim, and Kahil jumped into their vehicle and headed toward Las Vegas. They followed the reverse of the route that Uthal had taken the day before on his drive from Las Vegas to Hollywood. It was freeway all the way and they decided they should have no trouble getting away safely by the time of the detonation.

The Los Angles Ritz Hotel was tucked neatly in the corner of two freeways, Interstate 10 and 110, which made it easy to make a quick escape. The three jumped on Interstate 10 heading east, which wound around the South and then the West side of the downtown Los Angeles area. Eventually the Interstate headed due east.

Something was bothering Nawwaf as he drove off. He felt like he was being watched, but he couldn't identify why he had this strange feeling. He kept looking into his rear view mirror until it finally came to the point where his nervousness was noticed by his traveling companions.

"What's your problem?" asked Qasim.

"Nothing really," responded Nawwaf. "I just feel like we're being followed."

"Well the only thing I think will be following you is a highway patrol car if you don't slow down a little," replied Kahil. "We don't want to spend an hour chit-chatting with a CHP officer. We need to get out of here before that bomb goes off. And getting pulled over by a police officer won't help us achieve that goal."

"I didn't realize I was driving that fast," acknowledged Nawwaf.

Nawwaf reduced his speed, but he continued to feel anxious about someone following him. He continued to check to see if there was anyone behind.

Forty-five minutes into their travel time they arrived at the Interstate 15 interchange. This was the freeway they would use to head north taking them all the way to Las Vegas. They were finally getting to the edge of the greater LA area and the traffic was starting to lighten up. This was bad for the FBI because it made them more noticeable. Now Nawwaf noticed them.

"I'm sure that car is following us," Nawwaf stressed.

"What car?" asked Qasim as he turned around.

"The black Suburban," responded Nawwaf. "I noticed them before but now that they switched freeways behind us I'm convinced that we're being followed."

"Lose them," commanded Qasim.

"I'll try," answered Nawwaf as he migrated over to the high-speed lane. "How did anyone get wind of us? We were pretty anonymous. We shouldn't have raised any suspicions."

The FBI tail appeared to react to Nawwaf's identifying them because they started to speed up as if there was no longer any need to hold back. The chase game had changed to one of close pursuit.

Nawwaf saw the rapid approach of the FBI vehicle and he knew he was in trouble. He decided he would have a better chance of losing them if he was on the city streets so he tore across all the lanes of traffic and took the next freeway exit which happened to be exit 113, the Baseline Avenue Exit.

Nawwaf only slightly reduced his speed as he streaked down the off-ramp and made a dramatic right turn onto Baseline Avenue heading east. The car's wheels slid sideways and screeched as he made the turn causing him to slide across the lanes before he settled into the right hand east bound lane.

The FBI didn't fare much better. In their attempt to keep up with Nawwaf, they screeched around the corner causing their suburban to sway to the left, nearly throwing the vehicle over on its side.

Nawwaf checked his mirror and in exasperation complained, "They're definitely following us. They're still behind us and they're trying to catch up with us."

In another desperate attempt to escape his pursuers Nawwaf made a quick right turn onto Heritage Circle. He ignored stoplights and stop signs, narrowly avoiding several close calls with other vehicles. This turn was followed by another right turn onto West Grand Avenue. He thought that by jumping between streets he would be more likely to lose the Suburban that was tailing him. But he was unfamiliar with the area and his attempts to lose them also increased the risk of him getting lost.

A quick check into his rear view mirror confirmed what Nawwaf feared. He still had not lost them, and they were gaining on him. He took another quick right turn onto Independence Way, hoping he could enter a suburban area where he could rapidly make a series of turns and possibly lose these infidels that were chasing him.

In the back of Nawwaf's mind was the concern that this chase would cause enough of a delay that he wouldn't get out of the Los Angeles area in time to avoid the effects of the bomb. He was not ready to die. Not by the hands of the FBI, nor by the hands of the Ritz Hotel bomb.

West Independence Way dead-ended on East Yosemite Loop Road, and Nawwaf took an immediate right turn. He streaked past one street after another, each one indicating that there was no outlet, either to the left or to the right.

"What the heck have you gotten us into?" demanded Qasim. "Is there no way out of here? The name of this road, 'Loop Road,' should have raised suspicions right away. Have you trapped us in here?"

Nawwaf had managed to bottle himself up in a tightly knit community which included a circular road with numerous dead-end spurs running off of the main loop road. East Yosemite Loop Road swung north and became West Yosemite Loop Road, which headed south and looped around again to become East Yosemite Loop Road. Nawwaf could drive around and around in this loop for hours.

Off of the Yosemite Loop Road were fifty-five left or right turns Nawwaf could have made. Unfortunately there were only four of these turns that actually exited this circular community. All the rest of the turns would have ended in a dead end. Nawwaf had placed himself into a maze that was a no-win.

Nawwaf, not knowing what to do, followed the loop road all the way around hoping eventually it would exit somewhere. Once he realized it was a loop, he started to look for escapes.

On his third circle through the loop, as he was driving down the west side of the loop, he noticed West Constitution Way appeared to be a possible alternative for escape and he made a quick left turn. He followed this route out of the circle nightmare he had been in, crossed over Grand Avenue, and took a left turn on West Lincoln Loop Road. His frustration reached a peak when he realized he had just jumped on an identical loop circle maze. This was another Loop Road. No one would have imagined there could actually be two of these loop nightmares with nearly no exits. Nawwaf had managed to find both of them. This loop had fifty-seven possible turns and only five of them would lead to an escape from the nightmare.

* * *

The FBI agents in the pursuit vehicle were having very little trouble following Nawwaf's car. They debated whether it was more dangerous to start shooting, even though they were in a suburban neighborhood, or if it was more dangerous to allow Nawwaf to continue driving at high speeds through this neighborhood, also risking the lives of the citizens. They made the decision to do a standoff and wait for him. When Nawwaf accidently switched into the second loop neighborhood, one of the agents quickly jumped out of the Suburban with his sniper rifle and decided to wait for Nawwaf to complete the circle.

The FBI agent waited behind a tree, hoping he would soon see Nawwaf speeding around the loop and returning back to the point where he entered the loop. He heard the screeching of tires coming his way north on West Lincoln Loop Road. He prepared by taking aim in the direction from which he expected the car to come.

* * *

Qasim, sitting in the passenger seat, was screaming at Nawwaf, "Are you the stupidest person I ever met?" he cursed. "How can anyone be so stupid as to get us caught in two mazes? One maze wasn't enough, but now we have to find ourselves circling around a second maze. You're dumber than the infidels that are chasing us!"

Nawwaf's blood was boiling. This should have been such an easy escape. How did these infidels find him? Why did he have to put up with these stupid Muslim Brotherhood morons? Why did they even have to come? They've been nothing but a burden. When he requested help he wanted someone who could help, not someone he had to babysit. Now he was caught in this loop and rather than being helpful, these idiots spent all their time accusing him of causing this mess. In the end they'll probably all get killed anyway because of the bomb that should be going off in a couple hours. How could life get so messed up? Where was Allah when he needed him?

Qasim continued his rant, "Can't you find any way. . . ?" and then he went quiet.

The suddenness of the silence caused Nawwaf to look over at Qasim sitting in the seat next to him. In the middle of Qasim's forehead Nawwaf now saw a red spot which grew bigger as the blood oozed out. Behind his head was a bloody headrest. The back of his head had been blown out.

Nawwaf, without thinking, slammed on the brakes. He didn't know how to respond, and it didn't take him long to realize this was the wrong response. He had been turning a corner when he hit the brakes and along with the momentum of the vehicle, the car was thrown into a roll, tumbling over and over until it slammed upside down into a tree about ten feet from the FBI agent.

The agent, assuming everyone in the car had been killed, approached the car with his rifle pushed forward ready to shoot. At the same time the FBI Suburban came streaking around the same corner and pulled up to a stop next to the overturned car.

An unexpected shot rang out. Kahil, who was in the back seat of the car, had pulled his weapon and shot the FBI agent in the foot. The agent crumpled to the ground and a second shot from Kahil hit the agent in the front of the neck, causing him to asphyxiate.

Agents from the Suburban jumped out of their vehicle and a gun battle ensued between the FBI and Kahil. In the meantime Nawwaf had also successfully pulled out his weapon and had pushed the air bag aside that was hitting him in the face. Now he was also firing at the FBI.

The gun battle was a short one. Kahil received a barrage of bullets to the head and body. He was killed instantly. Nawwaf was also shot several times, but he managed to survive long enough for one of the agents to come to his side, strip away his gun, and hear him moan, "The bomb. I have to get away from the bomb," shortly before he died.

Chapter Sixty-Four

Ritz Hotel
November, 2017, Los Angeles, California

Livy didn't know where to start. She hesitated bringing Jonathan into the situation because of the tension between them, but she knew she had to remain professional. She made the call to his cell phone.

"Hello," Jonathan answered. "What's up?" His voice was cordial, almost as if he didn't know it was Livy that was calling.

"We think there is a bomb planted somewhere in this building, and we think Uthal, the third suicide bomber from Ann Arbor, is with the bomb," Livy explained. "We need to try to find it."

"What do you recommend?" asked Jonathan with a skeptical tone of voice. "A room to room search doesn't make a lot of sense. There are twenty-six floors we would need to search. That would be an impossible task."

"I'm going to try to work with the front desk to see if they can help narrow down the number of rooms we would need to search. And maybe we can go through the surveillance tapes and find Uthal when he came into the hotel. Maybe we can figure out where he went. Or at least narrow it down to a floor." From her previous inquiries Livy already knew Uthal was not a registered guest. So finding the room with the bomb would not be as easy as asking the front desk for a room number.

Just then Livy's phone started ringing. She told Jonathan, "I'm getting a call in from Alvin. I'll take that and get back to you. Why don't you come down to the lobby and help me try to narrow down our search."

Then Livy pushed a couple buttons on the phone and connected with Alvin. "Hello," she said.

"This is Alvin and I have bad news," Alvin started. "We caught up with the three Arabs that were leaving your building. It turns out they were definitely involved in the terrorist activities that have been happening here. Unfortunately, a gun battle left all three of them dead. But not before one of them said something about getting away from a bomb. So now I'm convinced there is a bomb in your building and Uthal is camped out with that bomb. It sounds like the explosion is imminent. I've asked all resources, including the local FBI office, to convene at your hotel and we're immediately going to start this search. Do you have any ideas how we can narrow the search?"

"I contacted Jonathan. We're going to go through the registration records and the surveillance videos to see if we can spot where Uthal went or where these other three terrorists came from since it's highly likely that he went to their room. With any luck we'll find something before the bomb goes off. I hope you have a bomb squad coming as well."

"I have both the FBI bomb squad and the local police bomb squad coming," he replied. But Livy had triggered a different question in Alvin. "Isn't Jonathan staying with you?"

"No. He's mad at me because of my Dragon Pit activities. He doesn't agree with what we're doing. So he's decided to stay away from me for a while."

"I'm surprised you even told him about it. We want to keep knowledge of our team to a minimum. He may inadvertently leak some information to the wrong people. That's too bad," responded Alvin.

He continued, "We'll be swarming you with support shortly, so be ready to give us as much information and direction as possible. We need to find this bomb."

"Agreed," replied Livy as she disconnected the call. Just as she was hanging up with Alvin, another call came in. This time the call was from Gerick Johannes of the Denver office. "Hello," answered Livy.

"This is Gerick and I just received bad news from the Denver office and I wanted to let you know right away," said Gerick.

"More bad news?" questioned Livy. "I can't handle so much bad news at one time. Can we spread the bad news out a little and not give all of it to me in one lump?"

"Sorry about that. This is really tragic and I don't know how to tell you this so I'll just be blunt and say it. Earlier today they found the bodies of Glenn, Cynthia, and their two children, along with the bodies of two of the kidnappers. They were in a house north of Golden. They had been dead for several days. Some children playing close by noticed the smell and the homeowners went in to investigate and found the bodies. It looks like everyone, including the kidnappers, was executed at point blank range. We're guessing the Muslim Brotherhood simply didn't have any use for them anymore and so they eliminated them. I'm really sorry to have to give you this news, but I figured it would be better hearing it from me rather than over the news."

Livy was stunned. She wasn't expecting anything quite so blatant. She had to sit down and collect her thoughts. The momentary silence worried Gerick and he asked, "Are you okay?"

"Not really." She was still in shock. Then, after another short pause she said, "Thanks for telling me. I really didn't expect this level of cruelty."

"No one did. No one did. I'm sorry to be the one to hurt you like this."

"It's okay. I'm glad you were the one to tell me."

"I'm coming over from Anaheim to the Ritz Hotel to help in the search for the bomb," commented Gerick. "I should be seeing you shortly."

"See you then," Livy responded. She shut off the phone and just sat there for a few more minutes digesting what she had just learned. She had just received an entirely new level of clarity of what exactly she was dealing with.

Just then Jonathan came walking by. "Are you okay?" he asked.

Livy told him of the death of Glenn and his family. Jonathan had only met them a couple of times and wasn't close to them, but he could see that Livy was shaken by their death. "I'm sorry," was all he could think to say.

Jonathan's arrival brought Livy back to the problem at hand. She jumped up, started walking toward the front desk, and said, "We better get to work if we're going to find that bomb."

Jonathan followed in her footsteps. As they arrived at the front desk Livy flashed her badge and asked for the hotel manager. She and Jonathan were escorted to a back office where they informed the manager they suspected a bomb plot and they needed immediate access to the hotel's registration records and their surveillance tapes. The hotel manager readily complied. He asked about evacuating the hotel. Livy deferred this request to Alvin who would be arriving shortly. In her mind, it really wouldn't make any difference anyway. If Nawwaf, who was on the outer edges of the LA area, was still worried about getting hit with the bomb, then what chance did anyone leaving the hotel now have? It had to be a nuclear bomb. It was probably better not to get everyone panicked.

Livy put Jonathan to work on the registration records, looking for anyone who checked in during the last couple of days and who may have had an Arab name or passport. He also used pictures of the suspects and started questioning all the hotel staff to see if anyone recognized the four individuals, Nawwaf, Qasim, Kahil, or Uthal. There were staff members that recognized the faces, but none of them knew the names or room numbers of these individuals.

Jonathan came to Livy after a frustrating search and said, "Apparently they used false names and passports. Several people have seen them, but no one seems to know their names. It's very frustrating."

Livy had also experienced some frustration in her search. She had spotted the individuals on the lobby videos but couldn't tie them to a specific floor. It was always in the lobby where she spotted them and the elevators and their numbers were hard to see from the angle where the monitors were located. Unfortunately the cameras in the elevators weren't working so they weren't any help either.

Alvin and his team had now arrived and they proceeded to start an evacuation of the hotel. They also started the futile search of the rooms going through them one at a time. It was a long and tedious process, but there didn't seem to be any better options at the moment.

* * *

Uthal knew he wasn't supposed to leave the hotel room. He wasn't supposed to leave the bomb unprotected. But he also wasn't going to set the bomb off without getting credit for the deed. He especially wanted his parents to know so they could be proud of him.

For some reason internet access in the room wasn't working on the room's television set. He wasn't sure why it wouldn't work but he couldn't allow maintenance to come to his room and check it out. A call to the front desk informed him that he could use the computer in the business center to send an email. He would have to leave the bomb in the room unprotected, go down to the lobby, go to the business center, and send a quick email. Then he would have to get back to the room as quickly as possible to again protect the bomb.

Uthal decided it was important to send that email and he moved the furniture away from the front door. He opened the door and peeked down the hallway. He wanted to see if the maid service was anywhere close by. He didn't want to leave the room if they were close and if there was a chance that they might be entering the room.

No one was in the hallway. It was completely empty. He decided to make a dash for it. He grabbed the pistol he had brought with from Ann Arbor, hung the "Do Not Disturb" sign on the outside of the door handle, shut the door, and headed for the elevator. Once he arrived in the lobby he headed directly for the hotel's business center and they immediately offered him a computer to use for his email.

* * *

Unfortunately for Uthal, the attendant at the Business Center recognized his face from the pictures the FBI had shown her earlier and she knew the FBI was looking for him. She helped Uthal to get settled in on the computer. Then she left the office and headed to the hotel manager's office. There she found the FBI agents and she informed them she had just seen Uthal.

Livy remained focused on the surveillance videos. She did a quick check on recent recordings and confirmed it was indeed Uthal who had just passed through the lobby and had gone into the business center. She tried to backtrack his arrival and found him coming from the elevator. But the floor numbers were not visible to the surveillance videos. Luckily the hotel had surveillance videos on each floor and now it was just a matter of going through each of the floors until she discovered which floor Uthal was on.

She started from the top floor, playing on the extravagant tendencies of the Arabs, and soon spotted him walking toward the elevator on the twenty-third floor. She turned to Jonathan and said, "I think the bomb is on the twenty-third floor, but I can't tell which room. We need to go up there and start looking. We can eliminate any empty rooms, but beyond that we really don't know who booked the room so we don't know what we're looking for."

"Let's go," Jonathan replied.

As they headed off to the elevator, the remainder of the FBI team was dispatched to the business center. They were trying to stay cautious, working their way toward the office by circling around both sides of the entrance. They wanted to make sure all exits were covered. But they were too late. They went storming into the business center with their weapons extended but the only thing they accomplished was to scare everyone who was in the office half to death.

* * *

Uthal typed his email message quickly and hit the send button. He wanted to get back to his room and protect his bomb. It wouldn't be long now and he was excited for the big event to happen. Allah would be so proud.

He rushed to the elevators, pushed the button to the twenty-third floor, and was off. Little did he know that right behind him, on the very next elevator, Livy and Jonathan were also heading to his floor.

Once he arrived at his floor, Uthal sprinted down the hall to his room. He was comforted by the fact that no one else was in the hallway. The maids had not gone to work on his part of the floor. The bomb should be safe.

Uthal hurried to his door and was about to insert the key when, down at the end of the hall near the elevator, two FBI agents, complete with bulletproof vests, stepped out of one of the other elevators. They spotted Uthal and immediately yelled at him to stop. He ignored the command and continued to open the door. Jonathan, one of the FBI agents coming out of the elevator, fired a warning shot over Uthal's head, hoping it would make him stop. Instead Uthal stepped into the doorway using the wall and the doorway for protection. He pulled out his pistol that the Muslim Brotherhood agent had given him and fired three shots back in the direction of Jonathan. Instinctively Jonathan had stepped in front of Livy to shield her. Two of the shots from Uthal missed, but one was true to its mark and hit Jonathan in the left eye. The bullet exited out of the back of his head and spattered blood and brain matter into Livy's face as she stood behind him. She was shorter than Jonathan so the bullet soared over the top of her head. But Jonathan wasn't as lucky.

Jonathan crumpled to the ground. Livy also dropped to the ground, taking a prone shooting position and took aim at Uthal but her shots were too late. The target was gone. Uthal had stepped into his room and shut the door.

Chapter Sixty-Five

The Bomb
November, 2017, Los Angeles, California

Gerick and Edward heard about the bomb threat at the Ritz Hotel in downtown Los Angeles and they were ordered to go directly there as quickly as possible to help in the search. Gerick was driving while Edward kept sending text messages. At first Gerick thought it was pretty normal, but after a while he started to get suspicious. It seemed like an abnormal amount of texting so he asked, "What's going on? Is there something happening that I should know about?"

"No," barked Edward. "Don't worry about it. It's personal stuff."

Gerick let it go. Asking any more questions would only end up getting Edward even madder. But he continued to be suspicious. He tried to peek over to see what Edward was typing.

Edward sensed Gerick leaning his direction and he turned the phone to make sure it wouldn't be seen. This made Gerick even more suspicious. It didn't seem like he was sending personal messages. Nor did it seem like he was sending FBI messages. Gerick, who was very good at texting while he was driving, grabbed his own phone and sent a quick text to a trusted agent in the Denver office. He asked him to track the messages that were being sent to Edward, and to forward anything suspicious. It wasn't long before the messages started beeping in. The very first forwarded message was very disturbing. It read, "They know about the bomb in LA and are going to the hotel to search for it. You must detonate now."

***

Livy crawled over to his bloody body and looked at his damaged face. Jonathan had shielded Livy with his body. He had given his life to protect her. He had paid the ultimate price. Livy was in turmoil. Her feelings were tied up in knots. She had just lost her best friend. But in a way he had already dumped her too. But regardless, she had previously had strong feelings for him for several years and it was hard to lose him, especially like this.

But then there was the bomb. There wasn't any time to feel sad or morn. That would have to come later. Uthal could be in his room setting off the bomb right now. She couldn't allow that to happen.

Livy called Alvin and told him what had happened and requested backup. She wasn't in a position to take on the search for Uthal alone because she wasn't sure what room he was in. Alvin had just arrived at the Ritz Hotel. "We're on our way," he instructed. "Don't do this alone or you'll just end up like Jonathan, and that won't help anyone. Wait till you have a team with you."

"I'll try," Livy responded. What she was really saying was that she'll wait a couple minutes, but that she wouldn't wait too long. The risk was too great. If she had to try to enter the room alone, then she would do it. Something had to happen and it had to happen quickly.

Livy decided to work her way closer to Uthal's room. She looked down the hall at the twelve doors on the side of the hall where Uthal had entered, and she realized she really didn't know which room was the right room. It happened so quickly. It could be any one of four different rooms. Livy decided she would have to wait until she had a backup. They would have to invade all four rooms at the same time. If they went into the wrong room the noise could trigger Uthal to set the bomb off and that could be catastrophic. All four rooms would have to be hit simultaneously.

* * *

Uthal burst into his room so quickly, he tripped on the carpet and nearly fell to the floor. He stumbled and recovered quickly and shut the door. Then he moved a table against the door and wedged it in order to make entry difficult.

He went over to the bomb to check it out and make sure no one had tampered with it. The bomb's trigger had a control mechanism which required the operator to punch in a special code. That code would then allow Uthal to set a timer for a countdown on the bomb. Without that code, no one would be able to set or change the timer.

Uthal decided he would start the timer off in case the FBI broke their way in. Then it would be too late. The bomb would already be set to explode. However, if the FBI didn't come in he could reset the timer again and again until the time arrived which had previously been planned for detonation.

Uthal punched in the access code "666". Then he proceeded to set the timer for fifteen minutes out. He pushed the start button and closed the cover. The bomb was live and ready. He checked the timer and it was ticking down to 14:55, 14:54, 14: 53. . .

* * *

Gerick sent a message to Alvin which said, "Edward is the mole. He is sending text messages to someone telling them what we're doing. I'll have his messages forwarded to you."

Gerick sent a second message to his contact in Denver and told him to forward Edward's messages to Alvin. Then he wondered what he was going to do about Edward. Bringing him to the Ritz could be dangerous. He may turn on his fellow agents and facilitate the detonation of the bomb. Bringing him there would be a big mistake. But Gerick wasn't sure what to do.

Suddenly the question of what to do was answered by Edward. Edward had drawn his weapon and it was now aimed at Gerick. He clicked the safety off. "What are you doing?" demanded Gerick.

"I know you know," replied Edward. "You're not fooling anyone. You know about me and I'm not going to let you tell anyone else. So here is what we're going to do. We're going to take a detour and head to Las Vegas. Highway 91 is coming up here and I want you to take the east exit and head for Interstate 15. Then get on 15 North and head for Las Vegas. We need to get past the San Bernardino National Forest within the next couple hours. You have a choice. Either you do this with me, or I do it without you. Either way is fine with me."

Gerick decided not to confront Edward right now when they were traveling at seventy miles per hour. If being shot by him didn't kill him, the resulting accident definitely would. So he decided that for now he would comply and head toward Vegas.

In the back of Gerick's mind he wondered, *If Edward thinks Anaheim is too close to the bomb, and he wants to get to Vegas, this must be a really big bomb. How much of the LA area is going to be destroyed? How many people are going to be killed? This is going to make the Orlando or the North Dakota explosions seem like child's play.*

Gerick's mind reeled with the thought of the danger that existed, both for him personally, and for LA as a whole. He was sitting next to one of the key players behind this bomb. He was sitting next to an FBI mole working for the terrorists. He was sitting next to a traitor.

* * *

Alvin and three of his agents were the first to arrive on the twenty-third floor joining Livy in the hallway close to the elevator. Alvin went immediately to the body of Jonathan and kneeled down to see his condition, but it was obvious he was gone. Then he reached over to Livy, gave her arm a comforting squeeze, and whispered, "Sorry." Next, looking down the hall, he asked, "Where is he?"

Livy answered, "Not exactly sure which door. It's one of the four doors on the left numbered 2312, 2314, 2316, or 2318. I think it was 2316 but I'm not positive. The shooting started right after we stepped off the elevator and I was never able to get a good look before he disappeared into his room."

"Then we'll have to hit all four of them at once," replied Alvin. Livy nodded. "We'll wait till we have at least two assets per room." Again Livy nodded. Then, turning again to Livy, he asked, "Are you okay?"

"I'm fine. It's always a shock to see this happen to someone close to you. But we have a job to do and I'll just have to do my grieving later."

Alvin gave her arm another squeeze. He always enjoyed any kind of physical contact with Livy. His interest in her was more than professional, but he had to keep on a professional face.

Just then another elevator arrived, this time with five more agents. That brought the number of agents up to ten including Livy and Alvin. Alvin stood up and had all the assets huddle around him. Then he explained how they were breaking into four rooms at once, two agents per room. He assigned two agents to each of the four rooms and he and Livy would go one each to the two rooms in the middle. He wanted the two of them to cover the rooms that would most likely contain the suicide bomber.

He explained the procedure. They were to go to each of their respective doors and avoid the peephole. Then, standing to the side, they would put gum over the peephole. Next they would put a small amount of explosive around each of the doorknobs. Once everyone was ready, they would look toward Alvin, and when he saw that everyone was ready, he would trigger the explosion of all four doors at the same time.

The process was standard operating procedure, but Alvin wanted to rehearse it to make sure they were all on the same page. The agents moved out to their respective doors. In less than a minute they were all ready to trigger their explosions. Then the unexpected happened. Room 2318 started to open their door. The agents in front of that door quickly forced the door all the way open and pushed their way inside, pistol extended.

* * *

"What the heck?" barked out the room's single occupant.

The agent put his index finger in front of his mouth, indicating the occupant should keep silent and stepped into the room. He shut the door behind him and in a whisper proceeded to explain, "We have a situation outside and you need to stay inside until we resolve this."

"Okay," replied the room's occupant. He could see that it was an urgent situation with the potential of physical harm, and he preferred to not be one of those individuals getting harmed.

"Stay as far away from the door and from this end of the room as possible," continued the agent. "The best thing for you to do would be to go into the bathroom and lay down in the bathtub." The resident nodded and headed toward the bathroom. Then the agent and his partner left the room and joined one of the teams at one of the other doors.

* * *

Alvin, who was in front of room 2314 looked toward rooms 2316 and 2312 to confirm they were both ready. Then he gave the signal. Three simultaneous loud explosions blew off the doorknobs on each of the rooms. For room 2312 the explosion knocked the door wide open only to find a couple in bed, the woman sitting on top of the man. She screamed and jumped off, quickly covering herself. One of the agents went into the room and explained the situation and sent them to the bathroom for cover.

Room 2316, the one Livy was at, turned out to be empty. The room had been booked but its occupants were not in the room. But for room 2314, the door surged and immediately bounced back. Something was wedged up against the door not allowing it to swing open in spite of the missing door handle. This was a bad sign and the agents knew it. Immediately gunfire erupted from inside the room. The agents quickly moved away from being in front of the door but it was a fraction of a second too late for one of the agents who took a hit in the arm.

Now the entire team of agents surrounded room 2314. Alvin was hesitant to spray the room with bullets since he might accidently hit and trigger the bomb. They were in a standoff. But it was a standoff they couldn't afford. They had to get to the bomb. They realized that inside the room was a suicide bomber who didn't care if the bomb exploded early.

The next strategy would have been to use gas canisters and masks, but those weren't available so they had to work with the equipment they had at hand. Using a snake camera, the agents poked the camera under the door in the hopes that they might be able to see the terrorist. The furniture that was blocking the door also blocked their view. Next they poked the camera through the hole in the door created by the explosion. They couldn't see anything. But Uthal must have seen the camera because he fired a couple more shots through the room's door.

"Where are the shots coming from?" asked Alvin in a whisper.

"Can't tell," the agent replied as he maneuvered the camera around to a new position. "He's hiding somewhere. Can we do something to draw him out?"

"Can you see the bomb?"

"Yes. It's the size of a large suitcase and it's sitting on the floor in the center of the room."

"Show me," instructed Alvin. Looking at the monitor, he suggested, "If we can get him to stand up we can spray the room from the waist up thereby avoiding the bomb and still hitting him. Let me know the minute you see him."

* * *

The agent just nodded. Alvin instructed the agents to be ready to spray the room at waist height and up, but no lower, as soon as they received a signal from the agent with the camera.

The camera was inserted further through the hole. This allowed for a larger sweep of the room but the agent was also hoping the camera would draw Uthal out and cause him to fire a few more shots. He kept scanning the room for another minute with nothing new happening. Then he saw movement behind the couch. It looked like Uthal had peeked over the top of the couch. The agent focused his attention on that area hoping to see movement. Suddenly Uthal grabbed the end of the camera and yanked hard on it. Apparently he had crawled around in the room until he was at the point where he could grab the end of the camera, and he was trying to break it off.

The agent wasn't able to see Uthal, but he assumed he was standing up in order to be able to pull at the camera. The agent gave the signal anyway, and a volley of bullets flew through the wall and into the room followed by a crashing thump. Alvin assumed this to be Uthal falling to the ground and he gave the signal to attack the door. After a lot of hitting, pushing, and thumping they were finally able to push away the blockage behind the door and make their way into the room. Uthal was indeed laying on the floor next to the door, his upper body riddled. But he was still alive. He held a pistol in his hand and struggled to take aim, but one of the alert agents immediately kicked at the pistol and knocked it out of his hand.

Alvin and several of the agents went directly to the bomb and saw that it was ticking down. They had nine minutes and forty-seven seconds before the bomb went off.

Uthal used his final breath to yell out, "Kill the beast. Kill the beast." Then he went quiet with a smile on his face.

"He must have met his virgins," exclaimed Livy.

Chapter Sixty-Six

It's All about Revenge
November, 2017, Los Angeles, California

Gerick knew he needed to let Alvin and his team know that there was urgency in finding and disarming the bomb. Edward's need to get out of the area made this obvious. That had to mean the bomb was going to be detonated soon, and Gerick was worried Alvin didn't know about it.

Gerick had been trained for this possibility. He knew how to manage a hijacking where the passenger was pointing a weapon at the driver. The formula was simple. First he had to distract the passenger enough to where he was able to push the child safety switch which deactivated the passenger side air bags. Then he needed to find something to run the car into, like a tree or a power pole. He would crash the car in at the right front corner, causing all the damage to occur on the passenger side of the vehicle. As he was about to crash he would pretend to lean over for protection, but what he was actually doing was to push the seat belt release button of the passenger.

Following this formula the passenger would probably end up with his face etched into the front windshield of the car while the driver was safely protected by the driver side airbags. That was the formula, but nothing ever works out exactly as planned. He was driving a rented Chevy and they're not known for their passenger safety record. Gerick selected the end of the railing he was going to hit. He gunned the car toward it. He pushed the seatbelt release button and crashed hard into the end of the railing. But the seatbelt didn't disconnect as it was supposed to and the car didn't crumble only on the passenger side as anticipated. Instead it accordioned and flipped over the railing and landed on the roof of the car on the opposite side of the rail.

Gerick was safe. He was protected by the steering wheel and door side air bag as expected. But flipping the car still caused him to get banged up a bit. Edward didn't fare as well. His legs were broken instantly as the car compressed in on him. Then, as the car flipped, the seatbelt finally came loose dropping him on his head and instantly breaking his neck.

Gerick loosened his own seatbelt and crawled out of the shattered driver's side window. He was bruised and banged up, but nothing was broken. He stood up, surveyed the damage making sure Edward was gone, and sent a text to Alvin.

* * *

Alvin's phone beeped a message causing him to snicker. "What's so funny?" asked Livy. "I'm not seeing a lot to laugh about with only eight minutes and twenty-three seconds left until we're all dead."

Alvin responded, "I just found it funny that Gerick just sent me a text informing me there is a bomb that's about to go off somewhere in the hotel. He's a little bit late. Also, apparently Edward was our mole."

"No kidding?" replied a sarcastic Livy.

Three agents were focused on the bomb. They were trained in disarming bombs and they knew what to look for. One of the agents spoke up, "This thing can't be disarmed. Once it's activated it also activates several sensors. If we try to move the bomb in any way, the sensor will trigger the explosion. Or if we try to tamper with the cover plate that is on the bomb, we'll also hear a big boom. The only way to disarm this bomb is to enter the three-digit access code. And we don't know the code. The only one that would know that code is laying there by the doorway dead."

"What type of bomb is it?" asked Alvin, already guessing that it was a nuclear device of some kind.

"Nuclear. Low yield, but large enough to take out half of LA. I'd guess about half the impact of the Hiroshima bomb."

"So covering it or throwing it in a swimming pool won't help?"

"Not a bit. Burying it in a deep hole would work, but not when we have so little time left."

A second agent was running through the numbers, trying one number after another to see if he could get the access code by trial and error. He was entering about one number every three seconds, which meant that he could get through about twenty numbers a minute or about one hundred sixty numbers in the remaining amount of time, but there were a thousand possible combinations and there just wouldn't be enough time to try them all. But he had to try. No one else seemed to have any better ideas.

Alvin looked at one of the agents and said, "Search the body and see if you can find anything on him that might give us a clue what the number might be." Then turning to another pair of agents, he commanded, "Search the room for any clues. Maybe someone was dumb enough to write the code down. Yell out any three digit numbers that you find."

Six minutes nineteen seconds.

Livy spoke up, "Are there any magic numbers in Islam? Can we try his month and day of his birthday? How about his address? It's probably a number that's easy for him to remember."

Agents started searching their databases and making phone calls, blurting out numbers they wanted tried as soon as they learned them. But still no luck.

Four minutes forty-seven seconds.

Livy continued, "Did we check the email he sent earlier. Are there any clues in that?"

Three minutes fifty-one seconds.

"What about the room number? What about his wife or child's birth date?" Livy didn't know if he was married or not but she wanted to check everything. The agents were all scrambling to come up with potential numbers and the agent with the bomb tried all the combinations as they were blurted out. But still no luck.

Two minutes eighteen seconds.

Livy kept brainstorming for ideas. "What did he say when we entered the room? What were his last words?"

"Something about killing. Kill something," Alvin struggled to remember.

"Kill the beast," one of the agents blurted out.

One minute twenty-eight seconds.

"Does that mean anything to anyone?" asked Livy, desperate to get an answer, not really knowing if this was a clue or just the ravings of a delusional psychopath.

"Kill the beast is something you hear a lot in fantasy and mythology," suggested one of the agents. "But I don't see that giving us a number."

Fifty-eight seconds.

"It's in the Bible too," blurted Alvin. "Revelations talks about the beast."

"That's right," yelled out one of the agents in excitement. "I remember that passage and it also says something about the 'number of the beast'." He ran to the nightstand, pulled out a Bible and flipped to Revelations. "I have no idea where to look." His voice was despondent and frustrated.

Thirty-three seconds.

Livy jumped in, "You're right. They made movies about that number. I remember that number. It was tattooed on the demons. What was that number?"

Nineteen seconds.

"I remember that too," replied one of the agents. "It was something like 600."

The agent at the bomb put in the number 600. "Nope."

Twelve seconds.

"That's not it," replied another agent. "It had three digits the same. Like 333."

The agent punched in 333. "Nope."

Eight seconds.

"I remember now, it was 666. The number was 666," yelled out an excited agent.

Four seconds.

He punched in 666. "That was it!" yelled out the agent in excitement. "The bomb is now on hold and I'm going to shut it down."

The excitement in the room was so thick even a knife wouldn't have been able to cut through it.

Livy, without thinking, ran over to Alvin and threw herself into his arms and started to bawl. The stress of the day had just been too much. Jonathan getting killed in front of her and now the disarming of the bomb had all been too much. She was overwhelmed, as was everyone else in the room. They narrowly escaped death, and now they had time to realize how close they came. Livy needed the comfort of a hug, and Alvin was the most available. He had no intention of resisting.

Alvin interpreted the hug very differently. He wanted more. In spite of the cruelness of Jonathan's death, he had always hoped he could be his replacement. This might finally be the opportunity.

* * *

It was the day after. The entire FBI team was still on a big high after successfully diverting a major terrorist attack. It was subdued because of the disappointment and pain of having lost several agents and close friends. Additionally, Livy and Alvin were distraught about what had happened to the Dragon Pit team. Brian and his family were in hiding. Glenn and his family were dead. Jonathan, even though he wasn't an official member of the team, had taken a bullet for her. He had most likely saved her life by his actions. There were several other agents who had died and although they weren't close friends, they were still members of the team. Then there were the police and firemen who were caught up in the battle in Ann Arbor and had paid the ultimate price.

The Islamic community also mourned the fact that so many Muslims were killed in the battle. Even though many were the misguided terrorists, they were still people and had lives and families and would be missed by someone.

A nuclear explosion in the middle of Los Angles would have resulted in millions of deaths, and not just dozens. Disarming it was an immeasurable success.

Livy, Alvin, Gerick, and the FBI team that remained in LA were all meeting for pizza at a specialty pizza shop in Hollywood known to be a hangout for celebrities. Across the street they could see the studio where the Dr. Philosopher show was taped. It was a time of mixed feelings. It was a time for toasting success and a time for remembering the team members who had paid the ultimate price. It was a time for celebrating that they were still alive.

It was finally a time for relaxing, free from the stress everyone had felt the previous few days. Alvin and Livy were sitting at a table with several other agents when they simultaneously received a text message from the director of the CIA which read, "I have communicated with the director of the FBI and we agreed that you need to hear this immediately. There has been a contract put out on Alvin Foller and Livy Cobar accusing them of being instrumental in interfering with the will of Allah. The contracts finger you as being the leaders of the NERDS who attacked Medina, the mosques in Detroit, and Mecca. I'm not sure where they came up with these ideas, but nevertheless it's out there and someone believes it. And the contract specifically states that anyone, meaning any Muslim who wants to be a hero to Allah, should take it upon themselves to make sure the two of you do not see another sunrise. Because of this contract it is extremely important that the two of you disappear immediately and go to one of our remote safe houses."

Livy, in shock, looked over at Alvin and mouthed the words, "Did you get that message?"

"Yes," he said. Then leaning over to her so only she could hear, he said, "We need to slip out of here immediately. Let's get rid of any tracking devices like our phones and get to a safe house. Apparently we must still have a mole somewhere in the FBI. Edward was sending texts to someone and I think it was someone on our team. So we need to get away from our team. We have to get away from anyone who may know us."

"Agreed."

"Let's move," Alvin urgently requested and the two of them, attempting to avoid being noticed, casually headed for the door of the pizza parlor and departed.

Chapter Sixty-Seven

The Hide-Out
November, 2017, Belize

Alvin and Livy needed to disappear. They couldn't trust the internal workings of the FBI any longer. There were spies within the FBI. The Muslim leaks were so big the two of them knew they were both at risk. Now that they had successfully prevented and destroyed a terrorist cell, they knew there would be Muslim terrorists that would be out to destroy them. They had been designated as the head of the NERDS and would be a target for future terrorist assassination attempts. It was inconceivable to them how anyone figured out they were indeed the head of the NERDS, or Dragon Pit as they preferred to be called. How did their enemies come to that conclusion? Or were they just guessing?

Livy had lost Jonathan. She thought his death was dreadful, but she didn't miss the relationship. It really wasn't going in a positive direction. Now she was extremely excited about a potentially new relationship with Alvin. She had always felt close to him. She had secretly hoped it would someday be more than just a working relationship. But she also believed that personal and working relationships didn't mix well together. That's what damaged her relationship with Jonathan. It turned out Alvin felt exactly the same way. But now that everything was out in the open, and Alvin and Livy had to lay low for a while it seemed like a perfect time to see if there could be more to their relationship.

Alvin had proposed that the two of them hide out together for a while. His proposal was a little backhanded. As he and Livy drove off toward the LA airport he said, "Livy, I've always thought the world of you, more so than I have ever had the right to think. Anyway, we both need to get away for a while and lay low until this whole thing blows over. I'd like to propose we do it together."

He hesitated to see what her reaction would be but she wasn't ready to give her feelings away. All she said was, "Go on."

He continued, "Okay! I'll be frank. I would like to have a relationship with you outside work. I would like to spend time with you and see if there can be more to our relationship. What do you think?"

Livy was filled with excitement. She hadn't imagined Alvin felt the same way about her and to hear that he was interested excited her. But she wanted to know more. "Tell me exactly what you think we should do."

"I think we should run away somewhere together. We should hide out for a while and see if this blows over. If nothing else, we can at least watch each other's backs. Maybe we can get a place together. I don't mean we should share the same bed. I mean maybe a two-bedroom apartment somewhere. I'd love to date you and see where it goes. If it works out, then great. If it doesn't, then we part ways with no hard feelings. But since we both need to disappear, I thought this might be a great opportunity to test out the potential of a relationship. What do you think?"

Livy's excitement could hardly contain itself. "I know the perfect place. I know just where we should go."

"Perfect," replied Alvin. "Let's go! We can't go back to any of our old stomping grounds. They will be watching for us at all the FBI offices."

"I agree. Let's go to the airport."

They arrived at the airport and grabbed the first flight to Belize City using fake passports and fake names. They had to spend a couple hours in the airport waiting for the flight. There weren't that many connections heading out in that direction. Eventually they boarded and arrived in Belize ten hours later. At the Belize international airport they went across the street from the airport to the car rental mall to pick up a vehicle. Thirty minutes later they were off and running on their adventure together.

The travel time from Belize City to Hopkins by car was about two and a half hours. It started at the Belize International Airport which was to the northwest of the city. They headed north on the Northern Highway completely avoiding the city. Later they would turn south toward Dangriga. About six miles short of Dangriga they came to the Southern Highway. They traveled along at sixty miles per hour when, unexpectedly, an ewe jumped out on the road forcing Alvin to slam on his breaks and bring the car to a screeching halt. Livy, who was dosing, jumped and was startled awake. When she saw the ewe she cussed and said, "That was a stinking rude way to wake me up."

"No kidding," replied Alvin jokingly. "That woke me up too. I was in the middle of a good nap when that stupid ewe jumped out and made me pay attention!"

They continued on this highway and turned off toward Hopkins. Livy was excited to finally be in her favorite town in Belize. In town they stopped for dinner and after dinner drove to the Jaguar Reef Lodge. This was where they would be staying for the next few days while they finalized the preparations of their new home. They would be moving out to one of the islands on the barrier reef. Interestingly this reef was the second largest reef in the world and was believed to be an extension of the Great Barrier Reef in Australia.

Out on the reef was an island owned and controlled by the Smithsonian Institute. It was a prime location used for marine biology research. Additionally, unknown to anyone else including the staff at the institute, the island complex also included a CIA safe house and it was this safe house that was being prepared for Livy and Alvin. They were going to be in a beautiful location living on a Caribbean island with a beachfront house and their own boat allowing them access to the mainland any time they wanted to go. Life didn't get much better.

The Jaguar Reef Hotel was a beautiful location. The hotel was located on the Caribbean beach just off the barrier reef. It had three swimming pools for anyone who was hesitant to swim in the ocean waves. It included lounge chairs and hammocks, and had glass-bottomed kayaks for the more adventurous. Livy feared once she was settled into the hotel she wouldn't want to leave. But she was also excited about finally setting up house with Alvin. Living here in a semi-remote portion of Belize, right on the Gulf of Mexico on the edge of the Caribbean was going to be an incredible life. If you had to hide out, there wasn't a better location in the world.

Chapter Sixty-Eight

The Next Cycle of Terror
November, 2017, Los Angeles, California

Uday, the Muslim Brotherhood member from Los Angeles, was also the Imam at the local mosque. He was extremely upset at the failure of his Brotherhood members. He was angry at how they wasted his only nuclear bomb. He was promised that it would result in something big and that didn't happen. So on Friday, at the next weekly mosque prayer meeting, he was committed to start building his own network for revenge. He felt he must make up for the failure of his companions. If it was going to happen, he would have to do it himself. He felt the need to rebuild the organization that had been lost and he knew just how to do it. He was going to learn from the mistakes of Sami and Shihab when he organized his own cell. He was going to learn from the mistakes of Nawwaf when he created his own model for revenge and when he identified how it was going to be executed. He was going to do it right. He would not fail and he was not going to involve those idiots from Egypt. This time revenge would be taken and it would be grand. It would be memorable. This time the revenge would make Allah proud. He knew just what form it would take and it was going to be a surprise to everyone.

* * *

Gerick had held on to Edward's phone. He hadn't had the chance to turn it in for evidence. Hearing a message beep on Edward's phone, he took it out to see what the message was. He was surprised to hear a message come through because he had thought all the key players in Edward's cell had been eliminated. Opening the phone, he read the message which must have been sent the previous day during the heat of the conflict. For some unknown technological reason the transmission had been delayed and just came through now. It read, "We are in the room with the bomb, but the bomb is safe and the timer is ticking." Gerick was stunned. One of the FBI agents in the hotel must have sent this message. He checked the timing of the message and learned it was sent about the time that Gerick and Edward were also in the heat of their struggle.

Gerick was in shock. He thought he had eliminated the FBI mole when he eliminated Edward. But now he learned there must be a second mole. He wondered if there could possibly be an entire network of moles. Disappointed, he realized the battle wasn't over. He now shuddered to think that this was probably just the beginning. That one of the agents that was with him at the pizza parlor right now celebrating their success had actually been plotting to destroy it as well.

As a consultant, Dr. Gerhard Plenert has facilitated organizational transformations all over the world including Asia, Latin America, Europe, and the Middle East. He has worked in numerous countries including England, Australia, Malaysia, China, India, Japan, Saudi Arabia, Germany, Ireland, Mexico, Brazil, Vietnam, and of course the United States and Canada, and many more.

As a professor Dr. Plenert was a tenured full professor at California State University, Chico, and a professor at BYU Provo, BYU Hawaii, the University of Malaysia, the University of San Diego, Utah State University, and Washington State University. He was awarded numerous academic achievement awards.

In his private life, Gerhard is a world traveler having visited nearly every continent. He has published 16 business books focused on Organizational Process Optimization. His books have been endorsed by individuals like Dr. Stephen Covey, and by companies like Black and Decker, AT&T, and FedEx.

Gerhard has taken his passion for reading mystery / suspense novels and is now writing his own series of novels. He enjoys integrating his travels into his novels to bring reality to some of his adventures and experiences.

He has published novels including a mystery / adventure series title "The Templars" and "Montana Rising" and a fantasy series titled "Small World". "Dragon Pit" is the first of a new "suspense / thriller" series of books.

He lives in Virgin, Utah and has been married to his wife for over forty-five years. Together they have eight children and fifteen grandchildren.

www.ingramcontent.com/pod-product-compliance
Lightning Source LLC
Chambersburg PA
CBHW070835260626

47170CB00007B/2380